Darkness Brings The Dawn

Erik's Story

BY

Jodi Leisure Minton

Bloomington, IN
authorHOUSE™
Milton Keynes, UK

AuthorHouse™
1663 Liberty Drive, Suite 200
Bloomington, IN 47403
www.authorhouse.com
Phone: 1-800-839-8640

AuthorHouse™ UK Ltd.
500 Avebury Boulevard
Central Milton Keynes, MK9 2BE
www.authorhouse.co.uk
Phone: 08001974150

First published by AuthorHouse 4/25/2006

ISBN: 1-4259-2979-6 (sc)

Library of Congress Control Number: 2006903465

Printed in the United States of America
Bloomington, Indiana

This book is printed on acid-free paper.

I want to express my appreciation and thanks to all those wonderful tarts that gave me support throughout this entire project spurring me on because of their love for Erik and Gerry. You know who you are. You will find many hidden messages within these pages that only you will understand

Preface

Much *phan-fiction* has been written about the renowned opera ghost, first made famous by Gaston Leroux in his book *Phantom of the Opera*, and later by Andrew Lloyd Webber in the stage musical by the same name. There is much speculation, both for and against, about many so-called known facts, and whether the opera ghost really existed, and if he did, what was his fate?

Besides the stage play, I had the privilege of viewing *The Phantom of the Opera : The Movie*, numerous times, starring the Scottish actor Gerard Butler. For many years, I had been interested in writing and had made several attempts, and although I had recently continued with that dream, upon seeing Gerard's portrayal of the Phantom, it so inspired me that I was compelled at first to write a short story, that soon blossomed into a full scale manuscript for a book. That the character of the Phantom in the movie version called to me as a writer, is a phenomenon that is hard to explain. After all, I had seen the stage play before.

What left a lasting impression on my senses and conscious mind, and undoubtedly unconscious mind as well, was Mr. Butler's tremendous talent as an actor in this amazing role. The Phantom became a living, breathing person with a soul and spirit that one minute made you soar to unbelievable heights, and the next made you weep. That Mr. Butler's singing voice was beautiful and melodic, only added to the drama. You became truly *wrapped up*, not only in the Phantom's sorrow and his pain, but came away with the realization of how dreadful a large slice of humanity views such individuals. You empathized! And in the end, you desperately, so desperately, wanted to make it better!

There in lies the premise of my book. What happens to the Phantom at the end of the movie, when the lights come on, and you ultimately go back to reality? In many ways this is a typical romance story, with all those entities that a romance story must have to enter that category, and be appreciated by the masses that stream to the bookstores to buy them. But make no mistake! This is not your usual romance. Within these pages lie the deep, wrenching, and often dark and brooding thoughts of a man who has suffered a most despicable fate, telling of how he strives to reconcile, not only what a lifetime of cruelty has heaped upon him with a terrible vengeance, but how he will deal with those horrific events that he alone, caused in retaliation.

Much of my food for thought was gleaned from Gerard Butler's awe-inspiring performance. Through his eyes, his expressions, and his mannerisms, I was able to feel not only what the Phantom was thinking on the surface that made the scene flow to perfection, but what he felt deep within his tortured soul. I merely continued where the movie ended, and took the story to my interpretation of its fruition. Although the book was written to stand entirely alone, to truly understand where I am going with this character, I would advise that you view Andrew Lloyd Webber and Joel Schumacher's film…*The Phantom of the Opera: The Movie*, and experience Gerard's magnificent performance. Only then will you understand the extent of *my* character. Seeing the stage play alone, an entirely different medium and entity unto itself, will not get you to where I want to take you. I wish you not only an exciting viewing experience you will never forget, but hopefully in reading one also!

This book is devoted in spirit to Gerry Butler, and his unending dedication to all his characters, whether fictional or non-fictional. Drawing from many of his own life experiences, he gives these characters human and emotional persona that is within all of us, using his genuine, heart-felt ability to give his audience something to take away with them that lifts the spirit and *makes your soul take flight*. That this is a cherished gift to be savored, is undeniable. He has given me that wonderful inspiration to once again reach for a dream, helping me to believe, achieve, imagine, and ultimately inspire others! I bow to you, my dear friend!

Jodi Leisure Minton

Life (is) wrought with barriers and crossroads of chance.
(But) TIME and CHOICES make us whole!

Excerpt from a poem written for Gerry Butler by
BlackOperaMask

To everything there is a season,
a time for every purpose under the sun.
a time to be born and a time to die;
a time to plant and a time to pluck up that which is planted;
a time to kill and a time to heal.
a time to weep and a time to laugh;
a time to embrace and a time to refrain from embracing;
a time to lose and a time to seek;
a time to rend and a time to sew;
a time to keep silent and a time to speak;
a time to love and a time to hate;
a time for war and a time for peace.

Ecclesiastes 3:1-8

Chapter One

PARIS...1871

Shattering the mirrors had been an impulse! One that symbolized to Erik, regardless of the cost, that which must be left behind! It had been a cathartic moment, where the world he had known for a lifetime was broken into as many shards of glass, as lay scattered upon the cold floor of his home. He had stepped through the hidden doorway, and the last 20 years of his life had vanished, as if it had not really happened.

He wanted relief from the pain in his heart. His body felt numb, as if it no longer belonged to him. Tears ran down his face in ribbons, and the salt stung at his eyes. In resignation, he closed his blurry eyes to the impending darkness, allowing the gloom that surrounded his new world to shroud his senses also. His hand touched the damp wall in many familiar places, as he walked rapidly along the narrow corridor, his footsteps echoing almost silently, as practiced feet knew every ridge and bump of the rocky pathway beneath his boots. As he neared the obscured and tiny entrance to the massive cave network, where the underground river was hidden from the outside world, Erik felt a cold breeze blow in upon his wet shirt, and he unconsciously pulled the ruffles of the garment together for warmth, where it had once gapped haphazardly open to his waist. His britches and boots were wet as well, and the icy coldness that invaded his body triggered the stark reality of his situation, which suddenly seemed like a sharp slap across his face, as cold facts entered into his thoughts once more.

Where had he gone wrong? He wanted to push the events of the last few months to the farthest recesses of his mind, but his heart ached unmercifully. Only moments ago, it seemed that time had stood quietly still, or perhaps it was just that he had willed it to do so. Why had Christine come back to return the ring? At first, almost against all rational thought or reason, for just a split second in time, he dared to believe that she had returned to him! He saw in her eyes a confusion of wanting to convey to him something important, as an eternity of emotions and unanswered questions rapidly passed between them, but it was gone in a moment, and as he watched her fade away into the stone passageway, he knew he could never have called her back! Was the ring a token of what had transpired between them, and she wanted him to always remember, or was it merely a symbol of what could never be, and returning it would somehow help her to forget? Would he ever really know the answer to this paradox? She wanted her freedom from him, and now she had it!

Shafts of moonlight filtered in from the opening in the rock, and Erik's steps slowed cautiously, as the moss covering the wet sheetrock made progress through the passageway more dangerous. He gritted his teeth as he thought about what lay before him. He mentally calculated his turbulent situation. He knew what he needed to do. The plan had been set into motion by his own unorthodox and persuasive actions, and the obvious, disastrous turn of events, and there could be no swaying from his unalterable decision, or from his newfound fate, even as he wished it could be otherwise. He was certainly no fool! At least when it involved the evolution of his home, he thought angrily, not actually wanting to delve into those issues that might certainly dispute that statement, and with that reasoning pushed to the back of his mind, his mood was growing darker with every footstep toward an uncertain future. There had always been the chance over the years of needing a rapid escape. He had constructed his world as safe as possible, with the knowledge he had gleaned over innumerable years of self-teaching in architecture, design and construction, building a haven that included underground passageways and barriers to keep intruders out. The locks, pathways, and underground tunnels, not to mention the traps and hidden labyrinths, all fitted with mechanical devices, were hard for the inexperienced to navigate. But it was not totally foolproof. It could be entered into from the opera house, and from the outside, if one were to stumble upon the secret entrances. And for this reason, Erik had long ago set plans into motion that would hold in readiness the necessary components for leaving, if such a need ever arose. But he had never ventured to use them. He had grown comfortable and accustom to his dark world, and the two main ingredients that sustained the very life force within him, and both had been right here in the opera house itself. His music and his Christine!

Erik's eyes pierced through the dim light, searching the shadows for a small, buffered inlet along the narrow waterway. Cocking his ear upward, he heard the drone of voices in the distance, alerting him that the city was still buzzing with the burning of the opera house. A faint clanking could be heard from the water pumpers, as buckets were undoubtedly being filled to douse upon the fire. A pungent smell of burning wood and cinder wafted acidly in the air, invading the confines of the small opening, causing Erik to cough and his eyes to sting, bringing forth tears for yet another reason. Time was a crucial factor. His foot hit upon the object he was searching for—a tall timber sticking out of the water and rock, to which a length of rope lay idle. Bending on one knee beside the timber, he picked up the rope that disappeared into the murky water, and gave it a slight tug. An object loomed into view from a short distance away, and Erik pulled it closer to stop at the water's edge. Yanking aside a dark colored tarp, he uncovered a small wooden boat, modest in its appearance, yet sturdy and laden with a moderate amount of supplies. He wanted to be far away from Paris before morning. He slipped silently into the boat and secured a paddle.

Hours later, Erik pulled the small craft closer to the riverbank. His body was weary, and his mind needed refuge from the night's events. The full moon was high in the sky, and its beam cast an eerie shadow across the river, engulfing the side he navigated in almost total darkness, leaving the opposite bank shimmering with dancing lights that sparkled upon the ripples in the water, lending just enough light to secure his passage. Trying to focus his eyes on the scene around him, Erik stretched out an arm, catching his hand upon a small tree branch, and pulled the boat into seclusion, amongst the reeds and a small gathering of bushes. No one would find him here, he reasoned, with growing satisfaction towards his own safety.

His eyes adjusting to the darkness, he could barely discern the mound of supplies packed tightly in the bottom of the boat. Rummaging about, Erik found his heavy lined cape. His body was shivering from the cool breeze that had blown softly on the water for what had seemed an eternity, but wanting to put a decent distance between himself and the confines of the city, had spurred him to forgo the luxury of obtaining dry clothing. The temperature of the cave, in which he had lived, had been unchanging, never affected by the weather on the outside, and he had seldom needed his cloak, except when he had left the security of the lair, and more often than not, it was needed for concealment from prying eyes, rather than for the purpose of warmth.

Erik wrapped his long, hard torso in the confines of his cape, much like a cocoon, and stretched out as comfortable as possible into the bottom of the sparse little boat. He fleetingly thought of the lushness of the padded seating in the gondola, as his tired body settled upon the hard timbers the small craft was constructed from. He had been used to the quietness of his musical domain, that rarely had a sound emanating from its overwhelming vastness, unless you accounted for the dripping of water as it trickled along some of the walls, or the gentle lapping of waves from the river, as it crested at the rivers edge just below his quarters. His music was the only sound that reverberated off the walls, and what he composed and sang had been for Christine alone. Shaking himself free from his current thoughts, Erik tried to concentrate on the hum of crickets, that in an absurd way mimicked violins. The last thing he did, before drifting into a restless and fitful slumber, was to extract the white mask from a sack and place it familiarly upon the right side of his face. His hair was in rampant disarray without his wig, and he could come to terms with that more easily, but to go without his mask was something he perhaps had to accomplish more slowly! Gingerly he pulled a large, dark, tarp, formerly used as a ground cloth for painting stage scenery, over all of his body and the needed supplies. Hopefully, he thought, this would protect everything from the penetrating morning dew. Sleep overtook his senses, and for a few precious hours of needed escape, rendered his mind blank to the tortured thoughts that were the past. The future would be tomorrow.

Something about the way the boat rocked, startled Erik out of his needed sleep. Water was lapping at the sides with a force that concerned him, and he wondered if the wind had picked up during the night? Perhaps he needed to tie the boat more securely? His body was stiff from the morning dampness, and he shifted heavily, bumping his left side up against something softer than the thwarts of the boat. He sat up abruptly, and two large saucer blue eyes were staring back at his steely green ones in fear and disbelief. The small figure started to flee upward, but Erik, with a cat-like swiftness, caught the lads wrist in his large left hand with a vice-like grip, and pulled him back down sharply into the bottom of the boat, causing the rather dirty urchin to mutter a most indecent remark from under his breath. Shyly, the lad looked up at the tall menacing man towering over him. *Mon Dieu*! What did he have here, Erik thought suspiciously, unconsciously raising his right hand for a fleeting moment to touch the mask that covered his face, lowering it just as quickly, figuring what did it matter now. The boy had already seen him.

"It's okay, lad. I'll not hurt you," Erik assured forcefully, seeing that the boy was genuinely frightened that he had been discovered, and probably scared half out of his wits at the sight Erik was sure he presented..

"I didna mean to steal anything, *M'sieur*. Beggin' your pardon, but I was just seekin' a small space to rest for the wee hours of the night. I didna know that anyone was sleepin' in the idle boat," the boy piped up boldly, a small wince evident on his face, as Erik still held the lads wrist tightly in his grasp. Absently he let the boy's arm fall free, feeling a twinge of guilt, as he noticed the red hand print he had left on the tiny arm.

Erik perused the lad skeptically. He was tall enough, Erik thought idly, but he had a chalky paleness about his skin that made Erik believe perhaps the boy was a bit sickly. He had no muscle to speak of; he was rather frail and wafe-like; his frame was poured into breeches that were far too small, and the tattered leather vest that he wore, fit so tightly around his chest, that Erik couldn't fathom how the lad could even breathe. He wore a brown woolen cap pulled tightly down to his eyebrows, letting not a bit of hair out to prove its color, and the almost girl like features of his face were smudged with a bit of soot. It was hard to tell where the dirt ended and the child began. Erik thought perhaps the lad was somewhere between the ages of twelve or thirteen, but with little experience in that area of living, he could not be sure.

" I don't want to bother you any longer, *M'sieur.* I'll just be on my way," the lad offered, but did not stir, or seem in the hurry that he was verbally conveying.

Erik raised his left eyebrow in amusement. Perhaps the lad was hungry and looking for a handout. He certainly looked like he could use a cartload of meals under his belt to fatten him up. Well, he certainly had food to share, and the boy seemed content to sit without constraints, and didn't shy away from Erik's appearance. The lad had seen his mask, and the aftermath of what lay exposed with his wig off, yet didn't react as if it was out of the ordinary. So be it, he thought!

The sun was just starting to stir on the horizon, and pale yellow light filtered into the secluded hiding place, yet all around them, trees still hid the small boat from prying eyes. How had he been discovered, Erik wondered? "Where are you from, lad?" Erik asked thoughtfully, wanting a lot more information. Something about the lad was vaguely disturbing, but Erik was hard pressed at this very moment to put his finger on just what made him uneasy.

"Oh, here and there! No place in particular," the lad offered nonchalantly, almost as if to imply, that this kind of knowledge was not to share with a stranger. A bit irritated, yet unable to think of a good reason to press the lad further, Erik slipped lithely out of his cape, and his crinkled ruffled shirt front gapped open to his waist, revealing a wide muscled chest and a taunt belly that disappeared below the waistband of his brown britches. He faintly detected a smothered gasp from the lad, but when he glanced once again in the lad's direction, the boy had turned slightly toward the supplies, and his eyes were cast downward, as if searching for something in his vest.

Thinking once again about the food, and for the first time noticing a small rumbling coming from his own empty stomach,

Erik reached over in front of the boy, his right shoulder coming in solid contact with the lad's left thigh, as he agilely retrieved a small waxed box from beneath the damp tarp, casually flipping open the lid to reveal a treasure of cheese, wine and dried fruit from within. The boy pulled away sharply as Erik straightened, and it seemed to him that the lad appeared to be a bit skittish. "I assure you, lad, I don't bite, and I don't mean to hurt you," Erik offered again quickly, but with some impatience creeping into his low masculine voice. The boy looked at him carefully, with chin pointed downward, and eyes not quite fully open, but slightly downcast and hooded. Perhaps it was the mask that scared him after all, Erik decided, but before he had a chance to offer words of assurance, the lad spoke up anxiously.

"I don't want to bother such a fine gentleman as yourself, *M'sieur*, but I am *v-e-r-r-y* hungry. Can't for the life of me remember when I ate last. I dinna have anythin' to give in payment for a meal, but I could make the boat tidy, and perhaps gather a pile of wood for a fire," the lad offered with hopeful enthusiasm.

With growing absurdity, Erik pondered the current situation. There wasn't enough stuff to need tidying up, and he dare not risk a fire. He had momentarily thought the boy afraid of him, but it seemed not to be the case. Something about the lad still puzzled him, yet he knew not why. The boy appeared to be from nowhere and willing to help. Why not take advantage of a small gift just dropped into his lap. His own circumstances were cloaked in secrecy. Why should he believe the lad's should be any different? The boy was talkative and friendly, and the sound of another human voice did wonders for his otherwise dark, monotonous mood. If this lad would agree to go along with him, on at least part of his journey—a helping hand that could go unnoticed into the busy marketplace of a city now and then for supplies—would certainly be most advantageous for making a smoother transition, while in his precarious, predicament of the moment. Perhaps they could help each other. He'd post the question to the lad after a small repast of food, to show the boy he was serious. A little something in the lad's belly could go a long way in persuading him of the merits of such a partnership.

"What do you call yourself, lad?" Erik asked, trying pointedly to put the boy at ease. The lad sat there unmoving, an awkward silence stretching before them, causing Erik to search the boy's face, wondering both at his hesitation, and why he didn't want Erik to know his name.

"Jake," the lad volunteered belatedly, a high-pitched squeak to his voice. A slow pink flush rose in his pale cheeks, as his unprepared answer was offered. His downcast eyes shielded the fact that a scowl played across Erik's classical features. Yikes! It hadn't even crossed Jake's mind to think of a name to give to the stranger. He dare not tell this man what it really was! "What might I call *you, M'sieur,"* inquired the lad in equal response, hoping to slide through the oversight he had just encountered.

Jake still kept his head slightly lowered, giving Erik's eyes more access to the top of the lad's tightly knit woolen cap, then a genuine studied view of the actual features of the child's face, and he wondered why the boy appeared so shy, when moments before he almost seemed bold. "Erik, will be fine," Erik said matter-of-factly, selecting a piece of tangy cheese from the waxed box, and balancing the bottle of wine gingerly on the mound of supplies. He offered the food to the boy.

"But I can't call a gentleman by his first name, *M'sieur*," bulked the lad insolently. "It just isn't done," Jake protested. His tiny face lifted abruptly in defiance, knowing what was proper, and what was not. A fiery sparkle was evident in his eyes, as he offered the knowledge that he wasn't stupid. What he knew—he knew! And that's all there was to it!

Erik almost laughed at the lad's independence showing through in his emotions. That was the spirit he saw in the lad only moments ago! "Well, it's done here. My name is Erik," he chuckled, a twinkle in his green eyes, as he offered the food to the boy again.

With a suddenness that startled both of them, the lad grabbed at a moderate size piece of cheese, and fairly stuffed the entire morsel into his mouth in one swift swoop. Erik instantly ascertained, that chewing such a large portion was going to be more than a monumental task, since the lad's cheeks stuck out in both directions, and his eyes were wide in belated recognition of what had just transpired. He could see the boy gulping, trying to keep the situation under control, and in spite of himself, Erik laughed out loud.

"Easy, easy! There is more food where that came from," he chided, thinking that the boy must have truly been starving. He offered the bottle of wine to the child, then pulled it back, thinking again upon his decision. But the lad seemed to be choking, so he offered the bottle again. "Here, wash it down with this."

Jake took the bottle in both small hands, grasping it tightly around the neck, and put the opening to his lips. Turning it straight upwards into the air, the red liquid spilled forth rapidly, sliding not only down his throat like a red-hot poker, but spilling negligently down his chin, and onto his clothes. Erik reached over hastily, grabbing the slippery bottle out of Jake's hands. The boy coughed and sputtered, spewing the offending refreshment, as well as half chewed cheese over Erik's white, ruffled shirt and bare chest.

"*Mon dieu,*" Erik shouted, rearing back in surprise, and jumping awkwardly to his feet. The little boat rocked precariously back and forth with such a force that Erik lost his footing, his thigh colliding harshly against the gunwales, pitching his towering frame sideways, causing him to fall over the side and into the water with a gigantic splash.

Jake immediately came up out of his seat, both hands covering his mouth in disbelief, as he stared horrified into the river. Erik had gone under the water once, and when he came sputtering up to the surface, he gasped for air. The white mask was in one hand, and the other was wiping water off his face. When he stood up, the water was not more than four feet deep, leaving most of the drenched shirt hanging off his massive shoulders, and clinging transparently to his skin. Erik took a couple strokes with his free arm, then began wading toward the riverbank. His face was uncovered as the mask lay limply in his hand, and his dark ebony hair was plastered over his head in all directions, covering most of his deformity, except for that on the right front of his face. Jake had a clear view. He looked at it long and hard, even if just for a moment. It didn't look that bad, he thought. He had actually seen worse. But he understood that the man didn't think so, or he wouldn't wear a mask. It was the nasty scowl that was plastered on Erik's face, and the dark foreboding glance he shot at the boy, that gave Jake pause to be worried. He shrunk his little frame down into the bowels of the boat, which not being large, didn't hide too much.

Erik came forward, his body dripping water onto the supplies, as he searched for a towel to dry himself, and a change of clothes to improve his newly acquired foul mood. "I can wash the wine out of your shirt," Jake offered timidly, wanting to be helpful, yet not wanting to further anger this man who had shared his food, and not just shooed him away like many others would have done. He was truly sorry, but he didn't know how to make up for this disaster.

"I doubt my shirt's in need of washing *a-n-y-m-o-r-e*, lad," Erik retorted in an even tone, with an obvious emphasis on certain words, letting the boy know most effectively, that he was presently not in a frame of mind for talking. Silently, Erik carried the articles he'd been seeking to shore. He stripped off the wet, clinging garments, dried his taut, muscled body that glistened with a golden hue, as water droplets were caught by the peeking rays of the morning sun, and put on tight, black britches, a conservative white, linen shirt with sparse buttons down the front, and black riding boots that ended just below his knees. All the while the lad kept his back turned staunchly to Erik's view, and it seemed to him, that the lad was acting as if *he* were the one to have been pitched into the cold water. Once again, before returning to the boat, Erik applied his white mask. He wasn't ready to give it up...just yet! As the lad heard Erik approach, he turned around.

Jake stared at this tall imposing gentleman, who to him appeared handsome, with or without the mask. It was all a matter of opinion, what you saw and what you didn't. Knowing that it might anger Erik further, he still felt compelled to make a statement. "It doesn't look all that bad, *M'sieur*," the boy offered sympathetically. "You don't really need the mask." He knew it was bold, and he mentally prepared his mind for a rebuke, and stiffened his body just a little if the man struck out in anger, but what he had said was true, and he had been brought up to accept the truth.

"You try my patience, Jake," Erik shot back with little conviction. The day hadn't even begun and already he was tired. "It would be best if you just leave me be." He vaulted over the side of the boat in one fluid motion and seated himself at the stern. He noticed the stiffness in the lad's manner, and that he seemed unyielding in his statement. " It's just a tool to hide a part of me, that I'd rather the rest of the world did not see," Erik stated flatly, no emotions revealed in his tone, as years of decency and compassion had been withheld, leaving him unfamiliar with the sentiment. He left it at that! Perhaps someday he wouldn't feel that way, but today he did. "I'm going to be traveling a very long distance. If you have no other pressing business needing your attention, would you want to come along?" Erik had said it, and given the boy a choice. Either he came along, or he didn't.

Chapter Two

They had made good progress down the river during the early part of the day. The boy had readily agreed to come along. To Erik's surprise the lad had almost seemed anxious, and somewhat excited about the idea of leaving the vicinity quickly, bouncing in the boat with gleeful intent before he realized not only might he spill Erik back into the water, but perhaps himself as well. A stormy look on Erik's face, and a stern remainder informing the lad that he had only *so many* dry clothes, made the lad sit quietly, almost like a statue, for the better part of an hour before he finally relaxed. All this gave Erik just cause in wondering, what was so distasteful in the boy's past to make him want to leave the vicinity in such a hurry? Had the boy no family.... anywhere? Despite the most unique and misfortunate events of their meeting, Erik rather liked the child. He knew that the boy could be very helpful in his journey. But he also knew, deep down, that he had once before enjoyed taking care of a child, and watched her grow into a woman, and he had not found it unpleasant. It might not have been in the conventional way that most people would imagine, but he had played a significant role in bringing Christine to where she was today in the world of music...certainly *not* in the world of love, he thought with little humor, a deep ache suddenly knotting his gut as he remembered in a flash... all those memories. Both good and bad! He had whispered through the walls to her...suggestions. When she should retire! That her voice needed rest! What she should wear! Making sure she practiced on a daily basis the operas that he alone had picked for the theatre to perform, so she would be ready when the time was right. An opportunity that he made sure *became available*! He had structured her life in innumerable ways that even she did not know about, and most duly accomplished through the guise of Madame Giry. Christine was the woman that he had eventually grown to love, one that he believed had some inherent understanding of the pain inflicted on him by the world, for she heard it in his voice when he had sung to her, and when they had sung their strange, sensual duets, and he was certain that when he had finally revealed himself, that she had developed an undeniable physical attraction to him. He believed that in another timeframe, most pointedly one where Raoal did not have a part, he might have actually guided her gently to discover the real man behind the monster. He desperately needed to erase the pain—that silent, yet excruciating warning against danger that alerted the body to flee from further injury, not distinguishing between physical or mental, for it did not matter. Music and love were not factors anymore! They were in a past life that was totally swept away, brutal and agonizing rejection telling him unequivocally that he would never let them enter again. Prying his mind resolutely from the past to the present, Erik shook his head in silent determination, almost as if he believed that in doing so, he could extract those memories from his mind. He had to force his mind to concentrate on what the coming evening would bring.

The waterway had served its purpose. He had needed to leave Paris by a route that no one either suspected or believed possible for him, and although it had not been the fastest route that he could have chosen, it was the one that could be taken at a moment's notice. He couldn't keep horses in readiness at all times. But now he wanted to go overland, and the immediate necessity of that plan would be to purchase a wagon and a pair of horses, for the next part of his journey.

Jake sat silently in the boat. Leaving all behind that was familiar, was hopefully a step in the right direction. Everything he had loved here was gone, and all that remained was what he despised. His father had taught him to be independent, beholden to no man, and to make his way in the world on his own terms, no matter what the circumstances. This stranger was a means to an end that suited the design of his own separate plan, and he meant to take advantage of it in full measure. Erik was an impressive figure in the very least, and although Jake knew nothing about the man's past, one he likely wanted to keep secret, Erik seemed genuinely kind, and for now, that was all that mattered.

Halfway through the day, Erik pulled their little craft to shore. Instructing the boy to gather wood for a fire, he settled himself in the boat, rolled out a leather saddlebag that would fit on a horse, and extracted a map that was folded many times over. He studied it for several minutes, then called to Jake.

"We'll rest here for the afternoon," he said matter-of-factly, his eyes unreadable to the boy. "This evening I have something that I want you to do," Erik added wittingly, and the look that he gave the boy, and the tone of his melodic and commanding voice, made Jake's heart race a little faster, as his mind played with the idea of some new adventure.

The stable was dark and portentous. Only a few ribbons of pale, lucent light filtered easily through small cracks between the boards, from a little shack connected in the back. Mud had fallen out of the crevices that kept the cold of winter out, and Jake could smell the burning oil, and the putrid smell the oil made, when a lantern was not cleaned after each use. He rounded the building, lifted the large rusted latch that kept the gate secured, and pulled the door wide enough to enter. "Anyone here to attend?" he yelled as loudly as he dared, for fear of waking the entire countryside. Erik had instructed him to get the job done, but not to draw attention to himself needlessly.

"What yer wantin'," came a booming voice from the direction of the dim light near the back of the stable, and was followed immediately by a meaty looking man with a snarl on his features, and dressed in filthy clothing. Jake almost jumped back in fright, but he had a mission to accomplish, and he needed to talk to the stable master.

"I'll be needin' a good wagon, and a pair of horses, and a talk with the stable master," Jake let out with a rush, realizing that he had been holding his breath.

The man eyed Jake up and down with distain and laughed a crooked smile. "Oh, lad, the stable master isn't here right now, but I have just what you are needing," and reached out to grab the boy by the collar, pulling him over to the sorriest looking pair of nags he had ever seen in his life.

Jake squirmed free and looked incredulous at the man, as if he were totally daft. "Those horses are too old and rundown," Jake exclaimed, knowing that the man was trying to dupe him into purchasing horses that were unsuitable. He knew good horseflesh when he saw it, and this wasn't it!

"And what do ya have on ya. laddie, to be paying for all of this," the man said with sly menace to his voice. "Ya can't just sass-shay out of here without a good chunk of coin."

" I have enough," Jake remarked pointedly, "but I need something better than this," he said, indicating the two old nags.

"Well, let's just be takin' a look at what ya have there," the stable-hand weaseled, and lunged forward, grabbing the boy by the back of his britches, trapping one small arm, and lifted him high over his shoulder, all the while Jake making every attempt to kick his legs in all directions, and beat at the man's head with his free arm.

A loud commanding voice came out of the darkness in the direction of the doorway, and the stable-hand spun around with the lad dangling off of his shoulder, feet pointed in the direction of the rafters. "Boy, I told you to bring the wagon and horses posthaste. Not to play around and keep me waiting."

The ominous, dark figure stepped forward to the edge of the shadows, and the stable-hand could see a dangerous looking gentleman wrapped in a black, hooded cloak, his face totally obscured, from both the darkness and the angle of his hood. He caught a silver glint that bounced off the tip of a sword, which dangled meaningfully from beneath the bottom edge of the dark cape.

"Give the man the money you have, lad, and collect the two large bays there, and that carriage," the man said, pointing a black gloved hand in the direction of what he wanted, and with a forewarning message in his tone, that no one would have even considered disobeying.

The stable-hand put the boy down gingerly, looking up with some fear in his eyes, but the man in the cape was gone. "I'll be needin' all the fixin's to hitch the bays to the wagon, and one saddle thrown in," said Jake, confidence in his voice that the stable-hand would now take his own requests seriously.

The frightened man did as he was told, agitation showing in every single movement, as he prepared the fine horses that he had hoped to keep for himself, yet in fear that if he didn't do what the man had commanded, he would certainly be back, and dealing with *that* man was not to his liking.

Erik waited outside in the shadows for the lad to finish his business. He had calculated that the boy would have some trouble, but it had all gone as he expected. He had been there when he was needed, but had not had to be a part of the dealings, yet still accomplished what he wanted. And his identity had not been jeopardized.

With some sense of expediency, they brought the horses and carriage back to the place where their boat was anchored. Erik wanted to keep not only their presence a secret, but also the direction in which they had departed. First walking the rig a fair distance from town in the opposite direction, then circling around and riding the rest of the way in a more attention-drawing pace, Jake studied Erik out of the corner of his eyes. With that black cape thrown negligently over his broad shoulders, and a wicked looking saber belted tightly to his left hip, Erik looked so different and so...so...dangerous. And with that mask, and his black hair flying in the wind, Jake thought that perhaps the Prince of Darkness was a far better analogy.

Upon arriving, Erik unhitched the bays and tied them loosely to the back of the carriage. "I can help with the horses," Jake offered, knowing that he had lots of experience from helping his father, the head stable master of a large estate just north of Paris, but was not wanting to give Erik that information about himself.

"You did a fine job back there," Erik commended, not pausing in what he was doing in preparing the horses for the night. "It's late and I want to get an early start. It's best you get some sleep."

Jake was disappointed and tried again to persuade him. "But I really know what I'm doing when it comes to horses," Jake said hopefully.

Some irritation evident in his voice, Erik repeated himself. "Stretch the blankets out over there under that tree, Jake, and get some rest. I want to get an early start." With that, Erik turned back to what he had been doing, expecting to be obeyed. Jake did obey, but Erik heard him mumble something under his breath, and Erik had to smile. The boy had done well, and he had more than enough spunk.

The night sounds played softly, intermingling with a light breeze blowing in the tree-tops, and Jake lay awake listening to the occasional nickering of the horses. His skin fairly itched on every inch of his body possible, and it kept him from sleeping. His clothes reeked from every kind of substance known to man, and it was time this foolishness was over. *She* wanted a bath, and *she* wanted one now!

Erik lay asleep on the blanket beside her, his heavy, even breathing telling her that he was in a deep slumber. She turned her head to look at him. His tall muscular body was stretched out on his right side, his arm cradling his head as a pillow, his mask almost obscured from her sight in the crook of his arm. Moonlight shining in between the tree leaves played across his relaxed features. Thick, black hair hung down to below his ear, and a few errant stands fell over his forehead most appealingly. Long black eyelashes closed over those green eyes that seemed to bore into her every time he would study her—those times he thought she wasn't looking, like he was trying to fit together the pieces of a puzzle. A puzzle she was afraid he would finally solve. And then he would send her away.

They had camped for the night beside the river's edge. She slipped carefully from beneath the cape Erik had given her for the chilly night. Silently she crept to the back of the carriage, where the horses were tethered. She nuzzled her cheek to the first bay's nose and patted him affectionately behind his ears. His mane was long and black, and flowed half-way down his neck. Jake knew both bays were horses to be proud to own.

She untied the bay, pulling him up along side the boot. Climbing on the back of the carriage, she swung one leg over the horse and hung tightly onto his mane. Slowly she started to move away from the camp. She just wanted to feel the cool water on her skin and brush the filth out of her clothes, and she wanted to do it in private. She couldn't let Erik find out that she was a girl. She would be back before he even knew that she was gone!

Suddenly the bay reared alarmingly, its front legs pawing the air, as Erik's towering form caught the reins, yanking the horse's head back around towards the carriage. Jake went flying off of the back, and landed with a thud in the dirt. "Ouch," she cried, tears welling up in her startled eyes, as her backside began smarting with a throbbing vengeance from the hard tumble.

"And where do you think you are going?" Erik said with malice in his voice, while tying the horse once again to the carriage. He stalked over to the boy, his eyes full of fury. He grabbed the boy's arm in a bruising grip and pulled him up from the dirt. Erik stood facing the boy, his eyes cold and accusing, his face inches from Jake's. "I don't take kindly to anyone stealing my property," he barked out, causing the boy to tremble a little in fear.

"But I wasn't stealing," Jake offered innocently, not knowing how to explain what she was doing without giving her whole charade away. And she couldn't do that at all cost. Not likely he would believe that she just wanted to take a midnight ride for pleasure!

But Erik wasn't listening. His temper was clearly beginning to erupt. He pulled the boy over to the blanket and flung him roughly to the pallet. "When I say to get some sleep, I mean what I say, boy." Silently he stalked off. He was infuriated with the night's newest events. Just when he thought he could trust the boy, he tried to steal his horse and take off on his own.

Jake sat in silence. Her eyes stung from the tears she held back, not wanting Erik to see her crying. Her backside hurt and her pride as well, and she knew she couldn't begin to explain. She honestly believed Erik was not the kind of man to cross, and now he thought her to be a thief. Think what he wanted, she had absolutely no choice, she assured herself. She repeated this reasoning several times just for good measure, heaving a final sigh of resignation. He would never trust her again. Jake lay on her side, curled up in a ball, and pulled the cape over her body to hide, silent tears running down her dirty face. Avoiding Erik until morning was a good thing! Of that she was certain!

In the morning they started off just before dawn. Erik was in a black mood. A storm had thundered wildly in his mind for the better part of the night, as he sorted things out. He didn't understand why the lad had wanted to leave, and even more so, why he would steal his horse. He thought he had been kind enough. The lad seeming content to enter into the adventure of the journey with enthusiasm, and that had made Erik smile more than once. He knew the boy had cried in the night, for he heard an occasional small sob come from beneath his cape when the boy was sleeping. Somehow, he would have to find out more about Jake's past, and why he was so untrusting of Erik's genuinely given friendship. Hopefully that would supply the answers. But then Erik also reasoned, that the boy's behavior was not unlike everyone's he had ever encountered. He had forced his thoughts away from this perplexing situation, needing sleep, but they had ultimately drifted back to the nagging sensation that somehow the lad was not what he seemed, and Erik vowed that somehow, he would unravel this strange tangle he seemed to have stumbled upon.

Erik hitched the two fine bays to the carriage, and packed the supplies into the boot behind the seats, before Jake had even stirred. The boy was wrapped tightly in Erik's cape, only the top of his hat showing. He nudged the lad's shoulder with his foot to get him awake. Looking at the lad sleeping, Erik wondered why the boy insisted on keeping his hat constantly pulled down to the tip of his eyebrows, and his vest buttoned tightly to the neck, even in the heat of the day. He supposed it had something to do with his frail appearance, and that he must be cold, even when the day sweltered with heat. Erik disliked that the lad's clothes were stained and rather filthy, and although he had suggested that the boy take his clothes off, and wash both himself and his garments in the river, the lad had refused, saying he would catch his death if he did so. Erik didn't press the lad further, but sooner or later the boy would have to relent, or he would begin to smell like the sewers of Paris. Within the next day or so, if the lad continued to stay, they would have to purchase him some spare clothes.

Jake felt the side of Erik's boot gently touch her on the shoulder, signaling that it was time to leave. Sleepily she stirred from the confines of the cape, rubbed her eyes and stretched her arms, shaking off the stiffness of the night out of her bones. It had taken her many hours to fall asleep, her emotions running the gamut, and her temper this morning was less than perfect. She was totally disgusted with herself for believing that she could outwit him, leaving herself so vulnerable, and almost exposed. Such foolishness on her part would never happen again. She was dirty and itchy! That would be the price she had to pay for her disguised identity. She would just have to live with it for now. But somehow, she promised herself, she would find another way to take a bath in private. Preferably when Erik was otherwise preoccupied. Offhandedly, Erik handed her pieces of bread and fruit, and made preparations to get underway. They traveled most of the day in stony silence, only saying a word now and then that was absolutely necessary.

The road was bumpy and narrow, and plagued with numerous ruts and potholes, many which were so large that they swallowed up the entire length of a coach wheel. Erik did his best, zig-zagging back and forth now and then, selecting the best possible section of road for the smoothest ride. The bays were feisty, and the muscles in Erik's arms and shoulders were in constant motion, as he struggled to keep them in line. The springs on the carriage were a bit wanting, and whenever the road became slightly cumbersome, the carriage careened from side to side alarmingly. Just before noontime, when they were about to stop and rest, and take in a small meal, a rabbit dashed across the road in front of the bays, and the horses both bulked, rearing slightly, causing the carriage to jerk sharply to the side. A loud metallic snap was heard from the rear of the coach, and the carriage dipped on the back right side, as the wheel came off from the hub.

Jake slid down the seat in the direction of the door and smacked the panel hard with her hip, giving off a squeak of surprise, as once again, pain shot thru her already bruised body. Erik, up on his feet, strained with the reins, pulling the horses to a stuttering stop, and the carriage shifted to the right at a dead stop, almost landing the carriage into a lake near the curve in the road.

"Are you all right," Erik asked the lad, concern in his voice as he glanced momentarily in his direction, decided he seemed okay, then turned and vaulted over the half-door and ran around back to survey the damage.

Jake climbed down with some difficulty, her hip and backside smarting from two falls in less than a day. She looked at the damage also. The right, back wheel had come off of the axle, which was easily fixed, but the metallic band that held the wood together had snapped in two.

"I'll just have to fix it," Erik said, more in irritation that it would impede their progress, than that it would be hard work. He didn't seem concerned that he could accomplish either. But Jake wasn't so sure! The band was metal. What was he going to use in place of it?

Erik instructed the boy to build a really, hot fire. It was high noon, and the sun beat down with its fiery rays that scorched everything that it touched. What could he want with that? It was hotter than blazes outside. Who needed more heat, Jake thought, trussed up in hot clothes and totally puzzled, but she didn't want

Erik's wrath crashing down upon her head, so she did what she was told.

Erik stripped off his shirt in the penetrating heat, hung it on the carriage, and bent to his task. First he wired the band together, then set it in the hot fire to heat. Erik snorted to himself. If the outside world only knew how he had mastered this talent, he thought dryly, for he had used this method dozens of times, when constructing many of the grates and barricades that made up the barriers and locks before entering the lair. While waiting for the band to turn a white, hot hue, they ate some cheese and fruit, Erik downing a half bottle of wine for good measure. He then extracted the band from the fire with a gloved hand, and pounded it to a rounded shape with a mallet. He fit it over the wooden wheel, and placed it back on the axle, by lifting the carriage using a lever.

Jake took all this in with avid fascination. How did Erik know how to do all this? As she watched Erik work, she was totally aware that his hard, muscled body glistened with sweat, and the sinewy muscles of his abs, back and arms rippled as they accomplished their task. His ebony hair was in disarray over his entire head, covering even part of his mask, and with his hair falling over his forehead, she swore he looked almost like a little boy in costume playing dress-up… playing at the game of being a man. One dangerous and very intriguing man, to say the least. Jake swallowed hard, a little giggle escaping involuntarily.

Erik looked over at her sharply, wiping the sweat from his face with his left hand, raking his fingers through his tousled hair, and pushing it backwards over is head. "And what is so funny," he said, questioning, his green eyes colliding with hers so harshly that it penetrated her senses, making her flinch. Perhaps he should have asked the lad to help him, Erik thought belatedly? Something to occupy his time, since he was so bound and determined to be helpful.

"Oh, nothing," she said simply, making a little puffing noise, hoping to evade any more questions on his part. In embarrassment, she turned around to look out over the lake, hoping to escape where her thoughts had been wandering. She didn't possess the finite skills or worldliness that most women knew about men, but she was certain that this was a man who would be sinfully, and seductively possessive in a very primal and sexual way to any woman that he decided was his. And that thought totally fascinated her. That she was attracted to him, was something she absolutely refused to think about!

Erik was done. His chest prickled from the salt that had dried on his skin. The lake water appeared cool and inviting. He wanted a bath. He hated being dirty. Those years of his life in the gypsy camp, he had been forced to live in squalor, and the stench of unwashed bodies and obnoxious odors had been almost intolerable. He remembered jumping into the crystal clear water of the river under the opera house, the first opportunity that he had, and not knowing how to swim, he had almost drown. Erik eyed the boy with interest. The lad had a dirty face, and his clothes were caked with dust, and about anything else he could think of. Jake had been sitting on a rock by the lake, watching Erik perform his task, but now his back was turned, and Erik smiled to himself with evil intent. There was no time like the present, and a better opportunity may never again present itself. Erik stalked silently up behind Jake. His arms snaked around the boy, clutching him tightly around the chest, lifting him up swiftly off the rock.

"Time for a good dunking. The dirt is so thick on you, lad, that I think if I allowed you back in the carriage that the wheel would break from the weight, and I don't have a fancy to fix it again," Erik laughed, taking long strides towards the water.

Jake kicked wildly, uttering the most offense language Erik had ever encountered. Erik waded into the water up to his chest. Jake flayed his arms wide, knocking Erik's chin hard with the force of his elbow. Erik's head rocked back and he cursed, when biting his tongue gave him the taste of blood in his mouth. Not to be deterred, Erik dunked the lad once down to his neck, at the same time pulling at the buttons of his vest. Jake sputtered and kicked, but the water impeded his movements. Erik dunked him again, letting the boy's head go below the surface of the water for only a few moments, but long enough to render him calm, and pulled not only his vest over his head, but along with it came his shirt and hat as well. Satisfied with this accomplishment, Erik began to laugh. "All you need now is a good scrubbing"

To Erik's surprise, a long cascading mane of dark red hair came spiraling down from the boy's head. What Erik felt next, gave him more than a moment's pause, as his face drained completely of color. Two plump mounds of flesh pressed accusingly against the arm that he held around Jake's chest. *Mon Dieu*! He let Jake go, like his skin had been burned by a cinder. Jake rounded on him, fixing her large blue eyes on his, humiliation and venomous rage showing at the same moment, and started pummeling Erik's chest furiously with her tiny fists, like her actions would make any difference. At first Erik just stared at her in silent, awestruck denial. His mouth hung open just slightly, and his lips were full and expressive. His startled eyes took in every bit of what was visible above the water, and then some, in the crystal clear water of the lake. This was not a boy, and she was certainly *not* a child. His mind reeled with conflicting curiosity and wariness, at the implication of what he had discovered. Knocked back to extreme reality by the continuous assault upon his person, Erik grabbed her tightly against his chest, pinning her hands between them, able to feel the fiction of her taut young breasts familiarly against his own sensitive skin, their hard pink nipples puckered from the cool water, branding him with silent torture. He inhaled deeply, barely able to exhale.

"Stop your fighting and I'll let you go," he said cautiously, his mind still trying to assimilate what his body was already accepting with a fervor that assaulted his senses most pleasantly.

Jake let her body become still. Keeping his promise, Erik let her go. She grabbed at the shirt and vest floating on the water in a humiliated huff, and started wading toward the shoreline, her clothes clutched tightly to her chest. Over her shoulder, she threw him a sharp retort. "I told you I wasn't stealing your horse, you pompous ass. I just wanted to take a bath in private." With that, she came out of the water, exasperation evident in every movement she made, and disappeared out of site behind the carriage.

Erik watched in total fascination. She had thick red hair that came to just below her waist, hiding most of the view of her lovely back from his observant and piercing eyes. Her body was petite and fair, and her shapely backside swayed back and forth in her obvious agitation, giving Erik reason for the vague grin that played at the corners of his mouth. Why hadn't he seen the signs? Everything was right there in front of his face. Of course hindsight was always better than foresight, he reasoned, with a deep suspicion that this was the calm before the storm. Everything made sense now, and nothing made any sense at all! This would certainly explain why she drew away from him every time their bodies accidentally touched. But why did she tout herself as a lad, and what was her real story? What was behind her need to leave the area so quickly? Erik had many questions, and he wanted some answers. And there was no doubt in *his* mind, that he would eventually get them. No doubt at all!

Chapter Three

Jake fumed at being dunked so callously into the water. Exactly who did Erik think he was? He had ruined everything. Now her charade was ended, and he would not want a girl to continue the journey with him. Ooh, her blasted luck! If she had just gotten away on his horse, she might have kept going into the night. She chastised herself for not staying near Paris, and taking the advice of good friends that could have helped with her beastly situation. Now she was stranded, without any money, and had no idea where she was. Just look at her now, she thought in rising consternation, growing distain for her predicament emanating from every single pore. She felt more like a drowned rat than a proper human being. What was she suppose to wear while her clothes were drying, she fumed hotly, sharp irritation rising to the surface when she thought about Erik's bold and blatant stare, when he so horrendously unearthed her coveted secret? Mulishly she stomped at the ground in irritation. How dare he man-handle her that way! An electrifying spark had shot right through her body, when he had crushed her against him, skin to skin, but she was positive now, thinking with total reason, that it was merely from the shock.

Silently she mulled over her immediate need. Since *M'sieur High and Might* had put her into this particular mess, he could just help her out by sharing his clothes, she thought rationally, feeling some better almost instantly. Cautiously she rounded the edge of the carriage, and grabbed Erik's white linen shirt off the back boot. For a split second, she thought about incurring his wrath by her action, but her need for something to wear ultimately won out. Quickly she stripped out of her wet breeches, donned the shirt and grabbed up her dirty clothing. Silently she slipped away, hopefully undetected, and walked down the sandy shoreline in her bare-feet, stopping at a sunny area with a little brook running off into the trees. The clear water trickled and bubbled over the rocks, and carried a fresh spring aroma. Her spirits lightened as she took in the beautiful afternoon. The smell of fragrant tree blossoms wafted on the air, and the thought of being clean, once again, seemed almost like a dream, making her laugh like a child, kicking sand into the water with her bare toes.

"I thought you might like this to use in your bath."

Jake jumped, startled by the deep, melodic voice behind her, for she had not heard his silent approach. She whirled to face him, oblivious to the appreciative effect she presented to him, his eyes immediately turning a dark emerald green.

He held out a bar of soap. When she just stared at him, and made no comment, he placed the soap on a large rock, gritted his teeth to stave off a barely suppressed hunger of...wanting to crush her delectable form against his own and take those pouting, full lips in a bruising kiss. Instead, he turned on his heel, and went back to the carriage.

Jake felt unnerved. Seeing Erik stripped to the waist, his hard, sinewy muscles and wet britches soaked from the water, leaving absolutely nothing to the imagination, his male arousal all too obvious, caused her mind to spin out of control. Why did her senses seem to leave her body when this man came near her. The very idea that thoughts of a sexual nature invaded her mind in connection with a virtual stranger was disconcerting in the least...and utterly preposterous. He was way too much unleashed male intensity! Determined to push those thoughts from her mind, she decided not to think upon them again. No way was she going there! They were the musing of a very foolish girl, and would get her absolutely nowhere. More likely than not… into a hot bed of steaming coals. Oh! Not the best choice of words. Besides, she knew Erik's mind. He would send her away when it suited his purpose! In a heartbeat!

Jake shrugged out of the shirt and slipped into the crystal, clear water, warmed pleasantly by the sun. It felt heavenly to wash her wild, unruly hair, helping to raise her sinking spirits. Using the bar of soap, scented with a mild sandalwood, she washed her itchy body and her filthy clothes. When she came out of the water, she let the warm sun dry her pale skin, then slipped back into the linen shirt. Not wanting to linger overlong, fearing Erik would be displeased and anxious to be underway, she went back to the site of the carriage. But he was nowhere to be found.

Erik had left Jake at the water's edge, his mind a mixture of confusion. Seeing her shapely form in *his shirt* was almost his undoing. He couldn't pry his eyes from the enticing picture that she disclosed. There she stood, her spirited little body almost naked before him, yet just hidden enough to tease his imagination, with brutal clarity. Even with her petite form, long slender legs peeked out from the shirt's length that ended just above her knees. Her taut, full breasts clung suggestively to the linen, for her body was still wet from their brief interlude in the lake, and Erik could tell by the flash of silvery sparks in her eyes, that her emotions were still out of control. Before doing or saying something that he knew without a doubt, he would later regret, or encouraging the heightening of her fiery countenance any further, he left abruptly, his own emotions ignited more than he would ever admit.

Daylight had been swallowed up by the previous events, and evening would be upon them in several hours. Erik made the decision to stay there for the night. He entered the clearing by the lake with his arms full of firewood. He also had bathed and changed into dry clothing. He looked around to see if Jake had returned, and found her once again, sitting on a rock beside the water, drying her hair in the sun, her clothes slung over a tree branch to dry.

"I trust you are feeling better, now that you are scrubbed," Erik said conversationally, walking up to where she sat, and depositing the firewood on the ground.

"Yes, but no thanks to you," she proclaimed, lifting her chin jauntily into the air.

Erik shrugged, his face unreadable. "I merely did what I thought necessary," he said, impatience for her childish manner clearly evident in his authoritative voice.

"Be warned, *M'sieur*, that if you try such a stunt again at my expense, not only will I leave when you aren't looking, but with your horse as well, and you'll surely be out of luck," she added, clearly a warning in the stiffness of her posture.

Erik's body tensed at these distinct words of challenge, and the humor fell from his face. He stepped towards her. "You had best not try it, *ma cherie*, or you will rue the day that you do. Leaving, with or without my horse, is entirely out of the question. It's too dangerous," he added with silky menace, his jaw twitching involuntarily, as his eyes stared down at her darkly with explicit meaning. He had to admit it; she was a little vixen of the highest order, when her dander was up, and the word "trouble" came unbidden to his mind. Again, there she sat, half-naked in his shirt, with her red hair flying about her face, trying to tell him what to do. It made a multitude of fantasies flash unbidden before his eyes. Belatedly, he realized that her half-broken accent was gone, and that she spoke with distinction, and in a manner indicating formal learning.

"And exactly when did you become my keeper," she retorted, hotly. She had come down off the rock, her small body posed with arms akimbo, and her eyes shot open hostility at being treated like a child. "I'm quite able to take care of myself. I have managed to reach the age of seventeen without your help, and no doubt will continue to do so," she added.

Seventeen, Erik thought! Well now we're getting somewhere!

Erik's gaze rested mockingly on her face. "So old," he replied easily.

The sarcasm in his voice stung her, but she put her chin up and replied, "And I have experience in areas that you couldn't begin to fathom. I know how to survive," she said suggestively, letting him interpret that anyway he chose .

"What is your *real* name and what are you running away from?" Erik asked pointedly, figuring they might as well have it out right here and now.

She stared at him silently, as if deciding whether to speak. "Not that it's any of your business," she finally offered, "but I'm escaping a fate worst than death. Being forced to marry a man that looks like a monster, and that I despise," she spat out with such venom in her voice that it made Erik flinch, the color momentarily draining from his face to an ashen hue, as he realized the implication of her words. He ran his hands negligently through his hair, his face a cold mask beneath the visible one. Ignoring his first question, she showed him her back, returning to her previous task. In the scheme of things, she reasoned rationally, what did a name matter, anyway.

Bitterly, her caustic words sunk into his senses. Erik wheeled around, kicking over the pile of firewood with an impulsive gesture as his temper flared, but he left her alone. He saddled a bay and angrily rode out of camp. Her words had cut deep. He had once hardened himself against the cruelties of the world, but to hear it thrown so blatantly into his face, caused inexplicable grief. At this moment he felt naked and vulnerable, and he did not like that humiliating feeling. Why did he care? This was no different than what he had faced many times over, as the world handed out its unjust vengeance. Erik's eyes were seething sparks, as they peered dangerously into space, and his body remained numb, his mind unconsciously tightening the woven protective barrier around his heart. He had let his heart, instead of his reason, rule his actions once before, and it had nearly made him go insane, causing him to do things he now regretted, but could never change, and he swore it would never happen again. He had several times entertained the idea of slaking his unsatisfied lust upon a common whore, but his sensibilities as a more refined and learned gentleman smothered those radical desires, wishing instead for the companionship of that one soul that could share more than just the baser urges of the body, but those of the soul also. Erik dug his knees into the horse's flanks, letting the bay's gait guide his own pace, as they spirited across the sloping hills. His instincts took over while his mind spiraled without restraint, his dark brooding emotions delving deep into his inner soul. This half-child, half-woman might despise him, he thought hostilely, and think him grotesque and scarred, but whether she agreed or not, he appointed himself her *keeper*, from herself, as well as from the dangers of traveling alone. And at this moment, he was the one in charge. With that arbitrary decision set clearly and irrevocably in his mind, Erik slowed his pace to take in his surroundings. He had left the safety of the opera house many, many nights, to ride the adjacent countryside around the outskirts of Paris. Several times he had stayed away a week or more, enjoying the openness of the wilderness that contrasted so harshly with the darkness of his world. But each time he had gone back willingly, for it was there that his heart was enslaved, and another soul had heard his pain.

When Erik returned, the late sun had passed below the tree-line, and a light breeze brought a chill to the evening air. Erik stepped out of the shadows, where his soul was accustom to dwelling, and made ready to take on a small, stubborn termagant. He added fuel to the fire that had long since settled into low burning embers. His dark mood had lessened, and he realized that he was hungry. They had both missed an adequate noonday meal. He pierced three fish, threading them on a makeshift skewer, and placed them over the red coals. Catching fish in the river, where the water entered the labyrinths below the opera house, had been a past time he had enjoyed as a boy, but he hadn't done it in a very long time.

Jake had heard him return and was wary of his presence. What had made him so mad, that he had left in a rush of fury? She had watched him ride the big gray beast into the distance, and she could tell that he was more than angry. He had asked her a simple question, and she had given him a truthful answer. Partly anyway! His handsome face had turned to stone, like she had done something terrible. She didn't understand him at all. Could he have been *that* mad, just because she wouldn't give up her name? A name just wasn't that important! She came over to the fire, the tempting smell of the roasting fish more than she could resist. She was hungry and he knew it!

Erik handed her some fish and fruit. Jake was wrapped in a blanket to keep the chill of the evening at bay, for all she still wore was his linen shirt. There had not been enough warmth left in the day to completely dry her heavy clothes. He thought she looked charmingly innocent, with the firelight dancing across her child-like features, but experience had proved otherwise. A child she was *not*, and the question of innocence was yet to be tested. She could be a little hell-cat—that he knew first-hand, but whether he could really trust her...he didn't think so!

"I want to make an early start. We have wasted half a day. I want to reach the outlands of *Le Harve* before darkness tomorrow," Erik informed her.

Silently she listened. They had not spoken much since his return, saying only what was necessary to get the meal done. She studied his demeanor through eyes half lidded, trying to understand this complicated stranger. He was dressed neatly in light tan britches that hugged his thighs and hips so tightly, it was hard for Jake not to stare. A white ruffled shirt hung loosely from his broad shoulders, and gaped open negligently to his trim waist, where the dark dusting of hair upon his chest trailed a line downward, disappearing into the waistband of his britches. Her mind became all befuddled as utterly preposterous thoughts jumped to the surface… like what it would be like to run her hand down that rock-hard chest, or have his naked body stretched out over hers. And his eyes in the firelight were breathtaking and …mesmerizing. She was aware he was watching her, his gaze not in the least guarded. Startled somewhat back to abject reality when he blatantly stared at her full breasts, that strained against *his* shirt, where the blanket had fallen toward her waist, she flinched at the intensity of his smoldering eyes. She was so confused. Everything was so complicated. This man had so many facets to his disturbingly, mysterious character. One minute he seemed rugged and ruthless, and the next he was gentle and kind. Who was he? Where had he come from? And where was he going? What happened that he wore a mask? Jake knew she should be helping with the dinner tasks, but sat in silence with her troubled, unanswered thoughts, drugged by the very sight of him, unable to move until it was time to retire.

"Come over by the fire, Jake. The night wind blows cold, and we need each other's warmth," Erik insisted, for she had settled against a tree alongside the carriage.

"But we can't share the same pallet, Erik. You're a man," Jake said, a hesitation in her voice that told him she was warring with her convictions, and stubborn to boot.

"Well, it didn't seem to make any difference up until now, did it?" Erik shot back, amusement clearly laced within his tone. Jake couldn't see his face in the closing darkness, but it sounded like he was mocking her. He had his nerve!

"I'll be just fine, right here," Jake insisted, not willing to budge an inch, her stubborn pride outweighing her reason. The night wind blew steadily over the water in the direction of the shoreline, and her body shivered from the cold.

Suddenly Erik's tall, massive body loomed above her, dripping with danger. He bent down with a lightening speed that surprised her, wrapping his arm around her tiny waist and lifting her up easily, balancing her on his hip, as he strode back to the fire. Unceremoniously depositing her on the blanket, he said rudely, "If you think I'm going to let you have the chance to slink away in the night when my back is turned, and taking my horse, you must think me a total fool."

Jake scrambled to her feet, stubbing her bare toes on his hard boots. "You can't tell me what to do," she screeched at him boldly, her blue eyes dark burning embers in the light of the fire. This was not the way it was suppose to be, she fumed inwardly, agitated at how he seemed to always maneuver into control. She sensed danger pouring from every part of him, tempered with a very loose restraint, and most likely only corralled with tight discipline. Perhaps it would be wiser not to stir the beast, she thought, but bending away from her own stubborn pride was not one of her strongholds.

"Is that so," Erik said evenly, his anger beginning to subside, taking in the sensual appeal of this incredibly beautiful woman, who without question, would be sleeping beside him. His mind gave a moments pause, digesting whether he could really handle the close proximity of their bodies, now that he was set upon this dangerous course. Just thinking about it made his breathing turn ragged. He closed his eyes momentarily and took one long, deep breath, resigned to a night with his emotions tethered under very tight control.

"I despise you," she explained in defiance, a flush spreading over her face as her body betrayed what she was saying. Her entire body ached in places she didn't know existed. And it tingled also! And all because of him! But she simply wouldn't go there! She had wanted to sleep as far away from him as possible. Damn, the man was irritating...and so impossibly fascinating.

"So you have stated before," Erik said dryly, annoyance in his tone, as he tired of her repetitious triad. She tried to maneuver around him, but he pulled her down next to him, as he settled upon the pallet. "Struggling will only make it harder, Jake. So give in and go to sleep," he growled. He was tired from the long day and needed rest.

Yielding to his request, that was more like a command, she finally gave up. Scooting a small distance away, leaving a space between their bodies, Jake settled with her back towards him, and tried to relax. But Erik had other ideas. If he couldn't feel her next to him, she could sneak away when he was sleeping. He put one arm around her waist and pulled her slight body against his own. She gave a small gasp, but didn't resist, or try to move away.

Jake wiggled slightly in his grasp, as if to make herself more comfortable. The close intimacy of her nearly unclothed body, made his male instincts react most uncomfortably. Involuntarily, he pulled her backside tightly up against his groin and her back solidly against his chest. His nostrils flared at the scent of sandalwood in her hair and his manly parts became exceedingly tight in his britches. He found an indefinable feeling was tugging at his conscience from two different directions. One part of him wanted to let her go, and not force her to stay with him, when she obviously despised his appearance, and the other wanted this woman-child most desperately. She was nothing but trouble, he told himself savagely, and would probably be his undoing if she stayed. It was sheer madness, to even think about delving into such foolishness for a second time. He had hoped against all odds, once, that he could have some kind of normal love from a woman, and he had found out most unpleasantly that he could not. That any woman could see through the monster that his face represented to the world, and love him as a man, had simply been too much to ask. Protecting her would have to be enough!

Jake could feel the steady beating of this man's heart, who held an arm about her ribs like a tight band. She felt tension in his body, his muscles twitching along the length of his frame, like he was making a concerted effort to keep himself under control. With a muffled groan, she felt him reach between them and re-arrange himself in his britches, yet she still felt a distinct hardness that continued to press quite alarmingly against her bottom. Exactly how was she suppose to sleep with *that*, not too subtle remainder of his blazing masculinity?

And she didn't understand why he was so mad. Her emotions were whirling. Everything seemed like a double-edged sword. She felt a sickening feeling in the pit of her stomach, both at the thought of being sent away, and the newfound feelings that were raging in her innocent body for this dark, foreboding man. She felt a power in him, like strangely or magically, he could make her do his bidding, and it was frightening, yet somehow, ultimately exciting also. She began to tremble, both from some unknown fear and from the chill of the night air. As if sensing her thoughts and feeling her fear, Erik gathered her more tightly against his hard chest, enfolding them both within the confines of his cloak. The heat from his massive body began to penetrate hers, giving her a warm glow, as her shivering subsided. And finally they slept.

Long before day-break, Erik hitched the horses to the carriage and made silent preparations to leave, before Jake heard nary a sound. The sun had many hours yet, before showing its fiery glow on the horizon, and the air was damp with a misty dew. Suddenly Jake was lifted gently into Erik's strong arms, his cape still wrapped about her slender form, and her cheek was pressed against the hollow of his neck. Sleepily she looked up into his face, confusion in her eyes. Involuntarily, her hand came up to gingerly touch his mask with her small fingers, and slowly ran them over the side of his face to his ear. Erik flinched instinctively, turning his head away only slightly, and her hand came to rest only on his mask. She left it there for a few silent and tenderly shared moments, then let her hand slide down to rest on his bare chest, where she felt the rapid beating of his heart.

"What are you doing," she finally asked, bewilderment in her voice.

Depositing her on the seat of the carriage, Erik replied. "Stay right here until I tell you otherwise," he said, a tightness in his tone that told her not to question.

"But I'm not yet dressed, and it is still so dark," she commented, still not understanding.

"Your clothes are not yet dry and we must be underway." With that simple explanation, he jumped lithely into the carriage. A second later, the bays lurched forward, and once again they were on their journey.

They traveled a long distance before stopping. The road was smoother than the previous day, and Jake found herself dosing more than she was awake. For some odd reason she was still very tired, like the night had been extremely short, and since the sun was not yet up, it was impossible to know how early they had left. Erik seemed preoccupied with the carriage and getting to their destination, so she left him alone, and kept to her own thoughts.

In Erik's opinion, they hadn't taken their leave early enough! After a few badly needed hours of sleep, he had awakened to Jake's small body moving suggestively against his own in restful slumber. Her *borrowed* nightshirt had inched upward, leaving her backside bare against his groin, and his own hand had settled down onto the smooth skin of her bare thigh. The raging fire this had caused, within his already tense and agitated body, ignited an unbearable need to experience those unknown pleasures he had sought once before, but was denied. His mind told him otherwise, but his body sought those pleasures again, with this small creature that was unwillingly worming her way into his soul, yet obviously hated him for what he appeared to be on the outside. She had laid in sleep so innocent and warm, wrapped snugly within his arms, oblivious to the havoc that ravaged both his body and his soul. If he hadn't done something drastic, like distancing his own body from hers, he would have not been responsible for his actions, and the sorrow it would have caused them both would have been unbearable to face. He had taken everything into his own hands with Christine, trying to persuade her to the decision he ultimately wanted her to make against her will, even when he knew it could not be, and it had been a disaster. He couldn't let that happen again!

Chapter Four

Jake had watched Erik handle the horses throughout the long monotonous day. They had traveled with only one stop from before daybreak, for the necessities, and for her to retrieve her clothing, and Erik did not seem in a mood for any conversation, informative of otherwise. His expression was haunting, as he stared into space with an almost pout upon his lips, like he was concentrating deeply on something from another time and place, or perhaps about the journey ahead, yet seeing the road at the same time. It was just another one of those strange things about him, to make Jake wonder what was really inside of this man.

Suddenly, Erik pulled the carriage off the roadway and into a small opening between the tree-line, coming to a stop at the side of a small clearing, protected from the road and surrounded on all sides with tall trees. He looked over at Jake, taking in her appearance, moving his eyes up and down over her slight body several times for good measure, and in a way that totally unnerved her, for his expression was first one of appreciation, but rapidly turned to annoyance, and she didn't know why.

"We are nearing the village of *Dorne*. I want you to go there and purchase a few supplies, and buy yourself some clothes that are appropriate for a female," he said with such purposeful meaning, it left no doubt in her mind, that he disapproved of her boyish attire.

The idea of getting out of her rather tight fitting outfit seemed welcome, and it made her almost giggle remembering how she had obtained it off her pompous neighbor's wash line, when she had left in a bit of a hurry, but it also gulled her to think that Erik could dictate exactly what *he* thought she should be wearing. She had rarely worn clothing becoming a female, even though there had been a few times it was necessary, like at her father's funeral, but that dress had been black, and not something she would ever wear again. Politely she answered, but with some distain in her tone, "If you insist, I will do as you suggest, but such clothes are not appropriate for traveling, and not something I usually wear."

This made Erik wonder skeptically, what *did* she usually wear, and why she would not normally wear female clothing. "And why is that?" he asked, wanting the information he had been seeking for several days now, but had not yet been able to obtain, because of her obvious stubbornness. At least that's the way he saw it!

She had another thought! Why was he always trying to pry out of her, what she didn't want to give, and once again making demands of telling her what to do? Finally she decided, perhaps one small piece of information might help persuade him in letting her take care of the horses. She answered in both an informative and appeasing manner, " I have been taking care of horses for many years, and dresses are not exactly suitable."

Erik's left eyebrow arched in astonishment and some realization, yet casually he countered! "Female attire is all that is required for this journey, " he said adamantly. "I will give you enough coin to make your purchases, but be wise about your selections. The daytime is hot and the evenings are cool." With that information, he left the carriage and started unhitching the bays from their harness.

Not to be denied, after so willingly giving Erik some knowledge about herself, Jake also started to unhitch the other bay, talking softly to the big beast and stroking his neck affectionately. The large bay reacted kindly to her gentle touch, and Erik had to admit begrudgingly, that she did know how to handle the large beast. Inwardly he smiled, realizing that this slip of a girl had lots of surprises. He just wondered how many, and what would come next, and more importantly, how much trouble it would cause him?

Erik readied his bay with a saddle. He knew it was a big risk to let Jake take one of the horses, but he really had no other choice. It was several miles into the village, and she would have a list of supplies to buy. She wouldn't be able to carry all of it. It was day-time, and he didn't expect her to have any trouble. He just wasn't certain, once she departed, that she would ever come back!

Before making out a list, Erik inquired of Jake, "Can you read?"

"Well of course I can," she said in irritation, thinking it was rude to even ask. Wasn't she talking now like she had some learning. That accent she had used before was a bit of a pain, she thought wickedly, thinking that she had pulled that off rather well... while it lasted!

Erik turned his head away and smiled, looking for some paper in which to compose a list, thinking to himself that she might try to be unladylike, but the need to be accepted as an equal was certainly there. He gave her the list, a bag of coins, threw in a few last minute instructions, and sent her on her way in the direction of the village, cursing that he couldn't, at present, do this for himself, without removing his mask. When he went across the sea to England, he would have to do so to obtain passage, or risk his story being reported even that far north, but for now it wasn't necessary, and he was silently content, because he wasn't ready to tackle that problem in his mind. Darkly his mind turned to waiting, not certain Jake would even return. If she didn't, she had money to start again from whatever she was running from, and a good horse and saddle in the bargain. Yet her final words were still ringing in his ears.

As she road away, she looked back, catching the look of resignation and loneliness on his face, like he believed she would never return. "You have to trust me sometime," she said simply, and with that she had broken into a swift canter, her fiery red hair trailing behind her, and he knew immediately that she was truly a very experienced rider.

Jake couldn't believe her luck. Erik was sending her off on another mission without him, and with the full knowledge that she was indeed a girl. The idea that he wanted to trust her made her happy, but it confused her also. He was always so disgruntled and mocking, that she didn't know from one minute to the next what he was thinking. She thought he wanted a boy to help him, and she wasn't adverse to that idea. Her father was always confessing that she should have been one. But now Erik demanded that she dress like a woman. There just was no reasoning to what a man really wanted, she decided in disgust, yet a little smile graced her lips at the thought that he wanted her dressed as a girl, instead of a lad.

Entering the town, Jake looked all around and spotted the mercantile halfway down the main street. Many carriages and wagons were in front, and it was easy to tell that it was the hub of activity. She left her horse hitched outside and entered the establishment. Immediately her senses were treated to many various delightful aromas. Bayberry and baking cinnamon came to mind first, bringing back memories of her childhood, watching the maids of the manor house dip candles, and the cooks bake delicious fruit pies that unknowingly had disappeared off the windowsill several times. Her father had chastised her unmercifully, making her take one back that had not been bitten into, and she had learned her lesson well. Never show her father a pie that was not half eaten.

Jake went about her tasks with seriousness and purpose. She didn't want to spend all day at this. Shopping had never been one of her passions, just a necessary part of living. She picked out several outfits—a springy flowered day dress with puffed cap sleeves that ended at her ankles, a light woolen skirt with a simple linen blouse more sensible for traveling, and shoes that were appropriate with both. She also purchased a nightgown that would replace the linen shirt of Erik's that she had been wearing. The nights were cold he said. Okay! Check that off her list! Lastly, she found an outfit that was more to her liking. It wasn't on *his* list, but there was more than enough money, and it was most certainly on *hers*. Gathering up her new clothing, she bought the other supplies—wine, cheese, bread, dried meat, and some fresh fruit. She added a few spices just to make the food more interesting. She spied fresh meat pies cooling on a countertop, and had them wrapped separately, thinking that Erik would probably like the taste of fresh cooked meat as a welcome change. A young store lad helped her tie the packages to the back of the saddle, and she was on her way. She had to travel more slowly for fear of damaging the food and everything coming untied.

When Erik saw her coming in the distance, his tense body started to visibly show signs of relief. As her figure became recognizable enough to make out her attire, his jaw clenched tightly, and his face took on a stormy expression. She came right up to him and slid down out of the saddle with ease, both feet hitting the ground in unison. She was dressed in tan men's riding britches that hugged her figure most alarmingly to his mind, and a casual pale, yellow, linen shirt that also fit quite becomingly across her obvious assets. She seemed not a bit disturbed about this captivating wardrobe, that was cinched tightly at the waist with a broad leather belt, and finished off with brown riding boots that ended just below her knees.

"I don't recall that outfit being on the list," he said, his eyes narrowed a bit, but appreciating what he was seeing, regardless of what his mind thought, and trying to ignore what his body felt.

"Whose list are you referring to? My list was different from yours," she replied saucily, throwing him the money pouch with the coin left over. Immediately she went to the task of removing her purchases, stretching over the horse's rump as she reached for the packages.

Belatedly, Erik noticed the black ribbon that tied her red hair back at the nape of her neck. He came up behind her and yanked it out of her hair. She whirled around, startled at his callous action, and the black look on his face and the anger in his eyes, gave her a moments pause. "I don't like black.....on you," he said, a cold harshness in both his tone and his attitude, that she was unable to think of a suitable retort. She just dropped the subject and went back to what she was doing, more puzzled about Erik than she had ever been before.

They went through the supplies and packed away what wasn't needed for the evening. It was just about sunset, and once again, they had missed the noon meal. Both ate the delicious meat pies with relish, making only small talk that avoided the earlier incident. Jake tried to reason why Erik had been so mad. He was upset about her getting the men's clothing, as she figured he would be, totally prepared to take the consequences of that, but ripping the ribbon out of her hair didn't make any sense. It was something a girl would wear.

Erik was sorry for his actions. He knew it hurt her, but seeing that black ribbon had made him snap. What was he suppose to tell her? Not the truth! He said the first thing that came to his mind, and in the end, it was not exactly inaccurate. The day was late and morning would bring going into *Le Harve*, something he did not relish doing. But it had to be done. They must get some *real* sleep tonight. No small feat there! How that would be accomplished he had absolutely no idea.

"Bring the blankets, Jake, it's time," he said, irritation in his voice more at what he had been thinking, than at her.

"Time to be trussed up like a turkey, you mean," she said sarcastically.

"It's cold, Jake, you know the routine," Erik shot back, knowing that there was no question that he could trust her, but he wanted her near him, and the cold night was reason enough for him to make it happen. The folly of it all is what played on his mind, but not deeply enough to make him change it.

"I'll be there in a minute," she said entirely too sweetly, he thought. Why was she giving up so easily? Then he knew the reason. She came out from behind the carriage in the most god-awful nightgown he ever hoped to imagine. It was made of heavy flannel, hung to her feet, and was buttoned up to and tied snugly around her neck.

"Well, I see my money was well spent," he said with little humor.

"You did say that the days were hot and the nights were cold, did you not?" she supplied pleasantly. As if on cue, the wind picked up at that moment, blowing its cold breeze harshly into the clearing, and the treetops bent, scattering a few pine needles into the chilly air.

"I did at that," he mumbled, laying down on the blanket to get comfortable for the night. He held out his arm for her to join him on the pallet, and when she did so, he smiled in the fading light from the fire. He pulled her close, as he had so easily become accustom to doing, and was surprised that knowing she would not sneak off in the night, helped him to relax, as he had not been able to do before. With the events that were to happen on the morrow playing deeply on his mind, he drifted to sleep easily.

Jake was able to relax completely in Erik's arms for the first time. She did smile a little about the nightclothes that she had chosen, knowing that it was as much a joke on her part as the obvious reason—for warmth. It would not ordinarily have been her choice, but the temptation was just too much to resist. For her it had been a big day. She had been free, doing what she knew best—riding a horse, and she now was confident that Erik trusted her. Before she knew it, Erik's wonderful warmth had invaded her small body once again, and she was asleep before she knew it.

Erik felt her hand gripping his softly. Distant music played a lonely melody, engulfing his senses in a myriad of kaleidoscopic images. The smell of candle wax hung heavily in the air, and white spirals of smoke billowed upward, disappearing into the vaulted cathedral ceiling. In the soft flickering light from a hundred yellow flames, he languidly drank in the beauty of her long tresses, the curve of her full sensuous mouth, and the silent wonder encapsulated in the darkness of her searching eyes. A secret, unfulfilled longing drew him onward, and with a low lyrical intonation, he sang to her, the sensual, melodic words weaving a story where monotonous darkness turns to shafts of brilliant light. He wanted her understanding for the dark secrets that caused his pain, and to reach into his tortured soul, where one can dwell far beyond the realm that the world can see. As if unbidden, cymbals crashed violently and glass splintered, sending him back into the gloom of denial and despair. His world was falling, and the sweet aroma of a single rose, once a pleasing fragrance to his senses, stung his nostrils like smoke turning to acid. His body thrashed unwillingly, as he fought to escape the pain once more. His soul was returning to face the tortures that he had fought, with all his energy and being to lay to rest.

Jake was awakened from the haziness of slumber by the violent movement of Erik's body. She turned towards him in hesitation, no longer restricted by his arms to keep her near. The low set of the moon allowed but a hint of light, and she couldn't make out all of his features clearly, but he seemed to be sleeping, his body supine with both arms flung out to either side. He mumbled something in a low anguished tone, but she couldn't make out the meaning. He still wore his mask, but the rest of his face did not look relaxed. Carefully she leaned over his torso, placing her hand upon his bare chest, where the shirt was parted to his waist, and felt the burning heat that engulfed his body, and a fine sweat lay upon his skin. Suddenly she was alarmed! Did he have a fever? Gingerly she placed her hand to his left cheek, where fine soft hair had begun to grow, feeling an inferno of heat there also. He did not awaken to her touch, and that more than scared her. She left his side for only a few moments to find a cloth, and doused it with cool water from a corked jar. Folding it lengthwise, she laid it across his hot neck, pressing it down gently with her hand. He brought his hand to hers, touching it softly and then her arm, as if caressing a lover. With her other hand, she touched his forehead, smoothing his hair back from his face. Then she touched his mask, sliding her hand down its length to the cloth on his neck. Cruelly her wrist was grabbed by Erik's strong hand in a tight, bruising grip, as he reacted violently to the kindness that she had offered.

"What the devil is going on here?" he shouted, scaring her out of any sleepiness that might have lingered.

"I was just helping to make you comfortable," she explained. "You are burning up with fever," she added, wanting him to understand what she was doing and why.

"I do not have a fever," Erik proclaimed, laying back down in unexplained exhaustion, not understanding why he was so tired, but knowing that his mind reeled with the memories in his head, and that any reminiscence of sleep was fast disappearing.

"You were talking in your sleep and thrashing about. And you woke me up," Jake said a little harshly, not liking the way he was accusing her of something, but not knowing exactly what.

"Well, get back to sleep. It's still the middle of the night, and you might have slept most of the morning, but I did not," Erik pointed out with emphasis, gathering her body once again against his own in the usual manner, and with no uncertain meaning to his efforts.

Jake tried to will her body to lay still, but Erik's seemed extremely hot, and he held her tighter than before, restricting her breathing. She wanted to believe that she could lay here beside him without it affecting her, but she knew that her feelings for Erik were slowly changing. Feelings that had been foreign to her nature, and her set principles, and entailed wanting this man in a way she had never experienced before. Her defenses were crashing down, and she knew it! She had hoped he would tell her his story and confide in her, but she also knew that their friendship was fragile. And she couldn't even be sure that he really wanted her around as a female, instead of a lad, even though he wanted her dressed like one. He had been more than adamant about that!

Erik could feel Jake fidgeting against his groin. Her shapely backside made his male instincts react involuntarily, even through that unsightly nightgown, and his blood rose close to the boiling point, bringing his body to the verge of acute sexual agony. Was he never to have a moments peace from the bounds of this accursed arrangement, he thought, wondering with increasing alarm and uncertainty if the sweet, yet unwelcome tension growing in his body could be kept under his control? Not even certain he wanted to control it. His mind was still reeling from his dream, and he was in no mood to be tempered. In one swift movement, he turned onto his back, pulling Jake across his body to lay against his left side, her nightgown hiked up to just below her round, tempting bottom, and her thigh thrown over his in a suggestive manner.

"Enough," he said in exasperation. "Be still, and go back to sleep."

For a moment Jake was stunned. But the closeness of his body was comforting and she didn't resist. Without any effort at all, she snuggled in, making Erik realize that this was perhaps not the best solution either. In the moonlit blackness of the night, his eyes gleamed darkly with emotions and instincts, long leached beneath a disguised exterior. His nostrils flared at the scent of her hair, and her soft slight body pressed appealingly against his own, made his senses whirl in a more urgent way than before. But once again, he silently willed his mind to be rational and take control. She might welcome his warmth, but she was adversely affected by his appearance. Sleep would not come easily.

Jake settled herself in sleep, curving comfortably into Erik's hard masculine body, resting her head in the hollow of his neck, her hand resting on his chest. His head was turned towards her, his mask covering the exposed side of his face. In unconscious sleep, innocently she placed the palm of her hand against his jaw, just below the mask, and her fingers rested on the hard surface that hid his secret.

This time Erik did not pull away. He put his hand over hers and turned his head to touch his lips to her palm, kissing the small hand with tenderness and feeling. Gently he pulled her body closer, his other hand resting on her bare buttocks to press her tighter against his thigh, her left knee pressing against his groin with searing effects. Jake felt his touch and stirred sleepily, moving her head slightly to nuzzle her face into his neck.

"This situation isn't working," Erik said aloud in a husky voice, mostly to himself, his breathing labored and heavy.

"Do you mean to send me away then," Jake mumbled into his neck, at first not understanding, but reality sinking in slowly as she lifted out of her slumberous state, feeling his hand upon her bare skin in a most familiar place. A most shocking place!

"Because I'm a girl, instead of a lad," she added, disappointment clearly evident in her voice. "I can be a boy if you would like," she added quickly. "It doesn't matter to me."

Erik chuckled lightly, turning her on her back and leaned over her suggestively. He pressed his lean, massive body slightly against hers, his face inches away, green eyes glowing in the moonlight. "I'm not wanting you to be a lad, my sweet. And there in lies the problem," he added with emphasis, his breath upon her face, heavy and ragged. Lying down beside her, he pulled her chest flat against his own, the suggestion of wanted intimacy more than obvious, even through her flannel nightclothes. There was no doubt in her mind that his body was primed and ready. The heat emanating off his muscular frame and the intense, darkness of his eyes spoke for themselves. Erik wanted her! And the thrill was exhilarating and totally frightening.

"Well then, treat me like a woman, Erik," she challenged with brashness, hardly knowing the contents of her own mind, yet her lips having a will all there own. She placed her hand to the side of his left cheek, the hair of his short beard soft to her fingers, and again put her face into his neck, but this time she put her moist lips to his warm skin, making his body shutter in response. Thinking that he didn't like this, she looked up at him. His eyes were closed and he drew in a long, ragged breath between clenched teeth. His lips were in such a sneer, that she thought he was in pain. When she stopped, he opened his dark smoldering eyes and looked at her beautiful face in the moonlight. He laid his fingers against her soft cheeks, placed his lips to hers tenderly at first, then with more pressure as his passion deepened, and she felt the hard mask against her face. Gently, she placed her hands between them and pushed away.

"Please, Erik, take the mask off," she asked in a low, gentle voice, but with a bit of pleading in the inflection of her tone.

Erik sat up, turning away slightly, and hung his head for a few long silent seconds, then turned back slowly. "It's not something I'm used to doing," he almost whispered, a wretched anguish in his voice.

"But it's not needed here," Jake said softly and sensually. Kneeling in front of him, between his legs, she laid her hand on his left cheek, then traced her fingers along the length of his full, sensuous lips that were a part of every expression he made. "I'm not repulsed by your face," she assured him, wanting him desperately to believe what she was saying. To help him understand, she wrapped her arms tightly around him, and held her cheek against his bare chest, resting there for several moments. When she looked up, the mask was gone, and his right hand was covering where the mask had been. His eyes were downcast, and his head was turned slightly away, but she could see the tears in his eyes.

Erik had removed the mask as she had asked, but he knew what that would mean. The mask was his defense against the world, and it gave him the power to cope. His breathing was heavy and painful, crushing his chest like a huge boulder lay upon it. He couldn't look at her, and his hand was frozen against his face. It was one thing when he had thought her a lad, but she was a woman. A very beautiful, exciting and sensual woman! And he was a monster, a gargoyle, like the ones that sat on the roof of the opera house. *Beauty and the Beast*, he thought in disgust. She would be repulsed! How could she not? Even if she thought she wouldn't, he knew she would.

Then her hand was on his, soft and gentle, slowly, yet purposefully, prying his fingers away from his face, revealing the horrible secret that lay behind them. His world stood still, as he let her take his hand away. She laid her cool hand over his rough, deformed cheek, the skin pocked and pinched, with bulbous areas where the veins stood out and little or no hair grew. Gently she turned his face towards her, and felt his body shake, as if the earth had moved beneath them. His dark hair fell negligently over his head, errant locks trailing down over his forehead, and his eyes had a pleading, almost demented look. He sat like a statue, holding his breath, daring not to breathe, knowing the reaction that had always come.

His tears melted her heart. Leaning into him, Jake placed a long, lingering kiss upon his soft full lips, as she cradled both cheeks in her small hands. At first he didn't move, paralyzed more from the shock than from the feeling. Suddenly both Erik's arms circled tightly around her small form, and before she realized it, *her* kiss had turned to *his* kiss, and the demanding pressure he commanded reigned in every aspect of her soul. He pulled back to look at her for only a moment, as if questioning reality and his own sanity, then leaned in again to capture her mouth. His tongue parted her lips easily, and languidly he explored her sweetness, the sensation new and inviting. Stealing the breath from her mouth, he forced his tongue deep, numbing her will to resist, lazily giving her a taste of what undoubtedly would lie ahead, if she were to let him continue. He was telling her with his tongue, what he wanted to do with the rest of her body.

When she made small whimpering noises, he broke the kiss. He shifted their bodies to a lying position and pulled her tightly against the length of him. She could feel the raw masculine tension that was evident even through his clothes, and her realization was renewed that not only did she want this man, but he wanted her also! She felt as if she was being reeled in, drawn like an insect into the spider's web, to be encased in a cocoon where there would be no escape. Yes, she thought! That was exactly where she wanted to be!

Erik trailed his warm lips along her neck and kissed a spot behind her ear, then tasted the sweetness of her skin with his tongue. He wanted to touch his tongue to every inch of her luscious body. With raging emotion, he said softly, almost in a whisper, "My custom has been to take what I want, and not give anyone a choice, but for once, I need your consent. If this is not what you want, then stop me now, for I'll not ask you again." His breathing slowed to almost nothing as he held his breath, fear and anticipation stretching an eternity in only a moment, as he waited for some reaction.

He got his answer. Jake leaned her body closer against his, grazing her moist lips into his neck, then upon his deformed cheek. Erik groaned deep within his throat, as the needs of a lifetime came spiraling to the surface, making his body shake as he fought to get these new, unfamiliar feelings under control. He wanted to love this bewitching creature as he had never loved before, and he wanted it to be right for both of them. The forced confinement with her had been pure, excruciating agony, yet he needed her, demanded her closeness. He'd been to hell and back, and now she was giving him permission. His own needs and passions as a normal man ran strong and vibrant, years of forced isolation making his lust run hotter and more rampant than most. His concern was to handle her with care, providing her exquisite pleasure, not unnecessary pain. He wanted to believe that he would never have to let her go, refused to let her go, but that decision was for another moment. Tonight he would drown in her touch, drugged by the indescribable sweetness her body would give him, and he in turn would show her the secrets that lay dormant and untouched just below the surface within her womanly body, knowing with certainty that she would be wanton and passionate. Tomorrow was soon enough to think about anything else! Tonight was for loving!

In the dim light of the fire, Erik carefully started to remove Jake's nightgown, letting it fall to her waist, marveling at the beautiful body that was unfolding before his eyes. She was long and lean, yet possessed all the womanly curves that made her body so seductive to his view. A storm thundered wildly in his mind, as he sorted out the inner feelings that were hitting him like a giant tidal wave. Slowly he pressed her half-naked body against his own bare chest, feeling her soft, yet womanly curves melt against him, bringing a need that he knew would not be denied.

Jake mind was whirling. Helping Erik out his shirt, even as he was helping her, they were touching as she had never known before. Had never wanted to know, but now she did! His lips were on her lips, tasting and biting and teasing, then her neck, and then her breasts, and she thought she would die of something akin to pleasure, but she knew not what. The electrifying shiver that raked her body when his hot mouth took one taut nipple, made the air leave her lungs in one quick escape of breath. It seemed like many long moments before she could breathe again. His body was powerful, yet his demands were gentle, and she knew he was fighting for some kind of control. That which would make the experience last, and somehow bind them both together. And that thought was not distasteful at all. She wanted to be bound to this mysterious stranger. But she also sensed, that just beyond a thin barrier, was a man who could unleash pure male aggression, untamed and uncontrolled, if he so desired. And for one unreasonable moment, that thought sent a surge of excitement coursing through her entire body.

Erik's heart pounded in his chest. His nostrils flared as he breathed in the womanly heat from their lovemaking. Lazily he traced his finger against her moist lips, trailing it down her neck to that cleft where her breasts began. His gaze was smoldering as his mouth captured hers in a searing kiss, and his hands, that had been lifting her expertly out of her clothes, came up to caress milky white breasts shamelessly, teasing both nipples with his thumbs, making her whimper, even as his kiss deepened against her soft, moist mouth. Then his lips replaced his hands, taking each taut peak into his mouth in turn, sucking gently at first, then aggressively, nipping her with his teeth, making her senses reel as she was caught up in feelings that until now had been untested.

She could feel his rough, yet delicate hands moving down her body, burning her flesh as he hypnotized her mind. Her hands on his muscled shoulders, from removing his shirt, came down to his lean waist and tried to open the buttons on his britches, but her small fingers couldn't manage the task. Growling deep in his chest to have to give up her body for even a second, Erik did it himself, taking her body down with his lean, naked one, as he lay upon the soft blankets once again. His weight wasn't heavy like she thought it would be as he covered hers, balancing his full weight on his forearms, pressing his hard, male shaft into her thigh, reminding her quite unequivocally that there would be no turning back. Burying his face in the hollow of her neck, he kissed upward towards her earlobe, down her slim shoulder, reigning tantalizing kisses over every inch of her body that he could reach with his searching mouth. With his fingers fisted and tangled in her thick mane of hair, his tongue intensified each sensation to the fullest.

In turn, she played upon his sculptured torso also, tentatively at first, but gaining boldness as her hands became familiar with his body. Her hands and lips explored his muscled frame, trailing down wide shoulders, and a hard chest with light hair that tickled her nose and made her laugh. When her tongue touched the hard, protruding nub of his nipple by accident, the response she got from him was so intense that she continued, pulling gently and lifting his flesh with both her lips and her teeth, knowing now that the sound of him sucking ragged air between his clenched teeth wasn't pain, at least not the kind that was unwelcome.

"Let me love you, *mon amour*. Don't be afraid, for I won't hurt you" Erik murmured, his voice raspy with barely controlled passion. She could feel his hot, thick manhood pulsing against her thigh. Her arms encircled his neck, and her hands tangled in his thick, silky hair. She could feel where the hair did not grow on part of his head, but it didn't matter. She was lost in what was the makeup of this man, and she didn't want to be anywhere else. His knee slid between her thighs easily with her willingness to obey, and she felt his hand touching her intimately, his fingers finding the bud where her need was centered, creating a delicious, yet burning pressure within her body, knowing instinctively only he could grant deliverance.

Erik's body ached with a growing vengeance to be released, yet he desired to experience everything about her. To know, to experience, to feel—all that he had been forced to hold inside for what seemed an eternity. Gently he worked his magic, bringing her to the precipice, time and time again, her supple body squirming slightly beneath him, needing to be led to the pinnacle. Erik raised his head to look at her bright questioning eyes, his own glazed over with a dark and dangerous passion. Taking her hand, he slowly guided hers downward, showing her that touching him also, would give him pleasure. He groaned savagely, deep within his throat as her small hand wrapped around his hot, swollen shaft, and he knew he was forever lost. He could not allow this woman-child to leave him, ever. He needed her passion as well as her life, and he could only hope, against everything he had experienced, that she could somehow feel the same.

When he was certain he could hold back no longer, Erik said passionately, "Open your legs, *ma cherie*. It's time to love you completely." Silently she did his bidding, wanting to join with him as one soul, one being. Erik maneuvered his hips between her thighs, probing, rubbing the end of his shaft in the slickness he found there, preparing her for his entrance. Nudging slowly inward, he finally plunged forward with one quick thrust, stopping only momentarily as she gasped in pain. He knew he had come too far to stop. Covering her mouth in a bruising kiss, he inched forward slowly as he moved in a gentle rocking rhythm, sliding full length into her body, even as she began to move also. Slow strokes at first, that he could not stop, that he didn't want to stop, as he let the pain she felt subside. Her hands were around his strong back, tangled in his hair and touching his hard, lean muscled buttocks. Anywhere she could reach.

She heard his voice from far off whispering that he was sorry. At first the pressure had been intense, the thickness of his shaft, seemingly unable for her to accommodate, but one thrust forward, breaking her maidenhead, and one sharp pain, quickly mellowed into the most exquisite pleasure she had ever experienced. Ultimately, the pain did not matter, for her body had a need that she wanted him to fix. Turning on his side with her leg over his thigh, he quickly changed to a more rapid, rhythmic pace that he encouraged her to follow. His hand on her sweet derriere, ensured their united movements.

Together their bodies drew energies from one another. A driving force Erik could not control or explain, took over his entire being as it merged with hers, and in time he felt his body wracked with giant spasms as his seed jet hotly into hers, her own united spasms milking the very seeds of life from his own body. His heart pounded wildly erratic in his chest, his entire being satiated with unbelievable pleasure, and some kind of contentment that he had never experienced before. As he held her soft, and responsively in his arms, he knew the tension had gone from her also and he smiled. Together they lay entwined, their union unbroken. Their bodies were bathed in a fine sweat that glistened in the low light given off by the remaining embers of the fire. Erik pulled the cape over their bodies for warmth, from the breeze that he only now began to notice

He had played her body like an instrument, loved her to heights she had only imagined, and melted them into one. He held her naked body molded against his own, exhaustion a part of them both. He kissed her ear, whispering softly, " What can I call you," he said sleepily. "Jake just doesn't seem appropriate," he added softly, settling his hand around one firm breast, as he started drifting off to sleep.

"Monique," she replied simply. "Or Bonnie, if you like," she said, the words hardly out of her mouth before she was asleep also.

Monique was awakened by a frigid breeze upon her naked body, as the wind came under the edges of the warm cape. She did not feel Erik next to her, and she stirred in panic. Looking around the clearing, she saw him sitting on the ground, leaning against a tree, very still and perhaps deep in thought. It was still dark, but the moon was high, and the clearing was bathed in a shimmering light. Coming up behind Erik, she startled him, and he swung around suddenly, and what she saw startled her also. Tears were running down his face, and she didn't understand why.

"What's the matter, Erik," she asked softly, bending down to lean against him, wrapping the cloak she had about her shoulders so it enfolded his cold, shaking body also.

"I've never had someone to care for me," he said simply. "None that would allow me to make love to them," he admitted, hanging his head in some embarrassment, that this had been the first time he had made love to a woman. "I had someone take care of me as a boy, and looked out for my welfare over many years, but the relationship was different. More like an older sister" he added, giving her more information than he was accustom to sharing.

Gently she lifted his face to hers, giving him a feathery soft kiss on the mouth, and wiped his salty tears away with her lips, then looked into those sad green eyes, one perfect, one slightly deformed, both with an expression of need that melted her heart. "I'm here now," she said softly. "I'll take care of you," she added, knowing that more than likely, he'd be taking care of her.

Before she had time to create another thought, Erik had scooped her up into his massive arms, cradling her against his hard, bare chest, as her legs slid easily around his waist, her bare bottom against his skin creating a growl that came up from deep within his chest. Without another word, he took her back to their place beside the slow burning embers. Playfully she wiggled out from the cape, her nude body glowing in the dim firelight, bringing his own flesh to the height of readiness instantly. His dark, expressive eyes revealed with unmistakable fire, that he wanted to possess her again.

"Erik, Erik," she chided, " You make this most difficult, when you put on your clothes. Now I must undress you again," she laughed, and with his help, proceeded to do just that.

Erik groaned deep and husky, taking her into his arms. "One thing that I am certain of, *ma petite cherie'*. I will *never* have to divest you of that horrible nightgown, because it will never grace your beautiful body again." With that he entwined their bodies together and showed her new things that she had never even dreamed of doing—wildly wicked and delightful things, teacher and pupil learning together. Just before dawn they slept, cradled in each others arms, a new beginning a reality.

Chapter Five

The day was dawning with a gloominess that hung over the entire expanse of the sky, and the threatening elements fit Erik's mood perfectly. He was not looking forward to going into the seaport city of *Le Havre'*, especially in the daylight, and for the first time without the security of his mask. He had become dependent on it to hide his disfigurement, but more importantly, it gave him a kind of illusive power that he felt he needed under his own particular circumstance. Instead of seeing what was readily obvious on the surface, it presented a mystery that was buried deep within his very soul, lending him the tools to cope with a society that shunned the imperfect and the helpless, sending his own world into years of darkness and forced solitude. His attitude was almost one of anger, and his hands shook slightly, as he arranged the black cravat around his neck. Well he wasn't helpless now! When Christine and the masses had actually seen him in the flesh, the mask's intrigue had held the populace spellbound, giving him the leverage to accomplish his task. But today would be entirely different. In contrast to the many times before, wearing the mask today would be a detriment to what he wanted to accomplish. If news of the burning of *La Opera Populaire* had reached this far north, and the reasons for its unfortunate demise, wearing a mask might alert suspicions that would be most unwelcome. No! He would have to venture into this new future without it. At least for the time being! And the concept made his gut and his heart knot in a twisted agony that brought tears to his eyes, but he had set this course, and he would not sway. Let them see what they had always wanted to see!

But another deep and puzzling matter, causing almost similar responses to his already physically tortured body, was playing heavily on his mind. What about the girl? He wanted to take her with him, but he didn't know what her feelings about that would be. His body and his senses screamed with a sweet, as well as an anguished kind of punishment, that comes from being given a taste of a precious delicacy that could be ripped away before it was hardly consumed. Erik's jaw tightened with uneasiness when he thought about the possibility of Monique refusing, but she hardly owed him anything. What they had shared didn't bind her to him, like a master and his servant. He certainly couldn't force her to go! That kind of calculated strategy had almost been his undoing, events spiraling out of control in tragic proportions. As he looked back upon them in his mind, it almost seemed surreal. His overwhelming search for love, or perhaps the human touch, as his deprived existence perceived it, had taken over all reason, blacking out any thought of conscience—a conscience that had dwindled to nothing progressively, believing that he wanted Christine! Now, here he stood at a crossroads, not knowing which path to trod. Perhaps that one, that his new, rediscovered conscience urged him to follow, yet glared at him meaningfully from more than one indecisive direction, as he struggled to block out the events of the past. He couldn't really tell Monique the truth about himself, but he didn't want to blatantly lie. There had been tremendous false overshadowing of facts surrounding his real existence, which he did nothing to dispel, and it had brought him disastrous heartache and pain, so much so, that it ruined all he held important to the very essence of life within his soul. For this reason he decided it would be more prudent just to tell her nothing.

His mind sorely reeled with the events of the night before. Not that in their somewhat forced arrangement, mostly on his part, that the inevitable hadn't played out with almost precision and undeniable logic, like a well set powder-keg that lay in readiness, needing only that one flame to set it on a course that could not be easily stopped. But what had *really* happened between them? Was it just lust on his part, not wanting to be denied yet another time to that which he felt was his right as a man, or had he replaced his need for Christine so easily with a beguiling little creature that seemed to be weaseling her way into his heart as well. A heart that was still substantially wrapped in a protective cocoon, believing that any love found was really only a disguise, that would eventually rear its ugly face, just as his was, to put him in his place once again! He had to admit that although Monique presented herself at first as somewhat helpless and boyish, she had pleasantly surprised him in being gentle, caring and most definitely sensual; however, the little minx was exceedingly opinionated and independent. Qualities he found fascinating in the least, but the latter more than foreign to him when it involved a woman. And she *was* most definitely a woman, *not* the child he first thought her to be, he confessed, a little smile creeping across his face in spite of his somewhat black mood. He was far more use to being the manipulator than he cared to admit—devising the plan, carrying it to fruition, and to hell with the results. In the end, that too had been a disaster. Could he possibly learn from his own mistakes? That was a monumental demand to make on anybody, especially when his total departure from Paris would be difficult, almost astronomical to his mind, but he had no choice in the matter, and being forced did not compliment his usual, commanding temperament. Glancing over at the sleeping girl, Erik wondered what Monique's thoughts about last night would be.

Had she merely pitied him or was there more involved? They had definitely clashed at the onset, but in the end, she had welcomed his advances, and he *had* asked for her consent, surprising him most wonderfully with not only her luscious, enticing body, but actions that spoke of wanting to share a passion-filled experience also. He knew it was the first awakening of her true femininity, a fact that pleasantly pleased him, but was it something she would sorely regret this morning, when she came to her senses, that it had been with him? Almost fearful of the answer, his gut instinct upon arising had been to take one of the horses and flee...go back to Paris where he might rebuild his world after the fire...after everything had finally been forgotten in everyone's superficial little mind! He wanted to close himself up in that tomb, never to go above ground again, and shut the world out forever. But he knew he could not! It made him sick inside, almost to the point of retching, to think about what the day would bring. The stares! Hands closed over terrified mouths! Heads turned suddenly away in disgust, as he must show his face to an uncompassionate world. But there was no help for it! Mulling upon all the decisions he would have to make today, and the new experience he would be facing, Erik continued with a robot type attitude, the final task of making himself as presentable as possible, under such absurd and unusual circumstances.

When Monique awoke, Erik was not beside her. Her eyes searched the clearing to find him, stretching as she did so, noticing that her body ached slightly from all the glorious lovemaking of the night before. She smiled, remembering what a patient and gentle teacher Erik had been, awakening for the first time, those pleasures that she had fleetingly thought about, but never, ever wanted to pursue. She even had a moment of embarrassment, her face flushing with rapid pink color, remembering most vividly exactly what he had taught her, and knowing without any doubt, that she had responded most willingly to a new world opened up for her. Her father had always been so disappointed that she did not care about any aspects of being a woman, and the furthest thing from her mind had been courting, or taking a husband. It had been her father's darkest dismay that she dressed and acted more as a boy, causing him unmentionable distress on all too many occasions. But last night had been different! She had wanted

Erik to recognize her as a woman. Although he still presented as a man of many strange and evasive mysteries, she found… something about him… that was hard to explain even to herself that brought passion to her soul, and fulfilled a need she did not know existed. She hoped she had been successful in giving to Erik that something he seemed to be seeking. And whatever that was, be it of the flesh or of the soul, she hoped he would continue to need that from her. He had a gentleness of character that she desired in a man, not unlike her father had possessed, yet she recognized a dangerous and perhaps ruthless side to this strange man also! She had witnessed only a small part of what she was sure he must be capable of doing, if truly angered, yet contrary to reason, her worst fear was that he would send her away. She figured correctly that because of his face, Erik had been treated badly, and suspected that was an intricate part of the mystery surrounding him, but she found him fascinating, and…yes...mysterious, and some irrational need in her wanted to take care of this man. She knew nothing of his plans, or his purpose for being here, but she more than feared that the passion they shared before the dawn was just a temporary interlude, one that would inexplicably fade quickly for him when the events of his journey once again took precedence. That her presence was merely a coincidence that became convenient for his travel, and actually meant nothing otherwise.

Monique stood and turned in a circle trying to find Erik, the black cloak wrapped snuggly around her shoulders for warmth. She found him near the carriage, her eyes drawn to him like a magnetic force, and she was stunned by his appearance. She thought of a chameleon that changed to blend in with its varied surroundings, but some of his disguises made him stand out more eloquently! He was dressed in gentleman's garments, covered by a long black frockcoat, unbuttoned down the front. A tan brocade vest, layered over a frilly, white silk shirt, and around his neck a black scarf with a silver stickpin, could be seen under his coat.

Tight, black britches and black shoes finished off the outfit. But what drew her attention was the black wig. His hair was slicked back from his forehead, came down over and just below his ears, and had long dark sideburns. She actually liked the look, but his real hair was black also, and full on most of his head, and if arranged properly, could hide most of his facial deformity and be very attractive. Why did he need a wig? Why did he need this disguise, yet not wear the mask?

Erik spied Monique staring at him, and he came forward, the idea of speech almost painful. He searched for the appropriate words to explain. He gave a futile smile, involuntarily opening his arms to her, as his expressive green eyes stared in overwhelming wonder at the beautiful picture she displayed, bare feet peeking out from beneath his cloak as curly red locks flowed around her shoulders and back, a stark contrast to the dark background of his black cape.

"Erik, why are you wearing a wig, and why are you dressed like that?" Monique asked in bewilderment, but at the same time stepped right into his proffered arms to be infolded in a most welcomed embrace. He pulled her off her feet, burying his face into her neck, wanting wretchedly to cease to think, merely glory in the body that was offered so innocently and without question.

Erik took a deep, ragged breath into her hair, noting the sandalwood scent that continued to linger, thinking momentarily that she needed the smell of lilac or jasmine. Something more feminine! Reality taking over, he reluctantly set her on her feet, which settled charmingly upon both of his shiny shoe-tops, giving him the advantage of pulling her slight form tightly against the length of his in a most advantageous position, pushing her bare young breasts against his vest. Gingerly, he slipped his hands inside the cloak, enfolding his arms around her slight naked form, realizing immediately that his own body was reacting in a very willing way. He groaned audibly, deep within his chest, as Monique's hand wrapped around his neck willingly, also. With possessive hands firmly on her bare *derriere'*, he pressed her body intimately against his own, catching her warm lips in a crushing kiss. He kissed her time and time again, his tongue plundering the sweetness within. As his kiss deepened, he pushed her away only slightly, her arms still circling his neck, giving him just enough space between them for his hands to find her two ripe breasts. Lazily he gave them attention, teasing her nipples to hardness. Her body was a succulent nectar that a honeybee would savor, and he wanted to taste of it again.

Abruptly, Erik stopped, pressing her warm, supple body hard against him for a few lingering moments. "I fear, we will never make it to *Le Harvre,* if I allow myself to continue," Erik said harshly, with a huskiness to his voice that cried out with the passion he wanted to continue, but knew that he could not. With final purpose, he set Monique off his shoes and onto a soft layer of pine needles, holding her for a few lingering moments, as her swaying body tried to right itself.

Monique wasn't exactly sure what had just happened, but she knew it had been temptingly delicious, and she had wanted it to continue. Erik was looking at her rather sternly, but with a hint of pity. "I'm sorry, *ma petite*, that was rather unfair of me, now wasn't it?" he said apologetically, but his voice certainly suggested that he wasn't a bit sorry for his actions. She stared at him in puzzlement for a few seconds, then her eyes grew wide, remembering her question.

Watching the antics play over her face, Erik answered what she had asked with indulgence, the glazed over appearance of his eyes speaking to her only of abject indifference. "My reasons for being in *Le Harve,* require a little less scariness, for I will be dealing with a number of people," he said matter-of-factly, trying to convince himself with bitter irony, as well as her, that by wearing a wig that more of his deformity was hidden, presenting less of a horrific appearance.

"But, Erik, you don't scare anyone," she admonished gently, putting her small hand upon his rough and deformed right cheek, yet looking into telltale, sad green eyes that were not at all convinced, drawing on all the experiences of a lifetime of sorrow that knew otherwise.

Erik took her hand in his, leaning her up against him once again, as he peered down into her serious face. "Monique, I will try to remember those kind words you offer, but for my meeting today, it would be best if I did it my way," he said sternly, almost coldly, knowing the time had come to divulge his immediate plans of the day. "We will go into *Le Harvre'* together. I would like you to wear something very feminine. You did buy something besides that horrible nightgown and those riding britches, did you not?" he chided with an involuntary gleam of pure sarcasm gracing his eyes, causing her to wiggle against him. Still holding her hand, he caught her body with one strong arm, before she could easily protest.

"I bought a very beautiful day-dress, if you really must know," she retorted smugly, but the look she gave him was not one of defiance, but of apprehension that he would be disappointed. She didn't know why she wanted so badly to win his approval, yet the thought of his displeasure distressed her. There lingered a defiance in her nature that resisted his authority and command, yet when his unquestionable commanding voice, with its undeniably mesmerizing quality, bid her to do something, it was hard not to bow to his request, for even when her mind said no—her heart said yes!

"I'm sure it will do nicely," Erik assured her. " But it is most important that you look and act like a proper lady, not the hooligan that you are oft wanting to be," he finished meaningfully, pressing her tightly against him, feeling the heat of her naked body through his cloak, as once again she was obliged to struggle, her pride taking reign over her reason. " I have a meeting with my solicitor," he continued, dreading what must be revealed next. "Immediately thereafter, I will purchase passage to England. I do not plan on returning," he whispered softly into her hair, clutching her so tightly that his knuckles were turning white, fearing her reaction to this news.

Monique stiffened, a fear clutching at her heart at these unwelcome words. Erik was leaving France? But why? And why England? Her heart started pounding erratically in her chest as the implication of his words began to sink deep into her soul. Silence stretched out before them like an ugly prophesy handed down by the universe, yet had to be played out by those fools that were obliged to submit to its unalterable pattern. Her body began to physically shiver, as she thought about Erik leaving her behind. Tears welled up in her eyes, but she blinked them back, detesting her inability to control the flow, not wanting the satisfaction it might give him to see her cry. With a courage she did not feel, she asked, "Why must you leave France, Erik?"

Abhorring the very thought of releasing her and sighting the tears she so bravely attempted to hide, Erik endeavored to reply as honestly as possible, without really revealing the exact truth. "I have hurt people that I loved. I have no reason to stay," he said simply with no elaboration. "I would like you to come along," he added quickly, pausing only a moment in his repertoire, giving her no time to ponder his words, much less answer. He did not know what he would say if she refused, but would she leave France... her homeland? I won't beg, he thought dismally. Not even for companionship, much less love. He knew he would have to find the courage to let her go, if her answer was no. This time he would not scream, and yell, and make demands, but keep his pride intact, and just walk away with indifference, like he had done so many times to almost everything in his past! But...if he could just give her one simple reason to come along!

"It would be most advantageous to me, for reasons I would rather not reveal, if I were traveling with a wife. Would you consent to travel as my wife... for just a few days?" he asked abruptly, catching Monique completely off guard, as well as himself, for the idea had only just occurred to him.

Monique took a step backwards, breaking their embrace, eyeing him with what seemed to be complete distain, yet she answered almost in a whisper, "Yes, I will do as you ask...just for a few days." Her eyes were cast downward, and Erik couldn't see her face, but he guessed she would do it *only* because he had asked, not because it was really her desire to accompany him.

"Good, then it is settled," he said gruffly. "When this is all done with, if you wish to return to France, I will purchase your passage home and pay for your help. It will be enough to give you a new start," he said grimly, with an almost mechanical nuance to his voice that bespoke of a plan that went terribly awry—most definitely from bad to worst. "Get dressed, *ma petite, Le Harvre* awaits," he added, and seeing the horrified, painful expression on her face, Erik turned to hitch up the horses, giving her privacy to dress. His jaw tightened with a grim expression, as he mulled over the distinct feeling that he had not exactly explained his good intentions the way he had originally planned.

Chapter Six

Le Harve was a teeming seaport community situated on the northern boarder of France, where the Seine River flows into the English Channel. It was a thriving city with a huge import/export trade that kept the Parisians, as well as France, supplied with those frivolous commodities from around the world, deemed necessary to sustain even the most meager aristocratic existence. Flourishing with the newest industries supporting its growing expansion into the ever-disappearing wilderness, it had spread in a widening arc away from the waterfront, tall buildings totally obscuring any signs of shipping, if entering the city from numerous roads that intersected its boundaries. The main street was a large thoroughfare, with tall brick and stone buildings lining either side of the street, divided by a median of lavish trees and flowers, providing not only an extraordinarily beautiful view to its spectators, but producing an adequate causeway where two carriages rode side-by-side going in either direction. The temperature of the city was hot and steamy, causing the tempers of its many travelers and inhabitants to rise alarmingly, as they mingled and jockeyed for the most advantageous position to accomplish the goal of getting to their varied destinations. The traffic was stymied to a dead halt at the height of the day, and Erik, with a look bordering on quiet impatience, stood up suddenly, backing the carriage with precision, then swerved towards the right, maneuvering to squeeze between a grocery truck delivering its wares to the open marketplace and a wainwright's cart full to the brim with the odd assortment of tools for repairing wagons. Finally free of the crowded melee of congestion, he carefully steered their own carriage towards the shipping community, and down several narrower streets towards the busy docks.

The click of the horses hoofs and the constant clank, clank, clank of the carriage wheels on the noisy cobblestone streets, set Monique's mind into a trance as she reviewed the already short day. She had made herself ready to travel posthaste, sensing that Erik was in a particularly foul mood that bordered on some kind of inner rage, which totally puzzled her, for if it was directed at her, she could not fathom why! He had indicated his need of a *pretend wife* for the strange game he was playing, and although he encouraged her to participate, it was obvious his need of her was strictly as a business arrangement—paying for her services—then releasing her of her duties when they arrived in England. His words had stung her senses with unbelievable sorrow, realizing that his attention was again centered on his journey, certainly not wanting her physically or with any affection involved. She had hesitantly agreed to his plan, but with sad and quiet certainty that he meant what he had said. If a business arrangement was what he desired, then that is what he would get. No stings attached!

Erik's attitude as they traveled was tempered with some civility and even affection, yet there existed an uncomfortable undertone of guarded awareness to his surroundings. They had sat in companionable silence for most of the two hour ride into *Le Harve*, traveling at a slower pace when nearing the city itself, not wanting to draw undue attention. Monique sensed his revulsion and innate bitterness at having to go without his mask, and was finally beginning to understand. Half-a-dozen times the occupants of a passing carriage had openly gawked in rude manifestation, overstepping the bounds of common decency in doing so. Erik made no outward sign of noticing these rude acts, but she was aware that he had, quickly picking up on subtle body language that had become familiar to her, when something terrible seemed to be haunting him—a slight stiffening of his body, white knuckles that gripped the reins like he was sure the horses would bolt, but knowing they wouldn't, and that pout to his lips coupled with a stare that looked like he could not possibly see two feet in front of his face, yet the carriage never wavered from its path. Only a day before, she had been powerless to understand this bitterness that seemed to pulsate through his stiff and shaking body when he was forced to show her his face, but today her comprehension was complete, and the sadness she felt for Erik was one of tenderness and love.

Erik's control of his emotions had returned very slowly. He admitted reluctantly that he had not handled asking Monique to accompany him to England in the best possible manner, but she had agreed, none-the-less. She had looked at him in blank confusion at first, then seemed resigned to put up with him for awhile longer, most likely misplaced gratitude for separating her by distance from a situation she so aptly abhorred. Marrying a monster that she despised! Her resentful glance told him everything, so he naturally tempered his asking with the reassurance that she would be paid well for her services, and not left stranded in a country that was not her own.

The ever-present humiliation of exposing his face was wearing his nerves paper thin, yet the day's events had barely begun. His instinct had been to hide from people, calling darkness his friend, yet today he was forced to display himself in this obscene way in broad daylight. Facing the cruelty and scorn that loomed on the horizon, leaving him little dignity of being a member of the human race, gave him cold displeasure. Summoning the courage to continue, Erik concentrated his efforts on watching Monique. As they neared the city and the frequency of dwellings increased, the crisscrossing roadways became more congested. Erik noticed Monique's attention drawn towards the magnificent horses that pulled lavish carriages crossing their path. This, along with his limited knowledge about her association with these stately beasts, prompted Erik to ask cautiously, "Where does your fascination with horses come from?"

His commanding, yet mesmerizing voice, breaking out of the silence startled her. She stared at him in bewilderment at first, then with a mixture of emotion she couldn't explain, answering almost automaticly, yet with some trepidation, "My father was the head stable master for *Chapellae*, a large estate north of Paris. I grew up there, and was introduced to the saddle before I could walk."

"Won't your father be paralyzed with worry, wondering where his errant daughter has gone?" Erik replied, wanting to know more, yet fearful of her reply. He guessed she would eventually want to return to her father.

Monique thought about her answer. There was no reason keeping secrets any longer. Her charade had ended, even if Erik's had not; therefore she answered with the true sadness she felt, " My father is dead, Erik. I have no one that is searching for me." She seemed so inherently upset, that Erik thought it cruel to press her further, and although he felt genuine compassion, there was some deeper beckoning emotion that was wicked elation. Quickly, he changed the subject.

"How many dresses did you buy?" Erik said with a detached calm to his voice, yet his mind was strangely unsettled.

"Just this one and a skirt for traveling," she answered honestly, not understanding why it was important. She fidgeted in her seat, smoothing out the skirt of the delicately flowered dress, wondering if Erik had liked her choice. He had given her a genuine smile and an appreciative glance as she climbed into the carriage, but he had not spoken until now, and she was wary of his mood.

"And men's riding clothes plus one very ugly nightgown," he added in a mocking tone, still perturbed about the joke she had played at his expense…literally. There was no doubt in his mind that he would use *that* nightgown for rags to wash the horses.

"Items that I'm sure will come in very handy in the future, and not waste one franc of your money" she retorted with defiance, remembering his remark that the nightgown would never grace her body again. Well, he was totally mistaken!

Erik frowned and his hands gripped the reins tighter, quite aware of her meaning, knowing *that* infraction would not be allowed to materialize if he had any choice in the matter. Instead, he spoke absently, choosing to ignore her comment, " You will need a few more outfits for our voyage."

"Shopping again? Oh, Erik, I hate to shop," Monique protested, a truly pained and pitiful expression on her beautiful, yet childish face. She wrinkled her nose, searching his face with a hint of pleading, as if to say he couldn't possibly be serious.

In spite of himself, Erik's face broke into a smile. He had never heard of a woman who didn't like to shop. Recalling conversations overheard from his opera box, women fairly exalted in purchasing everything in sight, depleting their husbands purses with nary a thought to the consequences, nor the fact that money did not grow on trees. If it did, everyone would be clamoring to own a sizeable forest.

"It shouldn't be that tedious, *mon cherie.* I'll hire a cab to escort you to a ladies' dress shoppe, and when you have made your purchases, and my meeting is finished, we can meet for afternoon tea," he said with humor to his voice. "I can not have the gentry thinking I do not dress my wife properly," he added in simple explanation, hoping that by ending the afternoon on a pleasant note, it would make the evening easier, for there was no doubt about sharing a hotel suite as any conventional husband and wife. His wife would be by his side. Of that he was certain!

The idea of tea sounded scrumptious, but Erik's final words made her stiffen. Glaring at him with blatant stubbornness, she said unfeelingly, " Well, assuredly, we must present as a proper couple of beauty and breeding. Wouldn't want anyone to suspect we aren't what we pretend to be."

Erik's demeanor changed immediately, his body stiff and his expression unreadable, and she saw anguish flash in his eyes, just before they glazed with cold indifference, shutting her out completely. After that, they traveled in silence, Erik returning to his black mood and Monique sorry for hurtful remarks that were not intended to insult. Her unthinking words had not been directed at his face, but of course he took it that way. There was no way, at present, to convince him otherwise.

Abruptly the carriage came to a halt, jarring her out of her revelry. Two young livery boys dressed in like outfits came rushing forward, catching the horses from either side. Erik jumped down, giving them detailed instructions that Monique could not hear, then he came around to help her out. The sign above the building declared, Pontaine's Livery & Carriage House. Along the front, was an eloquently wide, gingerbread decorated portal, from which she could discern at least a dozen or more carriages and carts, awaiting their owner's return. The street was abounding with numerous small shops, and from the signs hanging out from their doorways, they belonged to—candle makers, tinkers, a small haberdashery, a quaint bookstore, and an interesting oriental tea shop. More colorful and artistic signs loomed in the distance, but she couldn't make out the names. Starring in wide-eyed fascination, Monique did not hear Erik call her name. She had rarely left the northern countryside where she was raised, and had never been to Paris. Everything looked like a storybook…big…wonderful…and magnificently exciting.

"Monique. Monique, I will meet you in three hours time at Belvous' Tea and Supper Club," Erik instructed, turning her to face him and handing her a piece of paper with numerous instructions written in a beautiful inscriptive scroll. He took her chin in his hand, tilting her head up to meet his searching green eyes, and what she saw, made her catch her breath. The tenderness of the night before, and his charismatic passion reflecting there, brought an unmistakable gladness to her senses. Softly he said, " Am I so ugly, *ma cherie*, that you will not have supper with me?"

Monique gasped, placing her hand in alarm on the arm that held her, "Erik, I did not mean..."

But he cut her off, not letting her finish, turning in the direction of the street, as the cab the livery boys hailed for him pulled up to the curb. He guided her to the enclosed, black brougham, leaving her side to give the driver directions to Pentier's Ladies Shoppe. "You will buy half a dozen outfits that a proper lady would wear, and those things that go with them," he said briskly, staring into her eyes with a no-nonsense expression. "A brush, a comb and whatever else you ladies need wouldn't hurt either," he said meaningfully, handing her a purse of coins, and she actually detected a little blush creep into his face, mentioning items that most men did not think about.

Suddenly he bent his head down to hers, catching her moist lips in a warm soft kiss. His arms wrapped around her waist, pressing her body intimately against his own, deepening the kiss, as a great need to possess her flooded his body, seeking to wash all the tortures and humiliation of the day away with the joining of their souls. But it wasn't the time or the place, and she heard him mutter an audible curse under his breath as reluctantly he let her go. He handed her into the cab, shutting the door behind her. Through the window he added, " The dress shoppe is across the street from the supper club. Please, *ma petite, be on time!*" With that, he motioned to the driver to be off, and the carriage careened onward, Erik watching as it disappeared down the narrow cobblestone street and out of sight, leaving him with an instinctive illusion of...danger... and he didn't know why! Dismissing his reaction as a ridiculous suspicion brought on by his own raw nerves, he turned around. Two wide-eyed livery boys, jaws hanging open in silent wonder, were staring in fascination and appreciation for the tall, imposing gentleman that had kissed the beautiful lady in a most unconventional fashion.

A brass bell tinkled in announcement, as Erik entered the solicitor's office of Bontonae & Seward. No one looked up from their tasks, except a middle-aged lady dressed becomingly in a bustled day-dress of the latest Paris fashion. When she recognized who he was, she smiled warmly, rising from her desk and came to greet Erik formally. "*M'sieur*, welcome, welcome! *M'sieur* Bontonae has been expecting you. If you would come this way," she said politely, spreading her hand to indicate the direction in which she wished to escort him. Located in an older refurbished building, the office was wide and spacious, and Erik appreciated the hint of Venetian architecture that was evident on this and many similar buildings. The outer office housed no less than eight cubicles where young lawyer apprentices were hard at work, digging for the information that made a large practice like Bontonae & Seward prosperous.

Erik was amazed by the warm welcome he had encountered. The lovely lady that now walked before him, had not even flinched when she had seen his face. He had never been here before; therefore, he was greatly impressed at Bontonae's insight into informing his staff of this one particular fact about himself, which Erik mentioned to the gentleman in his correspondence, it being a factor in some of his unusual requests. It had immediately put him at ease, deciding in an instant that his money had not only been well protected, but his choice of lawyers had been correct.

Upon entering a large inner office, Erik was immediately surrounded by a sparsely decorated workplace that had an atmosphere of getting things accomplished. The walls were lined with hundreds of volumes of books, and a large table set off to one side was laden with open pages, earmarked and folded, and papers were stacked in disarray, like someone had been laboring over a tedious problem. One large cherry desk was placed near the window, and as Erik turned in that direction, a small, rather thin, balding gentleman came over and extended his hand.

"Erik, a pleasure to meet you at last," *M'sieur* Bontonae replied, genuine feeling reflected in his voice. "I trust you had an uneventful trip from Paris," he said conversationally, motioning for Erik to take a seat in a burgundy leather chair beside his desk.

Uneventful! That was a gross understatement, Erik thought dryly, accepting the seat willingly. "Have you been able to complete my affairs," Erik asked, wanting to delve into the matter quickly. Money had never mattered to him until now. He had consulted on architectural projects around the world, strictly as a convenience to occupy his time and his mind in his lonely underground world. Everything had been handled by the law office of Bontonae and sent to a post office box monitored by Madame Giry. His actual artistic management of the Opera House for its pseudo manager, had been his real passion, along with the composition of his music, which in later years had culminated with the tutoring and management of Christine. That he had fallen in love with her had been an unusual circumstance, born out of a need for human companionship as a normal man with flesh and blood and feelings, and Christine's innate recognition of his loneliness and pain. He had survived on the salary of twenty thousand francs, doled out by the office manager himself and Erik actually smiled inwardly, knowing that his *silent boss* had at first given the money begrudgingly. Eventually he had realized that Erik had better taste and more experience in the arts and music than himself; therefore, he had reluctantly, but silently, given over those tedious tasks to the famed Opera Ghost! Unfortunately, he had not informed his successors, and there in began one thread in the chain of events that brought him to his present situation.

"*Oui, M'sieur,* it has been most easy to arrange what you have asked. The profits from your architectural consultations and the wise investments our company has made for you, have accumulated a very tidy sum. In fact, Erik, one could easily say that you are a very wealthy man.

"And what about the arrangements for England," Erik asked, grateful that his investigations into this lucrative firm had proved accurate, and thus no luck was actually involved in choosing a company to manage his affairs.

"That has been the most rewarding part, my boy," the elderly gentleman said, speaking to Erik in a familiar manner, as if he truly enjoyed revealing a plan that he personally had cemented together. "We have found a charming manor house just as you have requested, nestled in 1500 acres of rolling hills and forest lands outside the city of Cheltenham, perhaps a day's ride from London. You asked for an unassuming estate that was in some disrepair that an architect like yourself could rebuild and fit to your own specifications. An estate that was not near the city, but more secluded! Is that not correct?"

"Yes, that was my intent," Erik answered, still pondering whether *M'sieur* Bontonae had taken care of his most urgent matter. "And what about my identity?" he asked, uncomfortable discussing with a stranger about needing a last name. He had always signed his communications with the simple name of… *Erik…*, but revealed in his last letter, when explaining his wishes, his need for a new identity…. a full name, which he had never been privileged to know, would be a necessity.

Smiling intently at Erik, the gentleman continued, "In finding Pembroke Manor, I was delighted to discover that amongst its past history, there was a young man that disappeared about 15 years back and has never surfaced. Most believe he is dead, but your age fits him perfectly, and we have prepared papers for you to take on his identity, keeping your own given name. Along with the name, you inherit his title and his estate, so to speak, even though you have actually purchased it. You are now Erik Devereau, Earl of Pembroke."

Erik sat silently, a little stunned. This sounded totally strange and unnatural to his hearing. He had never really had an identity before. It had not been his choice to do this, but it was necessary in the scheme of the plan. After talking over the details and arranging for most of his money to be transferred to a bank in England, Erik set off to arrange details of his own—those necessary to have a wife, pretend or otherwise.

Erik waited near the tea house for over an hour, expecting Monique to show herself at any moment, and was irritated beyond reason when she did not appear. Thinking that she might actually still be shopping, he strode purposefully to the dress shoppe, swinging the door wide forcefully in his agitation, almost wrenching it off its hinges. His towering form stepped over the threshold, exuding a strength and power that could not be ignored.

Madame Pentier rushed to the side of the tall gentleman, dressed in immaculate black, his elegant clothes emphasizing his masculine physique, and when he spoke in a mesmerizing, musical voice, she hardly noticed the ugly disfigurement he bore upon part of his face. His eyes were dark and penetrating, and he stared at her with an inquiring attitude that commanded immediate attention.

"I'm looking for my wife," he said, glancing around the room in a searching motion.

"*Oui, M'sieur*, and what would your wife look like?" the lady asked attentively.

Erik paused for a silent moment, then answered easily, "A petite, redhead about this tall," he said, indicating with his hand just where the top of her head came against his long and lean muscular body.

Madame Pentier smiled knowingly, "Oh *Oui, M'sieur*, she was here sometime ago, and bought the most beautiful clothes. Much, much too shy, *M'sieur*. Did not want to spend your money! I had to encourage her by saying that her husband would want more striking gowns than she was going to pick for her beautiful figure. You will truly appreciate the selections," she rambled, pleased that she had been instrumental in clothing the lovely customer for this extraordinary gentleman.

"Did she indicate where she was going when she left, Madame?" Erik asked, more irritated now than before, knowing she had plenty of time to finish her business, and was perhaps once again trying to ignite his patience.

"*M'sieur*, she has been gone for almost an hour, asking where Belvous' Tea and Supper Club was located," she supplied quickly, seeing the dark irritation that was growing as the gentleman paced back and forth, running one strong, yet delicate hand thru his black hair in obvious agitation. " She had several packages in her possession, *M'sieur*. I asked if I could have them delivered, but she did not seem to know where that would be. I am sorry, *M'sieur*, but that is all that I know."

Erik thanked Madame Pentier and departed the shoppe, vaguely aware that a crowd had gathered on the street corner, beneath the tall, oil lamp that burned high above their heads in an iron basket. The shops were beginning to close their doors, and an early sunset was casting lengthening shadows between the walls of the tall buildings. Erik's earlier pleasant mood was fast disappearing. Either Monique had left him, not wanting to fulfill her bargain, or she was flagrantly defying his order to be on time. If that was the case, being trussed up like a turkey was the least of her worries. She should be more afraid of being the chicken that gets its neck wrung for being disobedient.

Erik leaned against the building, keeping an observant eye on the supper club, knowing he must continue to wait. Perhaps Monique just lost track of the time. As time swung by like a giant pendulum, ticking away in slow motion, Erik had a nagging fear that something was deadly wrong. The streets were almost deserted, and as the shadows grew long with unending darkness, Erik bathed in the overwhelming affirmation that he was once again in his own sacred and comfortable element. His hearing took on a sharper intonation, and his instincts became more honed. Voices from the alleyway across the narrow street drifted on the evening air, and the words *red hair* caught his acute hearing. Cautiously he crept forward in silence, skirting the building in the depths of the ghostly shadows.

"Was such a ghastly shame," one scraggly dressed women was saying, a cotton glove with absent fingers covering her mouth in pitiful dismay.

"What do ya think they want with her?" a younger girl inquired innocently.

"Most likely not for anything good," the first one added, not wanting to divulge the particulars that she was certain were true.

"T'was that Bartley crew, I'm tellin' ya, that finds wee lasses for those unmentionable brothels. Not likely she'll ever see the light of day," said another, her meaning quite clear without elaborating.

Erik stepped out of the enveloping darkness, materializing silently beside the circle of women, no hint from whence he came, his menacing face filled with a primitive, gut-wrenching fear at this latest discovery, yet he talked with an even unnatural calm, meant to instill power, "What red headed woman are you discussing?"

His haunting presence, and the mysterious way he appeared, caused one girl to run away screaming, and the others to stand in terrified silence, but one woman came forward unafraid, saying, " T'was a wee lass that was carrying many lovely packages from the dress shoppe there." She was pointing to Pentier's, and continued quickly, "Was not even off the curb when that Bartley crew came by with a carriage and snatched her right inside, driving away before a gendarme could even be summoned."

These incredulous words struck fear in Erik's heart. The premonition he had harbored of some huge impending doom crashing down around him like a building imploding, a feeling he had furiously tried to erase from his mind as ridiculous and unsubstantiated, had been absolutely authenticated. There was no doubt in Erik's mind that Monique was the red-headed lass they were discussing. And he was increasingly certain that her sassy and independent disposition would not lend kindly to her apparent entanglement, likely causing more harm than she could ever imagined. And that thought sent a demented rage coursing through Erik's already tormented body, bringing to the surface the jungle animal that would hunt its quarry until *his* thirst for blood was satisfied.

Asking a few more pertinent and valuable questions to the woman who spoke, Erik disappeared once again into the dark and foggy night as mysteriously as he had appeared. He realized that caution and time were the most important factors in considering his actions. Caution was a natural ally, giving him the advantage over his adversaries, where time was a lethal detriment, allowing these scum the ability to bring more harm upon the weak and unprotected. This had been a hard and tragic lesson he had learned very early, when caged and living with the gypsies. The faster he gathered the pieces of this puzzle together and solved this mystery, returning Monique to the shelter of his own protection, the better he would like it. That he would be unsuccessful was simply not an acceptable option!

Planning and discreet inquiries were the first step in expediting his plan, almost like creating music or building a form of architecture. He had secured a suite at the Spinx Arms Inn, between the heart of the city and the waterfront, wanting to be near the activity of both worlds, one where aristocracy lavished in elegance, and the other where the less fortunate put up with the acceptance of squalor. Carefully he laid out the tools of his trade upon the bed—a black hooded cape with hidden pockets that concealed his secrets, a full white death mask, and his ever-faithful Punjab lasso, made from a thin cord of twisted rope. A new accruement to his wardrobe was a gentleman's walking cane that hid a wicked and deadly, many-sided rapier. For what was to come, Erik knew he would have to draw upon all his instincts, his wits, and his knowledge. There was no doubt of accepting the challenge. Monique had gotten under his skin and he couldn't live without her! He needed answers and he needed them now! And somewhere in the dark and lewd bowels of the dank and steamy city, the Bartley crew did not realize that their fate had been irrevocably sealed, when they had the distinct misfortune of kidnapping the wrong, beautiful lady. The one that belonged to the Phantom of the Opera!

Chapter Seven

Darkness shrouded the city, and a dense and bone-piercing fog hung in the crisp night air, blurring the outline of any inhabitants foolish enough to frequent its cobblestone corridors. Doors were locked and bolted with window curtains pulled tight, hiding from prying eyes those home fires that burned in many a hearth. The storefronts of buildings and dwellings hugged each other so closely in this dangerous part of the city, that horse drawn wagons could not maneuver down the narrow streets, leaving room exclusively for the foot travelers only. Total silence greeted nightfall, except for the occasional familiar sounds that were routine for the docking areas on a busy evening, when a vessel pressed into a rigid time schedule might be loading its cargo throughout the bitter night.

Erik had gathered information from several sources. He started with the doorman at the Spinx Arms Inn, where he had found a suite to await passage to England on the paddle steamer *La Bentra,* leaving *Le Harve* within three days. And that left him precious little time to accomplish the task of finding Monique. His mind was ravaged with the unthinkable, that he would be unsuccessful, or if finding her whereabouts, her spirit might be broken, or worse yet, she might be dead. He was all too aware that her unusual zest for independence, most unlike a proper young lady of station, and that irritating knack she possessed for raising his ire at any given moment with her unreasonable actions, were going to bode ill for her situation. And the thought of being thwarted in his efforts, his black mood could probably be measured on a scale between the depths of hell and sanity, right around the mark indicating his desire to snuff out the existence of those responsible with a cold and heartless irrelevance. His greatest advantage was that he was more comfortable in the darkness. Those places, where activities lent more to bright lights and cherry atmospheres, caused him anguish and emotional torture as people shrunk back at the appearance of his scarred face, trying to hide their disgust and horror in their unsuccessful efforts to pretend not to notice. Because of his elegant dress as a titled gentleman, they were often forced to be polite, but he could see it reflected in their eyes, their unmasked expressions, and often in their actions as well, that they believed he should be locked up somewhere, not exposing himself to the gentle side of humanity.

Erik was here at *La Mason des Amour*, trying to find the collaboration that would send him on a certain course. He had positioned himself at the end of a long oak bar, a gathering place made available for gentleman to converse before being united with their chosen lady for the evening. It was situated between the common parlour and a room set aside for gambling, where a man more than likely would find his purse wanting than obtaining a quick fortune. Erik's second stop had been a prominent eating pub, where the maitre 'd was know to have specific and valuable information on any form of entertainment that a person might want to engage in… proper or otherwise. Making quiet inquiries into the best establishment for a gentleman to find solace for the flesh, giving a wife a reprieve from her usual duties to her husband, he was given several specific names. Wanting to substantiate these claims, he went to the most prominent one first.

Erik was not adept at striking up a frivolous conversation, but he needed detailed information, so consciously he made a valiant effort to look interested in his surroundings, giving over his attention to a portly, older gentleman leaning on the bar beside him. The man was dressed as gentry, and his red, cherry face was ogling the scantily dressed ladies in the parlour as eager men vied for their attention, making their choice and paying the exorbitant fee for a few hours of pleasure.

"I am searching, *M'sieur*, for an acquaintance of mine that would not likely be able to afford such a fine establishment. Where would one find a similar business, but less expensive in nature," Erik interrogated under hooded eyes, bringing his untouched brandy glass to his lips, pretending to consume the dark liquid in his hand.

"Well my boy, that would most assuredly be down in *the maze*. But I'm warning you, *that* is not a place to venture into alone. There are those that would be more than willing to help you out of your purse, leaving you bloody beside the curb," he said indicatively, looking at the tall, muscular young man closely, Erik's features partly concealed by the dimness of the light in the room, then deciding that the gentleman could probably take care of himself. "But if you can't be persuaded, and are foolish enough to go down there, you might look at a place called *Le Jeux*. It's the best known and most likely place where a gentleman with less means would take refuse." The man looked at Erik oddly, noting his fine dress and aristocratic stature, wondering why a gentleman would actually choose to go there alone. Let his friend find him, was his own thought!

"Do you know anything about a group know as "the Bartley crew," Erik questioned further, thinking this man seemed to know his information rather well.

"A meaner, more disgusting lot can't be found in *Le Harve, M'sieur*. It's rumored, they supply *Le Juex* with girls off the streets....those needing a home you know.... but a more refined lot than the average trollop. If you take my meaning."

Erik did, and the idea of degrading a woman for the sake of another made him grunt in disgust. He had heard enough! Erik laid his untouched glass of brandy down on the bar, his anger masked behind eyes that showed total neutrality. Thanking the older gentleman for his time, he took his leave, saying he would consider the man's warning before venturing into *the maze* alone. Having the *exact* information he needed, he departed quickly.

The maze was the red light district of *Le Harve*, where during the day, activity appeared ordinary and serene with dozens of shops, markets, and eateries in plentiful supply, exulting in the daily routines of living. At night the atmosphere changed to a scheming and illicit cauldron of humanity, where crime was rampant and shady activities were in abundant supply, creating the spiraling downfall of the human spirit.

Le Jeux was a somewhat disreputable bordello run by Madame Truveaux, mostly for those of the middle class, but a higher-class gentleman now and then graced its doorway... for a variety of reasons. Sometimes it was a matter of insufficient funds for the classier establishments, like *La Mason des Amour*, but occasionally, it was because a gentleman with particular odd tastes could... for the right price... buy the time of a *special* lady, that was not available at other, more reputable houses. Such was the case on this particular night!

Erik pushed open the creeky gate that led to *Le Jeux*. Sheer red curtains hung in the long windows, and tasseled lampshades spilled forth a soft yellow light that illuminated the wide front porch. Cautiously he entered the double portal, taking stock of his surroundings in one quick glance. A large foyer presented at the front of the house, separating into several small rooms to the left. A wide grand staircase lead to the upper levels, winding majestically along the right wall, and culminating at the top of the stairs into a spacious balcony, eventually disappearing on both sides into long hallways whose view was swallowed into darkness. Erik had the momentary thought that the old building must have been quite a showplace in its day, and that the old ornate architecture would be magnificent if properly restored.

A young girl in her late teens, dressed in a white silk wrapper flowing to her ankles, approached Erik shyly. She caught sight of the tall, almost dangerous appearing stranger, cloaked all in solid black as he entered, and she wanted to be the first to make his acquaintance. The cold wind whipped at the edges of his heavy black cape, revealing a plush gold lining to the obviously expensive garment. He wore black gloves on long masculine hands that held a silver-handled walking stick, and the collar of his hooded cloak was pulled high around his ears, adding remarkably to his raffish, almost satanic appearance. As he stepped forward into the harsh light of the chandelier, Erik's features were illuminated with stark reality, but his carriage and attitude were so striking and mesmerizing that at first glance they were almost overlooked. His black, ebony hair was slicked back from his forehead, and green piercing eyes bored right into your mind, rendering many speechless, not knowing if it was because of the stark revelation of his face or his totally commanding presence. Coming forward quickly, the girl caught a glimpse of his face in the brighter light of the foyer, and glanced suddenly away in embarrassment, casting her eyes downward. A moment later she lifted them again, greeting him politely, not looking directly at his handsome, yet distorted features.

"We are so glad to have you with us, *M'sieur.* I am Salene. Come into the parlour and meet the other girls," she said politely, taking his arm and leading him forward.

Erik followed her lead, noticing the white stockings that covered her long, slender legs being purposely revealed for his benefit from the folds of her open robe. His pulse quickened and a flash of pain surged through his body, remembering Christine's white stockings that he had all but forgotten, and now the memories started flooding back with a terrible vengeance. He closed his eyes in torment for only a moment, trying desperately to repel the images from his mind, needing to concentrate on the present.

Taking one long searching look around the room, not finding Monique among the many girls lounging upon couches and soft stuffed chairs, entertaining dozens of other men of various professions and means, if their attire was any indication, Erik turned casually to Selene. "Might I have a word with the Madame of the house. I actually had a more special girl in mind." he said with direct purpose. Politely Selene nodded in deference to his special request, leaving Erik standing alone.

"*Oui, Oui, M'sieur,*" came a voice from behind him. Erik turned around to find a middle-aged lady, rushing towards him eagerly, her hands in the air as if expressing delight.

Erik nodded, acknowledging her presence.

"*M'sieur,* you can have the pick of any of our young ladies. The price is very reasonable," she said, sweeping her hand across the air, indicating the ladies in the parlour.

Erik's teeth ground together and the muscles of his jaw tightened in a rhythmic motion, trying to bide his time and play out this tedious game. He didn't want just any girl...he wanted Monique...and he wasn't here for the purpose she indicated!

Gathering his wits about him, he spoke softly, but with determination, "I have a certain one in mind, Madame. I was told you had a new girl called Monique, and that I should ask only for her! A red head with a special price, I believe!" Erik added meaningfully, suggesting he was a customer that would pay more for the right kind of lady.

Madame Truveaux frowned for a moment. The new girl did have red hair, but no one could possibly know she was here, and she wouldn't be ready until tomorrow night. Suddenly her face broke into a smile. What would it hurt, she reasoned. The gentleman wouldn't know the difference, and the girl would certainly bring a very tidy sum. She just hoped that Jarvis hadn't gotten out of hand, as often happened, and that the young redhead was still presentable.

Smiling to Erik, she replied sweetly, "*Oui, Misieur*, we have a lovely new redhead, as you have mentioned, yet untouched I might add. Her name is not Monique, *M'sieur*, but Bonnie. They are one in the same."

Not quite understanding that message, Erik sighed inwardly, a frown furrowing his brow. With sinking despair, he feared that his search for Monique would take longer than he had hoped. It could take days to visit the numerous houses. He had figured with all hope, knowing how bewitchingly beautiful Monique was, that she would be considered very special indeed. But also knowing how troublesome she could ultimately be, they might well agree she was more trouble than she was worth. And in spite of himself, even under such desperate and horrible circumstances, a slight smile tugged at Erik's mouth. Yet something else nagged unrequited at his memory, but he knew not what. Climbing out of the daze of his unconscious musings, Erik caught the last of what the Madame was saying.

"…..and a bonnie lass she is, M'sieur. If you agree, she can be ready in a few minutes," she added, waiting impatiently for his answer. Erik didn't know why, but something stirred his curiosity. He agreed silently with a nod of his head.

"If you would just make yourself comfortable in the parlour," Madame Truveaux suggested politely. "I will have Millie come for you shortly," she added, hurrying off in a fluff of activity.

Erik stood impatiently at the window, his back to the occupants of the parlour, his mind trying …desperately…to search for that piece of information that would bring this puzzle together. Why had he agreed to this? Something in his mind said he must know for sure. The girl's name was Bonnie…not Monique! Why did that name sound so familiar? A foreshadowing of something played at his thoughts, but before he had time to reason it out, Millie came for him. He was led back into the foyer and over to the grand staircase. A swarthy man of medium height leaned negligently on the banister, eyeing Erik appreciatively.

As he put his foot on the first step, the man spoke. "Let her know who's boss, Gov'ner," he drawled in a broken accent, and Erik caught a whiff of his foul and disgusting breath. When Erik glanced his way, the man tipped his fingers to his forehead, winking suggestively. "Like the chaste ones, do ya Gov'ner. If the lassie don't behave, she'll be answering ta me! You can remind her of that," he said with emphasis, trying to assume importance.

A sharp voice came from the hallway, under the stairs, "Jarvis Bartley, get in here and leave the fine gentleman alone, or *you'll* be answering to *me*!"

Erik's whole body twisted around menacingly, his dark green eyes boring into the man's face, burning an image in his mind of the corpse whose doom he had already determined. His intense glare so unnerved Jarvis that he shuttered, turning away in agitation, imagining with an uncomfortable feeling that someone had just walked over his grave. Erik knew he would have to wait to settle his pressing business with Jarvis Bartley. His first priority was finding Monique and getting her once again under his protection. With Bartley in the vicinity, he had the unprecedented feeling that he was very close indeed, and that prospect sent anticipation coursing through his entire body with a sweet and undeniable turbulence of emotion! Slowly he turned back, following Millie up the stairs. Erik was escorted down a long dark hallway, far into the depths of the house. Silently he was handed a key to a door, and suddenly he found himself standing in the corridor alone. As he stared at the door, soft words of love came to his mind, "...Bonnie, if you like." He put the key in the door, his senses reeling with the discovery that he might have found the final illusive puzzle piece he was seeking.

Erik entered the room, locking the door quietly behind him. The only light came from a small lantern placed on a table by the bed. It glowed softly, casting streaks of shadow and light across the walls and ceiling in a swirling motion, as the flame wavered from the breeze of opening the door, giving the room an eerie appearance. The windows held dusty brocaded curtains to mask the existence of the bricked-up false opening, trying to convey to the customer the sense of a bedroom appearance, yet not allowing the girl to escape, or the gentleman not to pay his bill. Erik could barely make out the pathetic figure of a small girl huddled on the bed. Her skittish form moved in terror to the far side when he turned around, and all he could see in the pale light were two tormented eyes staring back at him.

Monique saw the stranger enter the room and she stared in misery and fear. He was tall and ominous, phantasmal in the shadows, like some cruel monster that could ravish her person with no thought of tenderness or feeling, and right then, the outright reality of her situation struck with a blinding thunderbolt. She shut her eyes in silent grief, turning her head into the pillow, trying with all her imagination to shrink into nothingness, as her mind flashed back with the images of how she had come to this pathetic state.

Monique stepped off the curb, encumbered with three large packages, wishing Erik had been there to help her. How did he think she could manage all this alone? It wasn't her idea to purchase new garments, and all of them gowns for a fine lady. What would she do with them in a few days, she thought in vexation. Not likely she would need them after that. Britches would suit better for what she had in mind…a job in a stable! She had been exceedingly embarrassed when Madame Pentier had asked… where… she would like her purchases sent, and she had stuttered and stammered that she did not know. One small detail that Erik had not supplied her with, she thought in irritation. And the look the Madame had given her was priceless, for she had glanced more than once at the naked finger on Monique's left hand—the one where a proper wedding ring should be worn. Monique was sure the lady thought her to be some man's mistress, whom he was lavishing expensive gifts upon for her appreciated services. The idea of making Erik pay in some appropriate manner for that embarrassment was uppermost in her mind.

As she was idly thinking, a huge carriage jolted to a stop beside her, blocking her path, splattering mud and water over her pretty yellow dress and making the packages fly in all directions as she tripped on the slippery street. A door swung open quickly, and a man jumped down from the interior, taking her around the waist, appearing to help her up. But as he did so, hands from inside the carriage grabbed her arms, propelling her upwards as the first man pushed her forcefully in, slamming the door behind as he entered also. Rough hands pressed a wet, scented cloth against her mouth, stifling her cries for help, as strong arms squeezed the breath out of her lungs. Violently she kicked at the bonds that held her immobile, but a cloudy haze started fogging her brain, and her eyes closed involuntarily, as blackness overtook her senses.

Hours later, Monique felt a stiffness in her body from being handled roughly and lying still in a cramped position for several hours. She heard voices from far off in the distance, becoming louder and more distinct as the seconds ticked by.

"Ain't she a fine one, Jarvis. Looks a bit hoity-toity for her own good. She should bring a high price," Millie said, not a lick of sorrow for the pretty young girl curled up in a heap on a cot.

"Ye be teachin' her the proper etiquette for entertainin' our special clientele, and no sha-nana-gans 'bout this one! I want the

Madame ta let her work tomorrow night," Jarvis warned. "I'll be wantin' a cut of her price, and I ain't wantin'ta wait too long."

Through a foggy haze, Monique lay on the pallet listening, hoping they would not realize she was awake. What she heard struck terror in her heart. She was going to be used as a lady of the evening! The very idea seemed totally preposterous. They couldn't make her do such a thing. Could they? Warily she looked for a way to escape. If she could just get out the door! She stood up shakily, making a valiant effort to bolt across the room, turning the knob and swinging the door wide. Franticly she darted out into the empty hallway, glancing quickly in both directions, seeing nothing but one closed door after another in the narrow corridor. Before she had a chance to make a rational decision, Jarvis caught her around the waist, pulled her roughly back into the room, and flung her violently against the wall, holding her shoulders painfully immobile with two strong hands.

"An' just where do ye think ye be goin', missy," he shouted angrily, his teeth bared in anger. "Ye be worth a lot of money ta good ol' Jarvis, here," he spat, venom in his tone.

Monique strained violently to free herself, kicking at his ankles with her feet. His arms pinned her tightly, assuring her compliance. With savage desperation, she turned her head, catching his hand with her mouth, and bit down with renewed vigor, sinking her teeth deeply into his flesh. He yelped in pain, releasing her, and jumped back in disbelief at her boldness. He looked down at his hand, blood welling to the surface from a track of perfect teeth marks imprinted upon his flesh.

Advancing upon her in growing anger, Jarvis swung his hand back and forth, walloping her soundly across the mouth with hard knuckles and the palm of his hand, sending her reeling backwards across the room and into the dark corner. Monique whimpered in pain, sliding to the floor, her lips split and bleeding. But Jarvis wasn't finished. Though eyes filled with tears, she saw Jarvis towering over her, slowly removing his belt.

"A good beatin' will show ye I mean business, and not ta cross me again, lassie, or I have more where this came from," he warned. Placing one boot on the small of her back, and pushing her body flat against the floor, he pulled up the thin chemise to her waist. Raising his arm high over his head, he brought the belt down hard across her backside and the back of her bare thighs repeatedly, until Millie finally came up and caught his arm.

"Don't mark her too much, Jarvis," she pleaded, fearing for the girl's life. Jarvis had a bad temper and sometimes he didn't know his own strength. More than one girl had met her maker at the peak of his wrath. "Won't be good to anyone, if she is battered senseless. If you want your money from the Madame, you better hold off," she added, hoping to cool his anger with that one important statement.

Jarvis pulled back, seeing that the girl was out cold anyway. "Well, clean her up, an' find something for her ta wear the gentlemen will like, and teach her how ta paint her face proper when she comes to. She better be ready ta work tomorrow night." With that he stomped out of the room, leaving Millie to clean up the mess. What was Jarvis thinking, she thought. It would take more than makeup to cover the bruises he had left on the girl's face that certainly wasn't pretty anymore.

When she awakened, the rest of the day developed into another bad dream. Her sore body ached so unmercifully that it was almost impossible to sit, the raw welts on her thighs and buttocks screaming with pain, yet she was forced to endure instructions on makeup and given rather explicit examples of what a man might want her to do. A few days ago she would have shuttered distastefully at all of them, and still did at some, but occasionally she had allowed her mind to drift back to Erik, and those images of their glorious lovemaking were very pleasant, helping to numb her mind. It was only when she was forced back to reality, and the idea of sharing any of those experiences with a stranger that almost made her retch, sending her entire body into agonizing torment that made her shutter with revulsion. And so the day continued, Monique in a virtual fog of oblivious existence.

Within only a few pain filled hours, Millie pulled the girl over to Jarvis. Monique had been instructed to dress hastily in a white transparent gown with a shear, blue wrapper that exhibited her long slender body to anyone's view. Quickly Millie had applied heavy makeup to Monique's face, hoping to cover some of the ugly bruises, telling her there wasn't time to waste.

"And, if you know what's good for you, missy, you'll not cross Jarvis, for he hasn't shown you his mean side yet… when he's really angry," Millie warned Monique, who had shrunk in silent terror, when Millie indicated there was a change in plans. That she was to meet her first customer…*tonight*…just couldn't be true! Monique had immediately retched the contents of her stomach onto the floor, and Millie had slapped her harshly also, her face stinging from the pain and her salty tears.

"Madame says the bonnie lass has got to work tonight, whether she's ready or not. Has some fine gentleman downstairs that's askin' for a redhead and a girl unschooled in love. Probably can't get what he wants uptown, so that's why he's coming to us," Millie stated, a bit of disgust in her voice, but no remorse for the girl.

Jarvis stared at Bonnie evilly, his face inches from hers, " S'pose he be wantin' a virgin or a new one he can teach his way? If ya ain't one, lassie, ya better be actin' like ya are. An' don't ya be makin' a fuss. Treat the gentleman nice and do exactly what he asks, or ye'll be answerin' ta me personally." With that he smacked her hard on her sore bottom for emphasis, reminding her what he could do if she didn't obey, and pushed her into a spacious room she hadn't seen before, locking the door from the outside.

"Take her in a drop of laudanum in some wine, ta dull her senses, or she might just bite the customer also, and then t'wlll be pittance ta pay," he said to Millie, rubbing his bandaged hand, and stalking off down the stairs in a huff.

As Erik stepped forward the girl whimpered, "Please, *M'sieur*, ask for another girl." Her voice was so muffled in the pillow held tightly against her face, that Erik could not recognize her voice.

"Is your name Bonnie?" he asked in a low, melodic voice, wanting desperately to know if it was Monique, but the girl seemed so frightened that he was genuinely afraid of pushing her over the edge of sanity.

Erik took the room in two strides and sat down heavily on the bed. Inhaling sharply, he held his breath, fearful that the wretched creature was not Monique, yet fearful that she was! Anger rose in him, gripping him with a turbulence of rage as his brain assimilated the magnitude of his discovery. If this was Monique, what had they done to her? With agonizing discomfort, slowly Erik reached out to touch the terrified girl, but she shrunk back in fear, a ragged sob escaping her lips.

"I won't hurt you, Bonnie," he coaxed, hoping she would turn his way, but when she didn't, he reached again, pulling her frail and battered body closer, wanting to see her face. She resisted, but he was stronger, and carefully he cradled her against his chest. Placing one hand under her chin, he turned her tear-streaked face towards him, and when he did so, his heart wrenched in both sorrow and relief, for Monique's blue eyes stared back at him with the dull gaze of drugs and pain. Slowly he exhaled, the tightness in his chest exploding, for his instincts had been correct.

As he studied her eyes, his anger was now complete, for he was certain she did not recognize him. Tenderly, Erik pulled her onto his lap, brushing the stray tendrils of wet curls away from her face. Gaudy, thick makeup and rouge mingled with the tears that trailed down her lovely features, and her lips were spit and bleeding. One eye and cheek had ugly purple bruising that would take days to heal, and Erik knew all too well, he would have to shield her from the horrible comments of others. His existence over the ensuing hours had been a living hell, not unlike the prison that kept him chained to its boundaries for what now felt like centuries. He would have given anything to find her. And now that he had, a feeling of possession took over. Patiently he soothed her, stroking her hair, trying to wash away the fear with the musical timbre of his voice. Softly, he whispered, "Monique, *mon amour*, it's Erik. I've come to take you home."

As the stranger reached for her, at first Monique had been afraid. Jarvis had warned her, when a man came to her, to hold her tongue or she'd know another beating. And she believed him. But how could she allow another man to touch her? She only wanted Erik! He was kind and gentle, and although he didn't actually love her, he treated her with respect and taught her to be a woman. Her body hurt and her mind was numb. She wanted to be held in Erik's loving embrace! And she just wanted to sleep. In sleep she could hear his soft and beautiful commanding voice calling her name.

Monique drifted in and out of consciousness. Erik gently undressed her, divesting her of the obscene costume she was wearing. Seeing the raw strap marks on the pale skin of her buttocks and thighs, brought his anger to a measured fury that was quickly spiraling out of control. Using water from a pitcher on the bureau, he washed the makeup off her face and dried blood from her lips, kissing gently over the bruises, ending with one long, lingering kiss upon her swollen lips. In doing so, Monique responded, sliding both her arms around Erik's neck, murmuring his name softly, but her eyes were dull. He realized she did not see him, but merely remembered their lovemaking as a dream, and pleasantly that made him smile. At that moment he felt an overwhelming rush of true and unconditional, compassionate love for another human being, and Erik was stunned by his revelation. He didn't just want to protect her from those that would do her harm—he wanted Monique by his side for eternity. Did that mean he was learning to cope with the loss of his past? When he had really thought about Christine, if not presented with a blatant reminder... like the white stockings. Not for several days, and that realization gave him hope. The love he had in his heart for Christine could never be extracted, but it would lay dormant and safe, a lesson learned that he would cherish to his dying day, but this was a different lifetime, and he realized the tangible love he had to offer was for Monique!

Erik knew the time was growing short. It had been late evening when he had finally made his way to *the maze* and he didn't want to linger. He still had a lot of unfinished business that needed his undivided attention. He had hired a brougham for a considerable amount of cash to venture into *the maze*, to lay in wait at the entrance at exactly one o'clock, and he chafed to get Monique to safety. Erik pulled her frail body into his arms one last time, brushing her forehead with his lips. Taking her left hand in his, he slipped a magnificent ruby ring encircled with diamonds on her wedding finger along with a solid gold band. Spreading a rich, dark blue cape, which he pulled from beneath his own cloak, neatly upon the bed, Erik wrapped Monique's naked body snuggly within, making sure nothing but her bare feet were exposed, allowing the cape to come over her shoulders with her arms free, then tied it at her throat. Picking her up gently in his muscular arms, he headed for the door.

There was a loud gasp from the parlour, bringing not only its occupants spilling into the foyer, but Madame Truveaux as well. The dignified, yet dangerous appearing gentleman with the scarred and beautiful face, was carrying his consort down the eloquent staircase wrapped in a lush velvet cape. Her left arm rested on his right shoulder, and her head lay against his chest, her long red hair flowing back over his arm. Her eyes were closed and she seemed to be sleeping. The gentleman's face and his posture had a look that bespoke of true bodily harm befalling anyone that got in his way.

"*M'sieur,* did you not like the girl?" soothed Madame Truveaux, thinking Erik was unhappy with his choice and bringing her back, so to speak. "You can pick another if you like," she offered hastily.

Erik gave her a dark sardonic look of pure hatred, but did not speak, continuing down the stairs. His cape was thrown back over his shoulder on his left side and attached to his hip was a deadly looking rapier that indicated most pointedly that he meant business. Clearing the stairs, he started for the front door.

"*M'sieur,* where are you going? You haven't paid for the girl," the Madame cried in panic, not understanding his intention.

Erik continued without speaking, all eyes staring in his direction. Again Madame Truveaux spoke, seeing her money disappearing as she watched. "*M'sieur,* you can pick another girl and you haven't as yet paid," she said in earnest.

Erik turned for only a moment, his eyes dark with barely contained fury, and within that moment everyone knew the magnitude of what the stranger was capable of doing. The ominously, foreboding look Erik unleashed upon the Madame, told her immediately the gentleman was deadly serious. Slowly he spoke, enunciating each word with clarity and emphasis,"I- do- not- desire- another- woman. One- is- quite- enough, Madame! And I'll *not* be paying for the pleasure of bedding my own wife!"

With those words, a hushed murmur was heard from those watching in the foyer. The expensive ring upon the girl's left hand and the beautiful cape had not gone unnoticed. By the time they turned around again to look, the girl and the stranger were gone.

The alleyway behind *La Jeux* was dank and steamy with raw sewage emitting an offensive smell that made a body gag. A door stood open at the end of an elaborate labyrinth of alleys, each connecting to another, swallowing up those unfamiliar with their system. A lantern swinging above a makeshift table, cast a dim light on three men playing cards, each one in turn more loathsome than the other.

Jarvis was sitting on a barrel, studying his cards with apprehension. Be damned if he'd let that scurvy lad across from him win again!

"Come on, it's your turn," Pierre fussed, kicking at the barrel in which Jarvis sat. "What's the matter, your head aching' like your hand," he laughed, remembering the little she-cat that gave the boss so much trouble.

"Just be holdin' your tongue, laddie, for that bonnie redhead will be getting' her due soon enough, and when she's all spent up and ugly, I'll be takin' my turn also," he offered, thinking he had done a fine job this month, filling his quota of girls for the Madame. Wasn't always so easy finding a *good looker* as he liked ta call them, ta introduce them into the profession. Once in a long while, he had ta resort ta more drastic measures, takin' matters into his own hands, ya might say! He noticed Millie's new girl enterin' Pentier's Dress Shoppe and since he was sorely desperate, he had laid in wait, taking his opportunity when it presented. His salary was kinda on a commission of sorts. If he delivered only part of the package, his reward was nothin', but if he found that one *special lady* for that odd assortment of gentry that wanted ta play those particular games that no one mentioned, then he was handed a hefty bonus. And they almost always wanted a virgin! If tonight's customer was dissatisfied, he might just try her out himself.

Erik shrunk back against the stone building, peering into the darkness with the uncanny night vision of a jungle animal that hunted its quarry in the darkness of night. Patiently he waited for his prey. Confrontation always brought forth his darker tendencies, the thrill of the hunt providing a catharsis for his pent up frustrations. His pulse bounded within his neck as the excitement of the moment heightened, leaving him somewhat shaken at the impact this night would present. He had promised himself this would not happen again, but upon finding Monique and discovering her condition, he was more than willing to make swift work of her captors. Obviously they had no idea who they were dealing with.

A cat screeched behind him, jumping off a windowsill, turning over a small wooden bucket as its four feet hit upon the ground in unison. Jarvis looked up in interest, "Françoise, go out and see who's out there. I'm expecting Dupree ta come by with my money any moment."

Françoise, sitting cross-legged against the back of the chair, gave a sigh of disgust, getting up reluctantly. "Don't you be lookin' at my cards, now," he warned, knowing Jarvis was a cheater when he thought no one was aware. He shuffled out into the alley, turning his head in both directions and seeing nothing, sauntered up the alleyway toward the street. A thin lasso whirled silently through the air, sleekly eliminating the man in question, his body sliding down the side of the brick wall in a crumpled heap. Erik did not look back.

Several minutes passed and it was Françoise's turn. "Where did that young pup go?" complained Jarvis in irritation. "I'll be whoopin' him good, if he don't mind his elders." Jarvis said, looking down at the best hand he'd had all night. He chuckled to himself, certain he would come out the winner. "Better get yer scurvy self in here if ya want yer cut of the money" he shouted from his seat, and when he looked up at the shadow of a figure in the door, a scream stuck in his throat.

An apparition of his imagination loomed ghost-like in the doorway. He watched in frozen panic as a thin rope shot out expertly from the figure's hand, choking Pierre in one quick motion, snapping his neck in a grotesque fashion. Pierre fell backwards onto the floor. Unable to move, because of the deadly rapier inching into the cloth of his thin vest directly over his heart, Jarvis stared in both fright and fascination. Was this a phantom of his mind or a man? The image was clad completely in black, the satanic face covered in white with ugly veins covering its surface. The opening around his glowing eyes was as black as coal, and his head was concealed by a hood. The figure inched closer, piercing the sharp weapon deeper, just enough to prick Jarvis' skin with ample meaning to hold him perfectly immobile.

"There must be some mistake here," Jarvis murmured weakly, his mouth dry as cotton, hardly able to eek out a word.

"I assure you, this is no mistake," the figure spoke, a sinister, naked fury in his voice, that stuck the fear of his imminent death right to Jarvis' soul. Helplessly he watched in petrified silence, as the figure threw a rope around a rafter in the ceiling, bringing a hangman's noose down to place around Jarvis' skinny neck. He pushed Jarvis over to a chair, guiding him with the rapier to stand on its seat, then pulling the free end tight, tied it soundly to the windowsill. Without emotion or guilt, Erik kicked the chair out from under Jarvis, whose body struggled and shook in rhythmic spasms. As the life dwindled slowly out of his disgusting body,

Jarvis glimpsed in recognition, the scarred face of the stranger in black, who had asked for the red-haired lady.

Nobody knew exactly what had happened to those three unfortunate scoundrels in the cold, dark alley, except those that were unable to tell their own story. All three culprits had been neatly executed with no sign left to accuse their tormentor, but if the truth were known, no one would morn their demise.

Chapter Eight

"She is sleeping, *M'sieur* Devereau," the physician advised, as Erik's black caped figure quietly entered the room and immediately strode to the bed, leaning over the bruised and battered form of Monique, so silent and immobile. His jaw was tightly tensed and the frown on his brow told the doctor that Erik's concern for his wife was deep and inclusive. "I have given her a sedative to make her sleep," he offered in explanation.

Erik turned toward the doctor, an inquiring look upon his features, yet the words he wanted to communicate were unspeakable! The doctor was a small, older man, with a shock of snow-white hair, and he looked at Erik intently, almost knowing what was going through the young man's mind. The gentleman's wife had certainly been through a terrible ordeal, he thought with empathy, and this unusual appearing, yet ultimately, commanding man was certainly lucky to have found her so quickly. "I do not believe there is any permanent damage. There shouldn't be any scarring, but I believe it will be most difficult for her to be up and about for several days, *M'sieur*."

"Was she raped?" Erik asked with difficulty, a raspy whisper invading his tone, as he forced out the words that he did not want to say.

Erik's eyes were filled with both compassion and concern for his wife, yet the doctor could detect pure, unleashed malice for those who would do his wife harm that it gave him a moment's pause before answering, realizing that this man seemed very capable of meting out punishment against those that deserved his scorn. "Are you on your honeymoon, son?" he asked with direct candor, wanting an explanation for his suspicions before making a diagnosis.

Erik startled for a brief moment, stiffening his body in reflex, then collected his scattered thoughts before answering, wondering why the doctor would ask *that* question. "Yes," he said hesitantly. " Monique just became my wife, "Erik answered half-truthfully, almost with irritation, thinking totally irrationally that since asking her to masquerade as his wife, they had not yet consummated the agreement, regardless of their completed passion of the night before. Mentally, he decided that little detail would be rectified at the first opportunity. Questioningly, he stared back at the physician, his disfigured, yet oddly handsome face an unreadable mask, wondering what this question had to do with his original one?

"She is obviously healing from first lovemaking, but there are no signs of bruising or assault, so I would say no, she was not raped," the doctor offered gently, noting that immediate relief captured Erik's features as his shoulders relaxed, and his face changed to an expression of concern, not anger.

He handed Erik a small blue bottle and a little round metal tin, giving him instructions to give Monique one or two drops of the liquid sedative every eight hours to help her sleep if the discomfort became unbearable, and to apply the salve to the wounds to keep the skin moist, not allowing it to draw tight, thereby relieving the pain. Erik, dabbling in the study of medicines, knew exactly what laudanum could do, and was sure Monique had been drugged when he had found her. He would not let her have too much, or she would become addicted. After she had obtained the needed rest to recover from her ordeal, he would find other ways to keep the pain from invading. The salve he would administer himself, knowing she would undoubtedly bulk at that idea, but she couldn't see to do it herself, and the idea of those administrations almost made him smile!

Erik nodded, thanked the doctor, and paid him for his services. His body was drained and tired from the complicated night's events. Looking down at Monique, charming and enticingly wrapped in needed sleep, despite the dark bruises evident on her face, he knew if he dare lay alongside to hold her in his arms, he would surely awaken her, seeking her passion that called to his soul. Relenting with a deep sigh, confident that Monique was truly okay physically, yet still fearful of her mental state, he heaved his weary body into a large stuffed chair beside the bed, resting his boots upon the coverlet and touching the long, soft tresses of her hair with the fingers of his left hand, assuring her nearness. He was asleep before his head rested back upon the chair, a degree of relief overtaking his being that granted the luxury of a few hours of complete oblivion, a means for healing his own battered senses, replenishing his spirit, and uncluttering his mind.

Hours later he awoke to the warm morning sun streaming into the large bay window of their bedroom suite, and he breathed deeply into long red tresses lying against his face, as his arms tightened around the sleeping girl pressed gently against his bare chest. Monique had cried out his name in the darkness, and he had laid beside her agitated body, giving her the comfort she was needing, yet the full impact of fatigue had overtaken him immediately, allowing him to drift back to sleep with a contentment that was consuming.

Arising carefully, Erik looked down at Monique's sleeping form snuggled comfortably into the folds of the comforter, and his heart was grasped with a longing that was totally indefinable. He had been playing at a dangerous game with his emotions, and had not been sure where he wanted to take them, or what fruition he desired for its end. He had, over many years, become accustom to being in control, and was finding that in spite of all his valiant efforts to the contrary, in this one volatile and complicated instance, it was not necessarily so! In looking back on his past mistakes and involuntary seclusion, he tried to sort out those feelings that were rapidly overtaking the essence of his soul, intertwining with aspects of his past, but more importantly, molding a pattern that could well dictate the path of his future.

From the beginning, Christine had become an enigmatic puzzle to his mind. An intangible part of his spirit, plunged into deep despair by the unfeeling throngs of humanity, had stubbornly sought to climb up from the darkness which invaded, seeking the companionship of another human being. It had allowed him to exist as a man, and not as a creature buried within the earth, living solely for the purpose of *existing,* and nothing else. And it had started out so…*simple*! An innocent act where ones talents inspire and nurture, giving something of themselves to another that defines them as a living part of humanity—a human characteristic in his tortured mind that cried to be set free from its forced restrains, as the creativity within his entire entity ached to be shared with another. Christine's youth at the time had been the ultimate medium, allowing him to be the Angel of Music she believed her father had sent to her, and he had not disputed that illusion. He had touched her with the power of his voice and his music, and somehow through that instrument of intervention, she had recognized his pain. But as she grew into a beautiful and desirable young woman, his natural instincts as a man, and those pleasures denied him by the world outside his own, had clouded his untested reason, evolving into a path bent upon possession and physical wanting, defying anything to stand in the way of his desired goal, regardless of the outcome. In the end, he did not believe Christine continued to think upon him as the monster she first believed him to be, but because of his own impromptu actions, and those beyond his control, he had not possessed the right to offer her anything, therefore letting go of an impossible dream. He could not inflict upon her what she did not desire from him, even though his heart believed part of her was torn between her choices. Once and for all he sealed the path she chose by not calling her name. There would forever be a place for Christine tucked deep within his heart, but his love for her had taken on a different form—one that desired her happiness, not his possession of her! She had taught him the ultimate meaning of love—how to give back without expecting anything in return, and from Christine he realized that was enough!

Erik sat down on the bed beside Monique, who lay on her side in a restful slumber, allowing her backside and bruised thighs to be free of the pressure of the mattress. Gently he tucked the coverlet around her neck that had slipped downwards, revealing two creamy white breasts. Her dark eyelashes, in striking contrast to her red hair, lay upon her pale cheeks, one rosy and one an angry purplish hue. He kissed each eye tenderly as she stirred beneath his mouth, but did not awaken. There was the overwhelming desire to take her into his trembling arms, kissing her sleeping body to wakefulness. Her breathtaking beauty stirred his loins and quickened his soul, leaving him helpless to the spell she spun so unknowingly around him. His years of forced celibacy were still a part of his being, and came crashing down around him with hardened retaliation, but the doctor had given her enough laudanum to make her sleep several more hours, yet her warm womanly form called beseechingly to his senses, and it was with great effort that he chose not to take advantage of touching her body again, as she lay in silent slumber. He had once again been given a woman-child to invade his life, like he was being tested by some higher power to see what he would do. The past could not be rectified, but the future was a clean slate, and what he would make of it was entirely up to him. Did he have the courage to try? That he wanted to, was a given, but did he know how to go about loving this beautiful woman that lay before him? Or that once again plunging forth with this most vulnerable step, that he would be successful...! By God, he *would* be successful, or something within his soul would die trying.

Both women were completely desirable in their own way. Christine was tall, slim and leaner in her young womanly figure, yet had a sheltered innocence that had totally encapsulated his desire for that which was denied and the unknown. Monique was shorter, petite, and very fair with more mature features that were full and ripe, screaming with a temptation that called to the very nature of his being with a gentleness that captivated his very soul, yet she possessed an independence and knowledge of the world that intrigued and sharpened his senses. Erik gave a little grin, realizing that even in her boyish clothes, Monique's body had called to his unconscious mind, at least when his eyes were wide open and not blinded by her ridiculous act of hiding her femininity, presenting a most alluring puzzle he sought diligently to solve, and was duly rewarded for his efforts with a most unique and daunting discovery. Yet the puzzle so easily solved, had turned into a perplexity of emotions that boggled his mind, sending the pieces scattering, and he wondered if even the magician in him could really find a way to put it back together.

Monique had from the beginning, even when he thought her a lad, presented with pure, unconditional acceptance, not turning away from either his face or his inability to share his secrets. And when the truth about her femininity had been most pleasantly revealed, she had come to him willingly, as a passionate woman desiring him as a whole man, regardless of his deformity, offering what had been denied to him, and cleansing his soul of a hatred that had entirely consumed him as he had grown to maturity. He had rationalized in his own mind that she needed him only for protection, and although that aspect had not been erased, as was obvious from her latest entanglement, he now recognized that his need for her had developed into an expanding love that he could no longer deny to himself, creating a vulnerability that stripped away all those defenses he had so carefully built up, to ward off the callousness humanity dared to punish him with, for being a freak of nature. Now his future happiness might somehow lie in Monique's hands, hinging on whether she could accept him with all his unknown faults and his obviously horrific past. His desire was great to secure her acceptance in its entirety, knowing the ugliness and horrors inflicted upon him by an unfeeling world were not his fault, but he, in his uncontrolled vengeance, had thrown back some unforgivable retaliation. And for the luxury of that entity of acceptance he was seeking, once again he would risk being shunned by the very person he would give everything to be allowed to love!

He didn't know what situation would present to tell her the details, or the reaction she would give at learning his horrible secrets, but he could not continue this lie if there existed any chance of keeping her by his side. He believed with a realistic certainty, if Monique ever found out the truth, or suspected on her own, she would hate him for not revealing the darkness that had encompassed his entire past. His mind told him it was ludicrous to offer the information, hoping that perhaps he could win her approval of becoming his *real wife* without such a revelation, but his conscience told him loosing everything was a risk necessary to bringing honesty to their relationship, and taking that first step in being the whole human being he had always desired to become, but did not really know how to be. Shaking his head in total bewilderment, he reluctantly realized that all this seemed so foreign to the nature of his previous existence. A lifetime of hate, pity and constant longing for what he had been denied had consumed him for a lifetime. How could it be erased so easily? Ultimately, he believed it resided in many ways within the mind of the girl laying so peacefully in sleep, and the outcome of that dilemma made him shiver with unbelievable fear, for his experience had been one of disappointment and refusal. Would this be any different?

Erik got up from the bed quickly, his thoughts burning his senses and the temptation to wake her becoming too great, and he knew Monique needed rest. He had arrangements to make for their departure to England, and other things to rectify before they could leave France. He changed from what remained of his formal evening attire, into a plain white shirt with buttons, black britches, a simple black vest and black knee-high boots. Over this he donned a black frockcoat. Gathering up his silver-handled walking stick, he departed the inn, leaving Monique in the care of a maid, arranged by Erik to sit with her in the suite until he returned.

Monique stirred in the fluffy confines of the quilt, thinking it felt warm and cozy where she lay, and a little smile came fleetingly to her lips, as she felt Erik's strong arms holding her gently as they slept. Suddenly she startled in fear, as her mind cleared from the haziness of her pleasant dream. Opening her eyes, she searched franticly around the room as horrible facts, non-summoned to her senses, started flooding her mind with a realness that made her agitated and afraid.

"Who are you?" Monique questioned hesitantly, seeing an unfamiliar woman sitting in a chair at the far side of the bedroom. Her eyes darted quickly around the suite in sudden panic. Spying the beautiful furnishings, and taking in the lavishly decorated bay window with the warm sunbeams streaming forth that danced brightly upon the patterned carpet, Monique felt somewhat relieved and momentarily unthreatened.

"*Madame*, your husband, *M'sieur* Devereau, asked me to stay with you until his return," came the gentle voice of the palour maid, as she neared the bed to see if Monique was alright. She was dressed in a black uniform, adorned with a starch-white pinafore-apron, and a round, white lace cap pinned in place upon her gray hair that was pulled neatly into a tight bun upon her head.

Monique looked at her in confusion for several moments. "*M'sieur* Devereau?" she questioned, wondering whom exactly that might be. She was so confused! Where was she? And who had brought her here?

Monique seemed so bewildered that it prompted the maid to offer, "Your husband didn't want you to awaken alone, *Madame*." Poor child, she thought with pity. The girl didn't seem to remember who she was, or that she had a husband! Just then a clear knocking was heard upon the parlour door, and the maid rushed into the next room to answer the intrusion.

Monique tried to clear her thoughts! Husband? Then her eyes grew wide in final understanding, and a little giggle escaped her mouth. The only husband she could think of...*real or otherwise*...was Erik, and that idea was pleasantly acceptable to her senses. But Devereau...was that Erik's last name? And how had she gotten here, and where had Erik gone? She needed him to explain!

Before she could think further, the maid returned. "The trunks have arrived, *Madame*," she said matter-of-factly. "I bid the men to settle them in the parlour, if that is satisfactory?" she asked, waiting patiently for an answer.

Trunks, Monique thought? But absently she answered, "Yes, yes, that is fine." Of what trunks does she speak, wondered Monique in curiosity? Quickly and painfully, she slipped from the bed, wincing as she did so, as sharp pain shot through her thighs and backside, reminding her instantly of the horrors of yesterday, yet her mind was befuddled even further in comprehending how she came to be here with Erik once again? Belatedly noticing with some amusement that she was completely naked, she tried ardently to remember the feel of Erik's arms around her, or was it all just a pleasant dream? Hurriedly she grabbed the quilt off the top of the bed, and wrapped it carelessly around herself, then ventured into the next room as if in a trance.

In the parlour sat two large, wooden, traveling trunks with silver initials embossed on their tops. One *M.D.* and the other *E.D*! Who did these belong to? Ignoring the maid, who seemed ready to protest her being out of bed, Monique went directly to the trunk with the initials *E.D.* and pushed open the lid. Fine men's clothing piled in two stacks lay neatly within the trunk's interior, and several pairs of boots were tucked at the side. She blinked and stared at the clothes. These clothes must belong to Erik, she thought. Erik Devereau! Then who was *M.D*? She opened the second trunk, and her eyes grew to huge saucers, complete understanding finally sinking into her mind, as she recognized the dresses she had purchased from Madame Pentier's Dress Shoppe. Erik certainly left nothing to chance in keeping up appearances, she thought with a slight bit of irritation, yet something within her prompted the idea to form that Erik would deny her nothing, and that small tidbit of information she secretly tucked into her unconscious mind for future reference. Rummaging through the trunk's contents, Monique noticed that not only was everything accounted for, but many delightful new things had been added—like lavender soap and perfume, items for fastening her hair, and several rather revealing nightgowns. In spite of herself she laughed, covering her mouth with her hand as she strived to stifle the noise. Was Erik trying to suggest to her that he didn't like flannel? Pulling out a pretty blue nightgown with a matching satin wrapper, she quickly disappeared into the bedroom to dress into something besides the bed linens.

When she once again entered the parlour, the maid was gone and Erik stood staring out the huge window, his back turned towards her, his tall impressive figure nearly taking her breath from her breast, as she took in his dark and authoritative presence. He turned as he heard her enter, his well fitting clothes accentuating his masculinity in detail, giving him that superior air of mystery that so deeply intrigued her, and she wondered fleetingly with irrational reason, if he would ever make love to her again. His eyes showed emotions she could not easily interpret, as he drank in her lithe form silhouetted in the doorway, the sun sparkling upon her wild, unruly hair and on her satin wrapper, emitting the bright fiery glow of an ethereal angel to his captured mind. He stepped forward, a genuine smile on his dark features. When he came close enough to block out the rays of the sun, and could distinguish the bruises on her beautiful face, his eyes clouded with anger, wishing he could make Jarvis pay all over again for his heinous deed.

Not understanding the hidden meaning reflected in his flashing dark eyes that suddenly turned to one of anger, Monique flinched self-consciously. " Erik, is that you? Really you?" she asked, her eyes filling up with tears, as the horrors she had endured invaded her mind, tearing down her courage and dissolving her earlier sense of well-being. Suddenly she felt dizzy and swayed unsteadily.

Erik came forward quickly, catching her against him, lifting her easily into his arms, and carried her to the bed. "Why are you up, woman?" he asked in irritation, yet totally appreciating the vision she had presented for his eyes to feast upon, thinking it was rather astute of Madame Pentier to suggest the obviously welcome additions to this lovely wenches wardrobe, knowing she would never have chosen them for herself. Clothing he rather planned on enjoying to the fullest. He decided immediately, with silent humor, that sheer material was readily more appropriate for his wife than the hindrance of flannel.

"I can't stay in bed all day, Erik." she rationalized, wiggling in his grasp for emphasis even as her arms came around his neck, not wanting to be controlled, yet glorying in the pure pleasure of his strong arms around her body once again.

"And why not? For the moment, that is the only place for you to be," he countered with reason, thinking she was already becoming too feisty for her own good. A simple matter he would change if necessary.

"Erik, I am not a child," she protested. "I can take care of myself," she countered, knowing it was totally untrue, but wanting to make the point, never-the-less. For some odd reason, even now, she felt she needed to have the upper hand.

He laid her gently on the bed, but she gasped as her bottom screamed with pain, and she curled up on her side. Knowingly he answered, "Oh, is that so! You haven't done such a good job so far," he retorted a little too sarcastically to her way of thinking.

Ignoring him, she rolled to her other side, turning her back. "I'm sorry, I don't remember everything," she said miserably, and the tears began to silently flow down her pale cheeks.

"It's okay love, you don't need to remember," he said gently, pulling her up into his arms so that her right hip rested carefully in his lap.

"Did you come and get me, Erik?" she asked in puzzlement. "I just can't remember." Shadows of memory swirled around in her head of a dark figure looming over her that she thought meant her harm, yet was kind and gentle, making her think of Erik.

"Did you doubt that I would?" he asked, incredulous that she could think him callous enough to leave her there to the horrors of men like Jarvis.

"I didn't know! I didn't think you could find me. I thought perhaps you went on to England without me," she answered truthfully, burying her face in the confines of his vest, unable to meet his eye with her disclaimer.

"And leave you there?" Erik said angrily, tightening his hold on her, disbelieving she could think that of him, making him truly angry for her doubting. In retaliation he answered, "You promised to be my wife, and it was too complicated to find another on such short notice. I expected you to fulfill the bargain," he finished callously, not meaning to intentionally hurt, but irritated at her none-the-less.

"Is that the only reason you came searching for me?" she asked, a true feeling of sorrow entering her soul, hoping without hope that her love for Erik would be returned.

"Should there be another?" he added softly, yet evasively, hating himself for voicing the words aloud, still fearing rejection for his new and fragile love, not yet able to share the feelings he so desperately wanted to convey. Instead, he held her tightly, not wanting to let her go, pressing her head against his chest and kissing her hair, just taking in the moment, knowing that she was finally safe. Gently he turned her face up to his, noticing the tears that stained her cheeks. Capturing her soft lips with a bold tenderness that melted her resolve, he made her mind forget that he didn't love her, merely wanted her passion. Her arms tightened involuntarily around his neck, once again lost to his mesmerizing spell, her body becoming the bowstring that played to his harmonious and sensuous cello, entrapping her in a musical duet that captivated her soul.

Erik was caught up in the pure wonderment of her existence. Carefully he turned her body to lay lengthwise against his solid form, crushing her full round breasts against his hard chest. He plundered her mouth for the honey he wanted, molding her against him as if he desired to occupy the same space, and began tuning her body to the fine pitch he ultimately sought to obtain.

Lazily he chuckled. "Although this nightgown is much more acceptable, I fear it must come off," he said, proceeding to expertly master the tiny buttons like they did not exist. Baring her creamy breasts to his view, he took each rosy tip into his mouth, sucking gently until she squirmed in his grasp, knowing her hands had unbuttoned his vest and played within the confines of his shirt, searching for a way to divest him of his clothes also. But quickly she groaned in pain, when her sore bottom accidentally touched against the rough bedding.

"Erik, I'm not sure this is a good idea," she protested. "My bottom hurts," she admitted, less embarrassed at her admission, than angry at the reason.

"I know, *mon amour*. If you will just trust me, I promise I won't hurt you. We will find a way around your...*predicament*," he said, laughing lightly in spite of her obvious embarrassment.

"You are a beast, Erik," she chided, punching him lightly with her tiny fists, little amused at his laughter at her expense. Then softening, she added, "But I trust you completely, my love." Burying her face in his neck and nipping him playfully with her teeth, she slowly trailed moist lips down his newly open shirt, and Erik noticed for the first time the endearment she offered, rather than just speaking his name. His clothes came off in an instant, and when he came to her, he was filled with a deeper passion than he had yet to experience. He was in total control, wanting to please her, as he knew she would please him. He pulled her nightgown over her head and feasted his eyes on the body that he hungered for in a distinctively primal way. He wanted her so badly that it actually hurt!

"Your sweet body is made for love, *ma petite*, and I want to love you again," he said in a raspy voice.

Without another thought, she took his face in her small hands, kissing his mouth and running her hands down the sinewy muscles of his arms, as he molded their naked bodies into one. She wanted to take away that strange pain that seemed to be reflected in his eyes—deep expressive eyes that sometimes, she was almost certain, hung his heart right out on his sleeve for her to see.

Suddenly he rolled onto his back and pulled her body against his own, his loins afire with a burning need that she flamed, yet could also extinguish. He captured her mouth with a hot, urgent kiss, deepening it rapidly with an eagerness that could not be denied, then trailed wet lips down the curve of her neck and onto her breasts with a hungriness that bespoke of the need to assure she was safe in his arms, trusting in the knowledge that he would never let her be harmed again. She in turn, came forth with a passion that said he could not possibly really exist in the flesh, and would soon vanish as in a dream, thereby giving him the pleasure he was also seeking.

Trailing her lips along his warm skin, she set his body on fire, and when she placed her small hand around his manhood, running her thumb along the ridge of his shaft, he growled deep within his chest in sudden surrender, his breath short and ragged through his teeth as her mouth and tongue played with his own nipples, bringing him to a fevered pitch that threatened to dissolve his own calculated control. With pure survival in mind, he gently lifted Monique up by her waist, pulling her across his body, one knee resting beside each of his hips.

"What are you doing, Erik," she gasped, leaning forward over his body, feeling both the thickness and length of his manhood pulsing thunderously against her flat abdomen, disbelieving what her mind was ultimately thinking. There was absolutely no way!

Erik gave a little grin, his eyes smoldering sparks caught in the afternoon sun that played with shadows over the ceiling, "Merely adjusting to the situation, *ma petite*." He caught one ripe peak in his mouth as she leaned forward, conveniently to his way of thinking, her hands flat upon his chest to steady her body. He chuckled deep and husky, before capturing the other. "I do not want to put undue pressure on that sweet little *derriere* you have."

"But love, we can not..."

Erik cut her off, " Trust me, *ma petite.* When I lift you up, help me love you," he suggested, his eyes glowing with a fire that told her he was completely serious.

But she wasn't convinced. "Erik, petite is the key word here. I am petite, my love," she explained, then looked downward meaningfully. "You certainly are not," she almost whispered, her eyes searching his for reassurance in her innocence of lovemaking.

Erik only chuckled again, lifting her as he indicated, and she did as he asked, helping his rigid shaft plunge deep into her body with an urgency of desire that immediately overtook both of them, sending shock waves through their bodies that played upon their already climbing fever. Carefully he tutored her movements, angling for the position that would produce the most tantalizing friction, as he combined his powerful thrusts with hers, bringing them both to the edge of an exquisite cliff, yet not quite falling over into the precipice. Instinctively she leaned forward, her breasts upon his chest, allowing his breath and tongue to tickle her ear, as the full power of his thrusts and his hands upon her hips guiding her movements, brought the bud of her desire to heights she had only imagined, spiraling them both into new feelings of unrestricted pleasure.

Together they flew, their spirits joined and their bodies united, tumultuous emotions unleashed as they climaxed in one indescribable explosion of passion. Satisfied and spent, Monique lay silently upon Erik's body, knowing that in passion he loved her. Erik held her tightly, unable to move, refusing to let the disappearing moment be broken. In contentment they slept, each longing for assurance from the other of a love they readily shared, but were each too proud and vulnerable to declare.

Monique thrashed her body wildly, trying desperately to break away from the arms that held her captive, the pungent sweet aroma on the cloth covering her mouth, clouding her senses and making her gag in protest. This time she would not allow Jarvis to beat her at his ugly game. Determinedly she held her breath, willing her tired body to fight him, twisting in his grasp to pound her fists at his chest and face. She would do better than a little bite on the hand, she thought with renewed vengeance.

Erik's sleep was invaded abruptly by a spiteful little hellion that assaulted him with fervor, catching his left jaw with a bone-jarring crack that momentarily disoriented him, forcing him to release her in defense of his person, and the idea of sleep completely vanished. The epithetical language that came from Monique's mouth as she fought him in sleep was all too familiar, and he smiled in spite of the pain that coursed sharply through his jaw, reminding him instantly of her fiery temper.

"It's Erik, love. It's okay," he assured her, catching her busy fists with both his large hands, pinning them against his chest as he pulled her close, stroking her hair and soothing her with his melodious voice. She quieted slowly, finally aware of her surroundings, and melted against him with an exhaustion that was full of relief, yet continued to clutch at his body for needed reassurance.

She looked directly into his face, a frightened and wild look in her blurry eyes that showed the confusion in her mind from what she had experienced. "I'm so sorry, Erik! I thought you were Jarvis, the man who took me," she said simply, an apology ringing heavily in her shaky voice.

He put one hand behind her head, drawing her lips down to his, taking her mouth roughly with his own, burning her trembling lips in a long lingering kiss, one that demonstrated his own, unique way of telling her he was there. Finally he spoke, almost in a whisper, his lips upon her hair, "I'm here now, he can't hurt you anymore."

"But I'm afraid, Erik. He was very angry and he beat me for disobeying him. He'll be looking for me because of the money," she said, her body still trembling in fear. "You can't protect me all the time."

"Trust me, love. Jarvis will *never* hurt you again," Erik said with such confidence, that Monique truly began to listen.

"How do you know Jarvis?" she questioned, unable to make the connection.

"I have made his acquaintance," Erik said noncommittally.

Erik's mind played havoc with his conscience. "If I had not asked you to come along with me, you would not have been in that situation. I should never have brought you here," he said. He quit talking, pushing away stray tendrils of hair that fell over her face, as he stared intently into her eyes, wanting her to understand the pain he felt for putting her into such danger.

"But I had no real reason to stay near Paris, Erik," she admitted, not wanting him to take the blame upon himself for what had happened. "And I really did want to come with you," she explained eagerly, wanting him to know that she desired to be with him, forgetting momentarily that he had only asked her along for business reasons. A little frown played upon her brow as she belatedly remembered his purpose.

"And exactly why did you need to leave so quickly, wanting to accompany me? What were you running away from, my sweet little tigress?" he asked pointedly, rubbing gingerly at his injured jaw, thinking perhaps now he would finally get a few answers to his long awaited inquiries.

"My father had died, Erik. We were certainly comfortable, but no money was left to save. A nasty old man that had lusted after me against my fathers wishes, thought he could marry me against my will, now that my father was gone. He was old and ugly and the thought of him touching me turned me to stone," she admitted, shivering at the very thought of him. Looking shyly into Erik's inquiring eyes, she said coyly, "I much prefer you." Her dark blue eyes were smoldering with her admission, and when he looked down into those liquid pools, his loins stirred involuntarily, and she felt his masculine body responding against her thigh. "Erik, you can't want... again?" she said in disbelief. How could it be possible to...?

"Oh, love, I most certainly do," he said wickedly. "But first you must show me that sweet little derriere," he demanded, turning her over on her stomach before she could find the energy to protest.

"Erik, please, no!" she pleaded, not wanting him to see the object of her pain, much less the shear embarrassment it would cause.

Erik surveyed the angry red welts covering her backside and thighs in long raw stripes, some worst than others, the skin broken in many different places. Angrily he cursed, venting his anger as he retrieved the small tin from the table in the parlour. While Monique waited not so patiently, he gingerly applied the cool, white salve, causing her to wince in pain, but he eased her discomfort with his mouth, trailing languid kisses from the small of her back up to her shoulders, then turning her on her side, taking two ripe breasts into his hands and teasing the pain from her mind with his fingers and his hungry mouth. Her hands in turn searched the ripples of his back, then his flanks, the hard muscular length of him...anywhere she could reach.

"I shouldn't have brought you here," Erik stated absently, his mind a jumble of fury, angry at himself for not keeping her safely within his view, and for not escorting her shopping himself...

wherever she needed to be. "He will never hurt you again," he mumbled, not realizing he said the words aloud.

"How do you know that, Erik?" she asked. "Is there something you aren't telling me? How did you find me and how did you get me out?" she inquired. "I need to know!"

Relenting for her peace of mind, he told her in skimpy detail just the facts she needed to know to satisfy her hunger for the truth, holding back that which he would rather not reveal, but she was not to be placated. "What did you do to Jarvis, Erik?" she asked pointedly.

"Nothing more than he deserved, my sweet," he said noncommittally, unable to meet her gaze.

"Did you murder him, Erik?" she asked, fearing the worst, realizing with abject certainty that Erik was not a man to be crossed, and that he would not hesitate to dole out punishment that he, as both judge and jury decided was just. Whether that decision was appropriate to all, did not seem to matter where Erik was concerned, if indeed, he appointed himself the executioner.

"He had it coming," Erik said, showing no remorse at all for his actions.

"A vigilante, Erik? Is that what you are?" she asked, not really expecting an answer.

"When it concerns you, perhaps I am," he admitted.

"You can't just murder when the mood suits you," she said rationally, yet her mind told her she wanted Jarvis to pay for his deeds, and she could not truly find the fault that her conscience should have demanded.

"Would you want what happened to you...*or worse*...to be forced on anyone else? These men murder and maim for the pure pleasure of it, not caring who they hurt with their game" he said, true anger in his voice at her seeming inability to see the need for his actions.

"Are you a dangerous man, Erik?" she asked unexpectedly.

"I can be," he said simply, offering no more. He wanted to explain to her...to tell her in detail about his past, but it would have to wait for another time. He had given her more than enough to think about. She needed time for the memories to fade and her mind to heal. There was always tomorrow. Today he wanted to erase it from her mind!

Monique could tell from Erik's demeanor that he was finished with this conversation. Strangely she felt safe in his presence, knowing now he would do everything in his power to protect her, yet she longed to know the entire truth about him. Would he ever trust her enough to tell her about himself?

In the end, she surrendered once again to his persistent attempts at bringing her body to a fever he wanted to flame. He took her more violently this time, like he wanted to purge himself of some demon that haunted his being, and when he was finished, his head rested on her shoulder, and she held him to her breast, realizing he needed her also!

Chapter Nine

Monique's eyes grew wide in fascination. Sheltered in the countryside north of Paris her entire life, she had never even seen the sea. And certainly never anything like this! Anchored at the huge docking area was the *La Bentra*, an iron, twin hulled paddle steamer that was built by the Thames Iron Works, constructed to carry passengers on a round trip from London to *Calais* and *Le Harve*, then back again after a day's stop over in *Le Harve* to load supplies. It was 180 feet long, largest in its class, had an engine in each hull, four smoke stacks and could manage up to 11 knots, using its two cylinder oscillating paddles. It had proved to be the most sea-worthy boat yet to be constructed to keep from rendering its passengers seasick, in the oft times turbulent waters of the English Channel. It had a capacity for 260 passengers, 100 that could obtain overnight double berth accommodations for the leisurely, three day, two night round trip.

Erik and Monique stood in line as husband and wife, nearing the custom's shed. The morning was already proving to be long, hot and steamy, leaving most of those awaiting passengers tired and out of sorts. The customs setup was a trial in keeping one's nerves intact, often enduring a *good cop/ bad cop* type of experience from grim custom officials. Passengers were warned of high penalties for smuggling contraband into England, such as tobacco and cigars, and could on the spot have their luggage searched for these illegal imports. Sometimes men would be separated from the women, both being subjected to body searches by agents of their own sex. Passports were often taken during the trip, allowing their owners to buy them back for an outrageous fee when they reached London.

Erik was being very protective of Monique on this first of three days that he allowed her out of bed. She leaned back against the length of him in respite, steadying her body, as he cradled her by placing an arm around her waist in the front, giving her some relief from standing continuously on her feet. Knowing she was weary, he commented, "I'd have secured a wheel chair for you, my love, if I had thought that would have been the answer to getting you through this long and tedious line, but somehow I think that would not have been the best course of action for your immediate problem."

"Oh, Erik, I'm fine, really! I'm just a little tired. But everything is so exciting," she exclaimed with enthusiasm, blushing a little at his mention of her rather particular need, remembering half a dozen carefully administered applications of salve to her posterior area and his rather unique and wonderful way of taking away the pain. He had pampered her to the fullest, insisting on meals in bed, barely allowing her out, except for necessary reasons. They were days and nights filled with sweet and gentle passion, Erik seeming to have an unquenchable thirst for their lovemaking, leaving her side only long enough to make arrangements for their passage to England. Not that she had minded, wanting to be by his side as often as possible, growing accustom to his overpowering presence, knowing she would miss him with a terrible vengeance when their time together was over. He had read to her, sonnets from an extremely old book, one he had brought with him from Paris, the low melodic timbre of his voice nearly hypnotizing her senses, making her desire him all the more. Another mysterious asset of this man who now haunted her mind!

There was a gleam on Monique's face that captured the overpowering excitement she had for this new experience, yet her mannerisms told Erik that she was still not well enough to spend the entire day on her feet. And he was adamant in his purpose of shielding her from the comments of those who might see the bruises on her delicate features, and make some ghastly, hurtful comment. "This will be over before you know it, and you can rest in our cabin," Erik encouraged lightly, noticing a pale face masked with her exuberance for the moment.

Monique had chosen a simple green striped poplin dress with a lightly quilted petticoat and a plain, heavier over-skirt that came down from the waist, circling in an arc along the sides and back, giving the impression of a small, but unencumbered bustle. It had pleased Erik that she had needed his help in fastening her dainty, yet revealing undergarments that conveniently for him laced in the back, pushing her beautiful full breasts up to be appreciated by his eyes alone. In fact, that appreciation had prompted him to take advantage of the moment, lifting each sweet mound out of their encasement, enticing each nipple to hardness and following immediately with his mouth, causing the act of dressing to come to a sudden, screeching halt. Erik had simply leaned her against the wall and her legs had wrapped around him quite naturally, their lovemaking swift, slightly violent, and precise, yet sweet and satisfying, neither completely removing their clothes. His sexuality was raw and perhaps touched on barbaric, but when kissed by this man she was certain she had been entirely consumed. He fulfilled every fantasy that now invaded her mind, since meeting this strange and fascinating man.

When they were done, Erik had let Monique's body slide down along the length of his in a primal seductive manner, taking her lips with a languid kiss, his velvety tongue claming her mouth for many long moments. "That, my sweet, is for the lovely, enticing little nymph that you are, stirring a need in me every time I see any of you revealed, or for that matter, covered up," he said suggestively, taking her mouth one last time, his tongue showing her most adamantly what he was saying was absolutely true and not idle talk.

"Erik, I didn't thank you for the exquisite ring," Monique said between breaths, holding out her hand to admire its brilliance behind Erik's back.

"The band, *mon amour*, is to assure everyone that you are my wife," Erik said with direct meaning. "The other ring is something I simply wanted you to have," he said softly, letting her go quite reluctantly to finish dressing, thinking to himself that she was indeed some sort of sea siren that was sent to capture his soul and drive his body to distraction, but certainly not against his will. A grin played involuntarily at the corners of his mouth as he watched her sash –shay out of his arms to don her dress, hoping that it fastened in the back also. Alas, he saw buttons down the front, that when closed, still showed off her charming figure to advantage, perhaps more than he would ultimately like!

"But it must have been terribly expensive…for just a few days of adventure," she continued meaningfully also, causing Erik to frown and turn his back to her in total frustration.

"It is something I plan on you keeping, my dear, when this *adventure* you speak of is over, but it was no more expensive than having to buy your wardrobe twice," he added, a bit perturbed at the turn in this conversation, away from love and her captivating body, and more towards her leaving him in England.

"Twice! Oh, Erik, these are not the same dresses that I bought?" she voiced in sudden realization, not having thought before how he had retrieved them.

"Madame Pentier was most helpful in duplicating what you had purchased, suggesting to add items that I believe are charmingly appropriate," he noted, a bit of sparkle coming back to his eyes that made Monique blush even in her distress over his words.

"I'm so sorry, Erik. I have caused you so much trouble," Monique stated, wondering *why* he would go to all this bother just to travel with a wife. "I think it would have been easier for you to have just gone on without me," she finished, glad that he had not, but dismayed at causing him trouble.

Erik was beside her instantly, taking her by the shoulders a bit too roughly. "If I hear you talk like that again, I'll beat that sweet *derriere* you have myself," he said forcefully, taking her mouth in a quick, but bruising kiss, his hot tongue plunging deep into her mouth. He pressed his hard body against hers in a most possessive way, making her knees grow suddenly weak. His demeanor was dangerous and dominant, reminding her of an animal stalking his prey. Her senses were quickly assaulted by a small over-shadowing of realization, of what he was capable of doing, if he was truly angry. "And don't ever believe that I won't," he added for emphasis, releasing her so abruptly that she was a bit stunned by his actions. "I have to arrange for the trunks to be delivered to the docks, my sweet. Do you think you can be ready in about an hour?" Without waiting for an answer, he grabbed up the black, day coat to his morning suit, and was out the door in an instant, leaving Monique to wonder at the words he had just spoken, and how to interpret his actions.

When it became Erik and Monique's turn to confront the customs officers, Erik handed them two matching passports. The officer flipped them open casually, glancing up at Erik with some annoyance when he noticed the special embossed gold seals, knowing that he could not antagonize these passengers as he had done many others, extracting extra money out of them that would be pocketed, for fabricated infractions and trumped-up fees, earning him a tidy extra wage daily for his efforts. Instead, he dutifully stamped the passports for *M'sieur* and *Madame* Devereau without much ado, handing them back hastily and sending them on their way toward the gangplank.

Erik was grateful for the guidance from the law office of Bontonae and Seward in judiciously procuring his passport, as well as the arrangements they had made for his passage to England, setting up at the last minute those documents also necessary for Monique. He had not enlightened them that Monique was not officially his wife, still a glimmer of hope that perhaps that disturbingly, unresolved, yet complicated detail, could somehow be rectified.

The huge paddle steamer was boused tightly to the pier by long, fat twisted ropes made of hemp, keeping both her aft and stern horizontal to the dock. A narrow, thirty foot gangplank was placed near the stern on the port side for boarding passengers, and a wider one at the middle, just aft of the large paddle wheel for loading supplies and luggage. A derrick, attached to a large rowl, was busy down the wharf, loading heavier supplies into one of the holds by way of a sling, while a half a dozen lumpers were busy unloading those import items that had been brought to *Le Harve* from London to be floated down the Seine River to Paris. Monique looked up at the beautiful white steamer with its brightly painted red paddles, a little apprehensive of this new experience, wondering if the sea would be too rough, knowing that this was probably nothing new to Erik, but it left her with just a bit of nervous trepidation.

Slowly Monique began to climb the steep, narrow gangplank that rested on the main deck fifteen feet above the level of the wharf, suddenly feeling the long morning wearing on her body, and she stumbled slightly on the rough wooden planking. She had barely righted herself, when Erik gathered her up into his arms without a moment's hesitation, carrying her the rest of the way with little effort. At the top he confronted the bos'n, who was checking passengers in by way of a long tedious list. He was quite formal in his attitude and dressed impeccably in a dark blue uniform, as were all of the crew, adhering to the boat's strict discipline and dress code. To Monique's amazement, Erik slipped into easy conversation with this man in perfect English.

"*M'sieur* and *Madame* Devereau! You will be in stateroom seven, which is located one corridor astern of the forward salon on this main deck. If you just follow the deck seating, your corridor is just after the chairs end." Noting that the man's wife was needing assistance, thinking that they both looked rather strange and beat up, but realizing that their cabins were of the extreme upper class, he added, "Do you need assistance, Sir?"

"That will not be necessary. Thank you," Erik said politely, yet rather curtly, clearly catching the implication in the man's eyes that he believed the gentleman beat his own wife, knowing that his own left jaw had a bit of purplish hue also, not to mention the right side of his face. Erik had been prepared for that attitude, but was not the least bit concerned about ever explaining. Let everyone believe what they wanted. It was certainly nothing new.

"Erik, you speak English!" Monique exclaimed, not totally surprised at just one more thing about Erik that was a mystery.

"And Spanish, and Italian, and a little of a few other languages," he offered, surprised at how easily he was able to reveal that information, realizing that he not only wanted to tell her things about himself, but that he was actually comfortable in sharing it with her.

"I don't know any English, Erik. How will I communicate on my way back home?" Monique asked, both fear and apprehension gripping her at the thought of Erik leaving her all alone and sending her back.

Erik's jaw tightened as his body stiffened, and unknowingly he gripped her more securely. Angrily, he stated quite firmly, "I will take care of everything...you need not worry! You will get home safely." With that, he had reached the door of their stateroom, bent slightly to flip the latch with his hand, and kicked the door open with his foot. He carried her in, setting her gently on her feet, but with some obvious frustration in his guarded mannerism.

The small, but comfortable stateroom was a genius in compactness. It had a wide built in bunk to accommodate two people, and along one wall was a built in bureau and wardrobe. The opposite wall contained a washstand with two round cutouts, in which were placed a bowl and pitcher for washing, neatly securing them from falling with the rocking and swaying of the boat. A small table came down from the wall with two small seats, the trio capable of being folded against the wall and secured. The wood of the furniture was polished to a highly smooth, glossy finish, leaving a hint of waxy aroma in the cabin. Adequate floor space was left over for traveling trunks, and sitting against one wall were the two trunks that Erik had sent to the docks before them. Fresh water and towels were replenished daily by stewards or maids, but the water closets were located in the hallways and shared by all the passengers.

Erik said to Monique, "I want you to rest. I will have a light meal brought in." With that he headed for the door, leaving her standing alone in the middle of the cabin.

"But Erik, I don't want to stay in here. I'm fine, really," Monique protested adamantly, wanting to see what was going on as the boat left port.

"It would be better if you rested, my sweet. It's been a long morning. Perhaps tonight we will venture out," he repeated, thinking she would stay put if he insisted. He left the cabin, confident that Monique would realize how truly tired she really was and follow his wishes.

A third day of being confined to her room, so to speak, even though the majority of that confinement had been in Erik's loving arms, did not sit well with Monique's sense of adventure. No sooner was Erik out of the room than Monique was peeking into the hallway to see if Erik's commanding presence had disappeared. Not sighting him anywhere, she slipped cautiously down the corridor, knowing that he would ultimately be angry, but she would deal with that later, eager to see the boat and what departing land had to offer.

As she entered the wide, highly polished main deck, there were numerous passengers leaning against the filigree ironworks railing that was attached to the bulwark, waving to people on shore that were waving back, celebrating their departure. Monique slipped into a free spot at the rail, leaning slightly over to view the longshoremen releasing the heavy ropes from their moorings, pitching them onto the boat as seamen reeled them into coils on the deck. The heavy gangplank was pulled onboard at a lower level and attached to the wall behind lower class seating, ready to be pulled out again when needed. Monique was enthralled with the moment. Overhead, seagulls winged their way over the water, and the sky was blue and clear, letting the sun's radiance touch on every shiny piece of metal or polished wood available, allowing the boat to appear to sparkle and gleam. Monique breathed in the salty tang of the ocean with its fragrant hint of seaweed and fish, and it gave her a renewed sense of vigor. The last few days had been trying, with horrible experiences invading her senses when least she suspected, yet her time with Erik had set a balance, allowing her to retain her sanity, knowing without his loving and caring touch, her mind would truly have been lost forever.

Suddenly, a body was pressed up suggestively against her back, and Monique was tightly sandwiched in between a group of passengers, pressing eagerly against the rail. "Well, pretty lady, I can see from your face that someone is not taking very good care of you," came a voice from her side, spoken in words that Monique did not recognize. "Perhaps I could do a better job," he crooned suggestively, bringing his rather handsome and smiling face into view of hers, and laying a hand possessively on her arm. Before she could indicate that she did not speak any English, the man was snatched away rudely, and Erik was standing in his place, looking at Monique with eyes and an expression that spoke volumes.

"I see that you need constant looking after, *mon amie*," Erik croaked out tightly, his fury just contained below the surface at her blatant disregard for his suggestions. His green eyes were almost black, the sun being towards his back, and she could tell by the expression on his chiseled features that he was exuding immense control by not yanking her from the railing. His jaw worked back and forth as he gritted his teeth, and his nostril flared just enough for her to notice.

Ignoring his fury and the fact that he was not pleased with her actions, she exclaimed with true excitement, "Erik, the day is so beautiful and the boat sparkles like it is adorned with diamonds. And I have never seen the ocean before." She glanced up at him again, just a hint of impish smile on her features, hoping to quell is anger. " Please, please, don't be upset with me," she pleaded, searching his eyes for acceptance.

Letting out an audibly deep sigh, like he had ceased to breathe as his fury had risen, Erik's attitude relented slightly, noticing the child-like enthusiasm in her eyes, finally digesting her words. "Did you never see the docks of Paris?" he suggested, thinking it rather odd that she had lived so close to the sea, yet never seen the ocean. Even he, in his seclusion, had ventured around Paris at night and the countryside of France, finding the ocean charming in its splendor in the moonlight.

"I grew up at *Chapallae,* Erik. We never went to Paris or to the ocean. My mother died in childbirth and my father just never had the heart to venture into the city or to travel alone. He always blamed himself for my boyish ways, and the rather unorthodox way he brought me up, but I certainly never minded, or wanted for anything. When papa died, I didn't really have anywhere to go. It still is not exactly accepted for a female to run a stable, *even though I'm much better at it than almost any man*, and it certainly rankled a few," she said with a little laugh, thinking back on the outfit she had worn when they had first been introduced, yet a bit of disgust thrown into her tone at those that would dispute her abilities, and her knowledge of running a stable most satisfactory.

Eric took in her words, genuinely surprised at her statement, thinking that she was as sheltered from the wonders of the city, with its architecture and modern technology, as he was from the pleasures of society and humanity. Somehow, he promised himself, for her sake, he would change all that!

Laughing, he spoke into her ear so only she could hear, "I can rightly believe that you probably ruffled a few feathers, *mon amie*! And somehow, I doubt that your father would have had any control over such a feisty and unruly little hooligan as yourself, no matter what the circumstances. But it's obvious with your father gone, that you still need constant looking after, and I'm most confidant that I'm the one that should do it!"

"You?" she voiced in astonishment. With that he guided her away from the railing, taking her arm very securely, leaving her no chance for protest or escape, and pointed her in the direction of the corridor, leaving her with the uncertainty of what he meant by his suggestive, but unexplained words.

"A small repast of food should be waiting in our cabin," he said casually, like nothing out of the ordinary had transpired. "And if that is not enough for me, perhaps you will be my dessert," he added in a low melodic and sensual voice, that promised of things to come, if she but behaved herself. When she looked up at his face, his eyes were smoldering sparks of dark green with flecks of gold floating within those mesmerizing orbs, and with a little smile on her face that was not lost to Erik's possessive eyes, she decided she would follow him anywhere.

The paddle steamer was constructed with three decks. The kitchen and elite salon that serviced the first class staterooms, were on the main deck, along with some higher priced middle class accommodations. The lower deck housed the rest of the middle class and lower class accommodations, along with the staff's mess room, sleeping quarters, and a less formal salon in which liquor was not served, thereby preventing day passengers that often traveled quite frequently, but imbibed too much, from bothering the other guests. A small top deck was merely for viewing, and had a tarp-like awning covering part of the seating for inclement weather. Many of the day passengers preferred this deck on hot, sunny days, spending only half a day to travel from *Le Harve* to *Calais*, or vise-versa, depending on which direction the steamer was heading. Heating was provided by steam generators in the hold, passing through coils to warm the air by way of passage through fresh air outlets, allowing the rule of no open fires aboard.

On deck the wind was whipping over the rails as the steamer continued on its journey up the coast to *Calais*. Erik leaned negligently against the bulwark railing, staring absently out over the shimmering water, its white caps rolling endlessly and disappearing only to surface again on the next wave. He pulled his collar about his neck to ward off the cold breeze. It had been a trying morning. He recognized Monique's enthusiasm for this *adventure* as she so irritatingly called it, to his mind at least, and didn't want to dampen her apparent sense of spirit. Outwardly, she seemed to be unaffected by her horrible experience in *Le Harve*, other than the obvious bruises, but Erik could detect something in her manner when she was sleeping and unaware, and knew instinctively that memories haunted her. He knew the signs from his own unsettled and haunting experiences that even now, years later, invaded his dreams, causing nightmares that drenched his skin and set his body thrashing with the silent horrors. He moved his jaw back and forth, still able to feel the result of her untimely dream two days past. How long would it take her to rid herself of these dreams, and who would console her if he allowed her to return to France? The thought that it might be some other man, grated on his nerves with violent denial, a most unacceptable solution to his mind. He had promised himself that he would not force her to stay, but how could he allow himself to let her leave? She needed his protection, and he needed her to stay!

Turning away from the sea, Erik viewed the passengers. There were many very finely dressed ladies and gentlemen strolling along the breezy, ornamented deck, many glancing away quickly upon seeing the appearance of his face. Erik was becoming use to the gesture, but it still tore at his heart, wondering why Monique in true honesty could tolerate his presence. It was something he would never fully understand. A sense of urgency in telling Monique about his past was building within him, knowing that the time was coming to an end when he could hide it no longer, leaving him once again vulnerable, creating a great sense of being afraid and uneasy. Being afraid was something he had felt deeply as a child, when his mother had refused to love him, hardly caring for his physical needs, relinquishing him to a gypsy circus out of...perhaps hatred. There his horrors had become twofold, but he had conquered that entity of fear as a young man, and the unaccustomed feeling of it resurfacing left him totally exposed. He was afraid that when Monique became aware of the true facts of what he had done, she would shun him like the plaque, running as far away from him as possible, and it wouldn't be because of his face. For some strange and unexplained reason that part of him didn't seem to matter to her. He had finally found someone that seemed to accept him physically, just as he was, but could ultimately be repulsed by what he had done, regardless that it was in defiance of the treatment he endured for his rejection and expulsion from mankind. In reality it made no sense! And that reality came with not comprehending even minutely how to begin in telling her his horrible and disgusting tale!

In defense of his rising, turbulent emotions that his mind rebelled to dwell upon, Erik turned his attention to the boat itself, admitting that it was indeed beautiful. The design and workings of this newly commissioned paddle steamer totally fascinated Erik's sense of construction, design, and architecture, letting his experienced eye take in everything at a single glance, storing it within his photographic memory, igniting his curiosity of exactly how she really functioned. All those years of constructing his own lair and the workings connected with the locks, traps and grates, came flooding back to him with fervor, something he had not thought about for many days. Memories swirled around in his mind, but they did not give him the uneasy feelings today of wanting to return. More that he wanted to banish the past and go forward with the future, sharing it with the woman he wanted more than anything to understand *why* he had done what he had done. Not that it was right! Just *why*!

Erik had left Monique to rest. She had drifted off to sleep after food for the body and food for the soul, the exhaustion finally catching up with her enthusiasm. He had looked at her in sleep and could not understand what had brought such a beautiful, accepting soul into his life? He wanted to feed the enthusiasm she had and not squash it because of his situation. She deserved to have fun, and he would see that it happened

Entering the cabin, Erik found Monique awake. "Are you feeling better, *mon amie*?" Erik said pleasantly.

"I feel much better, yes!" Monique stated, thinking Erik looked a little wind blown and troubled. "Where have you been? Is something the matter?" she questioned, searching his face for an answer.

"Just on deck for awhile to let you rest," he answered quietly.

"Erik, you didn't have to leave because of me," she said shyly.

"Would you like to dine in the salon for supper, *ma petite*?" he said suddenly, ignoring her concern and seeing her eyes light up immediately at his suggestion.

"Erik, could we?" she cried, flying off the bed and into his arms.

"Yes, *mon amie*, if it is your wish, we can dine in the salon," he said with a gleam in his eyes, as he clutched her warm, enticing, sleep laden body to his. "After all, you must have a place to wear those beautiful gowns you picked out," he confessed, a devilish grin upon his face, knowing that everyone's eyes would be drinking in her beauty, and he made a mental note not to leave her side for even a moment.

" Oh, Erik, I love you," Monique said without thought, placing a quick kiss upon his cheek, then spun around immediately to rummage through her trunk for just the right gown, quite childlike in her antics, holding each gown up to the mirror, turning several ways, then discarding it to try another. A smile was on Erik's face just watching her, and he laughed just a little, for he had not missed her declaration of love, but he wondered if she had? When she held up a royal blue satin gown with small capped sleeves and a rather plunging neckline, the dark, smoldering, predatory look Erik's eyes bestowed upon Monique made her laugh and shiver all at once. Turning away, knowing she had made her choice, she silently thanked Madame Pentier in her mind for persuading her to buy such an outrageous garment.

Supper in the salon was at eight and Monique tried to make her unruly locks adhere to the confines of the beautiful combs that were added to her wardrobe. Finally, in total frustration, she settled upon pinning it all up in a loose French roll, and inserting one large russet colored bone pin that she wove in and out to secure the long unruly tresses. She was not used to looking, or for that matter acting, particularly like a refined lady and giggled at the thought of even trying. Glancing down at her dress, she was suddenly aghast, for the neckline revealed far more than she remembered, and she tugged at it with vigor, trying to hide a bit more of herself.

"May I be of assistance," came Erik's amused, yet low, husky voice from behind her.

Monique spun around at his voice, feeling his hot breath on her neck. She had been so engrossed in getting dressed, and so excited about the evening that she had not really bothered to notice Erik dressing. And what she saw startled her for a long appreciating moment. Erik was wearing his white, half mask! But *why*? She had never seen him with both his dark, black wig and his mask together. She had never seen him so…so…so impossibly… *handsome*. He was dressed in impeccable, black evening attire—a coat with one button just above his narrow waist, yet unbuttoned, with long tails and a wide, black pleated cummerbund. His brown brocade vest was set over a white shirt, and a black ascot was tied around his neck allowing only a small bit of white collar to show. She was mindlessly speechless! His presence was totally mesmerizing! Just looking at him made her heart race erratically, and her mind turned immediately to mush! The words dark, dangerous, dominant, predatory and sexually aggressive all hit her like a brick wall. He was totally captivating.

Erik looked at Monique as she turned, his gaze becoming one of total desire and appreciation, as he also, drank in the beauty that she presented to him… and him alone. Her innocence and ethereal beauty never ceased to amaze him. Then his eyes narrowed, his concentration settling on full breasts about to spill forth out of her gown. "Perhaps another gown would be more appropriate," he said hoarsely, noticing the little laugh she gave as she realized his meaning.

"Erik, why are you wearing your mask?" she asked, ignoring his comment, but appreciating his reason for saying it. She had absolutely no intention of changing her dress. She smirked a little to herself, remembering her thought about making Erik pay for insisting she buy gowns that she could not use later, and making her feel so like a mistress in Madame Pentier's eyes. Let him squirm a little bit. He deserved it! Quickly she reorganized her thoughts. "People have seen you without your mask, Erik" she added in bewilderment, not understanding this newest action.

"I feel more comfortable with it on," he shrugged, noncommittally. He had thought about it in depth, and could think of no reason not to go back to wearing a mask in public. It was no different than wearing an eye-patch. He felt safer away from the shores of France. Its intention would merely be taken as a means to hide a deformity that many people had already seen.

"Erik, you don't need the mask. Why would you want to go back to wearing it? What made you wear it in the first place? What is so terrible about your past that you cannot share it with me? Please Erik, tell me! I know I'll understand," Monique pleaded, wanting to understand Erik's need for this security.

"It might be best to leave the past in the past," Erik said abruptly, taken off guard with her vigilant probing, yet legitimate questions, at a moment he was not prepared to answer.

"Why did you seek to know my story, but refuse to tell me your own?" Monique asked with some irritation, noting Erik's willing inability in giving her details.

Erik's eyes grew cloudy and distant as he looked into Monique's questioning ones. Abruptly he turned away from her, genuinely afraid to answer, not wanting the evening to end. "When I think you should know something, I'll be sure and let you know," he said with an almost stubborn intonation to his voice, yet Monique caught a glimpse of his face as he turned, and it showed a hint of true embarrassment for his answer, like a child being caught doing something he shouldn't and not wanting anyone to notice.

Monique was nonplussed at Erik's attitude. She had told him everything. Opened up with all those things that would surely make him send her back to France, yet he refused to share any of his own story. What could be that terrible?

Monique grabbed up her royal blue cape and suddenly all Erik heard resounding in the empty cabin was a soft click as the door to the stateroom closed behind her. Erik ran both hands over his wig, adjusting it with agitation in his movements. Why had he been so brash? He wanted to tell her! He wanted to tell her so badly that it physically hurt, deep around his heart and over his entire body, a strange sick feeling within of total helplessness. But would she...could she really understand? He would give her a few minutes to calm down. He didn't blame her at all. Suddenly his face had a little grin. He did have a peace offering. Something she hadn't given him time to present before igniting her fury. Perhaps it would help, he thought, little humor in his mind at the very thought of confronting her ire. Then he remembered the dress, and he was out the door in a flash, grabbing up a black box as he left. He would just have to take his chances with her fiery temper, and that reasoning gave him a moment's pause. Almost! The thought of her enchantingly, revealing dress winning out!

Chapter Ten

Earlier in the afternoon, the first mate had the unpleasant task of seeking out the captain. He straightened his tie and smoothed down his uniform as he entered the bridge of the *La Bentra*, carefully tucking his hat under his arm. He was overly nervous, knowing that the captain was not going to like what he was about to say. Clearing his throat he said, " Captain, Sir?" Patiently he waited for the captain to recognize him.

It was an exceedingly long wait. Captain McShane had been occupied all morning with innumerable things going wrong, and by the way his first mate was fidgeting, he suspected this was going to be another disaster. Finally, turning his attention away from the helm, he acknowledged his first mate's presence. "What is it, Howard?" he asked, more gruffly than he had meant, knowing that Howard was a good man and a hard worker, keeping the crew in line as needed.

"Well, Sir...," Howard started hesitantly.

"Spit it out, Howard. Don't just chew it," McShane prompted, thinking nothing could be as bad as one boiler leaking, and some of the cargo shifting from the poor packing of the longshoresmen.

"We haven't been able to find Fairfield, Sir. He is nowhere aboard ship. We've scoured the timbers of the entire vessel, but he just isn't here," the first mate explained.

"Isn't there anyone else that can take his place? I've heard others playing those damn pipes besides Fairfield. Don't make excuses, lad, just find another player," the captain commanded, turning around toward the helm, dropping the problem from his own mind, and into that of his first mate.

Howard knew he was dismissed. Frowning, he wondered how he would find a solution to this problem. By God, they were out in the middle of the frickin' water! And Fairfield played that organ so beautifully. A few other members of the crew dabbled at playing, but were a bit hard on the ears. He would just have to talk one of them into it. He had absolutely no choice. Music in the elite salon at dinner was expected by the guests!

Monique leaned against the iron railing that was trimmed with polished mahogany, staring into the blackness of the sea, its darkness uncovered by one wide path of moonlight that revealed shimmering waves cresting one upon the other with the look of rolling gemstones, showering a rainbow of varied colors onto the surface of the water, the low setting light of the moon stretching from the horizon to the hull of the steamer. The wind was blowing a gentle breeze through the spindles of the railing, giving a low whistling sound that blended with the oscillating paddles of the wheels, creating a rhythm of noise almost like music. Monique's heart was breaking with the overwhelming and unconditional love she had for Erik. She studied the magnificent ring Erik had given to her. Why couldn't he just trust her? She was so confused about everything, and could not understand Erik's attitude. She tried desperately to sort out all the reasons why he chose to hide his past. His face was the obvious one, but his face did not matter. Not to her! She had tried to make him understand that in several different ways, accepting him for the man she saw reflected on the inside, not just the appearance of his face. He was a man with many gentle attributes, yet there was a side of him that she was positive could be ruthless and cold. He had subtly admitted that to her, and demonstrated his mysterious powers by finding her, and dealing perhaps too harshly with her captors, yet there had to be a reason for his other, less explained actions that seemed to be buried within his past.

She remembered her father telling her about a beautiful black stallion that had been beaten and treated cruelly by its master. Everyone had called the horse a killer because he had trampled his master to death, and were afraid to come near. They wanted to shoot the horse because no one could handle the fiery, ebony beast. A young lad had befriended the horse in the field where the stallion had been put to pasture, giving him apples and sugar, and talking kindly to him. One day the lad came riding into town on the stallion and everyone was amazed, for the stallion seemed harmless and tame. Her father had said it was because the horse had been shown kindness, and that no beast or human was initially bad. They were forced to become that way because of the treatment of others. Something in Erik's past was so terrible that he was forced to have a ruthless and dangerous side, creating a mystery around himself that she had hoped, by showing him kindness, that eventually he would trust her enough to reveal.

Monique's chest felt tight with heartache. Erik said that he had hurt people that he loved. Perhaps he had a wife in France. He indicated only needing the appearance of a wife for his journey to England. He had made that explicitly known. This was only a simple business arrangement. Erik planned on returning her to France, yet there seemed to exist those unexplained times he genuinely needed her, and not just as his pretend wife. Nothing really made any sense. It was obvious he did not trust her, even now!

Erik came silently up behind Monique at the rail, sliding his comforting arms around her waist, pulling her slight form back against his chest. "*Mon amie*, I am sorry that I upset you," he whispered softly, his warm breath upon her neck feeling good in contrast to the chilly night breeze.

"Erik, I did not mean to pry into your life, but…"

"Shhh, love! It's alright. You have a perfect right to want to know about me," he said hesitantly, in an attempt at honesty. "I have almost forced you to accompany me here, demanding to know all about you, yet I offer you nothing about myself."

Slowly she turned around in his arms, looking up into his handsome face, his white mask stark white in the moonlight. "Erik, I just wanted you to trust me," she said simply, placing her small fingers lightly against the cheek of his mask, brushing her left thumb along his mouth tenderly, knowing instinctively that he wouldn't mind. His lips opened gradually as she did so, and he drew in a slow ragged breath, closing his eyes to the sensuous feel of sweet agony, as he breathed in the lavender scent of her hair, caught again in the spell she wove around him with her innocent acts of love and caring.

Erik pulled her into his arms, crushing her smaller form tightly against his body, burying her face against his chest so she couldn't see his face. "I do trust you, *mon amour*. And I want to tell you everything. I just have not found the right time or the right words," he admitted hoarsely, his voice cracking with the effort to pry those words from his heart. "Pl-e-a-s-e, just give me more time, " he pleaded, hoping she would somehow understand, his anxious confirmation of need not lost to her.

"I have all the time in the world, Erik," she said easily, knowing sadly that she did not. Soon their voyage would be over and Erik would send her home. But she loved this strange, yet wonderfully caring man, who pulled her in with his seemingly endless power, showing her kindness and protection, and she was satisfied that he admitted his trust in her. For now, that would have to be enough. He would tell her his past when he was ready.

Erik pulled away from her, and stepped back a pace. He pulled a black velvet box from under his evening coat, saying a bit shyly,

"You did not give me a chance to compliment that beautiful dress with just the right touch." Agilely he released a necklace and matching earrings from the black case. Monique turned away so Erik could pull the necklace around her neck and fasten the clasp. He bent down, placing his warm lips lightly upon the cool skin of her shoulder. "Something simple for the beautiful lady," he crooned softly. He pulled her back against the length of him, encircling her within the strength of his arms, both silently staring out into the vastness of the dark and merky depths of the ocean, each momentarily encased in his own thoughts, unknowingly neither vastly different from the other, yet each still worlds apart.

"Thank you, Erik, for giving me the chance to dress like a lady. I hope that you won't be hopelessly disappointed in how I look. I'm afraid I'm not very experienced at this," she sheepishly apologized, wishing she knew more. She had been around *Chapellae* all her life, seeing all the fine ladies and gentleman in their finery and at elegant functions, yet she had never, until now, wanted to know what she presently lacked in learning, and she sorely wished she had paid more attention.

"On the contrary, I believe you have all the experience that is necessary, in my way of thinking, *mon amie,* and need no other," he said with obvious meaning, placing one large hand over her small one, and sliding it suggestively and slowly across her breasts and up to her throat. "A termagant you can be… assuredly, but tonight a most bewitching and beautiful one. I fear if left to my own devices, I would be forced to take matters into my own hands, and we would not get supper at all—at least not the kind that is served in the salon. You are a witch, *mon amie*, and have stolen my soul. Do you intend to keep it?" he asked suddenly, his voice low and sensual, as he held his breath for her answer.

"Oh, once a witch has stolen a soul with her spells and her potions, it can never be returned. You are mine forever, M'Lord" she whispered, wishing that this silly banter between them was real, and not just frivolous talk.

"I see," he mumbled, thinking quite frankly, he had absolutely no intention of asking to be released from this witch's intoxicating potion or her binding spell.

Turning around, her mind suddenly anxious at the words she had spoken so carefree, but knowing they were really the true feelings of her heart, she smiled up at him shyly. "The necklace is beautiful, Erik," she said, touching the blue sapphire with her fingertips. As he held out the matching earrings, Monique slipped them on her ears with little effort, then straightened to look at Erik for approval, her blue cape slipping negligently backwards off her bare shoulders.

But Erik stared down at her with a silent frown, drumming his fingers absently on the wooden railing. His eyes were narrowed and his lips were set in a lop-sided pout toward the unmasked side of his face, as if he were totally unsatisfied with the outcome. The tear-shaped sapphire that sparkled in the moonlight, was nestled most becomingly between Monique's beautiful, full breasts, setting off the low neckline of her dress to its best advantage. Every single eye in the salon would be drawn to this exquisite bobble, and that daunting and unpopular idea, to his way of thinking, did not sit well with Erik's sense of possession, or lack there of, as the case may be.

Instinctively knowing what he was thinking, Monique laughed a little and standing on her tiptoes, placed an appreciative kiss on Erik's left cheek, glorying in the fact that he could be...well...jealous. As she did so, the ship's bell chimed eight times, making them aware that supper would be served. Taking her hand in his, Erik tucked her arm beneath his own and led her away from the rail, and over to the large double-door of the salon.

The dining area was large and opulent, the décor reminiscent of the Olde English, Tudor style of the Middle Ages. Decorating the solid white walls, crisscrossing with dark brown diamond-shaped edging, were the remains of stalwart weapons of battle— helmets and armor, swords and jousting sticks, spiked clubs of every kind, and many colored shields with the symbol of English households emblazoned upon their front. The sparse lighting came from a few dimly lit lanterns housed in glass, contained safely in metal filigree frames and placed in the center of some thirty-five formally displayed tables of various sizes, seating parties of two to eight quite comfortably.

Erik asked the steward in English for a table for two.

"I'm sorry, Sir, but there are no more tables for two available," the steward informed him politely. "I have two seats available at a table for six that is rather secluded along the wall. Would that be satisfactory?" He waited patiently for Erik's answer.

For some unknown reason, Erik unconsciously tightened his grip on Monique's arm, hesitating only a moment as he quickly processed that thought, not having entertained the idea of actually dining with other guests at the same table, mentally chiding himself for not making arrangements in advance. It had been a last minute decision on his part, and the enthusiastic response he had received from Monique with his declaration, had temporarily unraveled his usual, somewhat irritating attention to details. He could almost smile if the situation weren't so sobering, for the little minx seemed to be doing that to him all too often recently, successfully confusing his mind when he should be paying more attention. But he didn't want to disappoint her. This was to be *her* evening, and he had promised her dinner in the salon. Therefore, against his better judgment, and with a sharp tightening in his gut at this unfamiliar experience, he nodded reluctantly to the steward his approval.

The steward, dressed in a white dinner coat with blue trousers, led them forward across the crowded room, winding around several tables before coming to a large, round table for six, nestled against the white bead-boarding that decorated the long walls below a brown-colored chair-rail. An obvious hush of voices was evident throughout the room, even above the slow grinding of the engines that worked the paddle wheels, as heads turned in unison, perusing the unusual couple that passed. Male eyes were riveted to the bewitchingly beautiful red haired woman in the dark blue dress, her blue velvet cape hanging carelessly off her bare shoulders, drawing their eyes directly to the large blue sapphire between her breasts. The women, suddenly awestruck, were transfixed into a state of shear animal magnetism and profound suspense. Many had seen Erik on board without his mask, and it had almost frightened some, yet its addition exuded an air of mystery, investing this elegantly dressed man with the aura of danger, pulling them into his web of masculinity and suggestively implied sexual power!

The steward motioned with his hand toward two empty chairs at the table. Monique seemed excited and very wide-eyed at this new experience, taking in all of the room with avid fascination, neither aware of the attention from the other guests nor the initial whispering of voices. The steward introduced the seated guests, in English, as *M'sieur* and *Madame* Overland from England, along with their two sons Richard and Miles. In turn, he introduced the Overlands *to M'sieur* and *Madame* Devereau. Greetings were given by the older couple with a nod and a polite hello as they remained seated, but the two strapping lads, dressed in evening suits, stood instantly, leaning over the table to shake Erik's hand, neither looking directly at Erik with their greeting, both having eyes only for Monique as they quite elegantly gave their greeting also. The attitude of the room and this rather disturbing display of attention toward Monique was not lost to Erik! He knew full well what the addition of the mask could do, for he had used its pulling and significant power in the past, but he did not want to dwell on what his reactions might entail if this continuing admiration for Monique went further than his liking. At that moment he was exceedingly thankful that Monique did not speak a word of English!

Monique looked up into Erik's face that showed a hint of concern, as he bent to hold her chair. Seating herself politely, she leaned in towards his ear saying, "Erik, it will be alright." She knew this wasn't exactly what he had in mind. Something more intimate, perhaps, she thought, smiling to herself. And she had never actually been with Erik in a group of people, and believed this was something he did not like doing, yet knew instinctively that he had done it for her! She was glad he was here with her! The idea of an exciting evening, and her inexperience in dining in such an elegant atmosphere was so foreign, even though she had seen the lavish balls and festivities prepared at *Chapallae* a hundred times, she was sure she could never have accomplished this alone.

"I wanted you to have this evening, *mon amour*," Erik said softly to Monique, leaning ever so slightly in her direction, his eyes smiling at her, sensing her uneasiness.

Monique giggled a little, commenting in a hushed voice, "Oh Erik, there is so much silverware that I'm not quite sure which one to use, or when?"

He only chuckled, studying her meaningfully with the appraisal of a mentor and picking up a spoon nearest the edge of his place, he wiggled it only slightly, then proceeded to scoop up the fruit that was served with raspberry sorbet in a dish placed directly on his dinner plate. Knowingly she smiled, picking up the same spoon also, and delved ravenously into the delicious parfait.

A long silence was evident at the table while the meal was brought in, everyone busy arranging their own places. Finally, after the wine was served, the older of the two lads, spoke in French, "Madame, where have you traveled from and are you headed to England?" Noting that the couple had only spoken together in French, yet Erik had answered the steward and made his greeting in English, he assumed correctly that the lady did not speak English. Miles was a nice looking young man in his early twenties, with a neatly trimmed mustache and beard, his brown hair tied back in a queue.

Monique was startled at first to hear the young man speaking in French, and even more so that he was addressing her. She quickly swallowed some food, preparing to speak, when Erik answered instead.

"We are indeed headed for England, Sir, and have traveled from *Dorne*," he offered sparingly, not continuing further.

But the young man was not to be deterred. Again he spoke to Monique. "Are you enjoying the voyage, *Madame*," he said, ignoring altogether that Erik had answered, causing a frown to crease upon Erik's brow, knowing this question was hardly one he could foil easily, again being directed solely at Monique.

"Yes, the voyage is quite lovely," Monique said simply, realizing with some trepidation, that Erik would rather not delve into much conversation with the other guests. She rightly assumed that he did not wish to offer lengthy information.

Entering into the conversation, Mister Overland spoke to Erik. " Son, do you plan on staying in England long?" he inquired. He was a slight man, with salt and pepper hair. His wife sat silently at his side, seemingly too timid to speak.

Erik replied to the gentleman, "Yes, we are planning on taking up residence there."

With more interest the gentleman continued. "And where would that be, my dear Sir? And what brings you to England?" he coaxed politely.

Erik was becoming annoyed and uncomfortable in discussing matters about his affairs in England, but did not want to seem impolite, drawing more attention to himself than if he simply answered. "We will be taking residence near Cheltenham, Sir. I have architectural matters in which to attend." At the same time he heard Monique talking, this time to Richard, a younger looking, handsome young lad that appeared to be in his late teens, perhaps the same age as Monique.

"My dear lady, is this your first time on a paddle steamer?" Richard asked, eagerly taking in Monique's beauty, his eyes barely able to leave the cleavage where the blue sapphire was nestled, his youthful exuberance almost overwhelming.

"This is my first voyage," Monique answered, her face adding color most charmingly, yet becoming uneasy at the young man staring. Unconsciously, she leaned into Erik, seeking the safety of his person, even as he also became aware of the youth staring, and the ominous look he afforded the young lad, not only made the youth blush to a bright red hue, but he excused himself briefly from the table.

Suddenly, Madame Overland spoke to Monique in English, her cheery red face inquiring most interestedly. "My dear, do you have any children? My two boys have given me no end of joy over the years," she said, not realizing that Monique would not understand.

Erik, hearing the question, almost choked on the food in his mouth, needing a generous gulp of dark red wine to wash it down, its potency burning his throat like liquid fire. Collecting his rather scattered thoughts, he gazed at Monique with emerald eyes that smoldered at the very thought of such an occurrence, for the first time actually reminding him of the possibility. And the thought of that happening without his knowledge, and her leaving him without knowing the outcome, made him reconsider instantly some of his earlier decisions—most pointedly that of letting her leave in just a few short days.

"My wife does not speak English, *Madame*," Erik offered quickly in explanation. "And we are newly married," he said simply and sternly, yet the penetrating look he had given to Monique assured all it was absolutely true. Conversation lulled for the interim, Madame Overland totally embarrassed at asking such a prying and intimate question of an obviously newly married couple.

Monique, totally unaware of what had just transpired both over the table and in Erik's mind, blushed at the sensual look that Erik bestowed upon her, embarrassed that she could neither understand Madame Overland, or that Erik would leer at her with such open desire in his eyes right there with everyone watching.

Music began softly, almost hesitantly, emanating from a small pipe organ in the corner. Its harsh notes, although melodious and somewhat familiar, were interrupted by a choppy, unpracticed rhythm, offering to the listener an offending sound that prompted many to glance towards the organ in dismay. The player grimaced, making an effort to bring forth the appropriate tune, yet his untutored fingers were unable to give a smooth and harmonious performance. Tortuously, it drifted to all corners of the large salon as its maker became more bold and venturous in his playing.

As the sound of the organ drifted toward his finely tuned musician's ear, Erik's body was bombarded with a massive jolt of memories, shock waves invading his senses with a blinding force, shutting off his realization of both time and awareness. Candlelight flickering low, its burning aroma adding a familiarity to the scene within his mind, jarred his entire existence from the present into his turbulent past. He could neither speak nor hear Monique questioning, why an indescribable expression of pain was so suddenly reflected upon the unmasked side of his face? Unceasingly the notes clanked offensively in his ears. He could clearly hear the methodic beat of a metronome clicking, its pendulum swaying back and forth, as the offending notes neither stayed within their desired rhythm, nor met the crescendo that was intended.

Without warning, Erik got up from his place at the table, every muscle in his body taut, his thoughts clearly not in the present. He could hear the music playing in the distance, see the soft glow of candlelight with its pungent aroma of hot, oily wax that pulled his lair out of the depths of darkness, and smell the cool, luminescent water of the underground lake. Everything was still in its place…just as he had left it! Silently, he glided his way across the lair with the carriage of a man of authority and breeding, away from the massive swan bed where Christine was sleeping, and stood next to his magnificent organ. His playing would be the soothing lullaby that allowed her to sleep. He glanced down at the player who had invaded his space with a look of total clarity and meaning…ominous green eyes that did not frighten, but conveyed abject disapproval. Instantly the player scurried across the cushioned bench and was gone! Erik sat down at the organ, slowly placing his long elegant fingers gingerly on the keys, their cold familiar touch administering a rueful, almost toxic anesthetic to his shattered mind. He closed his eyes with longing, feeling powerless to resist the forces that were overtaking him. The present... the past…any existence became a blur as he started to play, the harmonious and feather-light notes filtering out across the hall like the wings of a dove, the melody unfamiliar to all who could hear, yet its spellbinding power soothing and hypnotic. A kind of ethereal trance spread throughout the smoky room as the guests listened, wondering who this man was that held them bound with his faultless technique and his magical power, pulling them into the depths of his intoxicating music!

Erik had breathed this music into his being for an eternity, just as he had inhaled the air that sustained his life, and its euphoric existence became the life-force that was his world. It had replaced that multitude of essential things that were heaped upon the ordinary man without care or appreciation, yet denied to him with scorn and refusal. It had been a refuse of retreat, blocking out the beatings, the repulsive reactions displayed at his physical flaws, and comforted him when his body raged with the lustful passions and physical needs of being a normal man, regardless of the sinful actions of the masses. Music looked blindly upon the ugly side of his face, and glorified in the side that was handsome, because he was the same man inside, whichever side you gazed upon. Music alone had touched his senses, aroused his passions, befriended his soul and caressed the very core of his dark and dismal existence. When he feared he would die within the dark abyss of loneliness, it was his music that pulled him from its dark, penetrating depths, calming his violent tempers and dark brooding moods. He craved with every fiber of his being to possess the life of a normal man. In his tortuous, lonely isolation, music had been his companion, his wife and his world, and eventually he had shared it with only one person!

Monique sat transfixed in her chair. Erik was acting strangely. He didn't seem to hear anything she was saying. It was as if he was somewhere else. Those mysterious entities...things from his past that were not explained... were somehow multiplying. He had never shared his love of music. Its poignant melody, so peaceful and beautiful at one moment, was now.... so sensual that she could feel it pulsing right through her body. It was as if he were talking only to her with the melody...making love to her with each note! It pulled her right into its compelling power and left her aching for more, not ever wanting it to end!

"Your husband plays beautifully, Madame Devereau," Miles whispered to Monique, leaning her way to catch her ear, pulling her abruptly out of her sensuous mood.

"Yes he does," Monique answered absently, her attention fully centered on Erik.

Empowered by the shear magnitude of his music, Erik heard the notes as if he were penning them to paper for the very first time, bringing forth emotions for the reasons they were written. He played gentle and sweetly at first, a medley of songs he had composed for Christine as a child, and then as a young girl, finally culminating into the sensuous, pulsing manuscript for the young woman he had grown to love…or desire…in perhaps a lustful, possessive way. The audience noticed the change in tempo and the more urgent, primitive melody. It had a compelling and seductive nature that pulled you into its rhythm, willingly, yet uncontrollably. Erik could see the colors of red and orange flash through his mind as the rich and provocative notes unfolded. He could feel the passions of a young woman as her first awakening into womanhood burst forth into full bloom. He was playing for Christine! His Christine! He could see her walking towards him as she arose from sleep, her white gown flowing in the candlelight, long legs bared to entice him, her eyes bright and seductive, teasing him. He wanted her to love him! He needed her to make him whole. Anger gripped him in an overwhelming power as his fingers flew over the keys. No! No! His head was exploding with the colors…the music…the memories. He envisioned every horrible day of his past as the notes resounded in his own ears, each disastrous situation turning into words that blended with the melody of the notes…*his world was shattered… love was gone… shunned and hated by the world…murder, murder, murder…betrayal and denial …why should he go on!* No! No! No! This wasn't right! It was *not* Christine! But where was, *she*? He could feel her! Sense her presence! He could touch her with his music! He could just barely see her through the mist that hung over the lake, if he just concentrated hard enough! She was his ethereal angel, his red haired sea-siren that comforted his soul, cradling him in love with her magical powers, finally setting him free from the bondage that engulfed him. In mechanical motion, Erik started pounding at the keys in a controlled rage, his eyes wide open, yet staring into space, causing the audience to shift uncomfortably in their seats, glancing at each other in sudden bewilderment.

Monique heard the beautiful and passion evoking music change, as Erik harshly and deliberately hammered on the keyboard, the melody still in perfect beat and harmony, yet becoming offensive and loud, as his dark, turbulent mood mounted, turning alarmingly in the direction of uncontrolled. She knew instinctively that he was in trouble! She didn't know why or how...she just knew! Rising quickly from her seat, she started threading her way between the tables towards the organ. Abruptly the playing stopped. Erik was standing at the organ in stunned silence, his eyes looking right through Monique as she approached, but did not appear to notice her presence.

"Erik?" she said softly, an almost pleading tremor to her voice, her eyes riveted upon his.

Without warning, right before her eyes, he disappeared in a cloud of red smoke! She blinked, her eyes wide in disbelief at what she had just witnessed. Where had Erik gone? He couldn't just disappear? Belatedly, behind her, she noticed that the guests were clapping loudly, showing their appreciation for the show that the *La Bentra* had provided for their enjoyment. Within seconds their attention was redirected back to their tables, and the man at the organ was all but forgotten!

Chapter Eleven

Monique was in a most urgent panic. Where had Erik gone? A soft rain had begun to fall, and the wooden decking was slippery with pooling water as she left the salon. Checking first their stateroom and not finding him, she grabbed up his cape without a second thought, and dashed down the narrow corridor toward the promenade deck, just beyond the first class cabins.

Oblivious of the distinct details of her surroundings, she did not readily notice a steward laying out towels in the cabins for the guest's nightly ablutions, tumbling negligently into him in her haste. "Pardon me, *M'sieur*," she said, with a quick, but absent apology.

Seeing her somewhat harried and bewildered state, Steward Bradford asked politely, "May I be of assistance, *Madame*?"

"Oh, *oui, M'sieur*! Have you seen my husband, *M'sieur* Deaveau?" she asked, a genuine state of panic notable in her tone.

"Not since his performance. The guests were very delighted. And the Captain was extremely pleased also. Might we ask him to play again?" Noticing her agitation and impatience at his rhetoric, Bradford offered, "You might try the lounge on the lower deck, *Madame*, for I doubt that anyone would be roaming the decks tonight. You can take the stairs over there to stay out of the rain," he prompted, pointing to a narrow stairwell, just beyond the last stateroom, before entering the uncovered deck.

"Thank you, *M'sieur*, for your help," she called behind her, taking the steps two at a time to the lower level, lifting her skirts high above her ankles and thinking that this would indeed be an opportune time to be wearing a comfortable pair of men's britches and riding boots.

Stepping just inside the double doors of the smoke filled lounge, Monique's gaze swept quickly over the patrons within, taking in the bawdy and boisterous atmosphere, the more casual dress, and the fact that most of the clientele were men engaged in gambling. She knew immediately that in Erik's agitated state, he would not be in here. As she turned to leave, a young man grabbed her arm, blocking her access through the doorway.

"Again, I meet the lovely lady whom no one seems to be taking care of properly," he said in English, but not in the soft, beguiling manner as earlier in the day. This time his tone was irritating, and Monique was in no mood to listen. She needed to find Erik and this man stood in her way.

Persistently, the young man started pulling her unwillingly into the interior of the room and away from the door. It was just too much! With a screech of pure rage, she snatched his hand from her arm by digging her nails into his flesh, stomping on his foot in the process for good measure, and raced out the door, leaving him momentarily stunned and unwilling to follow the little she-cat that had unleashed her claws. There were other fish in the sea that were willing to be caught! For the moment, he thought, his greedy senses unleashed and a gleam in his eye that boded ill for someone!

Finally out on deck, Monique didn't know where to turn. The wind was howling and the rain had turned into a heavier downpour, soaking within seconds, anyone that ventured into the open. Other than on deck, where could Erik have gone? Pausing only seconds to contemplate her decision, Monique started making her way around the promenade, clinging to the wooden walls of the cabin area with its small five inch overhang directly above her head, which did little in shielding her body from the pelting rain. As she made her way forward towards the bow of the vessel, Monique's mind was in a whirl of emotions. Darkness was broken only by the occasional flash of lightening, followed closely on its heels by the loud crashing of thunder that seemed to jar the very teeth out of her mouth, then rumbled away to nothing, disappearing into the distance blackness that encompassed their isolated, floating world. Her throat ached from the constant effort to hold back her tears. What had caused Erik to become provoked? His music had been beautiful, pulling her into the depths of its stirring melody with a fire of passion that she had never imagined. Where had he learned to play? There were so many questions that needed answers. Suddenly in her panic and fear, she realized she was angry. If Erik expected her to play his game, then she wanted explanations. The thunder and lightening echoed her mood, melding in a crescendo that called for the laws of nature to blend, unleashing their wrath upon the unsuspecting and helpless. Well, helpless she was not, and Erik was going to learn that in full measure if he expected her to keep her part of the bargain. He could not just disappear, leaving her behind, knowing neither his whereabouts nor how to explain his actions. She was totally infuriated!

As she rounded the corner, and into the open, Monique peered into the perpetual blackness, unable to see beyond her outstretched hand, the rain now falling in cold, glassy sheets, pouring torrents of water over the deck in a rapid swirling rush. A wide bolt of lightening rent the night just beyond the bowsprit, illuminating a tall black figure in sharp relief like a backwards lithograph. Erik stood with his back to the cabins, facing the bow, his gaze turned upwards towards the sky. He was shouting towards the heavens, something she could not distinguish above the howling of the wind, his arms outstretched, his hands balled into fists. Suddenly he bent forward over the bulwark, hanging his head and pounded one hand repeatedly upon the wooden railing. Leaning forward into the mounting squall, Monique tried desperately to make her way towards Erik.

Erik's body was trembling from the cold, but inside he was suffering from a profound discovery that haunted his being and raped his mind, and its impact caused him immeasurable anguish. He could hear the music echoing in his head. His hands covered his ears in an effort to silence the taunting melody without reprieve. He tried blocking out the continuous succession of scenes that spiraled unbidden before his eyes, torturing him with memories...bringing Christine to his lair...the myriad stacks of compositions he had composed on her behalf that gathered dust from neglect...duets sung together in perfect harmony and splendor...his massive black, ebony pipe organ with its silver pipes that stretched up towards the vaulted ceiling, and the monumental amount of draped mirrors that could unmask his secret. All had been lost with one destructive act...the burning of the opera house. He could taste the bittersweet irony of defeat, as he reconciled his mind to the realization that *music again consumed his soul.* With solid determination, he had vowed to banish it forever to the fiery depths of hell. It had been that connection with Christine that had sustained his twisted soul, but her denial of their love had broken the intricate thread that bound him to its magnificent splendor, catapulting him into a state of destruction that destroyed all his past. Yet now he found he craved music's alluring beauty, with a far reaching intensity that overpowered his original, selfish need to forbid its hurtful entity, and that thought was disturbing to the point of unaccountability. Now he rejoiced again in its illusive power, but for a totally different reason. It permeated and captured that part of him that was creative...that force that brought forth new beginnings, as well as laid down the old, allowing him the only peace he had ever known. It tore at his gut with final understanding. Falling to his knees in the swirling water, he screamed out in agony, his mind battling with the distant rage of losing the love of his past, yet discovering the daunting despair of perhaps losing the love of his future. He bowed his head in final submission, hot tears running down his face that mingled with the cold rain, as he sobbed, " Please, please, just make the music stop!"

Suddenly there was a pull at his shoulder as heavy cloth surrounded him. Startled, he rounded on the intruder, swinging his arm wide to keep his balance, knocking Monique down as she lost her footing on the slippery planking, causing her to fall on the deck against the metal bulwark. Lightening again lit up the sky, allowing for a few long moments, the appearance of daylight. Erik's eyes opened wide in astonishment as he saw Monique floundering in the water, bringing him suddenly back to grim reality. His thoughts were in a bitter turmoil of foggy existence. Why was she here? Crawling on his knees the few feet towards her, he pulled her up and into his arms, asking with an almost innocent tone to his voice, "What are you doing here?"

With the same astonishment, she looked up into his face, the pulsing rain clinging to his mask and eyelashes, his entire body soaked to his skin, and replied with monumental sarcasm, "I was about to ask you the same question, Erik."

Erik groaned inwardly, pulling Monique to a standing position along with himself. Wrapping his arms soundly around her shoulders, he guided them towards the bounds of safety, and out of the harsh elements of nature that for some alarming reason had momentarily complied with his mood. Suddenly, he felt guilty! He had ruined her evening. How it had happened he wasn't entirely sure, but bits and pieces were returning to his memory, and as they did, so did his anger. Anger at himself! Anger at his situation! And anger at Monique for being so stubborn!

Entering their cabin, drenched like two rats drowned in the sewers, both were ready to do battle with words. Erik, boiling over with both loathing for himself and this new set of circumstances he continued sorting within his confused and fragile mind, was totally livid that Monique would come looking for him, risking the possibility of bodily harm. He drew the first sword.

"And what was the meaning of coming on deck in the pouring rain?" he gestured dramatically, sweeping his hand upwards towards the ceiling. "You might have been swept overboard."

"Oh, and then you would have no one to boldly proclaim to be your wife," she countered. "What was the meaning of disappearing right before my eyes? And how did you do that?" she asked, gazing at him with suspicion, wondering oddly if he was some sort of magician.

With arrogance, he discounted her words, continuing to make his own point. "It is not necessary for you to know such things," he said, stripping off his wet clothing, flinging them in all directions, until only his soaked britches remained.

Monique stood transfixed in the middle of the room, relinquishing nothing, yet stared in admiration as Erik undressed. There they stood, not a room's length between them, yet were a continent apart in their convictions. "I did not know where you went, or when you would return! Nor anything about your music...and could not render even a simple explanation," she hurled at him, her temper seething just below the surface.

"There was no need for an explanation," he said simply, shrugging absently.

Monique tossed her head in exasperation, her hair coming untwined from its binding, and falling loosely about her shoulders. "No need for an explanation! I am told by everyone how beautiful you play, and I am so ignorant about my *husband* that I did not even know that he *could* play," she choked out, tears barely contained from springing loose, her determination rekindled with each incredible word he offered, not to let him have that satisfaction. "You take from me Erik, but you don't give back," she accused.

He knew she was right, but his pride forced his denial in his own mind. "You should have come back to the cabin. I would have returned in due time."

Monique's brows drew together. "In due time," she fairly shouted at him, her voice ringing with all the frustration she now felt. "What was I suppose to think happened to you, Erik? And how will I get home if something does?" She was trembling at the very thought of being left alone...more to the point...of the time when he would send her back to France.

Her words pierced like a sharpened rapier right through the center of his heart. His eyes suddenly flashed with all the wretchedness and humiliation that had been heaped upon him since his birth. She could not have hurt him more if she had keelhauled him right beneath this very vessel. She would leave him without even a thought, and again he would be alone. Was he so unlovable? Even his own mother had rejected him, he thought with mounting anguish! But his need for her was stifling. A kind of slow suffocation that now encompassed his soul. Couldn't she see his love and his need for her? Would he be doomed for the rest of his miserable life to never have anyone love him? Love him for who he really was, and not for who he seemed to be? His dreams and his nightmares were one in the same! He stood there for a long, silent moment, his body tensed like an animal ready to lunge.

Sudden anger overtaking his reason, Erik advanced on her, a look of total and overwhelming menace in his piercing green eyes that she had never experienced before, and it frightened her. "Don't you understand that I need you," he said hoarsely, the pulse in his throat standing out against the bright red flush of his neck, as he strained to keep his turbulent emotions under control. The thought came to mind of walloping her soundly, right then and there, but his vexation demanded compliance in a more effective manner.

Backing towards the door, Monique caught the latch in her hand behind her back. Boldly she questioned, "And what need is that, Erik? The one to possess my body or to play your mysterious game?" The pained expression she saw mirrored in his eyes even beyond the mask, almost made her weep, causing a twinge of momentary regret. But not enough regret to make her sorry, because her words spoke the truth.

Erik caught her roughly by the shoulder. "The need for you to be my wife," he cried, almost in a whisper, wanting her to understand that it was a bargain for eternity.

"To be your wife? And the possession of my body?" she asked cruelly. "A nice business arrangement where only you benefit," she added harshly, knowing this was not completely true, but angry once again at the callousness he displayed at her expense.

Erik's facial image changed from hurt to one that bordered on...revenge perhaps, if unnecessarily crossed. She wasn't entirely sure, for Erik had never before directed this kind of explosive anger at her, not even when he thought she was stealing his horse. "I need to know if you carry my child," he said without thinking, not meaning to broach that delicate, yet most agreeable subject in the heat of an argument. *Merde*!

"Your child?" she said in bewilderment, the entire idea totally unaccepted by her befuddled brain. Instead she answered, "You ravage my body, pay me for my services, then send me home when you've no need of me." By this time Erik was not listening. He was finished with excuses, whether giving or receiving. It was time for action.

She was shivering with cold from her wet clothes, but he did not care. Pulling her away from the door with avid irritation, he yanked her over to the bed in only two strides, feeling a tension in her body of constant resistance, yet she did not try to protest his control. With angry, jerking movements, he divested her of her clothes in rapid succession, letting them fall to the floor in a sopping heap. She was numb and distant at his unauthorized anger, saying not a single word, nor offering any loving response.

"I do need your body, *mon amour.*" Laying her unceremoniously upon the bed, he immediately pinned her squirming body beneath his own, assuring her acquiescence. "I need you to heal my soul. To make me a whole man," he choked out. "Our union erases the past from my mind."

"And what past is that, Erik?" she said coldly. "You have told me nothing," she added boldly, forgetting he would tell her in time, suddenly deciding in her own mind, that *in time* was right now! Determinedly, she tried to wiggle out from beneath him.

But Erik was stronger and bigger, towering over her in a cold, unsympathetic manner. Part of her was slightly afraid and part of her was not, knowing ultimately that he would never intentionally hurt her. Catching her wrists, he pinned her arms above her head with one hand, as he carelessly unbuttoned his britches, lifting his body only long enough to fling them to the floor. His rage was carelessly leashed, but he did not come to her in a gentle way. "Talking will come later, my little witch, that has taken my soul into her keeping. I need you *now* and the time has come to teach you that I am the one that is in complete control."

With those words his full weight lay upon her, his mouth catching hers in a bruising kiss, ending abruptly with a muttered curse, realizing he still wore his mask. Throwing his head back in irritation, he tore the mask off violently, along with his wig, his own hair falling over his head in dishevelment, loose wet strains falling carelessly over his eyes. Once again his mouth descended on hers, taking her trembling lips with the savage force of his possession, his tongue probing deep within to plunder the honey he sought to extract...that nectar that he pillaged for, time and time again with a hungering greed of a famished soul, until her head felt dizzy from the taking. He shifted slightly to his side, one hard muscled thigh anchored tightly across hers, pinning her downward into the mattress, allowing his mouth and free hand access to her breasts, sucking each peak and mound gently at first, yet slowly growing in intensity until he left his mark upon her skin, like the animal that stakes out his territory where no other beast dare tread. She tried to squirm from his control, his hand tight and unrelenting against her wrists, causing her some pain, even as his mouth bruised her tender flesh, but even the slightest movement seemed to rally his efforts, the core of his feverish sexuality pulsing against her thigh as a constant reminder of his ultimate intent.

"There is a need in me, *ma petite*, to show you that you are *mine*!" he whispered softly. "A possession that I can not in all good conscience part with," he choked out hoarsely, burying his face in her neck as he again pulled his body over hers, letting go of her hands as he did so.

Immediately, Monique's hands went to Erik's head, pulling it up and pushing his hair back from his eyes so she could see his face, as lightening streaked throughout the cabin. "There is no need to proclaim possession, Erik. I have come to you willingly every time."

"Oh, but there is my love. I must emphasize that *you belong to me*," he muttered with abandoned purpose, staring at her with liquid green orbs that penetrated right to her soul. He spread her thighs apart roughly with his knee. With little more than a touch of his rigid shaft against her unprepared flesh, he thrust deep inside, his sword sheathed neatly to the hilt in one stroke, surprising her not only with his sudden, brutal action, but taking the breath right out of her body as she screamed in pain, pushing her hands flatly against his chest, but he would not budge.

"Please, Erik, don't do this," she cried, tears springing from her eyes and running down her face to mingle in her hair.

Erik faintly heard her pleas, and felt her body tremble beneath him in painful response, yet there was an unfulfilled need in both his body and his soul, that spiraled beyond his control. All rational thinking or reasonable actions left his mind, as every part of his essence ached to show her...plead to her, the only way he knew how, exactly what he wanted. To tell her with his body all those words he was unable to express. He had tried, but somehow it just never came out right. That ugly part of him always got in the way. He looked for rejection and he was never disappointed. It was forever there, staring right into his ugly face. Yet, he needed her to love him! With little regard for her comfort, he thrust unceasingly, taking her mouth to stifle her whimpering. His conscience screamed that it was wrong to possess her in such a demeaning way, but years of denial took precedence. He would be her master, her lover, her protector and her friend. She must cry out her need for him also, just as he needed her. Only then would he know relief from the horrors of his past.

Monique's mind was in a blur. Why was Erik doing this? What was he trying to prove? Didn't he understand that he had her heart, and everything that comes with it? He was acting like a spoiled child that couldn't have his own way! Having one gigantic temper tantrum! But just maybe he was that spoiled child that had never been taught how to love. For some strange and enlightening moment, she reasoned that perhaps he had never been given love in any form, and didn't have the faintest idea how to give or accept it, and that extraordinary thought made her heart begin to melt. Just a little! As the initial pain eased and her panic ebbed, a slow tingling warmth gripped her body as Erik's first battering thrusts changed in their intensity, settling on a deep penetrating, rhythmic motion that reached all her senses, stirring those places in her womanly body that only he had ever seized, his sweet torture making her body respond in a treasonous way. Her breasts swelled and the bud of her womanhood was on fire. Her sheath clutched at his mighty sword with giant spasms at every thrust, sending her nearly over the edge. Her arms went involuntarily around him in silent surrender, as she raked her sharp talons over his sensitive skin, arousing a hiss of air through his teeth that had become so familiar. As he raised his head to look at sapphire blue eyes, caught like gleaming embers of a slow burning fire, as a faint touch of moon lapsed through the tiny porthole, triumphantly she smiled, thinking she would meet him with an answering passion. This game played by one, she thought with tempered reasoning, could easily be played by two!

Erik's breathing was heavy and labored, yet her warmth began to soothe him. He felt Monique's body reach up to meet his thrusts, her quaking womb sending him to the brink of loosing his self-restraint, driving him into an erotic frenzy, as she willingly wrapped her legs around his lean, powerful hips. His hands slid beneath her lithe body, cupping her backside, pulling her into him as they melded into one. But he was not to be denied. He would make her beg for mercy before he would yield, like a knight would demand in conquest, yet the burning on his back and shoulders from his own salty sweat mingling in her own marked territory, made him realize he would not come out of this unscathed. Each in his own way was determined to hold his own with the other, the age-old battle of the sexes settled in the bedroom. Monique wanted to show Erik that she was his equal, but Erik wanted to win.

The storm raged violently outside, pitching the large steamer back and forth against giant waves with a rolling motion that would frighten many a passenger this dangerous and catastrophic night, but in stateroom seven it only added to the intensity of the strange and volatile passion that brewed within. Thunder crashed with a deafening roar, but neither seemed to notice. Wide bolts of lightening illuminated the room at regular intervals, creating a psychedelic eeriness, allowing only a momentary glimpse of each other from the darkened room. Once again they each played the others body like they were tuning a fine instrument, the medley of their passion from within, blending with the poetic music of the storm until it became a full blown rhapsody.

Erik's body lay completely still upon Monique's, a raging fire of excitement flooding his being to the brink of overflowing. His chest heaved as he willed himself to remain in control. He was not yet ready to allow her to concede defeat. No clemency would be offered when his life depended on it. His face brushed against her hair, his flaring nostrils taking in the sweet fragrance of lavender that mingled with her tears. Tears he had caused, and he felt a momentary pang of guilt. "Is my love so distasteful that you do not wish to lie with me for eternity," he whispered softly, his open mouth, warm and moist upon her ear.

Monique was panting and breathless from their lovemaking, her womanly body budding with an indescribable force that splintered her very center. Her teeth nipped gingerly at his tender shoulder, avoiding those few places she was sure he would be aware of later. It was as if she did not understand his meaning. "Eternity, Erik? What is eternity? You mean to send me away when your game is finished!"

"Send you away? Damnation!" he cursed in denial. "A witch you are in truth. You twist my words with your spell," Erik growled, a pitiful sound of disgust escaping his lips as he rolled off her body, breaking their union.

Monique gasped at Erik's sudden movement, her body still screaming to be fulfilled. "And what about our bargain?" she said rationally. "The one where you were going to pay for my passage to France when your business was finished," she refuted in agitation, clearly knowing her own mind and what he had offered.

Ignoring her comment, he took another approached. "*I* do not mean to send you away. *You* are the one that is so determined to leave," he said in opposition, thinking it utterly irrational that she would not recognize that things had changed. He needed her!

"I am not determined to leave! You insisted on sending me back," she stated with conviction.

"I thought you wanted to return," he argued angrily, hardly believing what he was hearing.

"Only because you left me no other recourse. There is nothing left for me in France, now that my father is dead," she said sadly, remembering the events of the last month with a melancholy sorrow, knowing that nothing but problems awaited her return.

Erik's body lay against her, one thigh still claiming possession across her lovely torso, a fine misty sheen soaking her skin from the raging heat of his. "Well, that was then and this is now," he admitted reluctantly, his demeanor more arrogant than apologetic, his face showing in stark relief as a bolt of lightening lit up the room.

"And what exactly has changed?" she asked, not readily understanding.

"Nothing has changed, love," he evaded. "Nothing that matters anyway." His hands began to caress her, roaming over her swelled breasts and the concave curvature of her flat abdomen, as his mind wondered about vague possibilities.

"What do you mean…nothing that really matters?"

"I want you to stay with me regardless of whether you are carrying my child," he stated plainly, preparing to subdue her efforts if she tried bolting from his grasp.

"Carrying your child!" she cried, almost disbelieving it could happen. "But Erik, I can not be with child." His gentle persuasion nullified her attempt at wiggling.

"And why not? It's a very natural occurrence when two people engage in this most enjoyable activity," he chuckled softly, shaking his head, thinking how childish she sounded, discounting the fact that he had totally blocked the possibility from his own mind, needing a rather jarring reminder.

"But we aren't married," she cried, blushing bright red in the darkness, knowing full well that her love for Erik had determined her acceptance of him, whether marriage was offered or not.

Erik had to laugh in spite of himself, which made Monique squirm beneath him with renewed vigor to be set free. "Did you think our not being married would bar such an occurrence, *ma petite*?" he whispered softly, his warm breath caressing her face.

"Well, of course not," she said, peeved at the insolence of his question. Of course she knew it could happen. It was just the idea that he had said...well... proclaimed that he would send her home.

"Well then we are in complete agreement on something. You *will* stay with me." Lowering his head quickly, he lightly caressed her lips with his tongue to cease her talking, pressing a slow sensual kiss upon her mouth that lingered, his tongue tracing the outline of lips that were swollen from his attentions. Continuing downward he branded her pale skin with his feverish mouth, forging a path from the curve of her throat to her swelling breasts, sucking gently to bring out that sweet agony that shattered her senses, careening with desire to comply to his touch. Deftly he marked a trail downward over her flat abdomen, tarrying only moments in the soft triangle of red curls, until his mouth found that molten center where she ached to be released. Boldly he caressed her, with searching mouth and tongue, licking and searching, until she cried out his name, all modesty giving way to wanton abandonment, his conquest finally complete.

"Please, Erik, love me. Love me." She cried out in torment, surrender the only avenue of acquittal. Fisting her fingers in his hair, she strained against his mouth, her defenses against his shameless assault toppling in defeat.

Her submission made him smile, as he yielded his administrations. He pulled his body full over hers, taunting her, teasing her, his body suspended on his toes, his full weight denied. "What say ye, Milady? I could stop if you have a mind for it." Obstinately he waited, his body unmoving, allowing the intensity of her passion to build and smolder.

"Damn you Erik." She urged, tracing his lips with her fingers in the pale darkness, feeling the lines of laughter around his mouth, knowing with certainty that he would offer no quarter.

"Yes, Milady!" he tempted, teasing the palm of her hand with his warm tongue, even as the unyielding hardness of his own body pressed against her belly as he eased his body down, creating a need in him that demanded reprieve also.

"Sir Knight, bring forth that mighty sword you have and do battle," she plied with a seductive huskiness, her hand reaching between them, towards his belly, capturing that long, swollen weapon which he had chosen for the battlefield, the wisdom of his strategy not lost upon either opponent, yet neither declaring total defeat.

"T'is no sacrifice at all, Milady. Your wish is my command." This time he came to her gently as one to be cherished. Rolling onto his back, he brought her with him, and lifting her easily, he impaled her impassioned body upon his long, thick sword. Jolts of fire coursed through them…once opponents, now comrades-in-arms, their matching fervor seeking to bind them together as one entity. Powerless to resist, they yielded to the fiery heat within them. He kissed her with an eagerness that left her breathless, caressing her body and tantalizing her senses as the slow primitive movements of their union ignited her need for him. To him she offered a sanctuary where his soul could heal, denying him nothing. When they were satiated to the fullest, she lay within the comfort of his arms, their bodies not yet parted, yet spiraling downward with their fiery passion released.

"I want to marry you, love." He said, his hands wandering over her body unhindered. "I want you to have no excuse to leave me.'

"Marry you, Erik? Is there any other reason?" she asked lazily, hoping for some declaration of love, but not requiring it. She loved him and for now that was enough. In time, perhaps he would come to love her also.

"Because I need you," Erik stated flatly.

"To heal your soul, you say. To make you whole." She paused, laying a hand upon his deformed cheek, then nestling her face into his neck, warm moist lips kissing him lightly. "Erik, I don't know what all that means, but I have a good idea."

"I need you for many reasons," he admitted. "Of that I am positive."

"Does that include love?" she probed, wishing immediately that she had not said it.

"Love?" he said with a wretched questioning in his tone. "It seems I know very little about love, my dear. To me love is painful, full of spite and offers only denial," he said bitterly. Erik felt vulnerable in this simple, yet revealing admission…not yet ready to fully declare his love for Monique out loud. When he revealed his past she might well run from him. He could not in all honesty, declare love when she didn't know the truth.

The storm continued to rage with its ardent fury. A translucent moon reflected upon the tempered glass of the porthole, casting ghostly shadows over the walls and ceiling with each flash of lightening. Looking into Erik's face, Monique could see all the tortures of a lifetime mirrored in his mesmerizing emerald eyes, and her heart ached to erase from his mind, each and every torture he bore. She knew deep within his soul that he hurt from some unmerciful flogging of the mind, and perhaps the body, and it simply broke her heart!

Touching his face with both her hands, she kissed him tenderly, her lips for now offering that which he sought for release. "I want to marry you also, Erik… but," she said honestly. Immediately, Erik's body stiffened against her. Hesitantly, she added, "But, I don't know anything about you."

" I promise before the day is out, that you will know everything that you need to know," he whispered, crushing her against him as a jailor might bind his captive, fear welling up within him once again that what he was about to reveal would change everything.

"That is all I ask of you," she said simply, knowing in her own mind that nothing could ever separate her from Erik again!

Chapter Twelve

The storm continued its vengeance throughout the night, pitching the lumbering vessel back and forth between gigantic swells. The heavy winds whistled eerily through any opening or crack, its swirling fingers snatching the canvas cover from the top deck and hurling it along with anything else not tightly battened down, over the side and into the sea. As the winds had mounted steadily in the early evening, the deck crew had hastily gone to the task of tightening the hog-chains and securing the multitude of cordwood that was stored on the lower deck. Hog-chains were lines, manipulated with turnbuckles, that could be loosened or tighten as needed. To strengthen the structure of the vessel, a long beam known as a keelson was laid below the floor along the center, stretching from her bow to her stern. A wooden, vertical beam was erected upright from the keelson, usually about one-third astern of the bow, towering high above the top deck, much like a mast. To this beam, hogs-chains were attached, stretching in turn to the bow and stern, and also to each paddle wheel, giving the vessel greater stability and the paddles more security. This had been initiated in wooden hulled steamers and continued in those with iron hulls, although the hog-chains threaded beneath wooden steamers to keep her hulls from sagging were obviously not necessary, if the vessel's hull was built from iron.

It was the distinct duty of the engineer, situated within the engine room, to judge how much cordwood was actually needed at any given time, to keep the steamer on a steady course towards their destination. He controlled how much fuel was burned, knew how quickly the engine worked, and exactly how far to push the boiler, for if pushed too far, it could burst. He realized that the greater the pressure he could eek out of the boiler, the faster the paddle steamer would travel, and the steamship line was all about schedules. Being on time meant money! But an engineer had to be cautious. Paddle steamers were notorious for explosions in their boilers, if pushed past their maximum capacity.

Denison Crocket was a tall, lanky cockney lad that had spent ten years working his way up and down the Mississippi River in America, aboard some pretty fancy paddle steamers, tending the fires that allowed the gentry to take pleasure cruises for their amusement. He had returned to London just one year past, secured his job aboard the *La Bentra*, and genuinely liked his work. He worked hard, made a generous salary and he knew what to do to make this pretty lady fly! He liked the idea of plying a larger body of water, like the English Channel, and in a much bigger steamer, but it heretofore presented a bigger challenge. He looked hard into the embers in the boiler, keeping his ever-observant eye on just how hot it presented, and cocked an experienced ear to the sound of steam in the pipes. He kept his other eye on Fireman Wheaton as he dutifully stoked the furnace, that lower part of the boiler, with the proper amount of cordwood upon his own, explicit instructions. The constant, forward movement of the vessel would aid in diminishing how violently the craft was pitched back and forth by the crosswinds, but also cut down on the distance they might well be blown off course. Not to mention, keeping the passengers more comfortable. Hurrump, thought Crocket! Not an easy feat when the waves were breaking over the bow, dumping tons of water onto her decks. He just hoped they could keep the bloody ship afloat. He'd been in quite a few storms, but this was one of the worst.

From the doorway came a shout that could barely be heard above the howling wind. Crocket turned around to see a seaman stick his head around the doorframe of the boiler room. "Cap'n says we're loosin' ground there, Crocket" he yelled, his head bent just enough to allow streams of water to roll off his hat and onto the floor in a puddle. The intense heat from the boiler room immediately turned the tiny pool into steam, sending it spiraling toward the ceiling.

"How the devil does he think I can make the ol' girl go any faster? I'm nigh pushing her to the limits as it is. There'll be hell to pay if she decides to blow," called back Crocket, knowing that she wasn't quite there yet, but the ship was laboring more than expected, and it was taking an extreme amount of fuel to keep those paddles churning. If she was caught dead in the water in these waves, her wheels would be chewed to pieces.

"I'm just repeatin' what the Cap'n asked me to tell ya," called the seaman, ducking quickly out the door and back into the storm.

"Well, I suppose what the Cap'n wants, the Cap'n is used to getting. Bloody hell! We'll just see about that!" he muttered in agitation, getting up from his seat and going to the intercom to communicate with the man himself. He picked up the *speaking tube,* blew into the empty pipe several times, but got no response. Again he blew into the pipe, but again there was no response. In exasperation, he replaced the primitive intercom into its base, preparing to give an order for Fireman Wheaton to up the anty on cordwood just a smidgen. Not enough to let her blow, of course, but enough to give her a little boost. Before he could do so, the steamer shifted heavily to the starboard side. Stacks of cordwood, piled high in long bins along the wall of the engine room, shifted suddenly, dumping part of the contents onto the floor. Crockets keen ears, accustom to every noise associated with his engine, heard an unusual grinding sound coming from the wall directly behind him, like valves sticking in the pipes. If that happened, he thought with some alarm, the steam could neither enter the cylinder chamber, nor escape, building up pressure at both ends.

Deciding he'd better take a quick look, he yelled to Wheaton, "Ease off on the fire, lad. I want to check the cylinder." Quickly he opened a small door to where the cylinder was housed. It was here that the piston rods, extending towards the paddle wheels, were pulled back and forth by the steam, sliding the crank shaft, then turning a huge crank counterclockwise, and eventually turning the wheel itself. As he entered the small room, a loud crackling sound was heard within the cylinder casing, followed by the abrasive scraping of metal. Without another thought, he quickly dove back into the boiler room, landing with a thud upon the floor, nearly knocking Wheaton off his feet.

"Blimey, mate, what do ya..." the fireman began shouting, startled to find Crocket smashed up against the boiler in a ball. Within seconds, the edges of the cylinder box flew apart, the piston rod smashing into the wall just above their heads. There was a horrendous amount of grinding and snapping, as immediately thereafter followed a long chain of disastrous events, whereby the crankshaft split in two, dislodging the crank itself, that in turn snapped the paddle shaft that turned the wheels, bringing not only the paddle wheels to a screeching halt, sending anything not tied down into a forward motion toward the bow, including many of its passengers, but leaving the vessel dead in the water.

Within minutes, the captain was below, surveying the damage. "Did the boiler blow?" he asked, almost before he entered the doorway of the engine room at a decided gallop.

"No, Sir, it weren't the boiler at all. The cylinder casing blew apart when the valves stuck in her pipes," Crocket answered.

"Might be easier to fix than the boiler," the captain replied, relieved that it wasn't his order that caused this mishaps. He wouldn't have felt good about that!

"Perhaps," Crocket said, noncommittally, for he really didn't know how. They didn't have the right kind of equipment aboard to mend the metal shafts and no telling what those heavy swells, pounding against her iron hull, would do in damaging the wooden paddles. The draft on a paddle steamer was negligible, requiring only about 120 centimeters of depth, more or less, to clear the bottom. They were sitting almost flat on the water, with nothing particular to weight them down, and the sea would toss them around like an insignificant piece of driftwood.

Erik's head smacked hard against the headboard as his body shifted toward the bow of the ship with a forceful blow. "*Mon Dieu*," he swore, the words escaping his lips even before his brain tried to focus on his surrounding, his arms clutching at Monique's body by habit to assure himself that she was safe within the circle of his embrace. Within seconds he was fully awake, taking in the silence of the engines, and the halting of churning paddles that had ceased pushing water into their wake, that otherwise monotonous rhythmic noise that seemed to lull you to sleep, gone in an instant.

Monique stirred within his arms, but did not fully awaken, for his own body had kept hers from receiving a jarring blow, and she only murmured at him in a sleepy tone of voice, "What is the matter, Erik? Why are you awake?" She tried to snuggle her body closer to his, moving in an unknowingly seductive manner, making him curse again within his own mind, knowing he would rather attend to what he wanted to do, than what he needed to do, and that was find out what was happening beyond this cabin!

The large cumbersome vessel was not pitching into the swells as before, but seemed to be tossing from side to side in a more erratic manner, as the flat hull was carried over one large wave after another. Sliding from the bed, Erik reached for some dry britches and a casual white shirt, stuffing the tails negligently into the waistband of his pants. Pulling on boots even as he stood, he could hear the grinding and splintering of wood coming from somewhere astern of their cabin. It had to be the paddle wheels being chewed to pieces, and that thought gave him an uneasy feeling of certain doom.

"Where are you going?" Monique asked, noticing the rush of cool air upon her torso as Erik's warm body left her side.

"The engines have stopped, love. I'm merely going on deck to see what is happening!" With that he grabbed up his wig, placed it swiftly on his head with years of tedious practice and was reaching for his mask.

Monique sat up in bed, pulling the covers around her body to where only her arms and shoulders were exposed. "What do you think is happening?" she questioned, not really expecting an answer, for it was obvious neither of them could know, but a fearful tremor was evident in her voice, and Erik recognized the beginning of uncertainty creeping into her demeanor. He did not want to scare her further with what he suspected. There would be time for that later!

Coming to the side of the bunk, he sat down beside Monique. Tilting her chin towards him with the fingers of his right hand, so that he could see straight into her eyes, he said with an undertone of authority, yet concern, "Under no circumstances, *ma petite*, are you to leave this cabin." He stopped to let his words sink in! " If you do, it would only be because you were in the gravest of danger, and that I believe is very unlikely" he continued, with an emphasis that was not lost to Monique. He looked at her intently, knowing how stubborn and careless she could be when he wasn't watching, then added, "Will you follow my orders?"

Monique, a little frightened at the howling of the wind outside and the increased rolling of the ship, managed to muster up a small impish grin. "Oh, M'Lord, your wish is my command," she whispered, mimicking Erik's own words from their night of passion.

"Witch," he groaned, hating to leave her side when she was obviously frightened, wishing he could take her fears away by making love to her, but he was not at all certain that they weren't in danger, and he needed to investigate for himself to confirm his own suspicions. Grudgingly he arose from the bed, grazing her lips with his, as he did so.

"Please, Erik, don't be long," she pleaded, lowering her head a bit shamefully at her own recognition of fear.

"I will return just a soon as I know what the magnitude of the situation is that we are facing," he said intently, making Monique giggle, because Erik sometimes could be so ridiculously formal, but she knew it was most often when he was worried, or trying to solve some kind of puzzle.

"You mean what is happening on deck," she said slyly.

"Yes, isn't that what I just said, my dear," he replied, a frown playing on his brow, knowing that somehow she was mocking him, and that impishness in her tone made him rightfully wary that she would not follow his orders. He glared at her with something akin to a challenge, his feet spread wide apart and his massive body letting her know in an instant that he would deal with this topic later, if necessary.

Placing the mask on his face, he gave her one last glance. "Do not leave the cabin, *ma cherie*. I will not be happy with you if you do. Punishment is not out of the question, " he warned, fearing for their safety if all was going badly, wanting to protect her at all cost, under circumstances that may well be out of his control.

"And shall we choose weapons again, M'lord?" she bantered, making light conversation to hide her fear. Her question, in spite of his concern, made Erik blush, which only made Monique giggle again, and Erik wondered who had really won last night. In light of everything, he was not at all certain it was him.

Without another word, he left the cabin and plunged into a pandemonium of passengers running everywhere about the deck in their nightclothes. The boatswain and the first mate were yelling, trying to calm the passengers down, instructing them to go *back* to their cabins, to *stay* in their cabins, and to *keep* their life-jackets handy. Finally after several long minutes, the decks were thinned from anxious passengers, with only crewman remaining who had duties needing attention, and with the present situation, those duties had become numerous indeed.

Erik stayed on deck to survey the damage. A light, steady rain continued to fall, but the seas had actually begun to calm. Morning was peeking just above the horizon, allowing a dull light to sneak through the thick, gray clouds that blanketed the entire sky. He leaned against the bulwark, eyeing the splintered wheel on the port side, noting that not only were some of the flat paddles missing, but the paddle shaft was also missing, and the metal crank shaft was broken in two halves, the end attached to the wheel hanging loosely, yet banging incessantly against the wheel with each roll of the ship to starboard.

"Please, Sir, it is necessary that the passengers go to their cabins," came a voice from behind him. Erik spun around, momentarily startled, his mind intently working on calculating what would be needed to repair the damage.

The boatswain waited a moment for Erik to respond, but when he didn't, he repeated himself. "The captain has asked that the passengers remain in their cabins. For safety," he added, seeing that Erik did not seem inclined to budge. "When the decks are cleared of debris and the weather is better, we will let everyone know," he said with emphasis, noting that the mask this man wore gave him more of an authoritative appearance than when he had come on board without it, and he gave a moments pause before pressing Erik further.

But Erik spoke before it was necessary for the lad to speak again. "Do you have an engineer on board that can repair the damage," Erik asked, the tone of his voice commanding enough that the boatswain offered the information freely.

"Engineer Crocket takes care of the engine and all its workings, but I doubt we have anyone on board that can rightly repair what this storm has done to her. We may have to get out the paddles and row," he joked, but immediately he realized his mistake with that remark, seeing a dark scowl sweep across Erik's serious face.

"May I have a word with your Captain?" Erik asked, his irritation obvious.

"Well, I'm not sure that the captain has time to talk to passengers right now," protested the boatswain, but the look Erik afforded him changed his mind rather quickly.

"I'll see if he is busy," the lad croaked out, wondering how he would explain to the captain that he was afraid to turn the gentleman down, or do his own job effectively.

Fifteen minutes went by, Erik using every second to roam around the deck and linger studiously on each and every bit of damage he was able to see, without actually climbing over the railing and getting right up on top of what he was after. Not that he wouldn't have liked to do that! But caution was the opposite of stupidity, and the rough seas and the rain were more than he wanted to tangle with!

"M'sieur Deaveau, is there something I can do for you," resounded the gruff voice of Captain McShane, coming alongside Erik at the railing. His voice had the tone of irritation, most pointedly that he must nursemaid one of his crew, seemingly unable to contend with one simple passenger. It was only for the safety of this gentleman that he came down from the pilothouse at all.

When Erik turned to face the Captain, he displayed his usual commanding presence, that demeanor that gave orders and expected them to be obeyed, and it was not missed by the captain's eyes. He had a silent pang of guilt for chewing out the boatswain so harshly, realizing that the lad really had little choice. M'sieur Deaveau did not look like he would take no for an answer, and that information actually made McShane feel better, rather than more irritated.

Erik spoke with both authority and knowledge. " I am an engineer of construction and architecture by profession, and have been surveying your damage. It will take a lot of hard work to repair, but it is not impossible. Your boatswain says you do not have a construction engineer aboard," he finished, merely stating the facts as he saw them presented.

The captain liked the straightforwardness of this gentleman, and a smile spread across his features immediately. Well, it appears this man was not just a musician. "You are correct, Sir, in your assumptions. The entire mess will be a trial in wits and imagination. Just finding parts aboard to replace all the broken ones will take invention and persistence. I too believe it can be accomplished. Are you offering your services for the job?" he said, without further ado or amenities.

"If that is what you need. Yes I am!" Erik replied, no hesitation in his tone whatsoever, knowing that he would be exposed for hours on end, to everyone's view, the task he was about to undertake somewhat monumental.

"My crew will be at your disposal," the captain assured him, extending Erik his hand in contract and friendship. "I will take you to meet Engineer Crocket, who will help you coordinate your efforts with the crew."

"I must first tell my wife that everything is alright," Erik said easily, liking the idea of Monique becoming his wife, but a frown creased his brow at the thought that there would be no time in the ensuing hours to reveal to her his past, and that both relieved his mind, as well as troubled it.

Erik met all those that would be involved in the planning. Engineer Crocket would be responsible for not only conferring with Erik on what parts needed replacing and finding the needed materials, but with finding those crewmen that would help in the repairs. Fireman Wheaton would be the gopher that made sure messages were passed along the line, and the proper equipment was available when it was needed. Not an easy task, when many tools would have to be improvised. In fact, the entire project would be a constant task of improvisation.

Erik was in the engine room, talking over the need of the furnace to meld the metal crankshaft together. "Both ends should be almost liquid, then extracted before it falls. Pounding them together with a hammer while they cool will give them strength. A metal mallet is best, but a wooden one will do," he instructed. He found Crocket to be a very intelligent lad, taking instructions easily, understanding what was said, then delving head first into his work.

"Seen it done before, Sir, but can't say I've done it myself. But I'll try it," he offered, a big grin on his face, willing to do anything that was asked, thinking that this gentleman was probably the brains behind a project, but would not readily dirty his hands with the actual work.

"That's not necessary. Just find everything that is needed, and I'll come down and do it myself," Erik assured him. It's not that he didn't trust the lad, but the crankshaft would be the most important element, taking most of the punishment and strain, and he wanted it to be done right. There was no time to teach here, as much as he would have liked to do so!

On deck the crew were busy with some of his other orders. It was his suggestion that since the wheels had not been damaged in like proportions, any flat paddles that were serviceable should be divided evenly between them. Those paddles that were missing would be replaced by using wood stripped from the outside walls of the cabin area and cut to fit. It was the only place on board where the wood was long enough for the makeshift paddles to be constructed in one piece, other than stripping boards from the decking. That would not be prudent, for if it rained, the ship would take on water below decks.

Within hours the ship looked like a construction zone, most of the crew busy at tasks they had never attempted, many trying things they had always wanted to do, but had never been given the opportunity. With Erik's guidance, they cut wood, angled them for fittings and bolted them into place. Both wheels had sagged, and tightening up the hog-chains had not established the proper angle to let the wheels spin freely. Erik was still thinking about that one. He had an idea, but that would be last on his list, after everything was mended and finally set into place. When something did not go quite right, or seemed impossible, the crew was pleasantly surprised to find Erik, a titled gentleman, digging in along side them, more often than not, accomplishing the task single handled. A few male passengers had volunteered to help, but most were from the lower class. The rest of them just gawked or went about their usual entertainment in the salon, like nothing out of the ordinary was happening, demanding food and drink on a regular schedule, somewhat peeved when the menu was cut in half to conserve on the kitchen help, the other half busy helping with construction.

Monique had watched the proceedings on deck for two days, helping serve the workers sandwiches and coffee, or a cool beverage in the heat. Today the repairs would be finished. She had wanted to change into her bitches and help, and had actually brought the subject up to Erik yesterday evening, when he had finally returned to their cabin after long hours of extra work. His words still rang alarmingly in her ears.

"A lady of station does not wear men's riding britches. *My wife* does not wear riding britches," he said smoothly, ignoring the look of surprise on her face that quickly turned to indignation.

"But Erik, I could be of help. I know I could," she argued, believing him to be totally unreasonable in his demands, knowing in her own mind that eventually, this one request on his part, would most certainly be broken, especially when riding a horse. A dress in that matter would be out of the question! She would concede only in this instance.

"We have enough help, love," he said with a heavy sigh.

He was tired and he didn't want to argue. He had come to their cabin for just a few hours of needed rest. It was too dark to see the wheels to continue their work, even with the lanterns provided. It was simply too dangerous to risk it. They would start again at daylight. Exhausted, he sat on the bed and lay back against the mattress. He closed his eyes and was instantly asleep, his boots still resting on the floor.

Monique looked over at Erik, and just shook her head. Sometimes he was so infuriating, always demanding his own way. Watching him work had been another valuable lesson dripping with mystery. She had heard Erik tell Mr. Overland something about architecture. That word she was certain of, whether spoken in French or English. And she overheard a crewman speaking in French call him an engineer. Putting two and two together, she assumed he was both. How else could he know so much about what he was doing here? First he was a musician, then… a magician perhaps...and now an architect and an engineer. And he spoke several languages. What else would she discover about Erik's past? He was a giant puzzle of mysteries that seemed to be unraveling, one by one, right before her eyes! And without him uttering even one word!

Monique pulled Erik's legs onto the bed, knowing she could never pull his boots off by herself. He wore only boots and britches, having shrugged his shirt in the heat of the sun, and had not replaced it when the night turned chilly. He had worked the entire evening in the boiler room, where a tremendous racket of noise had disturbed the otherwise quiet night, the incessant pounding of metal against metal allowing only the most hardy to sleep unaffected. Finally, he had emerged, his body drenched with sweat, coming to their cabin only to sleep. His mask was off and stuffed in his pocket. She figured the intense heat had rendered it impossible to bare, whether from not being able to tolerate its presence or that it would not stick, she knew not which. Either way, in her opinion, it wasn't something he needed. Lying there on his side he looked so handsome and innocent. What mysteries did he still have to reveal? She covered him with a blanket, turned the lantern down to a small flickering spark and snuggled beneath the covers against his chest. In sleep his arms came around her, pulling her body tight against his own form. As she drifted off, the thought lingered that tomorrow they would finally be underway!

Morning had emerged within a few short hours, and when Monique awoke, Erik was already gone. Hurriedly she dressed, throwing on a simple, light dress of gingham that buttoned down the front. She decided quickly to forget the idea of a petticoat, determining the material not too revealing, and her waist was small enough to go without a corset, and thankfully so! Yesterday had been stifling hot after the storm, the noonday sun baking everything on deck, including the workers. Most of the men had stripped off their shirts, but that was not a choice for the ladies. She wondered how she had ever survived those heavy clothes she was forced to wear when she had first met Erik. She remembered feeling so nauseated from the heat that she had actually thought she would become ill, but the shear determination of keeping her secret had spurred her onward! Now, knowing the outcome, it was all for naught, and smiling again, she was thankful. After grabbing a light breakfast in the kitchen of fruit and a hard roll, Monique went on deck with a pot of hot coffee for the workers.

As she left the kitchen, she heard one of the girls remark to another. "That masked man's wife is sure a dandy. Doesn't put on heirs around us common folk, both of them working so hard alongside everyone else, like they weren't gentry at all." Monique had to smile. She might not be gentry, but Erik certainly was, and still he gave of himself like few people she had ever met. She was proud to be his wife. Well…*almost his wife!*

The day wore on, paddles were bolted into place and a new crankshaft was installed in the portside cylinder chamber, which had been soldered with molten metal, that last detail that had kept Erik up most of the night. And two new paddleshafts had been rigged. As Monique watched, five men were manning a rope that levered the last enormous crank into place to connect to a paddleshaft. This would turn counterclockwise, the key piece that moved the paddles. One wheel had already been finished. This was the last piece needed to send the ship on her way. Erik had been working with a team to secure additional hog-chains at just the right angle to balance the wheels for spinning, when he was needed to fix another problem. In pulling the wheel higher the paddleshaft on the starboard side would not fit into its chamber and Erik was surveying the situation, making his suggestion of what was necessary to allow the crank to slide into its holding more easily.

Suddenly, the ship lurched to the starboard side as the salon emptied of dozens of passengers that had finished their noonday meal, several bumping into the men that held the rope steady, as the large crank was lowered onto its casing. Two of the men let go, being pushed rudely aside, unable to continue their tight grip on the rope.

The rope went slack, allowing the crank to sway dangerously out to sea. Wheaten cried out a warning, but it was too late. As it swung back, it slammed into Erik's left side, propelling him off the wheel, over the railing and onto piles of cordwood tied to the deck.

Erik turned around when he heard the warning, but all he could do was shield his face, raising his arms to protect his head. He felt the solid impact of the metal crank and heard bones cracking, his breath leaving his body with such force that he was momentarily knocked unconscious. He didn't feel his body being lifted into the air, or pitched into a broken heap on the deck. But Monique saw it all. She screamed, dropping the pitcher of lemonade she had been serving to the workers, and ran! No, she cried, not Erik! Tears clouded her vision, denying the possible. He can not be dead!

Erik wasn't out for a long time. His world had momentarily faded to gray, like he was walking through the white mist that appeared at dawn around Paris, the grasslands holding onto cloud-like vapors that clung to the ground before the sun burnt them off with its radiance. Then the pain had invaded, like a white-hot poker newly extracted from deep blue embers, branding his skin in numerous places, the idea of distinguishing one place from another seeming more ludicrous with each passing moment. Voices rose and fell in the distance, yet his world spiraled downwards into total blackness with the speed of a coin being negligently tossed into a dark sewer drain. Suddenly, hands were tugging at him, stirring his body to wakefulness, the searing pain making his head dizzy, as nausea threatened to engulf him. He tried to protest their actions, defending himself against them, but could manage little more than an audible grunt, and when his head started to clear, he saw Monique through a red haze, staring at him in horror, her face pale as a ghost! She was saying something important, he was certain, but he couldn't hear her. Again his vision turned to gray, and then to black, and he remembered nothing more!

Chapter Thirteen

Erik shifted on the bunk, pain assaulting every muscle in his body. He shivered with cold, but even with extreme effort he was unable to voice his need for more warmth. He could hear the distant humming of the engines and feel the slow, constant churning of the paddles, giving him a moment of satisfaction that they were once again underway. He thought he must be in his stateroom, but he wasn't entirely sure. His eyes were heavy, and one eye…his good one…felt swollen and glued shut. Neither eye would respond to his commands to open, and the frustration was not only overwhelming, but unending, giving him a real sense of helplessness. He was a creature of darkness, functioning in its depths with accuracy and ease, but right now he wanted to see! He had never been comfortable in total darkness, especially as a child, and that was why he had used so many candles. He couldn't hear anyone in the cabin and he wondered if he were alone. He tried to call out Monique's name, but his lips would not move. His throat was dry and it felt like cotton had been stuffed into his mouth, his tongue thick and unmanageable. Pain coursed through him like waves of agony, breaking upon the shore one after another, unceasing in their intensity with no way to stop them. He felt nausea overtake him as his head spun out of control with dizziness and he gagged, feeling that his stomach would hurl forth its contents in the next moment and then his embarrassment would be totally complete. And then it did!

Monique returned to the cabin carrying a steaming kettle of water. She went immediately to the basin, poured the water into the porcelain, washing bowl, mixing it with cold water from the pitcher, until it reached the tepid temperature she desired. She brought it over to the bed, clean towels hanging off her arm.

"Oh, Erik!" she exclaimed with dismay, realizing he had vomited over himself and the bed linens. "I should never have left you alone," she said, chiding herself for her foolishness. "I will have the steward get anything else I need," she exclaimed, more to herself than to anyone else, for no one but Erik was here, and she doubted he could hear anything.

A gentle knock was heard on the door and Bradford, the young steward, opened it gingerly. "Is there anything else you will be needing," he inquired, glancing toward the bed, noting the grayish tone to Erik's face that was visible beyond the white mask.

"Yes, yes," Monique cried, not wanting him to leave before helping her. "I need assistance in removing his clothes. His wounds need dressing and I'm not yet sure, where all of them are." She stated this almost matter-of-factly, like tending the wounded was nothing out of the ordinary. He thought she seemed too calm.

"Of course, Madame, let me help you get him comfortable."

Together they stripped Erik of all of his clothing, his nakedness seeming neither to embarrass or phase her in the least, his muscular body above his waist tanned to a golden brown from two days slaving in the hot sun, but the stewards face blushed brighter than usual, the idea of undressing another man in front of a woman just a touch unsettling, no matter that it was her husband. And he cared not to speculate about the fine scratches on his back and shoulders. That was strictly between a man and his wife. They moved his limp body easily, but the moans that emerged from his dry, cracked lips were pitiful, his face contorting in pain even with their gentle administrations, and it tore at Monique's heart to a point she could hardly bare.

When they had finished, Monique inquired about a medicine box, and a clean sheet to tear for bandages. The steward assured her that he would see to it, and left Monique to tend her husband.

Monique tucked a sheet and wool blanket up to Erik's neck. Some of his clothes had been wet from working in the water, trying to fit one accursed paddle into place that had not been obliged to fit, and she could see that Erik's body had begun to shiver from the cold. Lying there in the bed so helpless, Erik did not look dangerous at all!

She sat alongside his hips and started with his face. He had one very nasty cut on his right forearm wrapped in a bandage to stop the immediate bleeding, but that would need to wait. He had a deep gash along the left side of his face, just above his eyebrow, and extending back toward his ear. His eye was swollen shut from both the blood of his wound and the blow to his head, already turning a dark, ugly purple. Not likely he would see out of this eye anytime soon. Wringing out a washcloth in the steamy water, she applied some pressure to the oozing cut, dabbing at the skin around it to wash the blood from his face. Then she cleaned his lips, chin, and down his neck of the residue from vomiting. Each time she wrung out the cloth the water turned a darker red. Erik had so much blood over his face, chest and left shoulder, it was hard to ascertain how extensive his wounds really were. She washed them also, deciding no injuries were visibly present.

Erik stirred, trying hard to open his eyes. He knew Monique was there. He could hear her talking to the steward, and felt them moving him and removing his clothes, but the pain had been unbearable, sending him once again into the realm of blackness, but it has lasted for only a few moments. Or at least he thought it had. It was hard to measure time in a sea of tortuous pain.

He tried to speak, his lips moving, but his throat would not eek out one tiny sound. With every effort he could muster, he groped into the air with his left hand, unable to see, and only slightly hear, but knowing her hands where upon his face. Catching her wrist with his large left hand, he hung onto her, trying to stave away that sinking feeling that screamed to overtake his brain, sending him again into blackness.

"Erik, you are awake!" Monique exclaimed. She had been so intent on tending him, and investigating his wounds, she had not noticed the slight movements that said he was not still caught in oblivion. He moved his head at the sound of her voice, his face turning toward where she sat. She could see he was trying with little response to open his eyes. "Erik, don't," she soothed. "Lie still and let me wash the blood away. I must see where you are injured"

"It...hurts...so...much," he mumbled, his face contorting with each sweep of her hand and each breath that he inhaled. His face was on fire and his ribs hurt like hell, and so many parts of his body felt numb. Every movement he made, mostly breathing, reminded him of the beatings inflicted upon his torso as a child in the gypsy camp, caged like a wild animal to be gawked upon as a freak. Each inspiration set into motion a chain reaction of pain that took minutes to subside. If he could just breathe once an hour, perhaps that would be good! Warm, salty tears ran down his face, a tangible sign of his anguish, and she wiped them away with her cool fingers.

"Erik, I know that it hurts, but it must be done," she said softly, not halting for a moment in her work. The sooner his wounds were addressed, the better!

Knowing now that he could hear, she started talking to him gently, soothingly, explaining what she was about to do, just before she would do it! She had always cared for her father's horses in such a fashion, with tenderness, talking to them, even though she knew they did not understand, but it was the tone of her voice that would initially keep them calm.

"Erik, you have two cuts that needs stitching," she told him. Her voice was low and direct, but softly whispered. He didn't respond. Perhaps he had passed out again. She needed those bandages and she needed a needle and thread.

Next she examined the cut on Erik's right forearm, extending from just below his elbow, downward about eight inches towards his hand. It was a long nasty gash, exposing the bone deep within the wound. This was perhaps the most serious, but she had yet to examine his ribs that appeared to be greatly discolored when removing his clothes. She hadn't noticed any other obvious injuries, but then she wasn't finished yet! Before she was done, every inch of Erik's body would be examined, and then she would be satisfied.

The steward entered again after a small rap upon the door. "Here are the items you suggested," he said politely.

"Barely looking away from her task, she again inquired, "Is there anywhere to get a needle and thread?"

"I'm sure there are some in the medicine box, Madame," he offered. "There has been need of it before." He looked at this very young woman attending her husband, meticulously addressing a task that most women he knew would be incapable of performing, and his admiration for her spirit increased.

"Thank you," Monique answered. "You have been very kind." No more had she voiced it, than she was again concentrating on her work. Bradford slipped out of the room unnoticed.

Monique rummaged through the medicine box, finding the afore mentioned needle and thread, a few compresses, some burn ointment that would be of no real use, and not much else. No medicine of any kind was available, for pain or otherwise. That frightened her, because Erik needed a doctor. Her only choice was to keep his wounds clean and dry, and hope they would make land very, very soon. At least because of Erik, they were once again underway.

Monique used the needle and thread with precision. It was immensely more difficult than she had hoped, the needle being straight for conventional sewing, where the needles she had used at the stable had been curved in an arc, piercing through the two edges of skin with ease, but in the end she accomplished her task. With the head wound, she used small stitches sparingly, that would leave a very minimal mark. Erik didn't need any more scars, especially on that side of his face that he accepted as normal. She had accepted both sides unconditionally, and perhaps someday he would also. She removed his mask, washing the blood away that had run behind it, believing that the protection of the mask had probably saved any damage to the right side. He stirred only minimally, and she was thankful that oblivion had overtaken him again.

Dressing the deep gash on his arm was another matter. The edges were torn and ragged, and small splinters of wood could be seen inside the wound. If left inside they would cause the wound to fester. Monique took a pair of tweezers from her cosmetics and soaked them in a small bowl of liquor to cleanse them. It was the best she could do for now. Not having the appropriate supplies was more than irritating. If she only had him at the stable, all this would be so easy! Washing her hands in the liquor also, she carefully extracted every sliver of wood that she could see, pouring a bit of the liquid into the wound for good measure. She pushed the edges of the gash together and unceremoniously sewed them with long connecting stitches, tying it at one end in a big knot. No need to worry about scars here, she thought frowning, and it would be easier to cut open if that became necessary. Hopefully it would not! Finally she tore strips of sheeting and bound the wound firmly, but not tight, tearing the end lengthwise to bring around his arm, securing it with a knot also.

Erik's face looked pale. Even the left side, tanned by the sun had a somewhat grayish pallor underneath, and his lips had the slightest tinge of purple. His breathing was very shallow and labored, each short inhalation followed by a small grimace on his face, and that further worried Monique. She pulled the blanket down to his abdomen, noting the harsh discolored markings along the left side of his torso, several ribs being outlined with deep purple lines. The crank had swung wide and hit him full force on the left side, knocking him off the paddle wheel and onto a stack of cordwood stored on the deck. Her fingers touched his ribs gently, running over each rib in succession, saving the discolored ones until last, noting how guarded he was in his breathing, each breath cut short before it was finished, only to be repeated, time and time again, hardly giving him time to exhale. When she examined the discolored area, Erik body arched off the bed several inches, turning away slightly as he brought his knees upward, as if to protect himself by pulling his body into a ball. In doing so, he let out a loud groan of pure torture.

"Erik, no! Please, Erik, lie flat," she soothed in a low voice. Pulling him back was no small effort, his mumbling colored with cursing words at every motion. She placed a cool hand to his cheek, kissing his brow, and whispered words of love, that seemed to quiet him. Painstakingly she examined the rest of his body, finding bruises over his right thigh and hip, where he had landed on the deck, but detected no broken bones. She covered him again, adding another blanket. Not wanting to leave, but needing something for the pain, she went to look for the steward.

Coming out of the cabin, Monique met Captain McShane in the corridor. "Well, Madame, how is your husband doing?" he asked with concern, having conversed with Bradford, getting a most detailed and informative report.

"He isn't very good, I'm afraid, Captain," replied Monique, her concern quite evident on her beautiful face.

Her clothes were bloodstained and disheveled, and her hair was negligently tied back with a blue ribbon to keep the hair in tow, but loose tendrils were flying everywhere and the captain thought she looked absolutely charming. Mr. Deaveau was a very lucky man, and from what the steward was saying, she knew what she was doing.

"His breathing is very shallow, and his color isn't good. I'm sure he has several broken ribs. I need help in binding them, so he can be more comfortable, and a bottle of whiskey to ease the pain," she said, the rush of words coming out so fast that McShane had to smile to himself, realizing that the steward was correct. The little lady knew exactly what she wanted.

Together they entered the cabin and stepped over to the bed. McShane saw the delicate stitching on Erik's face and the bandage on his arm that wasn't covered by the blanket. He lifted the covers to take a look at Erik's ribs and decided that Monique was correct in her assumption, considering the labored breathing, and the pallor on his face. Her husband was very sick, and that didn't sit well with McShane, because he really liked this young man. He was a likeable and knowledgeable gentleman, who had stepped up and helped them out when they were in very dire straights. It would have taken many more days to accomplish what Erik had done in only two, and with their limited fuel supply, more time on the water could have spelled disaster in very tall letters.

"I'll send Bradford back with a bottle of whiskey. He will be more than happy to assist you. I think he's impressed with your knowledge of nursing," he replied, knowing that Bradford seemed almost smitten with the lovely lady, and it made him chuckle inside.

"Thank you, Captain. But I'm not a nurse. I just know how to take care of horses. I've stitched up many and have set their broken bones," she offered without a thought to how that might sound—a lady of station, knowing how to do such things.

The captain only smiled, "Well it doesn't really matter now does it, whether man or beast, the treatment seems to be the same!" With that he started for the door.

"How long will it take us to get to London," Monique asked, hoping to get Erik a doctor as soon as humanly possible.

"Well, that's our problem. We were blown considerably off course. We are hoping to land at Weymouth within a couple of days. The ship is making only 6 knots, which is only half of her usual speed, and Weymouth is a two day ride by carriage to London," he said, noting the concern in Monique's face at this information. "I'm sure Weymouth will have several fine doctors, and we will find one as soon as we land," he assured her.

"I just wish I had some medicine," she said.

"I wish we did also. I'll send Bradford back with the whiskey," McShane said, closing the door behind him.

The steward helped Monique pull Erik to a sitting position. Erik fought them at first, the pain so intense that he writhed in agony, but the effort cost him greatly, exhaustion rendering him only calm to the observer. Inside was a private hell of misery that was unlike any physical pain he had ever experienced. He felt their hands upon his body... not harsh, but demanding... making him do things that his mind rebelled at. It became harder and harder to breathe, like a tight band was encircling his chest until he thought he could not manage another breath on his own, yet when they finally stopped their torture and let him go, the pain amazingly eased to a more manageable level. Then they were at it again, forcing some vile liquid down his throat. It tasted like straight whiskey! He hated whiskey. Didn't she know that! A wife should know that, he thought, irritated at her actions! At first he refused to swallow, but she pinched his nose shut, forcing the fiery stuff downward, if he wanted to breath. They repeated this action half a dozen times, until Erik, fed up with this nonsense, spewed the stuff out of his mouth, making them stop.

"Oh, Erik, you are not helping matters," Monique cried, knowing he was awake, her displeasure obvious, even in her gentleness.

"I was... *not*... trying to help," he accused in a low raspy whisper, barely murmuring through clenched teeth. Finally they left him alone and he drifted back into the fog.

"He seems to be resting a bit easier," Bradford offered, noting that Erik's breathing had considerably improved.

"The binder is to give the ribs support and help ease the pain. The secret is not binding them so tightly as to cause a rib to puncture the lungs," Monique explained informatively. It was rarely used on horses, but she knew of one instance, and the filly had mended nicely. The idea of shooting horses instead of tending their wounds was just so barbaric. She was glad they didn't shoot people!

"Is there anything else you need? I could bring you a tray of food, and some more hot water to wash up" Bradford said, believing now that her husband was settled, maybe she could tend to herself. Not that she didn't look beautiful, but her clothes were a mess!

"Oh yes, that would be wonderful," Monique stammered, realizing for the first time that she looked a fright, and unconsciously her hands went to smooth down her wild, unruly hair.

"Coming right up," Bradford exclaimed, a big smile on his face as he went out the door.

Erik had drifted in and out of wakefulness, bouts of pain overtaking his senses, mingled with times where his body seemed to be floating. When awake the pain was tremendous, making him yearn for sleep to dull his mind, yet when he slept, his unconscious soul fought to be awake and in control. Thus the hours passed, two parts of his being warring one with the other, neither completely satisfied.

Erik heard a noise in the room. His body was fatigued, every muscle seemed to scream out with some level of pain, therefore he was not inclined to move. Laboriously, he tried to open his eyes. His left eye did not seem to function, but his right eye opened slowly. He tried to focus. At first everything was a cloudy blur, but steadily the room became clear. His eye roamed back and forth, trying to find her.

Monique sat on her trunk near the mirror, diligently pulling the tangles out of her thick damp hair. She had fretted over Erik's condition all night, and now with the dawn he was resting easier. That second administration of whiskey had finally allowed him to sleep. Not that he hadn't fought her tooth and nail to get him to swallow, draining the cup of misery to the dregs, but in the end she had managed to get enough inside, and out, to render him calm. He had slept on and off since then without moving. She had slipped from the room for only fifteen short minutes to care for her needs and wash her hair. Now she sat in a thin chemise, the cabin being hot, hoping to be presentable before Mr. Bradford, the steward, would bring the tea she had asked for at breakfast. She wanted to get something on Erik's stomach that would give him strength. Starve a cold and feed a fever was the saying! Well he didn't have a fever yet, and she wasn't taking any chances!

"You're beautiful… you know that?" Erik said, a raspiness to his voice, both from his dry throat and from the stirring of his passion. Monique whirled around at Erik's voice, her arms overhead as she swung her hair upward, wanting her neck free because of the heat. He thought she looked charming, her breasts pushed up, protruding forward, straining at the thin garment… enticing him even in his misery, and his loins involuntarily stirred under the covers.

She dropped the comb. "Erik, you're awake!" she exclaimed, thinking he would sleep a few more hours.

"Yes, *mon amour*, it is morning. Why wouldn't I be?" he answered irrationally, totally discounting his condition.

She came to the side of the bed, sitting down slowly, not wanting to jar the bunk. Laying a hand on his brow to assure herself that he was not running a fever, she gave a sigh of relief.

"And why do you sigh, my little witch?" he teased.

"Erik, you have broken bones," she said, arranging the covers under his chin.

"That seems apparent since I can't move," he said, noting how lovely she looked, as he drew deep into his nostrils, the clean scent of jasmine from her skin. Her chemise was unbuttoned well below the swell of her breasts and a groan escaped his lips. "At least that part which is voluntary can't move," he added, a sardonic grin spreading over his newly battered face.

Monique glanced up, thinking he was in pain, and seeing the grin, and digesting his words, looked down towards his loins. "Erik, you are impossible!" she screeched, appalled that even in misery, he could think about such things.

"Perhaps I need an ugly nurse, instead of one so tempting," he laughed, but the effort made him cough. Stabbing pain shot through his ribcage like a many sided rapier had just pierced between his ribs and struck his backbone, radiating its torture throughout his chest. His arms came up to hold against them, but the pain assaulting his entire body made him dizzy, and he pushed his head against the pillows as he writhed in agony. After several long moments, the pain subsided, and he was quiet once again.

"Oh, Erik, you must be reasonable," she chided, not knowing what to do for such intense pain. She had nothing to give him when the whiskey wore off.

"I will pretend you are ugly and keep my eyes closed," he said, trying to assure her that he was alright.

"If you don't behave, I'll blindfold you so you can't see!

"Well, I can hardly see as it is, but my nose isn't broken. You smell so-o-o good," again he smiled, but this time he refused to laugh.

"Erik, you are sick, and your injuries will take many days to mend. You must conserve your strength," she said, needing to persuade him against this tomfoolery.

"I am not sick, Monique. I'm merely resting, and I will be up and about by tomorrow. You will see that I am correct," he explained.

Thinking him again an irrational child, she said with placation, " Yes M'lord, we will definitely see."

There was a knock on the door and Monique grabbed her wrapper and went to answer it. Bradford had a tray of breakfast sconces, fruit, milk and tea. "Thank you so much," she said politely.

"Will there be anything else, M'lady," he asked, glancing at the bed. Erik was lying quiet, his eyes closed. "If there is anything you want, you just have someone find me. I'll check on you later to see if you need anything," he chirped, admiration obvious in his tone.

She placed the tray on the fold down table, and poured a cup of tea. Picking up a spoon, she sat on the bed beside Erik. He was lying back against several pillows that elevated his chest, making it easier to breathe than with lying flat.

"An admirer?" he asked in an all too jealous tone.

"Steward Bradford has been most kind in helping me make you comfortable," she said, dismissing Erik's tone as infantile.

"The one that helped torture me when pulling off my clothes. And tried to drown me with whiskey," he droned, more childish with every word he spoke.

"One in the same," she said, knowing it was useless to argue when he was in this kind of mood. "I want you to have some tea. You need something to build up your strength." With that she held a spoonful of tea to his mouth.

"I can't. One bite and I'll be emptying my stomach right in your lap," he said without ceremony.

"You have done that already," she smiled, knowing he would not remember.

A groan of embarrassment escaped his lips. "Well now you get my point," he said, refusing to open his mouth. But he stared at her, his one eye taking in every curve of her body with brazen amusement.

She was flustered by the way he looked at her. He was sick! He shouldn't be acting this way. Who was the nurse and who was the patient here? His attitude was juvenile, but his body was acting like pure, mindless, savage man. Did that bulge at his groin never cease? Her blue eyes looked deeply into his, and she leaned her body close enough to lightly touch him. They were once again playing a game and this time she was going to win. "Erik, I want you to open your mouth and take some tea," she coached softly, thinking there was more than one way to skin a cat.

He felt the heat of her body as she touched him and his nostrils flared. This was a deliberate and direct torment for a man, he thought, and he believed she knew it. Their contact was intoxicating. He closed his eye for only a moment at the frustration of not being able to take her into his arms, his mouth opening automatically as she commanded. Within moments the tea was gone from the cup and Monique sat with the grin of a satisfied Cheshire cat upon her lovely face.

"Happy now," he inquired, knowing she had won this round, but determined to win the fight. Within minutes, from the warmth of the tea and the exertion of their encounter, Erik was asleep.

Monique was able to get tea down Erik several more times, hopefully replenishing the fluids he had lost. He was still very weak, unable to stay awake more than a half hour at a time, sleeping hours in between. The day passed slowly, the heat making the cabin hot and sticky, even with the porthole open. She covered him with only a sheet, but he threw it off in his restlessness, and finally she just let him be, locking the door so no one would enter. Needing something to occupy her time, she rummaged thru Erik's trunk for the book he had started reading to her. She found the tin of salve he had smeared on her own wounds, thinking perhaps this would come in handy, and another small blue bottle. Taking a whiff, she almost gagged, the stuff smelling particularly vile, and she laid it aside to ask Erik what it was.

Monique was reading a funny group of sonnets, giggling at their humor, when she felt eyes staring at her. She looked up to find Erik awake. In his nakedness, his magnificently muscled body, battered and wrapped in bandages, blatantly showed an obvious need, but she had become accustom to this hunger he had for her, even in his pain.

Erik's piercing green eyes claimed hers with an unwavering gaze. He wanted her so badly. She was not a room's length away, and he could do nothing but stare. The lamp was low, and the room wafted of oil and wax on the breeze that blew gently through the porthole. These injuries were becoming one damn inconvenience. And he had one more need and didn't quite know how to ask.

Monique got up and covered Erik with a blanket, the heat of the day ended. "Erik, do you think you could eat something more substantial than tea?" she asked.

"I'm going to need...something..." he hesitated, a look of embarrassment on his face, his neck turning red.

"What do you need?" she asked, wanting to help in any way possible.

"Since I don't suppose I can make it to the watercloset, perhaps a jar would do," he supplied.

"Oh, Erik, I never thought about that. Why didn't you say something?" she said, embarrassed at overlooking that possibility.

"Well, I am now. What did you think would be the end result of all that tea forced upon me? It has taken its toll, my dear," he said, thinking her charming in her embarrassment, that blush to her face endearing, and taking his completely away.

She went for the door, saying over her shoulder, "I'll be right back." When she returned, she had a clear glass jar and handed it right to him, like nothing out of the ordinary was transpiring. She stood by the bed and waited.

Erik just stared at her! "Excuse me, but I have never done this in public," he said.

"Oh, Erik, don't be ridiculous, I've seen all of you," she chided.

"Not doing this, you haven't," he croaked, deciding that being bedridden had absolutely no benefits.

She smiled, and went to the door. "I've seen horses do it a hundred times," she said with a much too impish grin, and hearing him snort, she left the cabin to give him privacy.

When she returned, the jar was on the table beside the bed and Erik lay back with his eyes closed. "You could have found something less conspicuous," he murmured with sarcasm.

"For apple juice?" she laughed, and tucking the covers tight around his shoulders, left the cabin again.

When she returned about a half hour later, she had a tray of cheese, fruit and soup, with a bottle of wine tucked under her arm. Closely he studied her. Her hair was tied back in a ribbon with loose wisps flying about her face, one small clump falling into her eyes. She was wearing a pretty dress that buttoned down the front, and he could see by the outline of her curvaceous body that she had on only a light chemise beneath that peeked out the front, her dress unbuttoned alarmingly low, his mind instantly calculating *too low* to be wandering about the ship alone.

"Don't you think you should be wearing more clothes when you go on deck," he inquired with irritation, knowing he had openly stared at her during the repairs, as she helped serve the workers food and drink, thinking her figure was beautiful without those ridiculous corsets and bustles to obstruct his vision, but that was when he was able to protect her. Frustration was something he was quite familiar with, but right this moment it was eating at him with a punishing vengeance.

"What?" she questioned. "Erik, don't be silly. I have dressed like this for several days and you didn't seem to mind before," she said, thinking he could pass from the sublime to the ridiculous in nary an instant.

"I wasn't helpless in bed. I can't protect you this way," he said, his voice rising as his anger escalated at his accursed situation.

"Erik, calm down. I'm not in any danger. And if I were, there are plenty of people that would see to my safety," she answered with reason.

"Oh, like your steward," he snorted with annoyance.

"And Captain McShane, Mr. Crocket and Mr. Wheaton. And I can think of several others in the kitchen. Oh, Erik, you are being unreasonable," she sighed. She had become tolerant of his possessive moods, even flattered by them, but again he was acting like a spoiled child, but she was far too wise to mention it. She would blame it on his confinement in bed, knowing he would not tolerate it long, but unfortunately at the present time, he had no real choice in the matter.

Erik folded his arms over his chest. He hated to grovel, but he wanted to kiss her. She was driving him out of his mind, being so close, yet so far. He watched her as she set the tray on the table and opened the wine.

"Will you eat some soup? It will give you more strength than tea," she told him, hoping that he wouldn't defy her with his stubbornness.

"I would rather have the wine," he bulked, knowing his stomach rumbled, and he could smell the delicious aroma of the soup, but he needed some leverage. He liked pulling her chain.

"The soup will do you more good," she pleaded, knowing this would be another battle.

"One spoonful for a kiss," he bargained, his voice so much a whisper, that she almost did not hear him.

"Okay, one spoonful for a kiss," she said evenly, making no sign of being surprised.

She laid down the small spoon and picked up a large one. He swallowed the broth she offered in one large gulp, then looked at her in anticipation. She leaned over and gave him a quick kiss on the lips. Again she raised the spoon to his mouth.

"That wasn't a kiss," he complained, thinking he was cheated.

"What do you mean that wasn't a kiss? Of course it was a kiss," she said, trying her best to keep a serious face.

"It wasn't the kind of kiss I was thinking about," he said, his self control waning, wanting to grab her with his good arm, but she was on the opposite side of the bed and she had hot soup in her hands, and if she spilled it, it would burn that part of his anatomy that he would rather not injure. He swallowed the soup again.

This time when she leaned in for a kiss, his left arm came up to the back of her head, holding her lips against his. Savoring the kiss, he opened her mouth with his tongue, a groan of pure pleasure coming from deep in his chest as he did so, his tongue exploring hers. He took the soup out of her hands, setting it on the bed, and encircled her body with his arms,

"I have wanted to do this for two days, *mon amour*," he said, kissing her hair and then her ear, his moist lips grazing against her cheek, as his fingers played in her hair at the nape of her neck. He drew her close until her breasts touched against him, wanting her, needing her. She rested her head against his neck, pressing her warm mouth to his skin, lightly tasting him with her tongue.

"Erik, you are too weak for this," she pleaded, knowing that he needed to conserve his energy.

"Would you deny a dying man his last wish," he said with a faint, but husky laugh.

"Do not joke, Erik, you are not dying. That isn't even funny," she said stupidly at his ridiculous banter.

" I feel like I'm dying when I can't make love to you," he said, drawing his hands up and down her back, feeling the curve of her hips, bringing his hands forward to capture her breasts, noting the erect nipples beneath her clothes. He wanted to go further, but he could already feel his strength receding. Her hand rested innocently on his left thigh to steady herself, and he groaned, feeling the pleasure of her touch, as his loins were set on fire, stirring his need against her hand. He closed his eyes in sweet torture, and leaned back into the pillows in frustration, swearing out loud at his inability to do what he wanted.

"Erik, it will come in time. For now you need your rest," she said, giving him a very lingering kiss upon his mouth, one that made him raise his arm to pull her closer, but she gently slipped from his grasp, and he groaned again.

"I don't want to rest," he said, knowing she was right, but not wanting to be defeated.

"You are such a non-compliant patient," she said.

"Oh...and how many patients have you had," he asked, his mouth twisted in a smile.

"I have cared for many horses," she said smugly.

Erik snorted, "Horses again...that's a comfort."

Monique picked up the small blue bottle she had found in Erik's trunk and brought it to the bed. "What is this?" she asked, holding the bottle out for him to see.

"It is laudanum, *ma petite.* A very potent pain killer and sedative that is very dangerous. One drop will make one of your horses sleep for a month," he exaggerated.

"I wish I'd know about it before," she mumbled. "You wouldn't have gone through so much pain, if I had," she exclaimed, knowing she'd use it if it became necessary.

"Do not think of giving me that stuff, *ma cherie,*" Erik warned cautiously. "I do not need sleep that badly. One drop is enough to put a man down for half a day. I do not want to be drugged and helpless," he stressed vehemently. He closed his eyes, his voice starting to drift off as the exertion upon his body began to take its toll.

Monique tidied up the room, took the tray back to the kitchen after eating some supper herself, then snuggled into the bed beside Erik, being careful not lean against him in sleep. But he felt her presence, and with his quiet insistence, she moved closer, resting against his right side, her head in the crook of his shoulder. Together they slept a more peaceful sleep.

Chapter Fourteen

Monique could feel the heat steaming off her body like baking in the hot sun. The cabin was stifling, and her nightgown, tangled about her waist in sleep, was drenched from that salty sweat that only the beams of that scorching golden orb could bring forth, yet it was still night. Her right arm lay across Erik's upper chest, coming to rest against his neck, avoiding his ribs. He had insisted upon holding her near with his right arm, and she had finally consented, knowing she was the drug that somehow dulled his pain. She had positioned her thigh across his for comfort, and he had not objected, more that he had given forth a deep sigh of relief that she would stay close and not leave him alone. But now, awaking from a hazy dream she could barely remember, in which she was fighting with a man whose face she could not distinguish, she was quickly aware that something was wrong. She heard Erik mumbling, thrashing his head about, his entire body jerking in sleep, jarring her quite oddly awake. She felt his chest and then his cheek with the palm of her hand, the emanating heat threatening to incinerate her instantly. She leaped out of bed, turning the oil lamp up so she could examine her patient. His face had an ashen look, even as his body glowed red with fever, and his breathing was alarmingly shallow. His entire body was bathed in a deep sweat, large beads of perspiration covering his skin. First she checked the binder protecting his ribs, but it seemed to be in place, and then she noticed the bandage on his forearm. It was soaked with a dark yellow drainage that was creeping to the edges of the compress.

When she moved his arm to get a closer look at the wound, Erik cried in anguish, thrashing about in obvious pain, even with her gentle touch. As carefully as possible, she unwrapped the binding and removed the bandage. What she saw made her gasp in fear, a knot forming deep in her stomach as an alarm rang in her head with a sickening sound. The edges of the wound were an angry scarlet red, its borders straining to be released from the stitching. The area around the injury was shiny, the skin stretched so taut, if it had burst, she wouldn't have been surprised. But what struck fear in her heart were the dark red streaks climbing up Erik's arm towards his shoulder. She had to bring his fever down, and if she could not contain the infection, Erik would loose his arm, and perhaps his life.

She tried to make her mind think. What had she done in the past? Horses were one thing, but when it came to Erik, it was hard to function. She willed herself to take a deep breath! A local infection called for the application of heat. It seemed ludicrous at first to think of subjecting Erik's body to more, when he was already so terribly hot, but the wound must first be soaked to soften it, and then thoroughly cleaned. She rightly reasoned that there must have been splinters of wood left within the injury to cause it to fester. Quickly she set about her work. Pulling on a sturdy wrapper and tying her hair back like she meant business, she went to the kitchen for boiling water. As she entered, Marta was busy taking some sconces out of the oven for breakfast. Marta took one look at Monique, with tears springing from her sad blue eyes, and came rushing over.

"Oh, deary, it can't be as bad as all that," she crooned, wiping the flour off her hands onto her white apron. "Is that man of yours doing poorly? I heard he was awake and talking, and feeling a wee bit better," she said in a hopeful note. She came around the large butcher table to put her arms around Monique's shoulder.

Monique, not accustom to showing emotions in front of strangers, was so distraught she couldn't help herself. She immediately broke down in deep sobs. "Erik is running a high fever, and the wound on his arm is infected. He's going to die. I just know it. He needs a doctor and medicine, and…" she cried, hiccupping in her distress, the words coming out so fast, she could hardly take a breath.

"No, no, he isn't going to die," Marta chided. "You stop talking such nonsense. He is a strapping young man, that husband of yours, and I'll bet as strong as an ox," she said, leading Monique to a tall stool to sit down, and turning her head, she told Angus, one of the kitchen boys, to put on a kettle of water, and then to go break open a new barrel of ice.

"Ice!" Monique squeaked. "You have some ice on board?" She looked into Marta's face like she had just said the magic word that could possibly save Erik's life.

"Well, of course we do! It is put in barrels and packed in shaved wood chips to keep it from melting. That's how we keep the prepared food from spoiling," Marta said, laying a stack of towels within two bowls and put them on a tray.

"Oh, Marta, could we use some to pack Erik's body in to bring down his fever?" she asked, hardly believing this stoke of luck. She just had never thought about the possibility. Suddenly she felt some better.

"Honey, that young man of yours is kind of a hero around here, he is. We'd be floating heavens knows where without his help and all of us know it. At least those that have any sense about them know," she finished, and Monique knew at once she was talking about those passengers that seemed to be oblivious that anything out of the ordinary was happening when repairs were being made, demanding this and demanding that, like there hadn't been a storm that had ripped apart the only thing that was keeping them afloat and from drowning. Marta was a middle-aged woman who was in charge of the kitchen help, but she did some of the cooking also. She was kind of pretty in a rough sort of way, with chestnut brown hair that she tied up in a bun, and Monique had liked her immediately.

Suddenly the whistle on the kettle made its sing-song melody and Monique jumped, knowing she needed to get back to Erik. As she lifted the kettle and started to leave the kitchen, Marta was right on her heels with a tray of supplies. Marta threw a few words in Angus' direction…to get about six small blocks of ice ready for when she called. Monique looked back, questioning her actions with a perplexed expression. "Well, you didn't think I'd let you go back and tend that young man all by yourself, did you deary? I know a thing or two about taking care of the sick and injured, and figure a second hand could come in handy," she said, smiling at Monique who looked about to cry again, but this time out of deep appreciation.

When they entered the cabin, Erik looked positively terrible. He had shifted to his right side and drawn his knees up slightly towards his chest. His wig had come off and most of his face was buried in the mattress. He was shaking violently! Monique ran to the bed.

"Erik! You are shaking! We have got to warm you," she cried. She got another blanket immediately, and laid it over him.

He raised his head only long enough to look at her, "I'm so cold," he said. His teeth were chattering and he gritted them, his lips parted, but even that small effort cost him, again letting his head fall back upon the pillow, unable to say more.

She stroked his hair, damp from sweat, and murmured words to soothe him, kissing his cheek. This seemed to help, and some of the shaking subsided. Then she looked at Marta. "He's in shock. He can't possibly be cold, its simply stifling in here. The shivering is just that his nerves are raw from the pain. I need to redress the wound on his arm. It needs to have the infection cleaned out." She said this so factually and business- like, that Marta realized Monique was once again in control of her emotions. Now that she had her attentions directed towards Erik, she would be okay.

Together they set about their task. Marta prepared hot water in a bowl at Monique's request and soaked some towels. Monique set on the edge of the bed, her back to Erik, with his arm on her lap, staring at the bulging wound. Placing a hot folded towel against the wound, she waited.

"Where did you learn to sew like that, deary?" Marta inquired, a bit fascinated that this young lass had stitched up her own husband.

Monique laughed, thankful for the moment to have something to laugh about. "Oh, my father taught me to stitch up horses. Erik wasn't at all impressed that he is my first human patient," she explained, seeing Marta's eyes get a bit wide with this information, yet she gave Monique a very genuine smile.

"Well, I'd say he's a lucky man to have you for a nurse, knowing all you do and such," she offered, thinking this little lass had a lot of spunk in her petite little body.

Removing the towel, Monique examined the softened area, and began the job of removing the stitches. She worried her bottom lip with her teeth, biting into the flesh, as Erik stirred behind her, the act of her administrations causing him considerable pain. But she didn't stop in what she knew had to be done.

"Don't be worrying none. I'll be holding him still, if need be," Marta suggested, already leaning her body over Erik's legs that had shifted in his pain, bumping against Monique as she did her most tedious work.

As Monique cut the stitching open, pulling the threads out one at a time, those restraints that had held the wound together, thick yellow pus streaked with blood, oozed out, running down Erik's skin onto the towel beneath his arm. And on the towel, she saw a few specks of wood. "I knew I didn't get all the splinters out," she mumbled absently, to no one in particular.

"I'd say you did the best you could," Marta said, knowing Monique was beating herself up for not creating a minor miracle.

"Well, I guess I'll just wash it out good, and try it again, and hope for the best," she said, knowing that right now, that was all she could do. "But this time I have something to put into the wound," she said with more enthusiasm.

While Marta held a basin of hot water beneath Erik's arm, Monique washed out the deep gash half a dozen times with hot water, pouring a liberal amount of liquor over the wound, the bone evident deep within its depth. But this time she filled the opening with the salve from the little silver tin. Lastly, she once again sewed the edges of the wound together, but not tightly and more sparingly, so if more infection built up, it could drain out. It would leave a much more ugly scar, but to her it didn't matter. She'd rather Erik had another horrible mark upon his body, but his life spared.

Before leaving the room to fetch Angus and the ice, Marta helped Monique get Erik comfortable in bed. It pleased Monique that Marta did not flinch away from the appearance of Erik's face, or that part of his head that had no hair, when together they managed to pull him straight in the bed. He moaned, not wanting to move, and cried out in misery when they insisted, trying to push their arms away, but the effort was too much for his fever-ravaged body. Finally, he slipped back into that state where the body will not respond, but the mind can hear.

"It's too bad you have nothing for the pain," Marta commented sadly, thinking it such a shame to be caught so long upon the water without a doctor.

"Oh, but indeed I do," said Monique, a spark of excitement in her voice at her newfound discovery. "Erik was quite adamant about not wanting to take it, but Erik for the moment is not the one in control. I am!" she said with some amount of satisfaction in her tone. "And I plan on making some of that pain go away," she said. "I didn't want to use it until I was sure his breathing was less shallow, for it will undoubtedly make it even more so, but he seems to be resting better, in spite of the fever. I suppose releasing that infection may have helped somewhat. Right now he needs rest, and this should help that along," Monique exclaimed, holding up the small blue bottle of laudanum.

She put just one drop in a spoonful of red wine and put it to Erik's lips, opening his mouth with her gentle fingers, and slipped the spoon inside. He coughed a little, knowing this was something he did not want to do, but not knowing why, and in spite of himself, swallowed the red liquid easily. "Thank goodness I didn't have to fight him this time. I don't think I have the strength for it," she laughed lightly, looking at Marta. "Erik can be such a child when he wants to be," she said.

"Honey, all men are just overgrown children. They talk big and thank goodness provide for us, and become our protectors when necessary, but underneath, they just need the comfort of our loving arms to keep them safe. Just like our children do," she offered wisely, thinking that this was a very strange couple indeed, but there was something oddly intriguing about them both, and she had liked them from the very beginning. Angus came to the door, and brought in the 6 blocks of ice. They wrapped them in oilskin and packed them around Erik's body. There was nothing more to be done but wait.

Erik's body raged with fever all day and into the night. The heat of the day again kept the cabin stifling, and the ice melted quickly as the cabin began to heat up, no breeze coming in through the porthole. Marta and Angus brought fresh ice twice throughout the day, and sent a tray of food along with Bradford, who also checked in to see if she needed anything. Monique went from trying to catch a small catnap while Erik slept, to soothing him when he became restless. In his delirium, he would become angry with incoherent ramblings which seemed to possess him, yelling out broken sentences that contained a jumble of words that didn't make any sense…hideous gargoyle, gypsies, murder and the name Christine. At other times he was almost lucid, his demeanor quieter, and he would murmur in a low melodious voice that sounded sensual and seductive, and she was positive she heard the phrase…angel of music. What were all these ramblings, and what did they mean? Who were they directed to, and what did they mean to him? Only one thing kept her from falling into the abyss of despair throughout the worrisome hours of his illness, and that was his continuous repeating of her name. When she was near enough to touch him, and he had any strength, he involuntarily clutched at her, murmuring her name, like he needed reassurance that she would not vanish with his inability to remain awake. At these times she caressed him, sitting behind him, holding him against her body. She held his scarred face against her breast, smoothed back his hair, and kissed the top of his head. He didn't seem so fierce and mysterious now. He was more like a little boy—that overgrown child that Marta talked about, who needed her to love him—to take all those hurts away, that for whatever reason, the world had inflicted upon him. Long after the sun had set, and cool breezes blowing across the water had entered the cabin, lowing the temperature, Erik once again returned to the world of the living, wrapped in Monique's loving arms.

He remembered the most bazaar dreams. They had filled his senses with hatred and melancholy, yet finally serenity and hope. And it had seemed like a lifetime. Slowly he opened his eyes. The room was dark! A fresh breeze came in through the porthole, blowing a refreshing scent of ocean aroma into the air. There was just enough moonlight to see everything outlined within the room, each article a black and white relief of different shades of gray. Erik could hear the steady beating of Monique's heart against his right ear, her breathing slow and steady, and he knew she was asleep. He picked up the arm that lay over his shoulder, her hand upon his chest and kissed the palm lightly, his tongue unable to deny itself from darting out and flicking its moistness thrice upon its curvature, and then down her wrist, where he placed a long lingering kiss. Only slightly, she stirred.

He lifted himself upright slowly, taking efforts not to wake her. Holding his left arm tightly against his ribs, he sat on the side of the bed, a feeling of dizziness overtaking him immediately. For a few moments he waited. Carefully he inched his tall body over the side, and into a standing position, and walked the few steps to his trunk. Bending slowly to open it, he pulled out a pair of black britches, and leaning heavily against the wall, managed to painfully lift one leg after the other. He couldn't believe how hard it was to do one simple task. It was as if the britches had a mind of their own, twisting back and forth at will, and it was no easy feat that Erik finally managed sliding the pants over his slim hips, and into some semblance of modesty, not even bothering to button the fly. Silently he padded in bare feet across the floor. He slipped quietly into the corridor and down to the watercloset.

When Monique awoke, she literally was in a panic. Erik was gone! She quickly jumped from the bed, not understanding how he could have gone anywhere, and without her noticing, realizing she had been more than tired to sleep so heavily. He was just too weak to have slipped out right from under her nose! Grabbing her heavy cape, she threw open the door, letting it slam against the wall negligently, and ran down the corridor to the watercloset. She knocked on both doors, but there was no answer from either one. Without another thought, she ran out onto the deck. Low hanging oil lamps were strung on hooks, casting the empty decks in an eerie light that silhouetted dark shadows along the deck's planking, of the hog-chains and the huge beam that towered above the pilothouse. Monique looked toward the bow, but the deck was empty. When she glanced astern, she could see Erik's tall figure leaning against the railing, staring down at the huge paddle wheel churning frothy water in its wake and into the dark waters beyond. She ran to his side in relief.

"Erik," she cried, nearly out of breath, from both exertion and fright. "Why are you out of bed?"

"I just needed some fresh air, and to be upright on my own two feet," he admitted solemnly, like it was nothing out of the ordinary that he should do so.

"Erik, you have been very ill. I wish you would come back to the cabin," she coached, sliding an arm around his, and giving it a gentle tug.

"And what do I get, if I were to honor that wish," he said, feeling more dizzy than he could possibly have imagined, yet hoping that once his body were horizontal, he would surely regain some strength, unwilling even in misery to admit his mistake.

Monique thought about that a moment before answering. Erik had to be weak. She couldn't imagine how he was standing right here before her, acting as if he had not been sick at all. She suspected he was just putting on a front, trying to show her he was stronger than he actually was to once again gain control. "Erik, you can have anything that you want, if you just come back to bed," she answered sweetly, knowing he would be exhausted as soon as he hit the pillow.

"Alright, M'lady, if you will assist me, we will return to our quarters," he said lightly, but inside his brain, it was beyond his comprehension how he was going to manage even one step, let alone make it down that long corridor. But he was bound and determined not to let Monique see his pain, or what it had cost him to be so foolish. Each step was torture, his body so weak that he closed his lips and gritted his teeth in silence, willing himself not to utter a sound. His ribs didn't hurt all that much due to the solid binding, but the non-use of his muscles made every single one he seemed to own, scream at him in rebellion, but it was the dizziness in his head that made him feel strangely faint. He must at all cost, make it to the cabin. He could not embarrass himself by falling flat on his face. This whole business of being out of control simply chafed at his nerves. He was a fastidious man about his person, for obvious reasons, who did things just so, especially where his personal habits were concerned, and having to expose himself to heavens knows what during the last few days, just grated at his sense of privacy. He held on to Monique tighter than he realized, her arm around his waist, grateful even in his unacknowledged stupidity that she had come to help him. Silently they made their way to their stateroom, and when Erik finally sat down on the bed, he gave a genuine sigh of relief.

"Oh, Erik," Monique cried in exasperation. "Why are you so foolish. You could have hurt yourself."

"But I didn't, ma petite," he said, realizing that he hadn't totally fooled her, but he was immediately distracted by the incredibly lovely picture she presented to his starving eyes.

"You were lucky that you did not fall right over that rail and into the sea," she said, only half-heartedly mad, just relived that she had him back in bed.

He pulled himself back against the pillows, and studied her serious face, his eyes roaming over her brazenly as she busied herself, tucking the covers meticulously around him like he might break. The thought came to mind that she was too serious, as she chewed on her bottom lip in concentration. It was those little things that he caught her doing that totally fascinated him. He relished in watching her unguarded actions, when she didn't know it! Her facial expressions when she was doing something particular, or the way she tackled a task, no matter how meager, made his fever rise for another reason, and he could think of the perfect medicine he needed to make it all better!

And she was so indescribably beautiful, that it stirred his loins even through his pain. She had removed her heavy cape, and only her thin nightgown remained, its material so shear that he could easily see the outline of her body beneath. Lovely firm breasts with rosy, taut peaks strained at the material, the sleek lines of her torso disappearing down into that region that his entire body longed to encompass, and he was positive that the dizziness remaining was due to his most basic and primal need to love her. Finally, he spoke out of the shear necessity of resolving that issue, "I don't sleep in my clothes, love," he reminded her casually.

"Well give them over, and I'll fold them, and lay them in your trunk." she said absently, not catching the dark smoldering eyes that sought her every move with the elemental candor of pure lust.

"I don't think I have the strength to take them off myself," he said without moving. "Could you help me?"

"Erik, I knew this would happen," she said. "I told you this foolishness of yours would take all your strength. The very idea of going on deck alone was..." She had pulled the covers back and started to unbutton his britches, tugging them down as she did so, and his swollen flesh jumped right out into her hand.

He grabbed her shoulders before she could react, pulling her into his arms. "Well most of my strength has left me, but not all of it," he said in the most husky, sensual voice she had heard in days, and it immediately melted her heart. His eyes devoured hers with a boldness that took the breath right out of her body, arousing immediately every nerve fiber she possessed to a fine pitch that screamed possessively for his magic touch. He pulled her clothed body onto his lap, the thinness of her nightgown neither impeding the feel of her backside against the object of his need, nor shielding his desire for her. He kissed her hard and long, his tongue mingling with hers, making her dizzy also, and her arms came around his neck like she had done it for a hundred years. She leaned back in surrender against his right arm, but he did not feel the dull pain that lingered, the pulse in his neck and chest beating so wildly that time simply stood still within his mind. Her teeth and tongue nipped at the flesh of his neck and ear, even as his left hand slipped under her nightgown, seeking that part of her being that he wanted not only to inflame, but from where she would scream for release. His fingers found her wet and wanting, stroking her desire till she cried out his name, then probing into that place where his own pulsing flesh desired to be set free. He lifted her up and around to face him, straddling her across his body as he lay back against the pillows, his chest raised against the headboard.

"I need you, Monique, but I'm too weak to do much on my own. Please, love me!" he choked out, his breath coming out so slow, that she was sure he was in pain.

"Erik, your pain. We can wait until later," she whispered softly.

"The pain is from wanting you so badly, that my mind screams for our union. The pain is not of my body, but of my soul. Everything else pales against it," he said, his eyes becoming moist. "Please, please, believe me." He said it so wretchedly, that she knew he told her the truth. He needed her once again to heal him, but not in the physical way. In a way that she knew would take many days of reassurance, and years to heal. But as far as she was concerned, she had a lifetime.

"I do believe you, Erik," she said. He lifted her up slowly, helping her sheath his searching sword within her body, a groan of pleasure coming from deep in his chest as their bodies united. She loved him as he barely moved, setting his skin on fire with a fever that was most welcome, not missing any part of his body that was within her reach, and when their bodies were screaming for release, together they created a slow, but penetrating rhythm, that although not long and not rough, brought them climaxing together in mutual satisfaction. Neither one spoke, not wishing to dissolve the moment, silently slipping into slumber, the horrible events of the last few days culminating in a restful sleep that would hopefully bring a brighter day!

Chapter Fifteen

Sir Percy Langford stood impatiently in the stairwell of the lower deck, fidgeting from one foot to the other as he waited for Jules Madison to show his simpleton's face at his friend's bidding. Why was Jules always late? Percy thought of himself as quite the dashing rogue where the ladies were concerned, but if the truth were known, he was neither a titled gentleman, nor particularly liked by the female gender. He was the third son of Lord Tensley Langford, who had proved himself most unsuitable for a title of bearing, dying a pauper after submitting to the unhealthy pastime of excessive gambling and liquor. Percy had been forced to fend for himself at an early age, and had followed in his father's rather unwise footsteps with rapid succession, squandering the small inheritance that had been held in his name since his birth. This, of course, had sunk him into a most grievous situation immediately, with a long list of debt collectors always hot on his trail. But he planned to change all that! At present he lived a rather meager existence in private, presenting himself as a gentleman of means on the surface, pursuing the ladies in earnest. His only recourse was to catch himself a titled female companion with a considerable inheritance. Thus was his sole purpose of taking voyages back and forth across the Channel on a regular basis, upon the likely chance of landing such a coveted prize.

Jules came sauntering down the stairs at a leisurely pace, a half-eaten muffin in his hand. Its remains could be seen within, as he chewed with his mouth open, the crumbs splattered over his wrinkled shirtfront, which stuck out alarmingly from his bulging belly. He grinned stupidly at Percy, ignoring his friend's increasing frown.

"I told you to come straight away, Jules, not to lollygag around getting your breakfast," Percy admonished, exasperation clearly showing on his effeminate features.

"You never said I couldn't eat first," Jules argued innocently, never one to be far away from the comfort of food.

"Well, now that you're finally here, did you find out anything?" he inquired, having asked Jules yesterday to keep an ear tuned for hearsay in the galley that pertained to that man in the mask or his wife. Jules, being in love with food as he was, always made it a point to make friends with all the kitchen staff of any establishment that he and Percy might decide to frequent regularly.

"I don't know what you are wanting to know about them, Percy. And I didn't rightly hear nothing very important, except the man is doing rather poorly," Jules offered reluctantly. He didn't know much, but sometimes he just didn't think everything Percy was up to was exactly proper!

"I know what I'm talking about, you dolt! That article in the Review , I was telling you about, was a really big deal. It said some guy burned down an opera house in Paris. And I'm not mistaking that it mentioned he wore some kind of mask!" he said with conviction in his voice, hoping that Jules had found out more than he was telling.

"Could have been anyone, Percy," Jules indicated, not believing that someone who had committed such a crime would just be walking around in broad daylight.

"We ought to at least get the authorities to investigate it. And just as soon as we make land! There was also the mention of a possible murder," Percy said a bit heatedly, trying to convince his friend of the merits of his newest idea, a hair-brained scheme for his own personal advantage. Sometimes Jules could be so dense!

"I don't know! Mr. Devereau seems like a fine gentleman to me. The crew has been talking an awful lot about how grateful they are for his help in repairing their boat. You can't just go around accusing people," he said, thinking Percy was a little daft at times.

"You can't be too cautious, you know. He might actually be dangerous! I'm going straightaway to the police. You saw him playing that organ the other night. That article said the man was also an accomplished musician," Percy said, thinking that this one fact alone was convincing in itself.

"Mr. Devereau might be all that, but it seems to me he acts more like an engineer. He probably just plays for the fun of it." Jules said, stuffing the last bit of muffin into his mouth, chewing with vigor.

"Well you don't have to come with me, but I'm not letting this go, you big ox," he said, slapping Jules on the shoulder with his gloves. "He's been getting just a bit too much attention around here. The entire crew will stop singing his praises if I have anything to say about it. It's really just too much! Why should a guy that looks like *that* get all the glory?" Percy mumbled, irritation for the man clearly plastered on his face.

"From what I hear, he's stove up too bad to do anyone any harm right now," Jules offered helpfully. "Why don't you just let the guy be."

"Well, that's all the better, now isn't it? He won't be getting out of here too hastily then, will he? And that little wife of his might just need some looking after while her husband is detained for awhile by the authorities," Jules said smiling, a very smug expression showing quite knowingly upon his arrogant face.

"Oh! So now I get it. You've had your eye on that pretty lady ever since they came aboard. You don't really think that guy has anything to do with what happened in Paris, do you Percy?" Jules said in disgust. Percy was a good friend, but there were times when he wondered exactly why he tolerated his shenanigans.

"Well, that would be absurd now, wouldn't it? Of course I don't. But it sure gives me a right good reason to make that pretty lady's acquaintance. I'm sure she would thank me many times over and in a very nice way, I'm thinking," he said with a suggestive wink to his friend. "I know she won't miss that ugly husband of hers. Probably got stuck with him through some silly arranged marriage and is despising every moment of it. And I'll be right there, all helpful and all, to console her," he finished. "Are you with me or not?" He shot Jules a glance that said he meant business.

"With you for what?" Jules said, staring at his friend in bewilderment.

A shadow was seen just overhead and the soft click of a door, clamping Percy's mouth shut, as he and his friend moved their conversation to their private quarters.

Morning brought forth a sky that was overcast and ugly, ominous gray clouds hanging low, threatening to spill buckets of water upon those beneath. A chilling dampness hung in the air, making a body shiver with the penetrating cold that went straight for the bones. This particular morning, as the *La Benta* limped slowly towards port, all her passengers were more than happy to remain indoors, whether to relish the comfort of their own warm cabins on such a nasty day, or to partake of the food and entertainment supplied in the two salons.

Erik seemed to have had a more restful night with less noticeable tossing about in pain, and no rambling in his sleep that

Monique could remember. She had awakened to find him unmoving, his face turned towards her, his right hand beneath his head. Lying cloistered within the protection of his right shoulder, she slipped carefully from the bed, trying not to awaken him. Looking down at his face, his long dark eyelashes brushing against his skin, shielding those penetrating green orbs from her view while he slept, it made her catch her breath, tears springing to her eyes with the thought that she had almost lost him. It was still hard for her to believe he wanted her to become his wife. His real wife! Not just the one that he pretended her to be. He seemed to need her in sickness and in health. Wasn't that the way it was suppose to be? And there lovemaking was glorious, making her blush right down to the roots of her hair, thinking about the things she would allow him to do! She stifled a giggle. Morning, noon or night…it seemed to make no difference to him. When he wanted her, he wouldn't be denied, even when she knew his pain was severe, whether it was prudent or not. Not that she was inclined to refuse, for those looks he always afforded her were most persuasive in nature, melting her right in her tracks. He had yet to tell her about his past, circumstances putting that for the moment out of sight, out of mind, but when the time came, it would make no difference. She knew that she could not possibly live without him! Silently she dressed, stopping first at the watercloset to attend to her own needs, then visiting the kitchen to find something nourishing for Erik for breakfast. Come "hell or high water," one of her father's favorite saying, she was determined to help him regain his strength, and no matter what he thought about the fare of food she might chose, Erik was going to eat it. She was certain of that!

Upon hearing her leave, Erik had also risen, although much slower than usual, still feeling a distinct weakness from too many days in bed, and not particularly liking its hampering effects. This put him at a disadvantage immediately, bringing about an irritating mood from the onslaught. He managed to get partially dressed with some difficulty, when there was a rap on the door, and Erik went to answer it with his irritation at the forefront, thinking it was probably that steward again, wanting to know if Monique was in *need.* He swung the portal wide, more abrupt than necessary, dressed only in a pair of tight black britches and his wig, saying rather hastily, "My wife doesn't need anything." Captain McShane stood towering in the doorway, an amused expression on his face.

"I came to inquire about your welfare, Erik," McShane said with genuine interest, as well as amusement. "May I come in?" he asked, stepping his large frame through the doorway before Erik had a chance to answer. He had taken to calling Erik by his given name that first morning after the storm, when within the pilothouse, they had poured over countless detailed drawings Erik had made quite hastily, yet accurately, discussing matters dealing with the repairs of his ship. Erik on the other hand continued to give McShane the due respect he was entitled to as captain of this vessel, by addressing him as Captain McShane only.

"I understand that you are on the mend, and I'm glad to hear it. Can't say that we weren't all a bit worried there for several days," McShane said, stating a fact as true as he saw it. "The entire crew was kept abreast of your progress, and a few helped your misses with your care" he said, quite satisfied that many had been more than willing to help, yet he was also making light conversation, having actually come for an entirely different reason.

Erik was rightfully taken aback that anyone had been worried about his welfare, unaccustomed to such behavior from the masses, and blushed with embarrassment at this new feeling, not knowing exactly what to answer in return. Therefore he said nothing.

"The ship seems to be functioning quite well under the circumstances, and most of the thanks for that goes to you," the captain said without any hesitation.

Not wanting to take that kind of credit, knowing there were many people involved, Erik was quick to answer. "I believe there were quite a number of other people involved in her repairs, Sir," Erik offered, realizing without a doubt that he had the help of some very eager and dedicated members of the crew.

"Yes, and I appreciate them also, but without your knowledge to put this pretty lady back together, we'd still be floating out there somewhere," McShane said, making it sound like they were helpless without his expertise. "I'm just thankful you were aboard, my boy," he finished, noting the uneasiness that Erik displayed, thinking for some reason, praise was not an easy thing for this commanding man to swallow. In another situation they would certainly be equals, and therefore it was not hard to understand that concept.

"When might we expect to dock?" Erik asked, his embarrassment not yet quelled at this unfamiliar praise. Not only was he anxious to be back on track for getting to London, but most assuredly to be out of this blasted confinement. He was not a man to sit around idle for very long, and this was grating on his nerves with profound vengeance.

"We are steaming along at about half her usual pace, but making very good progress despite everything. I figure we should make port in Weymouth sometime after dark. We were blown off course and plan to dock at our home port. Hard to pinpoint the exact hour that might be, with the cross winds so uncertain this time of the year, and this weather so threatening," he offered, needing to find a way to broach his next subject.

Erik seemed deep in thought about what he had said, so McShane plunged ahead. "It has come to my attention that there are a couple of rascals aboard that are up to mischief. They are frequent passengers, and probably harmless, but I believe they could stir up trouble that would cause you time and perhaps embarrassment, and I do not want that to happen," McShane explained to Erik.

Erik immediately stiffened at McShane's words, his eyes taking on a defensive look that was not lost to the captain. "What kind of trouble are you talking about," Erik asked cautiously, alarm suddenly overtaking his entire senses.

"One of my loyal crew members overheard these two rascals talking about an incident that happened in Paris some weeks back regarding a masked man burning down an opera house. They know rightly that this is not you, but the one passenger in particular is a scoundrel and a bounder that preys upon unsuspecting women, and he has a fancy for your wife. It is his intention to alert the authorities about your presence upon landing, to make enough trouble for you that would undeniably get you detained for a number of days, and give himself the advantage of making her acquaintance, no doubt offering his assistance," he said quite frankly, without disguising the particulars.

Caught totally unawares with this unbelievable situation, the veins in Erik's neck stood out with a telling anger as his flushed face displayed a kaleidoscope of emotions that started with pure rage, and ended with an expression of total and undeniable menace towards these two individuals, his gleaming sea green eyes not at all unreadable to the captain, but all Erik could manage to say was, "I see."

McShane knew exactly what Erik was thinking, especially when it involved his wife, and was determined to stop what he was sure Erik had in mind. "Now I know that you are a man that could easily deal with the likes of these two quite appropriately, but since this is *my* ship, and *I* am the law here, it is up to me, and not you, to handle this situation," he said with force, his words chosen with care to let Erik know with certainly that he did not want the gentleman to interfere.

McShane had no doubt that Erik could met out justifiable punishment, and it was probably what those two scoundrels needed to put the fear of God into their souls, but he liked Erik too much to take the chance of this situation going awry, and something more serious coming out of this preposterous incident. He didn't presume to know Erik's business, or what his past might unwillingly reveal, but what he did know, was that here was a man that had obviously suffered a lot in some indescribable way, yet was not afraid to share his knowledge in a dangerous situation, no matter what it would cost him. He didn't know why, but he was positive Erik offering his help had cost him dearly, and it had nothing to do with his injuries. More like he was on display for the unfeeling and unmannered to gawk at. To those that mattered, he was a God sent!

Erik looked the captain squarely in the face, and could see this man meant what he was saying about not interfering. It enraged him beyond measure that someone was after the woman thought to be his wife. *The one that would be his wife*! It made his temper flare so alarmingly that it was with monumental effort that he managed to keep it under some semblance of control. It was against Erik's better judgment to let someone else deal with his affairs, especially where the person he loved was concerned, wanting to teach these men a scathing lesson they would never forget, but there was too much at risk, given both the confined space of this small floating vessel and the fact that he *was* the man they were talking about. Not exactly a piece of knowledge he would like to make public, his own demise an almost certain outcome. And for some reason, this captain had Erik's better interests in mind. This again, was totally foreign to his thinking! An uncomfortable feeling he could not readily explain, prompted him to answer, "I will honor your request."

Pushing forward before Erik had a moment to rationalize his thoughts, McShane continued, "I will give you instructions that will take you to an inn that is quite off the beaten path, but on the way to London. Just mention my name, and you will be quite warmly received. You need a few more days to recuperate, lad, before you should undertake a rigorous two day ride into London," he said with concern. "There are usually several phaetons that can be purchased at the carriage house on the landing. Be ready when we land, and I will make sure that our friends are unavoidably detained," he said smiling. "Something about their salon tab, that hasn't been paid in over two voyages," he added, a little humor creeping into his voice.

Erik took all this information in with quick calibration, realizing immediately that McShane might speculate upon Erik's past, but was taking him at the face value of what he was at that moment, and willing to help him for whatever reason. "I appreciate your help and will take your advice. I certainly do not wish to subject my wife to the likes of these men, or to provoke an embarrassing situation," he said, seeing that McShane face showed immediate relief. "Your help is greatly appreciated, and I won't forget it. We will be ready when the ship docks," he said simply, offering no other explanation, not believing McShane expected one. It was enough that the man offered his help. Both men shook hands, their admiration mutual, knowing that they would probably never meet again!

A light drizzle begun to fall as darkness descended, throwing about a chilly wind that whipped around in circles, disturbing anything in its path. It was just before midnight when the *La Bentra* backed into a slip at the Weymouth landing area, her crew relieved and grateful to finally make the safety of dry land for repairs. Heavy twisted hemp lines were thrown towards the wharf where longshoremen caught and tied them to huge iron fixtures, securing the huge injured paddle steamer tightly between two wooden docks for a permanent mooring. The gangplank was hauled out and placed on the lower level to unload supplies. Tomorrow in the daylight, it would be transferred to the upper deck for her departing passengers. On the pier, a few assorted carriages lay in wait for those few passengers that ventured to depart at night, most fast asleep in their cabins, two in particular locked in a make-shift brig.

Such was the scene when Erik and Monique came out onto the lower deck to disembark from the ship. "Erik, I don't understand why we must leave in the middle of the night, and in the rain, when you are still so weak? Can't we wait until daylight? No one else is leaving in the dark," she said in exasperation, not understanding this new unexpected action. He had said to have their things ready before dark, making her believe they would disembark in the early evening, but time had stretched on and the weather had turned impossible, therefore she thought they would wait until morning just like everyone else. Marta had mentioned that the salon would be serving a light breakfast to most of the passengers, not that Erik had agreed to partake of food beyond their cabin again. And where was Erik's sense when it came to his health? He was still in a weakened state, not that he appreciated hearing her mention it, but he had paced the cabin in a foul mood the entire day, eating nothing, hardly speaking a word, and barely acknowledging her presence. No amount of coaching had persuaded him to take even one bite of food, much to her exasperation. He only left the cabin once, to deliver some drawings that had occupied his time in the afternoon to Engineer Crocket. Something about a "better layout that would make something-or-other work more efficiently." Late into the evening there had been a knock on the door and the boatswain had mumbled something to Erik that had set him into action. He had told her to dress warmly, selecting casual attire himself, and she had followed his example. She had not missed that he had strapped that wicked looking rapier around his slim hips and wearing that long cape, he once again looked like the Prince of Darkness. He left for more than a half hour upon docking, as their trunks were taken away, coming back only to collect her.

"It's best we are on our way immediately, love. I do not have the time to explain to you now, but rest assured there is a very good reason," he said with conviction, his heavy black cape whipping around his ankles in the heavy wind. He shielded her from the slight rainfall by securing her within the confines of his cape, wrapping his left arm around her head and shoulders. They bent slightly forward into the wind, and rushed down the gangplank to an awaiting phaeton with two matching bays, a purchase Erik had made not thirty minutes before, and already contained their trunks.

There he was again, telling her absolutely nothing, but "rest assured there was a very good reason." Erik could be so closed-mouthed and infuriating sometimes, it made her want to scream! She settled herself against the plush leather seats of the carriage that could easily carry four passengers, its slanted top shielding them from the light rain that continued to fall. Erik sat down next to her, gathering up the reins when he was settled, and the four-wheeled carriage lurched into motion, the new bays stepping out smartly in their new harnesses. It took not more than twenty minutes through the cobblestone streets, before they were making their way out of town upon a dirt road that pointed in the direction of London.

They rode in silence and into the dark. Two small lanterns swung from hooks on either side of the carriage, near the top, permitting just enough light to see the road in front of it, but not in front of the horses. Those beasts went into the darkness blindly, no moon adding assistance, and Monique wondered how Erik knew where he was going. The lighter weight phaeton seemed to zip along easily, its sleek and graceful lines not lumbering over the ruts as their previous, heavier carriage had done, and Monique heaved a thankful sigh of relief. They certainly did not need to be fixing wheels at this time of night. She remembered a story her father had told her right out of Greek Mythology where Phaeton, the son of Helios, drove the Chariot of the Sun so recklessly that Zeus, fearing he would set the earth on fire, struck Phaeton down with a lightening bolt. And that was where these magnificent and graceful carriages had received their name. It was quite fashionable for the gentry in France to purchase them to show off their prize horses. Monique was thinking that, except for the rain that would surely accompany it, perhaps a lightening bolt or two would be helpful right about now, to let them see where they were going.

Erik heard Monique sigh and patted her knee, his own thigh hugging hers most familiarly, even though the seats was quite generous. Her closeness, and the expanding distance between them and Weymouth, made Erik relax a little, "It alright love, it won't be long, and you will be tucked into a nice warm bed,"

"It's not me that needs to be tucked into bed, Erik, and well you now it," she said heatedly. "I can't believe this couldn't wait until morning, when we could have found you a doctor." She had mentioned that first thing in the morning, Erik refusing point blank to even consider the possibility. "And you have been pacing like a caged animal all day, and with no explanation for that either," she went on to remark.

Stubbornly, Erik looked ahead at the horses, his mouth in a slanted pout beneath the white mask, he once again had applied to his face. A pout, she might add, that infuriated her when he simply ignored her, which was becoming an all too familiar habit. Monique slumped back into the seat, feeling rejected and helpless.

Taking pity on her, Erik replied, "It's not as bad as all that, *ma petite*."

"Yes it is, Erik. You don't take me into account for one moment," she said in disagreement.

"Of course I do, love."

"Then why don't you tell me anything," she protested. Getting straight answers out of Erik was simply impossible.

"Because the time isn't right," he said honestly, knowing this wouldn't do much to quell her inquiries.

"Will the time ever be right?" And when he did answer, he was evasive. "And do you still want to marry me?" she said faltering. She felt cherished, and he had an unquenchable lust for her, but did he still really want to marry her?

"Don't be absurd, love. Of course I still want to marry you," he said calmly in a lowered voice. "What made you think that I didn't?" he added in a whisper.

"You didn't answer my other question, Erik." That he said this so calmly, only infuriated her.

It was Erik's turn to sigh. "Yes love, there is a time for everything, and sooner than I would wish it, the time will be right," he said simply, an almost dejected sorrow to his voice. When he did tell her, she might just leave him. Hell, she might just get the authorities on him herself.

He was tired, and the activity of controlling both a carriage and a new set of horses was wearing on his weakened body. The thought of having to explain *anything* tonight made him almost nauseous, but he supposed it might have to be done. Suddenly, he felt not only weary, but totally exhausted. He had been holding the pain at bay with shear willpower to get them away from Weymouth, and the worry of the day had taken its toll also, adding into the mix Monique's rightful need for answers, all in all made for a rather motley mess of his shattered nerves, not to mention the abuse his body seemed to think he was affording it.

Monique knew when Erik desired no more conversation on a particular subject, and she rightly guessed that he was done with this one. She looked up at his features, and could see that his face was pale beyond the mask. Sweat was upon his forehead, even though the air was almost cold, and she believed he was probably again running a fever. When would he learn to listen to her? Having spent over two weeks with him...probably never! She almost snorted thinking back on them. He had the propensity for doing exactly what he wanted. Did he ever think about the outcome? She sincerely doubted it!

Suddenly the phaeton turned off onto a small road with only two ruts, where no carriage could have passed them. Off into the distance, she could see flickering lights through the trees, and after several minutes, the carriage pulled up alongside a very charming, but modest inn. A sign that swayed back and forth upon its hinges, as gusts of wind swirled around it, declared in bold black letters, *The Tavish McShane Inn.* Erik reined the horses in, climbing down in a manner that to Monique's experienced eye, where Erik was concerned, seemed filled with pain, although he said nothing. Tying the horses first to a hitching rail, he then came around to help her out.

"The name of the inn, Erik. It's the same name as our captain," she said in amazement.

"So it seems, my dear. A small detail he failed to mention," Erik said with a touch of dry humor.

"Captain McShane told you about this place?" she questioned in surprise.

"He did mention it in passing," Erik said, leading her to the porch of the inn rather rapidly, the rain increasing in its intensity. Swiftly he opened the double portal, pushing her gently inside. They stood in a quaint, but beautiful foyer, surrounded with furniture made from trees that had not been stripped of its bark.

The walls were decorated with the heads of bear, elk and moose and an assortment of hunting gear. She recalled to memory a similar lodge she had visited with her father some years ago, high in the mountains of France, when they had delivered some horses to a Marquee, who had purchased them from *Chapallae.* The pungent aroma of cedar emanated from a large fireplace that spread across the breadth of a small parlour to their right, and Erik glided her over to warm her from the dampness that clung to their garments.

"I will get us a room for the night," he told her. It was his intention to stay a few days to regain his strength, and explain about his past, but at present he saw no pressing need to give out that information. It could wait until they were alone.

Brianna McShane came into the foyer, just as Erik re-entered, and stopped dead in her tracks for one brief moment, taking in the most handsome and dangerous image of man she had yet to encounter, his commanding presence immediately discernable. A smile spread across her face immediately, as she came forward in welcome.

"Well, well, it is good to be out of the rain on such a troublesome night," she said. "Would you be wanting a room?"

"My wife and I would be obliged," Erik told her, realizing immediately that this woman was not in the least bit intimidated by his appearance. "I know it is quite late, but is there anyone that could see to our carriage and luggage. If that is not possible, it is quite understandable, and if you would point me in the right direction, I will see to it myself," Erik said politely in French, having been told that both English and French were spoken here, his eyes glancing momentarily in the direction of the parlour, where Monique bent forward, rubbing her hands together near the flames. Hearing what he said, Monique immediately rushed from the parlour, and spoke directly to Erik.

"Erik, you will do no such thing. Your ribs are still mending, and I do not plan on re-stitching your wounds. If anyone will unharness the horses, it will be me," she said, not giving a thought to how it might sound.

"You will do no such thing, *ma petite*," he said, amusement in his face at her kind suggestion, knowing it was completely out of the question.

"You still doubt that I could do so?" she asked heatedly, her impatience building by the second, not sitting by one more time while Erik made light of his still being weak.

Erik only chuckled, "Love, I'm not questioning your ability to do it. What I'm saying is, I won't allow it," he finished, totally dismissing the topic from his mind.

He wouldn't allow it, she fumed, stomping her foot just a little, but enough that he did notice. "You're a rotten husband, you know that?" she said under her breath, making Erik chuckle all the more as he turned back to Brianna McShane.

Taking in the harmless, but probably accurate banter between her new guests, Brianna suspected immediately that her husband, Ian, had sent them here. She never received guests in the middle of the night that weren't sent by Ian, and it made her smile discretely, lowering her head so they would not notice. "Please, there is no need for either of you to tend to the horses. Jon will bring your luggage to your room, and take care of the horses for the night." As if on cue, a tall husky giant came ambling into the foyer, like he was summonsed by a bell, his ruffled hair a dead give away that he had been sleeping.

"Jon, I'm putting this couple in the Canterbury Room. Be a good lad and see to their carriage," she said to him in English, not hesitating a moment, she turned back to Erik.

"Yes, mum, not a problem," he said cheerfully, like it was nothing out of the ordinary to be working in the middle of the night.

"And what would the name be… for the registry?" she asked, knowing that many of her late night guests were not what they might seem. Not that this couple wasn't, but Ian had an uncanny ability for sending her the…extraordinary!

"Mr. And Mrs. Devereau," Erik supplied to her, making him oddly uncomfortable that the ceremony for making that name appropriately legitimate had not as yet taken place. But it would, as soon as he could possibly arrange it! He would finally settle this part of his future once and for all. He would either be a very happy and contented man, or one doomed to be unhappy forever! And the thought of that made his entire body shiver, and not from the cold dampness of the night!

CHAPTER SIXTEEN

The ever expanding fishing community of Weymouth was a large seaport town, situated in the County of Dorset, and nestled between an abundance of rolling hills, vales, pastures and grasslands, dotted with the likes of horses, sheep and cattle. It was positioned along the southern coastal area of England, several days east of London by overland carriage. Evidence showed that Roman Galleys had sailed up the River Wey, as far as the town of Radipole, where they could easily be beached and their cargoes unloaded. Many Roman and Bronze Age remains were plentiful in and around the countryside. A large dam, built in the mid 1800's had been constructed across the expanse of the Weymouth harbour, to assist in maintaining an adequate water level in the upper reaches of the inner harbour all the way to Radipole, thus allowing those ships with a deeper draft the ability to sail into her sheltered waters. Weymouth, with its huge harbour, was a stopping off place for large shipping, and supported trade all the way to the Orient.

Sunlight filtered in between a small opening in the long damask drapes that framed the single window in the Canterbury Room of The Tavish McShane Inn, casting long shadows upon the matching damask coverlet that lay spread across the high poster bed, its occupants still abed. The late night had been short lived, dawn close on the heels of a house once again settling from the arrival of its most recent guests. The early morning dew that replenished the varied grasslands, and the crisp and refreshing salty air of the sea, had already waned, being replaced with deep penetrating warmth, as the sun rose high overhead, the day well into its hours of daylight.

Monique stirred within the circle of Erik's arms, his warm naked body still wrapped in bandages, pressing against hers in sleep. They had settled into their room in the wee hours of the morning, partaking first of a delicious cup of hot mulled cider to warm their innards from the dampness of their ride, Monique settling for one plain cup, while Erik had two, perhaps three, liberally spiked with brandy. She thought perhaps he was hoping it would dull his pain, for she could see by his slower movements that the pain remained, more than likely made worse by the long and tedious day. Their trunks had been delivered to their room without pomp or circumstance, Jon hefting each trunk individually onto one massive shoulder, carrying them with ease, and depositing them beneath the window within their room. They had ascended the stairs tiredly, both feeling the exhaustion from a day of waiting, one for her filled with excitement and exasperation, not understanding Erik's unexplained actions, and ending with the long ride from town to their destination. Upon reaching their quarters, Erik had immediately stripped off his clothes without ceremony, depositing everything within a heap upon a stuffed chair, including his rapier and cape, very unlike his usual neat and orderly fashion, and settled himself upon the bed, drawing a sheet over his naked form. Although he had indicated rather adamantly that he needed to discuss something very important with her before retiring for the night, when she returned from her ablutions down the hall, he had been fast asleep. He had looked so peaceful in his slumber, yet she was sure exhausted from the day also, that she had dared to remove his mask for comfort, laying her cool hand upon his right cheek, and he had turned his face towards her without fully waking, his arms seeking her instinctively, pulling her against the front of his body in a spooning position. Together they slept the unhindered *sleep of the dead*, that entity where the body feels safe in abandonment, and the mind rests with the disappearance of weariness, and the lifting of the spirit allows the soul to heal.

Monique felt hungry. At least she thought hunger was the cause for that strange queasy feeling in her stomach that had awakened her. It had been many hours since they had actually eaten real food. She made a small effort yesterday to concentrate on food, but her irritation at Erik had kept her from being very interested, and Erik had eaten nothing at all. Perhaps that was why the liquor he had consumed along with the cider had taken its toll so easily. She could almost giggle at that fact. He had actually given himself a most potent sedative without him even being aware. And she was certain it couldn't have hurt! He had once again acted so irrational and childish, endangering his health by his actions. Today she would have to look at his stitches and perhaps take them out. Her stomach rumbled again, and most distastefully to her way of thinking, leading her to the conclusion if she would eat something, she would feel better. Carefully she slipped from the bed, taking pains not to wake Erik, selecting a simple day dress and chemise, disposing rather quickly of the ridiculous idea of heavy undergarments like an uncomfortable corset and tiptoed from the room.

Descending the stairs, Monique saw that there were perhaps a dozen guests mulling about a bright cherry dining area off the main foyer, just opposite the parlour. Most of the occupants were casually dressed, and engaged in the pastime of talking and eating. Oh, dear, thought Monique, catching a glimpse of the food upon their plates. That did not look like breakfast fare, but more like lunch. They had slept through the morning, she thought with surprise! That idea brought an impish smile to her face, and then she laughed out loud, stifling it with her hand. What would people think? Sleeping the day away! And they were truly, *actually* sleeping!

Nearing the kitchen, she wondered whom she might ask to bring some food to their room? She wondered if anyone spoke French? Once again she was determined to encourage Erik to regain his strength. After all, it was a new day, and one way or the other, she would make Erik see reason.

"Oh my dear, you are up, and I'll bet quite famished," came a familiar voice from behind her. She turned to see the smiling face of Brianna McShane. Of course, Monique thought, this lovely lady with the dark snapping eyes and friendly face had understood her last night when she had spoken to Erik. She had been so tired when they arrived, the idea of being in an English speaking country alone just slipped her mind. That Brianna had spoken to them in French, she had entirely dismissed as ordinary.

"Well, I do seem to have a rather strange rumbling going on in my belly," admitted Monique, thinking that the smell of food made it worse. Right at that moment she wished immensely for a hot cup of tea and a large sconce. But breakfast seemed to be over! "Perhaps just a cup of tea," she said timidly, not wanting to be a bother.

"Of course, my dear. And would you prefer breakfast or lunch?" she asked, seeing that this slip of a girl, who was almost child-like in appearance, if you were to go by her size and her looks, although outspoken last night to her husband, did not seem to want to inconvenience anyone.

"Do you think we could have breakfast in our room?" Monique inquired. "Perhaps Erik will be hungry also. He didn't eat one morsel yesterday. I suppose worrying about getting along towards London, and completing his affairs. We lost a lot of time when our paddle steamer was torn apart by a storm." she said, a tired look of resignation on her face, thinking back on all that had transpired in just a few short days.

"Oh, yes of course! I just received a brief message today from my husband, Ian, telling of the damage to his ship. He comes home for an eight-day layover about every four weeks between voyages, so I did not know about the incident at sea or the storm. Sometimes it is better not to know, my dear, until things like that are over. I'd only worry, if I knew," she finished, a genuine smile on her face for one of Ian's passengers.

"Then Captain McShane is your husband," Monique replied in surprise, having thought perhaps her husband's name was Tavish, like the name on the sign.

"Oh, yes, for fifteen years now. I help his father run this small inn that has been in his family for generations. Ian has always been very fond of the sea, and his paddle wheeler is his passion," she said without reservation, and Monique could see in her eyes that Brianna did not seem to resent their arrangement.

"I saw a brass bathtub in our room," Monique said with longing. "We were on the steamer for days, and have been without a bath. And I know after Erik's illness, he might want one also," she exclaimed, the thought of being totally immersed in water and giving her hair a real washing, an absolutely heavenly thought.

" Just leave it to me. A tray will be brought to your room. A new water system has been installed, and there is a filling tube beside the tub. Just turn the small crank and water is available. Jon will bring a few buckets of steamy water for good measure," she told Monique. And with a little wink, she added, " Go back to your man."

Monique's heart gave a little jump. The thought of getting back to Erik did seem delightful, knowing that he would be lying there in sleep...warm, naked and inviting. She didn't want Erik to awaken and find her gone. Quickly she raced up the stairs, hardly able to stifle a small giggle of laughter that was threatening to emerge. She opened the door quietly, and could see that Erik was still there! Good! She was half afraid he might have heard her leave and come looking for her. She glanced briefly around the room. It was very spacious, furnished with a beautiful three piece, Chippendale bedroom set, consisting of an elegant high poster bed, an armoire for clothes and a seven-drawer highboy. A small commode table adjacent to the bed held a Tiffany oil lamp. An eating table with two matching chairs was positioned near the window. Hearing a light rap upon the door, Monique opened it to Jon, supplying two large buckets of hot water, and a young teenage girl that brought in a tray of food. Neither said a word, aware that Erik was still sleeping, completed their task quickly, and left the room with a polite nod.

Monique slipped out of her clothes and back into the circle of Erik's arms. She barely had a chance to give a contented sigh, when warm, feathery kisses were placed upon the back of her neck, continuing over to her ear, a wet mouth and teeth finally consuming her earlobe, sending shivers of pleasure right through to her bones. Strong hands cupped her breasts, teasing and kneading at will, and that huge beast that unmistakably grew hard, and thick, and eager, sliding persistently in a rhythmic motion against the cleft of her bottom, made it quite clear that Erik was fully awake.

Slowly she turned in his embrace. "I thought you would sleep the day away, M'Lord," she teased him, glad that he had finally had some uninterrupted sleep.

"And where did my nurse run off to, leaving her patient wanting?" he bantered, equally glad that their departure had gone well, and finally they were settled for a few days of rest. He planned on making the most of their uninterrupted time together. He would not leave here until she knew his past, and then if she was disgusted and appalled, retracting her love as all others had, he would take her back to Weymouth, and put her back on a ship where she had friends that could see to her comfort on her way back to France. It might prolong his stay, but what did he have to look forward to if he went on? Nothing that he could think of! He could marry her first and then she would be stuck with him. But he could rightly see that plan backfiring in his face. He would have a wife that didn't love him! In the end, after all he had done, that was probably what he deserved!

"Wanting for what?" she asked, with a feigned expression of surprise.

"I believe you know for what," he coached, pressing his hips against hers for emphasis. "Food, of course, what else?" he said with a husky, sensual laugh, pulling her lips to his, branding them, his silky tongue plunging deep within her mouth time and again, until she felt so dizzy, she was limp within his arms, barely able to put two coherent thoughts together. Feeling her stomach churn at this most inappropriate moment, made her remember another kind of food. She wiggled her body from his grasp.

"Might I entice you to have some breakfast," she said impishly.

"I believe that is what I was doing, love. Devouring the most delicious sweet meat I can think of," he answered, his breathing totally ragged. And to show her exactly what he meant, he pulled her full breasts against his chest, cupping her derriere so he could maneuver her hips as he wanted, her belly feeling the full effect of that pulsing giant of his loins. His body was warm and hard, and still laced with the grogginess of sleep, yet became intensely heated and fiercely savage as he continued. She was infinitely aware that this incredible man, who had done the most intimate and satisfying things to her, seemed to need something from her, in an insatiable way, that gave him strength. A treasured gift she was most willing to give, to him and no other. Suddenly his mouth sought taut ripe peaks, teasing each in turn with his tongue, sucking with an ever increasing intensity, until Monique said, "Ouch!"

Erik pulled away and looked up. "I'm sorry, *ma petite*, was I too rough? Perhaps I'm more hungry than I thought," he said, flashing her a most unguarded smile, one that hinted at concern, his hands now busy caressing her derriere, as he pulled her closer.

"No, I'm just a little tender," she admitted. "But I really did bring you some breakfast, and it is quickly getting cold," she half-heartedly scolded, still determined to make him eat. Cold food that was suppose to be warm would not be appealing.

"Well, perhaps we should have a little breakfast, before I partake of such a delectable dessert. One should never have dessert before the meal," he laughed, giving her a cocky smile, his eyes smoldering with a desire that was so unmistakable, she knew he would not leave this bed chamber until he had both. Delectable dessert indeed! The man could be such a tease, torturing her with his very words, and despite her queasy stomach, her desire for him flared, that she could almost forget breakfast in the tangible form. Almost!

Monique jumped from the bed and Erik watched in quiet fascination and appreciation as Monique, unashamed of her nakedness in front of him, prepared two cups of tea, set them on a small tray along with some food, and brought them to the table by the bed. She picked up a delicious looking breakfast cake, piled high with whipped chocolate creame and turned around to hand it to Erik. At that moment, Erik, thinking to enclose her sweet little body against him beneath the sheet, threw his arm wide to allow her to enter. The plate with the breakfast cake went flying, whipped chocolate creame spilling down the front of his chest, the plate settling most inappropriately within his lap.

Erik looked up startled, and then began to laugh…a deep, hearty laugh that brought tears to his eyes. Talk about breakfast in bed! "I see that I can have my cake and eat it too," he said, removing the plate and cake, placing them on the tray.

Monique looked positively mortified that she had spilled part of Erik's breakfast all over him. But Erik did not seem the least bit upset. He was actually laughing. He pulled her against him and kissed her so soundly, and with such scorching intensity, she could scarcely breathe. When he finally broke the kiss, she muttered with regret, "Erik, I'm so sorry. I'll clean this up, and then go downstairs and get some more."

But Erik was still chuckling, "You will do no such thing, my sweet. I have you warm and willing in my bed, and I see no reason to replace this breakfast." With that he leaned down, using his tongue to taste the delicious whipped chocolate that had transferred from his chest to her lovely plump breasts, taking those delectable peaks into his mouth, licking and sucking gently, until the sweet creame was removed. Looking up, he only smiled, eyes as dark as coals in the shadows that played across the room, the wind blowing through the half open window, whipping the damask curtains back and forth in its wake. His face had a most charming expression, one that bespoke of satisfaction.

"Erik, you have chocolate on your mouth," Monique said with giggling humor, wiping it gently off with a linen napkin, thinking he once again looked exactly like a small boy who had been caught doing something he shouldn't. But then, doing all these incredible, sexy and insatiable things with this dark mysterious man seemed somehow totally forbidden. It was as much the dangerous side of him that drew her in, as his gentleness, and the wonder of it all could be downright addictive. She had no plans to give it up anytime soon!

Erik only looked at her, a devilish smile spreading across his face, saying, "Perhaps you should join me and have chocolate on your mouth too." With that, he looked down suggestively, and then up at her, his breathing becoming heavy and ragged, the blue eyes of her oval face wide with surprise as she realized his meaning.

She lowered her eyes and head shyly, "Is such a thing allowed?" she whispered, her face flushed with astonishment at what she knew she wanted to do.

He cupped her chin with his hand, and tilted her face up to look at him. "It is allowed, *my petite,* and desired," he assured her. Lying on his back, he pulled her down beside him, guiding her hand to where he wanted pleasure, and felt her mouth follow. Sucking in a slow, ragged breath between his teeth, he closed his eyes as his mind spiraled to a euphoric state, thinking if he lived a thousand years, he could know of nothing sweeter. She gave him pleasure as he had often given to her, and when he thought he might loose his control and explode, he pulled her up and over his body, searing her mouth with his, tasting that delicious chocolate, that mingled with the honeyed sweetness of her mouth.

Before she could produce another thought, he had rolled her onto her back, covering her willing body with the weight of his own, his knee urgently seeking to open her thighs, his need to bury himself within the tight cavern of her womanly body overwhelming. She could feel that long, thick sword he had used as a weapon against her, probing for entrance, yet today she accepted its sweet torture with wild wanting, wishing to be no place on earth but here, wrapped within the union of his embrace.

Together they soared, each giving to the other that which they desired, their united movements first slow and practiced, giving away to abandoned wonder. The taste and feel of him set her body to a fevered pitch with an exquisite pleasure that made her lose herself completely to his possession. He seduced her with his mesmerizing touch, overwhelming her with his heady passion. For all intense purposes he seemed to be healed from his illness. His strength consumed her, and his stamina delighted her!

Erik had a need that far surpassed any Monique could have imagined. The friction between their bodies unleashed all those pent up emotions that he had been forced to suppress, for what seemed like days on end. His inability to maintain control…of anything…had so annoyed him in his lucid moments, that he felt an overwhelming need to prove to himself that he had not imagined the heights to which his soul had flown, when encompassed with her healing powers… that entity that only she seemed able to give him.

When their bodies were spent, and their trembling muscles were once again relaxed and tingling with sensation, they lay secure in each others arms, washed in the afterglow of their union, unwilling to break apart.

Erik kissed her hair, damp from exertion. "Is that hot water I see, steaming from those buckets," he asked, thinking a bath did seem prudent under the circumstances.

"Yes, Jon brought them up to help heat the water. You can actually draw cold water thru pipes running right to the tub," Monique said informatively, thinking it a most convenient invention.

"Really!" Erik said, his curiosity getting the better of him. He pulled her slight body off his massive chest, breaking their union, and he heard a slight gasp! "Don't worry, love, there'll be more where that came from," he said with a devilish grin in her direction.

She took his meaning, and playfully retorted, "You are far too conceited, Erik!"

Striding towards the tub, scrutinizing it carefully, he smiled, turning in her direction to give her the once over and then himself. "I think a bath is quite in order," he laughed, turning the small crank that sputtered air, then cold water flowing into the tub. He poured one and a half of the buckets in, felt the temperature with his hand, and turned the crank to shut off the stream. He held out his hand to her, "Come join me, love! Alas, I think there is chocolate left on both of us." With that he gave a hearty laugh, stepped into the tub, and pulled her in on top of him with a splash. They both broke out in laughter.

"Erik, you should not get your stitches wet," she admonished. "And I really should see to taking them out," she added, looking at his face, noting the small wound over his left eyebrow.

"Well, you are the nurse, my petite," he said grinning. "Or is that veterinarian, my love," he snorted. "And I believe it is your job to make me conform," he said, his breath a hot murmur in her ear, his teeth nipping at her earlobe.

"Erik, you are impossible," she said hoarsely, splashing water upon his chest playfully, unable to deny where his hands were searching. She sat facing him, sitting on his lap, her legs wrapped around his hips. The deliciousness of the hot water, and the wonderful slippery feeling of their bodies as they glided over each other, made her head giddy, unable to produce coherent speech. She could feel and hear the beat of his heart, as she lay against his chest, the closeness of his own nipples too much for her eager fingers to resist. He sucked in his breath between clenched teeth, nipping her shoulder in retaliation, then reigned wet kissed along her neck, stopping only when he caught her plump lower lip and sucked it sensually. She thought she would die of blissful pleasure.

There was a rush between her thighs as he began exploring, running those huge masculine hands over her bottom, into its cleft, his fingers coming to rest on her womanhood, caressing and probing until she felt all the bones had left her body. "I want to hear you cry out again that you want me, love," he whispered, his voice deep and raspy.

"I want you, Erik," she supplied too easily.

"Oh no, love! I want to feel you squirm and pant, and scream that you want me," he said. He lifted her slightly, entering her with a hard push, for she was tight and he was large.

She gasped, not realizing in her own, drugged state of ecstasy, that he too was ready. Very ready! He settled her down with a growing, needy pressure onto his hot pulsing sword, and the groan she gave only made him chuckle, a slow husky sound, deep within his chest. He moved his hips for added effect and she drew in her breath, his fingers not leaving that place where he set her body to a fiery pitch, and she thought she would likely incinerate, even surrounded by water. Her breath came in short little gasps as he moved her against him, his hands gliding her hips in a slow stroking motion, every nerve within her shealth reacting from the friction of his searching sword. Her head rested on his shoulder, her wet lips kissing him, biting into his neck and shoulder with her escalating need to be released.

When she could take it no longer, thinking she would surely die of …some word that had not been invented to describe her sensations, she cried out into his neck, "Please, Erik, release me! I love you! You're a drug to me and I need you!"

Erik was shaken. He had not expected her to declare her love in such an impassioned way, but a smile spread across his lips that she did. "There, there my love! We will be released together. I promise," he said hoarsely, taking her mouth to his in a bruising and scorching, savage kiss, then held to that promise, bringing them to an exploding climax.

Monique lay limp against Erik's body, hardly able to move a muscle. After a few minutes, he pulled her upright, smoothing back her hair. "Love, the water is getting chilly. We had better make haste in washing, or we will be needing more hot water, and I well suspect that might raise a few eyebrows," he said with a little chuckle, when her eyes became wide with his meaning, realizing the water had a bit of a…chocolate tinge.

They washed each other with the soap that had been left alongside a pile of huge fluffy towels, their caressing motions threatening to land them right back into passion, Monique noticing that Erik would have no trouble doing so again. She jumped out of the tub, avoiding his grasp, suggesting they wash their hair. Erik peeled off his wig with pleasure, rubbing his fingers in his hair like his head itched, letting her soap his head and rinse it free, not embarrassed that she touched him, knowing that she accepted him as he was. He pulled his long muscular frame out of the tub, wrapping a big fluffy yellow towel around his lean hips, and took on the task of washing her long thick tresses, using the last half-bucket of warm water to rinse the soap free. He then wrapped her sweet enticing body in a large towel as she stood up in the tub, and one around her hair, lifting her out, and carried her to the bed. She noticed that his towel in front stood out like a tent peg, and it made her go into fits of giggles, burying her face in the hair upon his chest, making her giggle even more.

"And what, pray tell, is so funny," he asked in a serious tone.

"Erik, you are always…so…ready," she supplied.

"Years of denial, love and that enticingly, beautiful body that I can not seem to get enough of," he said, his eyes looking at her with the darkest passion, but something else that she did not recognize. Perhaps sorrow! Sorrow that she was determined to prevent from overtaking him again!

"Let me see your arm, Erik," she said quickly, wanting to change the subject, into the present and away from what haunted him.

In examination, she saw that it had healed well, the edges parting only slightly, leaving a much smaller scar than she would have imagined upon stitching. As he patiently sat in a chair near the window, she used a small pair of scissors, cutting the stitches open, pulling them out one at a time. Erik only winched once, jerking his arm, the stitches having been loosened nicely with the hot water. Of course she had mentioned not getting it wet, wanting to soften it with *clean* water, but he had not listened. She would ask for some binding later, thinking it needed to be covered for a few more days.

Asking him to lay back upon the bed, she looked at the wound on his head. That one she was proud of! The tiny stitches were barely noticeable and she gave a little squeak of delight!

Lying with his eyes closed, Erik ventured to open his right eye to observe her. "A squeak of appreciation for your handy-work, or that you get the chance to torture me again?" he asked.

"Well of course that I get to torture you again. Oh Erik, you can be such a baby," she chided, wondering instantly, if perhaps it was not particularly prudent to remind him of acting like a child.

"Baby!" he said startled, his neck blushing red and his pulse beating rather rapidly. Suddenly he asked, "Isn't there something you should be advising me about that would curtail our lovemaking?" He scrutinized her body, but the heavy towel obstructed his vision. There was yet one issue to be resolved before he would ever allow her to leave.

"Letting you in on? Like what?" she asked, not comprehending his question.

He cleared his throat, not particularly erudite in such matters, but they *were* intimate. Had been for several weeks now! And he supposed he should know. "That monthly thing women do," he said, almost in a whisper.

Monique blushed right down to the roots of her hair. What made him think about that! Perhaps that he thought he would have to stay away from her. Old wives tales, but she wouldn't let him know that just yet. But thinking back, she realized with some horror that her time was past, and her stomach gave a giant leap! Very long past! Not wanting to think about such things right now, she gave him his own words in answer. "When I think you should know something Erik, I'll let you know," she said, and when she looked into his eyes, she saw hurt reflected there, because he had unmistakably caught her meaning.

She had quite effectively thrown his own words right back in his face. And perhaps rightly so, he thought with some anger, but yet understanding her purpose. To give him a taste of his own medicine, he thought with little humor! Medicine that was not particularly palatable! He held his tongue in silence, admitting defeat for the moment, but not willing to let the issue drop. He would have his answer soon enough!

They remained quiet as she took out the stitches on his head, having to dig for some of them, being so tiny, and he winched several times, catching her hand once to give it a moments rest. All in all, the wound left a very tiny, hairline scar that was almost unnoticeable if you did not know of its existence, and for that she was grateful.

Afterwards they dressed in casual evening clothes, she in a simple, but stunning, very pale, golden evening dress that was less revealing than her one in the salon, and he in tight black britches, a white silk shirt and black vest, and a velvet evening jacket of the deepest claret. He continued to wear his wig and mask. The afternoon had slipped by, and the sun was just beginning to set. It would be the dinner hour soon, and neither had actually partaken of any tangible food. They were both famished. He kissed her neck as he helped button up the back of her dress, but she could tell that he was still hurt by her words. He in turn, knew she was undeniably correct. He had yet to tell her anything! Something he promised himself, he would be damned, if he did not soon rectify.

A short time later they entered into the foyer, her hand held snugly between his chest and his arm. At that same moment, Ian McShane dropped his sailor's ditty bag to the floor with a thud, and wrapped his big burly arms around his wife in a tight bear-hug, right inside the front door, kissing her soundly on the mouth and swinging her around in a circle. Then he turned, letting her slide down the length of his tall torso to finally put her feet once again upon the floor, but not releasing her. Sweeping his dark appreciative eyes across the house, he said in a booming voice, "It's damn good to be home!"

Chapter Seventeen

Brianna McShane looked up into her husband's face, giving him the brightest of smiles with her dark enticing eyes, and said in a most charming and chastising voice, "Ian McShane, you were not suppose to be here until tomorrow morning. You come prancing in here like nothing's amiss, taking a girl by surprise and me looking such a fright! No warning, mind you!"

Ian dropped his arm from Brianna's waist, giving her a sound smack on the bottom. "Now Branny, love, don't you be giving me the devil! I was able to get away a day earlier, and all's the better for it, for you, my sweet little wench, will be warming my bed just one day sooner," he said, a twinkle in his eye.

"Ohooo, Ian McShane, you are incorrigible! We have guests all around, and you carrying on so," she said, blushing with a faux sense of embarrassment, while standing on her tiptoes to place a quick kiss on his cheek, then playfully pushed him away.

Ian gave another hardy laugh, his eyes filled with appreciation as he watched his wife go back to the kitchen, "I certainly hope so, my sweet darling," he said grinning. Then he noticed Erik and Monique as they entered the foyer, and bellowed in recognition, "Erik, I see that you made it alright, my boy! Was afraid you might have some trouble, the weather being so onery and unpredictable."

"Thank you, we had no trouble. Your directions were most explicit, Captain," Erik said politely.

"The name's Ian, Erik! We have no such formalities at the inn. I'm not a captain here," he said. Then he laughed, and the lines on his face crinkled. "My wife Brianna is the master, and she runs a mean ship, my boy. She cracks a whip the entire time I'm home," he chuckled, his grin widening measurably. He gave Monique a knowing grin, crooking one eyebrow, "Don't suppose you would know anything about that, my dear?" Looking at Erik, he added, " This little lady cracked a few whips herself, if I'm not mistaken."

Monique grimaced, believing Erik did not remember the extent to which she bent in making him conform to her wishes during his illness, but she did know that Bradford and Marta had given a full report. The Captain seemed to know everything that went on aboard his vessel. She gave a muffled groan, glancing hesitantly up at Erik, who was staring at her, but he wasn't exactly smiling. His eyebrow was arched, just like the captain's. Men, she thought, stifling a giggle against her hand. "Well, I only did what had to be done," she said in self-defense, lifting her chin into the air with mutiny on her mind.

Erik was quite well aware of the lengths to which Monique had resorted to make him become the *compliant* patient. His senses, despite his injuries and his state of helplessness, had been ever more alert than she had suspected, having been developed in a world of darkness. Although unable to stop her on several instances, most pointedly in giving him the laudanum, yet not wanting to stop her on many others, knowing she was more adept at knowing his needs at that moment than he knew himself, he was most unsettled at being so vulnerable. He vowed never to be vulnerable again to the extent that he could not protect her. That more than anything else, had grated sorely at his masculinity.

Ian looked at Erik. He seemed more rested, and in better shape then when he saw him last. "A few days in this bonnie climate, and he'll be as good as new," Ian said to Monique. "I hope that you two will join us for supper. Afterwards, if you aren't too busy, Erik, perhaps you might accompany me to look at a project I'm undertaking for bringing hot water into the inn."

After a delicious dinner of Brianna's famous Mulligan stew, served in a special dinning room for the family, Erik and Ian went off to the mill to survey Ian's new project. They spent the better part of the evening, mulling over his new idea, Erik sketching free-hand several drawings that were quite enlightening to the captain. Ian was delighted yet another time, with the superb knowledge and insight Erik had into design and construction, setting him on a better plan for heating and supplying water conveniently to the house. Erik's plans would be less costly, and more efficient.

Monique slipped out of bed, her bare feet cold on the wooden floor. Her entire body felt absolutely wretched! Waves of nausea washed over her with a ghastly force, and she was convinced she must be quite ill. Silently she pulled out a light gingham day dress from the armoire, trying to be as quite as a mouse, but failing miserably as the brass hinges creaked loudly upon opening and closing. Making a determined effort to hurry, that ultimately became a clumsy dash down the hallway to the watercloset, she closed the door just in the nick time, retching the meager contents of her stomach into the commode. Shaky, and a little faint, she sat back on her haunches upon the floor. Three mornings now, she thought with distress! And this the first time, when she could hold nothing down! The one thought that kept resounding in her mind, as the reason for this particular situation, was somewhat daunting. She had to be carrying Erik's child. It was certainly possible, for every sign was there. Even in her misery, she managed a little smile, because she couldn't be happier. But what would Erik think? He said he still wanted to marry her. Perhaps this would change everything? Did he want a child? Would he be upset, or would he welcome the idea? She still knew nothing about him. Getting up slowly, she leaned over the basin, splashed cold water in her face and rinsed out her mouth. She needed some serious time alone to think! She didn't feel like facing Erik just yet. Let him sleep awhile; he had come to bed very late. Silently she tiptoed down the corridor to the stairs, and in two seconds, she was at the front door and onto the long winding front porch.

A chilly crispness gripped the morning air, and a fine white mist hung at waist level between the lower branches of hundreds of pine trees that surrounded the inn, their aromatic needles not yet kissed by the sun's radiance, which soon would burn off the moisture as it filtered in. Monique hung over the wooden railing of the porch, her attention centered on the stone foundation of an old mill across the yard, its huge wooden wheel mostly missing from the half-wall that jutted up along the river's edge. Up from the mill, the small river broadened out to form a large duck pond that seemed inhabited with dozens of quacking goslings. On one side of the pond, small cottages dotted the water's edge, while on the side nearer the inn, a moderate size stable was located, stretching along the river. Monique's heart gave a little leap, as she noticed two horses grazing in a paddock outside the old weathered building, and a young groom slowly walking a beautiful ebony stallion by his halter.

Although the dew was still heavy upon the grass, Monique chose that cold, watery route to walk in her bare feet, wanting to avoid the rough pebbled drive that circled around the front of the house. Coming up alongside the groom, Monique questioned, "Is he broken to ride?"

"Oh yes! Probably the best in the stables, but very high spirited. Not just anyone can ride, Hurricane," answered the groom.

"He doesn't look all that fierce to me," Monique laughed, stepping in front of the lad and patting the big stallion on the neck.

She stretched on her tiptoes to nuzzle her nose to the furry velvet of his, and the stallion whickered affectionately.

"He's thrown off quite a few in his time, he has! The captain's pretty strict about who can ride him, but can't say as I've ever seen Hurricane take to anyone quite like he has to you," the lad said, appreciation in his tone for this small young woman that handled this large beast so easily.

"Think I could take him out for a ride?" Monique asked suddenly, the idea so delightful that she immediately felt better.

The young lad looked at her skeptically. Patting the horse was one thing, but riding him was another. He didn't rightly think the captain would go for such a ridiculous idea. And this little lady certainly wasn't dressed for it.

"I know how to ride quite well. Really I do!" she pleaded, looking at him with the most beseeching, sparkling blue eyes, taking him by complete surprise, using her feminine wiles upon him without either of them realizing it.

"Well, I suppose I could find a saddle," he said. "You just wait right here, and I'll see what I can do. Then you can change into proper riding clothes. And a few turns around the paddock to see if you can handle Hurricane, would be wise," he finished, turning his back, leaving Monique and Hurricane to get acquainted.

As soon as the groom was out of sight, Monique pulled Hurricane over to the stonewall that hugged the tree-line, talking to him gently. She lifted her skirt above her ankles, and climbed up to stand on the wall. Gripping the large steed's long thick mane along with the reins, she easily mounted the tall black stallion, the folds of her skirt bunched around her knees. Sitting bareback, her long bare legs hanging down on each side, she felt perfectly at ease. Squeezing the stallion's flanks with her lean, but muscular calves, they started off down the drive at a trot, just as the groom came running out of the tack room.

"Hey, wait a minute," he called out. "You might fall off!"

Laughing into the breeze and over her shoulder, she yelled, " My father said I was born in a saddle. I've been riding bareback since I was five. Don't worry, I'll be back soon!" And with that small tidbit of information to appease the incredulous look plastered upon the young groom's face, she turned forward, and didn't give it another thought. She needed to be alone to do her thinking. And her best thinking, and reasoning, was done on a horse. Just her luck that a magnificent beast like this would just fall into her lap! Giving a little laugh to herself at the irony of it all, she leaned forward into a cantor, her red hair flowing behind her in the wind.

Erik had been thinking how nice it would be to wrap his body around that sweet little minx. He planned on showing her, yet another time, just how much he not only wanted her, but how much he needed her...more specifically, how much he loved her! Last night had not worked out to tell her what she was ultimately seeking to know about him. Things that she had every right to know, and understand, before she became his wife. Every time he thought he would tell her, something came up to push it out of the way. But he couldn't put it off forever! There were certainly times he wished he could. What would her reaction be, when he told her of all the horrific things about his past? Those events that had been out of his control, and those that had not! Things he had done because his heart had been torn apart by what the world handed him for irrational reasons, or those he had done just because he simply wanted what he believed he could not have! The previous evening had ended quite late. It had been pleasant dining with the McShanes. Something Erik had never experienced before, and therefore he had been most willing to spend a number of hours helping Ian put together new plans and drawings for supplying the inn with a new hot water system. Monique had been asleep on top of the bed-linens, when he had finally come back to the inn, and he had been reluctant to awaken her. He knew that she had spent some pretty sleepless days taking care of him aboard ship, and recently, he felt she looked very pale. He had simply helped her undress, and they had drifted to sleep in each others arms. This morning he was looking forward to a little more delightful activity with the lovely witch that had taken his soul into her keeping, before he finally opened a book of horrors, and revealed all those things that might make her run from him and go back to France.

Erik shifted in bed, wondering when she would return. She had been gone for quite sometime. Suddenly he heard someone yelling outside in the front yard of the inn, and got up to peer out of the curtained window. A young girl was riding down the carriage road on a very big, black stallion. And the way she was riding seemed to Erik at first glance to be a bit foolhardy. She wasn't dressed properly, and she was riding bareback. Upon closer examination, Erik's eyes narrowed alarmingly, and his jaw tightened with agitation. *Merde'*! What the thunder was she thinking? Did she want to kill herself? He immediately started grabbing up clothes, threw on his wig and boots, and within a moments time, was down the stairs and into the yard, but the stallion was already out of sight.

Monique rode Hurricane down the rutted lane, away from the inn, coming out onto the main road within several minutes. Crossing over the road, she cantered gracefully across a long, narrow green pasture with sheep grazing at the opposite end, its boarders partitioned with low stone fences that followed the rolling contours of the land. Touching her heels to Hurricane's flanks, she fell into a faster canter, and coming to another stone wall, the stallion glided over the fence with ease. The exhilaration made her giddy! Taking a long, deep breath of air into her lungs, she could smell the saltiness of the sea as she neared high cliffs overlooking the water. To the right was a stalwart, cylindrical tower, or light beacon, made of sandstone that warned ships to avoid the treacherous rocks and shoals below. Sea gulls soared high above, circling, swooping down to trail inches above the water, until they swooped up their meal.

Coming to another higher stonewall that wound around the lighthouse, Monique dismounted, using the wall as a stepping stone for getting off the large beast. She stood on the wall, leaning against the stallion's side, looking out to sea. She watched foamy white spray shoot high into the air, as the water crashed upon the jagged rocks below. Was life like this—waves that were controlled by the tides, cresting on the shoreline, until some huge obstacle was in the way, sending the water and spray in every direction, except towards the shore where it was destined to end? Her own life had been routine and basic when her father was alive. And then he died, leaving her torn in many directions, not knowing which way to choose. None had particularly sounded attractive. She had taken the easiest way out. Running away! And her journey had brought her here. She was glad to have time alone to think. She knew Erik had dark and dangerous secrets that he didn't want to reveal. Would he be stubborn, and never tell her? Could she marry him and not know? Would he even let her leave, if he knew about the child? She would raise their baby alone if he did not want it... of that she was certain! This child would be a part of the man that she loved, and nothing would change that. Nothing! This child would have at least one parent that loved him.

She heard the thundering of horse's hooves behind her and turned around, not leaving the wall. Erik was coming at a very fast pace on one of his beautiful bays, and by the expression on his face, he didn't look particularly happy. She had to stifle a laugh and keep a serious face, because she could just imagine how he had to scurry around to dress, saddle, and catch up with her so quickly. So much for being alone to think!

Erik came flying off the bay, swinging his right leg over the horses' neck, and jumping to the ground in one fluid motion, catching his arm to his ribs as if in pain, doubling forward just a little when hitting the ground. He strode over to her angrily, and lifted her down from the wall, his face inches from hers as he spoke, "And where did you think you were going, dressed like that? You might have broken your neck!" Keeping his hands on her shoulders, he looked right into her dark blue eyes, his green ones spiting sparks of fire!

"Don't be silly, Erik. I know how to ride as well as anyone," she said, trying to make him see reason.

"If you had fallen off and broken your neck…how would I have known?" he said rather sternly. He gave her a little shake just for effect, but she had caught the underlying relief in his voice.

"Erik, don't be ridiculous. I would never fall off of a horse," she said calmly. " I'm too good a rider," she pointed out, shrugging his words off as unwarranted.

"Just see that you don't," he said, his temper finally waning, realizing that she was correct. She was a very good rider. It was just that she had left without telling him that had gotten his goat, and the fact that she was dressed like…*that*! She was entirely too…enticing…and anyone could accost her. The muscles worked in his jaw as he tried to decide if he would let her off without anymore scolding, but when he thought about how utterly beautiful she looked with her hair blowing about her in the wind, and the way her dress clung to her shapely figure, he decided he wouldn't. "You didn't inform me where you were going," he finally said, his voice calmer, but still intense.

"Well, I didn't exactly know where I was going, Erik, but you need not have worried. I would have come back in due time," she said with a little humor. The look she afforded him when she realized what she had actually said, was priceless. She was hard pressed to keep from laughing, thinking it wiser to swallow her giggle.

Erik blanched, his face without his mask, clearly stormy and nonplussed at her answer. She had an irritating knack of doing that...throwing his own words right back in his face. "Do you have a reason for needing to get away from me?" he asked, not understanding why she would not have told him she was leaving. "If you wanted to go riding, we could have done it together."

"I just wanted some time alone," she said simply, turning around towards the stonewall and the sea.

His annoyance completely gone, he put his arms around her, and pulled her back against his chest. "And why would you need time alone to think, love," he said, his voice becoming shaky as he thought about loosing her, from a fall or because she would intentionally run from him.

"I needed time alone to think about what I must do," she said.

"Do?" he questioned.

"That circumstances might make it necessary for me to leave," she said.

"Leave?" he choked out, spinning her around to face him. "Why would you leave? I promised to tell you everything," he said in a whisper. Had he waited so long that now she might leave without even knowing his past? Had he been so negligent of her feelings that he had ruined everything? His fear of loosing her had guided his actions! Would he loose her anyway? Would she even listen to him now?

Mustering up her courage, she decided there was no time like the present for revealing her news. "I didn't know if you would welcome a baby," she said easily, wincing a little as she looked up at his face. There! She had said it! She waited for him to become angry, and thunder at her again. Perhaps even become tyrannical and denounce the child. He didn't smile, nor did he frown, so she didn't know what he was thinking.

But Erik wasn't angry. He looked at her in stunned silence, totally dumbfounded, trying to decide if he had heard her correctly. A baby? Could it be true? Of course it could be true, he reasoned, as a tight feeling of exhilaration gripped at his chest. His eyes turned to the color of the darkest emeralds she could imagine, and he pulled her into his arms, crushing her against his chest with a melding force. He bent his head to sear her moist lips with such a hungry, savage kiss that it left her dizzy and wanting more, her knees so weak she had to cling to him to continue standing. Raw sexual energy oozed out of every pore of his tall, hard masculine body, and his need to take possession of her body was overwhelming. She was carrying his child. He fought to keep his reasoning at the forefront, wanting more than ever to put her body beneath him, and show her without words the love he had for the mother of his child. Even knowing the possibility existed, the reality of the situation was unequivocally mind boggling. As his lips trailed over her neck, sparking a wanton need within her, he mumbled in a husky voice, " I can not let you leave, no matter what the circumstances. My child must have a name."

That statement made her eyes widen! The circumstances! Of course it would be a concern to him… thinking the child could possibly be deformed like he was, "The circumstances do not concern me, Erik," she whispered, knowing she would love his child, no matter what.

"You might think different when you finally know the truth—when the truth becomes more obvious," he said with disgust, turning his back, fear gripping his entire body to the point he thought he might truly be sick, right there in front of her. His hands began to visibly shake, but he held them at his side, knotted into fists to keep them steady, willing himself to remain in control. The time had finally come to tell her! No more stalling or finding something to stand in the way, staving off the telling of his horrible revelation. It was time to face the music, so to speak, Erik thought with morbid irony.

"Don't be ridiculous, Erik, it won't matter," she assured him, placing a hand on his arm. She looked up at his face, and she could see that he had fear in his eyes.

"It won't matter that I'm a murderer, and I hurt the people I love most?" he whispered, his voice breaking, as he choked out those horrible words.

"Erik! What are you talking about?" she said stunned, shaking her head, trying to sort out his meaning.

What was he suppose to say? How should he begin? Suddenly he grabbed her hand and pulled her over to the wall, lifting her over to dangle her feet on the seaward side, then climbed over to sit down beside her. He stared out to sea, his voice hardly audible through the slight wind that whistled around the open grounds of the tall beacon light. "She hated me!" he said simply, his shoulders slumped, his head bent in total rejection.

Monique didn't understand. "Who hated you, Erik," she asked, confused.

"My mother did," he fairly screamed at the wind, turning his head away in embarrassment, unable to look her in the eye. Keeping his head turned away he barely whispered, "Don't you understand...she didn't want me...and that will not happen to a child of mine."

"Your mother...but why...?" Monique started to ask.

"Well why not, my dear! Who would want to live an eternity with this?" he said with anger, pointing to his face as he stared right into her eyes, his voice hoarse, his fury barely contained. His body was shaking as he turned his face toward the sea.

"I would, Erik…I love you!" she said, turning her body around to face him. Looking into those eyes that showed all the hurt of the world, she placed a hand on his deformed cheek, and kissed him sweetly on the lips. "I would…because I love you!"

"You're different!" he said in a suddenly subdued voice, hugging her to his chest. "You're the only one that has ever loved me."

"That's not true, Erik. There are many people that have concern for you. The entire crew was concerned about you welfare aboard ship. You were their hero!" she pointed out reasonably.

"Hero? That's rich!" he said belligerently, because he felt belligerent. " I've always been hated by anyone who could see me," he said wretchedly, not fully understanding why now should be any different.

"Who are you, Erik?" she asked, sensing he needed an avenue to start his story, but not finding a way to begin.

"Who did you think I was?" he countered, turning the tables, putting her on the defensive, instead of himself.

"That's not fair, Erik. I don't know! I met this man in a boat, running away from…something! You could have been anybody, I suppose, but by your manners and your learning, I thought you might be some titled gentleman. Perhaps a Lord or something," she said, not really knowing what to say. What did you say to a question like that?

Erik snorted! "A Lord, or something!" he spat at her. "Oh, I was a Lord alright! Lord over my own domain, deep within the bowels of the earth. I believe they call it hell, my dear," he said, his anger beginning to rise just thinking about it. He repressed his irritation as best he could, trying to keep his temper under control as he struggled vigilantly for the correct words. Words that would tell his story honestly, but not alienate her love. If such were possible!

Monique sensed Erik's tension building as his body became more rigid. "Erik, it's okay," she soothed. "I'm here to listen. Just remember that I love you. I'm carrying our child, and I need to know your past. And I'm not going to leave you." With those words she felt his body start to relax, but she sensed there was great anger inside of him that was surely going to come out. She steeled herself to hear the worst.

Slowly he began to unravel the tale of his past, not giving himself any quarter or offering any excuses, just the facts as mankind hands out the ever, popular inhumanity to those that are different. For the most part, Monique just let him speak, asking questions when she didn't understand, but letting him purge the anger that was a canker, eating at his insides like a sickness. A sickness that had also overtaken his soul!

"My mother hated the very site of me," he said, concentrating hard on trying to breathe as his words unfolded. "As far back as I can remember she made me wear a mask. I saw her rarely, and one day when I was about seven, I woke up in a cage at a traveling gypsy circus. I never knew how I got there, but my keeper taunted me for three years, laughing in a hideous monotone that my mother had sold me. To this day, I do not know if it is true!" he said, his eyes brimming with unshed tears. "Could you hate a child so much that you would sell it?" he asked, almost like he thought she should have the answer. Tears ran down his face, and he swallowed with great difficulty to continue speaking, his throat aching from the strain of trying to hold back more tears.

When she didn't answer, but only held his hand tightly, he continued. "I was an animal, Monique, kept in filth and squalor! Hardly ever given a chance to wash, and no privacy for any human functions. People paid to see me without a mask. And when I bulked at showing my face, my keeper beat me senseless. Sometimes he went too far, rendering me unconscious, and that angered him even more, taking it out on me twofold when I awoke. Viewers laughed, and spit, and screamed in horror at my face. They threw money into the cage and my keeper collected it. I was a *prize* moneymaker." He laughed, a most wretched sound escaping his lips. "They paid money for the privilege of seeing a horrible freak. A freak!" he yelled out, his voice rising. With those words, he was on his feet and swung around to face her. "Would you pay money to see a freak?" he asked, almost screaming, but he wasn't really expecting an answer. He was talking to himself, trying to sort out answers in his own mind. He held his right hand over the right side of his face, his fingers parted so he could see between them, forming a mask, and Monique let out a sob, tears springing to her eyes, blurring her vision.

Erik was dangerously close to the edge of the cliff, and Monique was afraid. In his agitation he might fall over the side. "Erik, please come over and sit down," she suggested, but he didn't appear to hear. He just stood there, looking down at the rocks below, his hand over his face, silence stretching out before them. For a frightening moment, she thought he might jump!

"Luckily there was one person that did pay, and she took me away," he said, his voice calming just a little.

Hoping to bring him nearer to the wall, and away from the edge of the cliff, she asked, "Who took you away, Erik?"

"Madame Giry! She was a young ballerina, a couple years older than myself, studying at the Paris Opera House. The night she visited the circus, I had a chance to escape by strangling my keeper with a rope, and she was a witness. But instead of turning me in to the authorities, she helped me escape, and hid me in the catacombs beneath the opera house," he said, his face showing distress. "I lived there for… over… twenty… years, Monique," he said, emphasizing each word. "Although it became my home, a place I grew fond of for many reasons, it was also a living hell, my own private prison. A place filled with the deepest, darkest, most dismal loneliness you could ever imagine, just because the world did not wish to see my face." Tears were streaming down his cheeks and onto his neck, and his voice was raspy and ragged, as he paced back and forth in front of her. His eyes were red rimmed and glassy, and he looked totally miserable. When she could stand it no longer, she stood up, grabbing his hands tightly, and led him back to the wall. Sitting down on the ground to lean against it for support, she pulled him down next to her with a huge tug. He followed with little protest.

"But Erik, you are a very learned gentleman. How could you live down there for twenty years?" she said, amazed at what Erik was unmasking. How had he been educated? He was an architect and a musician. Never in her wildest imagination would she have ever thought any of this. It was so incredulous!

"I was very resourceful, my dear. I educated myself," he said with a sneer. "I wasn't going to let the world take *that* away from me," he said looking at her with a deeply pained expression. "They took everything else away, but they couldn't take *that*."

"Is that how you know so much about... everything?' she said, amazement in her tone that he survived all alone, her own anger rising, and her heart shredded into small pieces that he had been treated so terrible.

"I changed the underground caverns into a home, but I devised traps and stopgaps so no one but I could enter, unless they wanted to risk their life in doing so. And living below an opera house, I suppose it was only natural to eventually be exposed to music. It was my way of communicating with the world, and eventually it became my *entire* world. Music was as much a part of what sustained me, keeping me alive, as the food that I ate," he said, searching her face for understanding. "I had nothing else for comfort in that dark and lonely place. For many years, in some bazaar way, it satisfied every need that I had. The world hated me, shunned me, and all I wanted was to survive. But there came a time when music alone was not enough."

"Where was your Madame Giry, Erik?" Monique asked, puzzled.

Erik put his hands up to his lips in a praying position for several minutes deep in thought, the silence thick and tedious as he contemplated how to explain the hardest part. How could he tell the woman he loved such horrible things about himself? But he knew he had no choice. It had to be done, once and for all, laid out in the open between them.

"Surviving was one thing, but one can not live like a rat beneath the ground forever, merely existing for the sake of being alive. I needed someone to talk to, or I would have gone totally mad." He laughed with a decided sneer of sarcasm, adding, "I suppose there are those that would say I did anyway!" He paused, taking a deep breath as if the worst were yet to come. "I needed just one human voice to give me joy! Some reason to go on living! Madame Giry had grown up to be the ballet mistress of the opera house, and had a family of her own. I was like a little brother in her eyes. She saw to my welfare, as best she could under the circumstances, but I was not exactly the easiest person to deal with. I gave her a lot of trouble. My learning advanced so fast that I could outwit her quite easily. I don't think she ever feared me, but I did demand she do my bidding. And for that, sometimes I am ashamed," he admitted somewhat meekly, but she could tell he wouldn't have changed his actions.

"Who did you talk to, Erik, if not to Madame Giry?" Monique asked innocently.

"About eight years ago, Madame Giry brought a young orphan girl to reside at the opera house to learn ballet. She was frightened and alone, just as I was. She would talk to her dead father down in the chapel, and one night I heard her ask him about the angel of music he had promised to send her. It became a fixation I latched onto. For five years I watched her in the shadows, whispering to her around corners and in her sleep. Singing to her. I don't know whether it just amused me at first, or whether I felt some kind of kinship with her, because we were both so utterly and totally alone, but she responded to my voice, and eventually began calling me her *Angel of Music.* During those same five years I began running the opera house in the music genre. A sort of silent partner that no one noticed. It started as a joke on my part, giving me some needed amusement in my lonely existence, but I unwittingly became known as the Opera Ghost," he supplied, and heard her gasp.

"Erik...the opera ghost! I once heard a story about an opera ghost in Paris. I always thought it was just a silly tale." she said, her eyes opened wide in wonder.

"Oh no! It wasn't just a tale. It was unmistakably true, *ma petite*! You're looking at the Opera Ghost in the flesh...better known as the Phantom of the Opera! And as I became more famous, I became much bolder. Moving stuff around! Things disappearing! Letting people catch glances of me when I wanted them to do so, to further the illusion. I had little to occupy my time beside giving Christine her lessons," he offered without thinking.

"Whose Christine?"

Erik gave a deep sigh, closing his eyes tight in defense, not wanting to contemplate what was to come. After several minutes, he finally took a long, deep ragged breath, then turned to Monique, his eyes pleading for her to understand what he was about to disclose. He pulled her body close, nestling her between his legs as they sat on the grass, his back against the stonewall. "Christine was the orphan of whom I spoke You have to understand, Monique" he whispered into her hair. "I was a man with a deformed face, who had been denied everything... everything, from a world that did not care. I *did not* have a deformed body, and I had all the needs that any normal man would have." He stopped speaking to let his words sink in. " Three years ago I heard Christine sing and her voice was that of an angel. I was stunned that anyone could have such talent in one so young. I started tutoring her, but never let her see me. What I didn't count on was her growing into a beautiful and sensual young woman. I became obsessed with her. I wrote an opera for her! I wanted to further her career, but more than that, ultimately, I wanted to possess her." He paused again when Monique looked up at him sharply, of course thinking the worst, he was sure. "I had been in control of my own world, and I wanted to control her also. And for several years I did, until an old childhood friend came to see her, and then my world fell apart. I became mad with jealousy, for I was about to reveal myself, and finally I did, wanting to convince her that I wasn't a monster," he said, his voice tight with self-inflicted pain as well as that handed to him by mankind. His arms gripped Monique like a vice, believing she would run from him, like Christine had done.

"It's alright, Erik, I'm not Christine, and I'm not going anywhere," she assured him easily, realizing instinctively, he was afraid he would loose her.

"She came to me as a willing student of music, but I wanted more. I demanded her love! But she was too young to understand the real pain of my existence. I craved love and physical contact. At first I thought that she understood, because she responded to my voice, but in the end it was an impossible dream of mistaken reality. She loved another. In my madness and desire of her I did some horrific things, setting into motion disastrous events. The world denied me that which I wanted...and that which I needed to be a whole man, so in turn I lashed out with a terrific vengeance," he said, his anger again mounting, as he remembered each and every moment of those horrible events. His shoulders were heaving with tension, and he threw his head back in agitation, looking up at the sky.

Monique could tell he wanted to get up, needing to vent his fury on his feet, but she was afraid for his safety, so she leaned her body hard against his chest, preventing him from moving. The awkwardness of his story was past them, yet she knew he had more. She settled her head into his neck, her lips upon his skin and murmured, "It's okay, Erik, I'm here to listen."

He hugged her hard, bringing his lips down to kiss her hair, his arms tight bands around her ribs. His words spilled out rapidly, like he needed to be rid of them quickly, or he would be afraid to ever say them. "I murdered a man who threatened to reveal my secret existence, and dealt too harshly with another, causing his unintentional demise," he said, taking a deep breath, then he talked more slowly. "For those sins I was hounded by the police, and had to flee for my life, destroying, and leaving behind everything I have ever known," he finished hoarsely, his body shaking as he sobbed out those last words of grief, his face buried in her neck.

Monique could feel his hot tears as they ran down her chest and over her breasts. She knew that this was only the beginning of what had really happened, but believed he would reveal more in time, giving her a better understanding into this man that was to be her husband. Slowly she ran her hands over the wet skin of his neck and onto his cheeks, lifting his bent head to meet her eyes. "It's alright Erik, I'm not going anywhere," she repeated. "You will be my husband, and we will have our baby, and I will love both of you," she said with finality. "I can only tell you of the great sorrow that is within me, for what has happened to you. I would have understood if you had told me a long time ago." Gently she kissed him, her moist lips kindling a slow burning fire that once and for all, began to burn away that cocoon which had surrounded his heart for a lifetime.

"Do you hate me?" he asked, his lips trembling as he swallowed hard, trying to hold back the tears that seemed destined to spill forth with his grief.

"I could never hate you, Erik. In fact I will always love you. I can not totally condone what you did, but I believe I understand your reasons, just as I understood why you dealt with Jarvis the way you did." She lifted her head to look directly into eyes that mirrored the deepest, most pitiful sorrow she could ever imagine, but a face that reflected relief that she could understand. "Life is not always fair, my love. My heart breaks for what has been done to you, and I will spend a lifetime showing you that there are those who love you."

"Will you love our child if he should look like me," he asked.

"Especially if he looks like you, Erik" she said with passion, meaning every single word. "It is not the outside that I see when I look at you, although I believe you to be very handsome, with or without your mask. When you are not screaming or shouting at me," she added with emphasis. "But if I am honest, it is the man you are inside that I have come to know and love," she said, her entire body flushing with heat, noticing the sensuous, fiery look that had entered his dark green eyes. If looks could cremate, she was sure she would be a pile of ashes.

"Did I ever tell you that I loved you?" Erik said, his voice trembling, husky with pent up passion and tightly coiled emotions that needed to be unleashed, knowing she meant every word.

"No, M'Lord, I don't believe you ever have. An oversight, I'm sure," she said softly, a hint of devilish sarcasm in her tone.

"Well, I am now! I love you Monique Devereau!" he mumbled, kissing her soundly, his tongue mimicking what his body desired more specifically. When he finally came up for air, he asked, "Would you like to become the wife of Erik Devereau, Earl of Pembroke, before we leave here?" Before she could answer, he pulled her body down to lie beside him in the grass, deciding that kind of information could be left for another story. His groin pressing insistently against her thigh, assured her of his most urgent agenda.

"Since we have already dispensed with the honeymoon, which I would be more than happy to experience again posthaste, and have a family on the way," he laughed, his eyes sparkling with true merriment. "Perhaps we should have the wedding."

"If it is your wish that we wed before leaving here, I would be most happy to present my child with his legal father," she said laughing, just happy to be in his arms.

He pulled his body over hers, resting his elbows on the grass and played with loose tendrils of hair that fell into her face. "It is what *you* wish, *ma petite*, that interests me."

"Yes, Erik, I would like to become your wife before leaving here. But how can we arrange it on such short notice?" she asked, thinking it would take too long, and Erik wanted to be on his way to London.

"I'm in no hurry to go anywhere, love. I want to be caught in the web of a witch that has me under her spell, and will *never* release me from its binding power," he said, a wicked grin spreading across his face, as he lowered his head to take one plump breast into his mouth, Monique having totally missed the fact that he had unbuttoned her dress. The sensation of his warm lips and tongue upon her already heated flesh, sent shivers of pleasure through her body, and her mind instinctively set upon willing him, never to stop.

Teasing her flesh unmercifully, he said through his teeth, "A warning to the wise, my love! I have been alone far too long, and tend to want control."

Monique only laughed, stroking the muscles of his shoulders, wiggling her body beneath him in a suggestive manner. "I am well aware of that, Erik," she said, with just a hint of sarcasm. "Not to fear, love, for I believe I have a trick or two up my sleeve that could bring you around to my way of thinking," she added, an impish intonation to her voice, which only added flames to his own growing passion.

"Indeed," he answered huskily, knowing what she said was undoubtedly true, but he'd be damn, if he would readily admit it.

She groaned, the fire within her body escalating with his persistent touch, " Say it again, Erik," she coached, a wanton smile of abandonment upon her face.

Erik broke free from one luscious peak to mutter, "Say what love?" And when she groaned again, he waited a few breaths, thinking, as a magician he too had a little bag of tricks. Finally he offered, "Yes, *ma petite*, I love you." And with those words confirmed, he promptly took the other peak into his mouth, and sucked ever so gently, not wanting to hurt her tender breasts, that to his touch seemed firmer than usual, giving them attention with passion and purpose, rendering her totally mindless of thought or reason.

His hand inched up her bare leg, finding that place between her thighs he was seeking. His head came up sharply, startled, "No undergarments, my lady? How scandalous!"

"I was not exactly meaning to go out riding this morning, when I was sick and needed some fresh air," she said saucily.

"You were sick this morning?" he said in alarm, casting her a quizzical glance, starting to lift himself from her body in distress.

Pulling him back down by his shirt, she assured him, "It is most natural to have morning sickness when you are pregnant, Erik." Lazily she ran her hands over his bare chest, grazing his nipples, pulling a groan from him that started deep within his chest.

"Then perhaps we shouldn't be doing this," he said in retrospect, trying to suppress his passion, a most comical pout upon his lips. She had to giggle, for this was the Erik she had grown to love—a gentle, caring man—a dark, dangerous and savagely sensual man—perhaps even a ruthless adversary if thwarted wrongly—yet in the deepest sense of the word, a child at heart. A child that was disappointed when he didn't get his own way!

"I'm no more than about two weeks along, Erik. Do you mean to leave me wanting for months," she said, a little smile on her lips, knowing that would certainly get his undivided attention.

"Months!" he said with a frown, a bit disgruntled at the very idea. "I had not thought about months exactly," he said softly. "Perhaps just until you felt better."

Monique laughed at his expression, knowing exactly what was going through his mind. "It's alright, love. There is no reason not to make love."

"That's a welcome relief," he said silkily, starting in right where he left off. "I dressed a bit hastily today myself, dispensing with both undergarments and stocking, and let me just say, that boots without stocking are not wise," he laughed, divesting himself of britches and boots within seconds, only his shirt remaining. In moments he had lifted her out of her dress, leaving it beneath her as a barrier against the ground.

Systematically, he began a languid, lazy assault upon her entire body, leaving no part of her untouched, quickly spiraling his own passion to a fiery storm of impatience, leaving her in an equally delirious need. He growled low within his throat, when his hand dipped between her thighs and knew instantly that she was ready to accept him, regardless of his faults and his past, she still loved him.

The sky was a deep light blue, white billowy clouds moving across in rapid succession, a light breeze blowing inland with the clear scent of the ocean. The day had warmed markedly, blending with the rising heat of their passion, their newly declared love blocking out everything except one another. The stonewall fencing hid them from view except from the sea, giving them the privacy they needed. Passionately and urgently they made love on the sweet smelling grass, as if it were their first time together, their bodies entwined, hands seeking, stroking and probing to give the other pleasure, mouths touching and tasting in their wake. When he entered her body with that part of his own that bound them together for a lifetime, their union was an electrifying joining that swept them into the realm of a kingdom that was not upon this earth. When time had passed, and their passion had ebbed, they lay in each others arms, content with being together.

It was past noon when two horses clipped slowly down the lane to the inn, two riders upon the big bay, the stallion being led along side, his reins in Erik's hands. When they stopped in front of the stable, the young groom came running out in heated agitation, and seeing Monique riding with her body pressed tightly and sheltered to Erik's chest, one strong arm a tight band that held her against him, and both her legs hanging to one side, he was prompted to chastise. " I just knew you would fall off," he said, noticing her disheveled condition.

Erik began to chuckle, unable to help himself. And the more he thought about it, and the closer he discerned her rather discombobulated appearance...her dress mussed, several buttons missing, and grass stained beyond repair, the funnier it appeared to him. Finally, he was laughing so hard that tears sprang to his eyes unheeded. He relaxed his grip on her to wipe the tears away. In utter disgust, Monique slipped from his grasp, and slid to the ground before he could manage to stop her. With a look of pure disbelief at the way both men were carrying on, having a good laugh at her expense, she sash-shayed over to the porch in a manner that bespoke of her growing irritation, played a little tattoo with her bare feet upon the porch, gave them both a hot, fuming glance and disappeared into the inn. Behind her, Erik watched with eyes that smoldered with barely contained passion and lust, for the only woman he had ever loved! The mother of his child!

Chapter Eighteen

Erik stared down the long hallway to where the library was located, his feet in total disagreement with his emotions. To pull off a small, yet memorable wedding in a fashion that he wanted Monique to remember with fondness, he was going to need some help. And ready or not, there was no time like the present! He was not a man who had often requested help from another, unless paying dearly for the service, except perhaps his adopted sister, Madame Giry, who had done many things from the kindness of her heart, therefore he was more than uncomfortable in asking now, but something inside himself told Erik that Ian would not mind. In fact, he was rather sure that the good Captain would be most amused at his current predicament. Like it or not, for Monique's sake, he would have to swallow his pride to make this happen.

Erik rapped lightly on the door to the library with his knuckles, getting an immediate response for entrance. He opened the door with some hesitation.

"Come in Erik," Ian said with a hardy welcome, motioning Erik to a comfortable seat beside his large oaken desk, yet near a blazing fire set in a small stone hearth. He immediately noticed a less than confident look on Erik's solemn face that was so unlike this young man, it prompted him to immediately inquire, "What can I do for you, Erik?"

Standing against the hearth, too much churning within his mind to comfortably sit, Erik put his hands together, touching his lips as if in thought, trying to decide exactly how to begin. No use skirting around the issue, he thought with turmoil, realizing he could not delay any longer. "I'm rather in need of a pleasant place to hold a...ceremony," Erik said. "Like... perhaps the gazebo down by the river."

"Well of course, Erik," Ian said easily. "What kind of...ceremony...are you after?" he added, a touch of amusement beginning to vaguely shadow his features, a suspicious gleam dancing in his merry eyes.

"It seems I'm in need of a place to hold a wedding," he said simply. "And perhaps some help in making the arrangements, like needing a preacher, and advice on posting the banns," he added, knowing that England had different laws about such formalities than France.

"Who's getting married?" Ian asked, totally fascinated, his suspicions rather astute that Erik hoped for his whereabouts to be kept anonymous, and his affairs to be discrete.

"It seems that I am...and Monique, of course," he said, totally expecting the humorous grin that rapidly spread across Ian's face.

Ian laughed out loud, his large frame shaking with not so silent hilarity. "I'd say, my boy, you rather caught me on that one. You do keep a secret rather well," he admitted, thinking that here was yet another profoundly disguised fact that kept him guessing about this rather mysterious and ultimately private young man.

"Bloody hell," Erik swore, a scowl on his features, unable to focus on anything for several moments. His ire was rising, but he had the good sense to know he deserved this most uncomfortable hazing.

His laughing finally subsided, Ian motioned Erik towards the chair, at the same time wiping moisture from his eyes. "Take a seat, Erik. I swear, I'm all ears, but I think you have some explaining to do. If you had come to me at sea, lad, I could have married you instantly, but on dry land, I have no such powers," he said in amusement.

An hour later, Erik left the library, seeking Monique. Coming downstairs, not finding her in their room, he located her in the parlour, washed and scrubbed from their morning exertion, curled up on a settee, and looking quite lovely in a pretty lavender gingham dress. She was reading a small book of poems borrowed from Brianna and written in French. He sat down alongside her and placed a lingering kiss upon her forehead.

"It seems I have been quite remiss in finding out some rather important details about the lovely wench I'm about to marry," he confessed, hoping she would forgive him this newest, rather touchy oversight.

"What kind of important details," she asked, her vexation having waned from his earlier display of laugher at her expense. Not that she had blamed him. Her clothes had looked positively unraveled. But that had not been because of falling off of a horse, like he let the stable groom believe. Not that he could discretely mention the cause…that she had been deliciously and quite thoroughly, ravaged by the man she loved. Twice! First gently, as their newfound excitement about their first child had been realized, then again, after a leisurely nap within each others embrace, where the sun and the warm feathery breeze from the ocean had lulled them to sleep. Upon waking, Erik's need for her had ignited into a savage passion, which he quite expertly transferred to her, knowing he had finally shared his past, and by some miracle she still wanted to become his wife, not patronizing him for his past indiscretions, but loving him for the man he was today. Upon returning, and after a leisurely bath, she had taken tea and a light afternoon luncheon with Brianna, letting Erik fend for himself.

Erik cleared his throat, a sheepish look of embarrassment upon his features. "I have made arrangements for a small wedding ceremony to take place, here at the inn, down by the river, in a small white gazebo."

"Oh, Erik, that would be wonderful. I saw the gazebo and the flowers around it are showing the first signs of spring," she said with genuine excitement. "And when might this take place?" she asked, the reality of becoming this dangerous, fascinating, and gentle man's wife finally starting to sink into her senses. He had already given her a gift that she wanted from no other.

"The day after tomorrow," he assured her. "As soon as the banns can be posted. Although the law requires three days for such an occurrence, the time can be shortened with the right incentive and a little bit of persuasion," he said charmingly, his eyes telling her that he would do anything to make this happen.

"You mean money," she said with a knowing grin.

"Yes, ma petite. Money seems to be the universal language," he said, placing a quick kiss upon her pert little nose. He had never cared about money one way or the other, even though he had most expensive tastes, but at this moment, he was glad he had the knowledge that would give him an avenue to provide well for his wife and family.

Shifting in his place beside her, he took her hands in his own and kissed her palms, one by one. With two fingers, he tilted her chin up so that she looked right into his searching eyes and asked, "With all the information I so unwillingly extracted from the bewitching and enticing…" his head ducked to kiss her palms again, then transferred to her sweet, moist lips, as he murmured against her mouth, "*hooligan*," then looked into dark blue eyes that had narrowed just a bit, " that is to become my wife, I believe I was terribly remiss in not ever asking for her surname." He laid his forehead against hers for a long, shared moment. "It seems it is most necessary for posting the banns," he said, his neck flushing with a scarlet color just remembering the reaction Ian had given him when he went to sign the paperwork, and didn't know his soon-to-be wife's last name. He swore it took the man five whole miserable minutes, in Erik's memory, to contain his mirth. But even with all his most unfortunate *oversights,* Erik believed that for some strange reason, Ian genuinely liked him. Is this what friendship was all about? Acceptance without judgment? Not having ever, in thirty odd years, had a true friend of the male gender to call his own, the feeling was very complicated, and extremely hard to comprehend.

"Och, my dear laddie," she purred in her most genuine Scottish accent possible. "My father was a MacPherson of Pitman," she said proudly, knowing her ancestry well. "I grew up in the highlands of Scotland until I was about six, and then my father took a job at *Chappallae.* He never looked back because the pain of my mother's death so destroyed him. He wanted to be far away from all the memories. But he always, affectionately referred to me as his *bonnie lassie*, and the name Monique is readily translated to *Bonnie* in the Scottish language of the highlands," she said, an engaging smile on her face.

A quick intake of breath through Erik's teeth, made her glance into his eyes, as for the first time it all made sense to him. The last piece of that unsolved puzzle that had evaded him for so long, neatly slipped into place, the understanding of its significance showing on Erik's face at her words. The name she had used at the bordello had never consciously registered in association with what she had revealed on that first night they had made love. It had been tightly stored in his unconscious mind to help him deliver her from the evils of a man named Jarvis, then buried immediately to be momentarily forgotten in his haste and need to take her to safety. He marveled at the ability of the mind to produce such miracles, extracting information that was needed in a crisis and storing away that which was not.

"My father always envisioned me having a true Scottish wedding with him decked out in all of his Scottish finery. I saw him wearing his plaid on several very special occasions. Once at *Chappallae* when he formally handed over a prized filly to a Duke in a political ceremony, and he swore to me then, he would wear his full regalia the next time at my wedding. My father was continuously prodding me to take a suitor," she said with little humor. "I'm very sad that he won't be here, Erik," she added with feeling, her eyes becoming momentarily full of sorrow.

"I'm very sad also, love. I wish he could be here with you. Ian and Brianna have agreed to stand up as our witnesses," he supplied, more for information, but hoped it would ease her pain, if only a little.

"Erik...?" Monique questioned hesitantly.

"Yes!" Erik replied, his eyes roaming intently over the petite and beautiful woman he loved, hardly believing she had agreed to become his wife and soon give him a child. He immediately noticed her hesitation. "Is something amiss? Do you feel okay? Do you want to change anything?" he inquired, becoming anxious.

"I don't have anything to wear!" she exclaimed with such delightful innocence, that Erik had to chuckle, a deep rumble that started in his chest, and ended with him shaking, as he took her into his arms and kissed her most soundly, his hands starting to roam with familiarity over her sweet, enticing body.

When he finally remembered where he was, not that it concerned him overmuch, he said with a bit of dry humor, "This declaration coming from a wench that hates to shop is most unusual. I had thought that perhaps you would want to wear your new riding britches, but alas, it would be confusing who was the groom. Then again I could have suggested that most becoming flannel nightgown, but alas again, I tore it up long ago," he offered, recalling it had been quite satisfactory in greasing the metal parts of the crankshaft on the paddle steamer, and for other odd jobs in making repairs, affording him a few smiles of appreciation, when he declared it was something his new wife would not be needing.

When Monique tried to punch his chest with her free hands, he only laughed. "Although I would be most willing to take you shopping, and buy you anything your heart desires, my sweet, Ian has assured me that Brianna would be most upset with me, if I did not leave those arrangements to her, since there is not sufficient time to have a new dress made. He was most emphatic that you were *not to worry*," Erik finished, searching her eyes for approval.

"Oh, Erik, you have thought of everything," she declared, giving him a quick kiss on the lips, then jumped to her feet with excitement. About to run off to find Brianna, she gave him a sudden glance, stopping in her tracks. He had thought of everything and the idea of a small outdoor ceremony was thrilling. "Was that all you needed to know," she asked, not wanting to be rude, but itching with the exhilaration of the moment.

"Yes love, that's all I needed to know. And I'm sorry that I didn't ask you sooner," he said apologetically, seeing in her eyes instantly that he was forgiven. "Now go find Brianna. I'm sure the two of you will find much to talk about."

With that encouragement, she quickly disappeared from sight and into the kitchen. It was only moments before he heard a screech of excitement when the two women embraced.

Erik went back to the library, preparing himself mentally for his next encounter with Ian. After writing her surname onto the banns documents, Ian commented, "A Scottish lassie by birth? I should have known. Red hair and a temperament to match!"

Erik explained that her father had recently died and about her sadness at him not being at her wedding. "Perhaps I should have taken her to my estate in England, and then journeyed to the highlands to give her a Scottish wedding, but I did not want to take her to our new home without being my legal wife," Erik admitted.

"Exactly how far are you willing to go to bring her back to her Scottish heritage? Being Irish and a Scotsman myself, Erik, I must tell you, that you can take a Scot out of Scotland, but you can not take Scotland out of a Scot. That she wanted to see her father at her wedding in all his fine regalia means her father instilled the heritage within her deeply, even though she may not realize it."

"I'll do anything for that lovely lass, Captain! She is my life," Erik said quite emphatically.

"Glad to hear you say that, Erik. You leave everything to me," Ian said with genuine satisfaction, and the look he afforded Erik gave him a momentary pause, but he dismissed it immediately, confident that Ian knew exactly what he was doing.

Brianna flipped open the heavy lid to an old trunk and rummaged through the contents for several moments. " I've kept this safe for many years, because I had the feeling that someday it would be used again, and I know it is exactly your size. There was a day, many years ago, when I was quite petite and slim," she told Monique, laughing merrily at her own buxom figure.

Monique looked around the sunny attic room. There were lovely old pieces of furniture pushed against the wall in matching sets. She supposed they were used now and then within the inn. These attic contents appeared dusted and shiney, and the room did not have the appearance or the musty smell of most attics. It looked more like a storage area, than a room for junk.

"Oh yes, here it is," Brianna said, pulling out a lovely ivory dress made of soft, flowing satin, with an over dress of delicate Belgian lace covering it from neckline to hem. The sleeves were capped, to be worn either high or off the shoulder. A thin, pink velvet ribbon wrapped around the ribcage just below the bust-line, culminating in back with a small bow, its long ends trailing down the length of a short train.

Monique gave a little gasp. The dress was exquisite. She had never worn anything quite so lovely. "Are you sure you won't mind letting me borrow this?" she exclaimed.

Brianna laughed, "It will be a treat to see you wearing my dress. You will be simply stunning, my dear. Hurry and try it on. I'm a bit taller, but a small adjustment in the hem will be easily accomplished."

Monique slipped out of her day dress and chemise, and Brianna helped her fit the wedding dress over her head. As Brianna hooked all the tiny buttons along the back, Monique peered into a tall floor mirror that stood in the corner. Her reflection in the shiney glass made her blink her eyes with disbelief. The figure looking back couldn't possibly be her.

Brianna gave a little laugh, watching the expressions play across Monique's face. "Honey, when Erik sees you coming down that isle, he isn't going to know what hit him," she said with appreciation.

"Do you really think so?" Monique said, a bit apprehensive, wanting desperately to please Erik, and not disappoint him. She had worn so few dresses, and been such a tomboy all her life, that she didn't know much about fancy clothes. She had told Brianna about her father, and how sad it made her feel that he wouldn't be here. All the trouble she had given him growing up, running the countryside in britches, she was quite convinced, this would have been his finest hour.

Brianna's thoughts about this delightful bonnie lass, were running in another avenue altogether. Monique was such an unspoiled child where her beauty and her expectations of people were concerned, that she did not see really how totally charming and breathtakingly lovely she really was. But Brianna could see in Erik's eyes that he knew, and was extremely protective. In turn, she could see in Monique's eyes and in her mannerisms that she positively adored Erik. Ian had told her about what this young couple had done aboard his ship when the chips were down and their help was so desperately needed, unselfishly lending a hand in any way possible, and what it had cost them in the end. Brianna didn't know what lay beneath Erik's mask, but obviously to Monique, it did not matter. He was a mysterious and most captivating man, and her Ian liked him very much. That's all the convincing that she needed.

Brianna and Monique took the dress downstairs to be hemmed, taking care that Erik did not see it, and made a few small plans about the wedding. Brianna wanted to serve an informal, yet intimate tea after the ceremony, with little tortes, cake and punch. In preparation for getting the bride ready, a room on the first floor was set aside for Monique to dress for the ceremony. The groom must not see the dress. It was simply tradition.

"Do you think he will be pleased?" Monique asked, still not entirely convinced that all this was really happening.

" I think that both of you will be very surprised when you meet for the ceremony," Brianna said lightly. "Neither of you will be disappointed," she added, thinking she could hardly wait till this most unexpected and delightful wedding took place. It would prove to be quite interesting. Thinking back on her own wedding, a fine ceremony in the old Scottish tradition, she had a large lump in her throat. Besides, she simply loved surprises.

Erik fidgeted with the towel around his lean hips, awaiting Ian to bring his clothes for the wedding, and the twisted tension in his gut presented him with the most distasteful assurance that he was more than a little nervous. He had vacillated back and forth a hundred times, trying to decide whether to wear his wig, his mask, both or neither. The question upper most in his mind was who was Monique marrying? The famed Opera Ghost, the man she had met in a small boat, sheltered within the bushes along a riverbank, or the man he knew she accepted in private, physical faults along with many, many others? Which man did she expect to find at the altar? She had assured him a dozen times that his face did not make a difference in her acceptance of him. Could he put his pride aside just this once, and give her what he believed she would want? Did he have the courage to exclude the rest of the world, regardless of what they might think, and just be himself. Monique was dressing downstairs with Brianna's help and he knew she would be a vision of beauty. Could he allow beauty to marry the beast? Did he have the right to present a false entity to the woman he loved in this most sacred ceremony that would bind them together for eternity?

A knock on the door ended Erik's battle with his conscience, and he bade Ian to enter.

"Exactly what is that?" Erik queried with incredulous speculation, somewhere between humor and terrifying horror, as Ian closed the door behind him, the most amusing, yet magnanimous grin plastered upon his own handsome face.

"This, my boy, is what is going to put a beautiful smile on your young bride's face, that you so befittingly honor her father. It took a bit of searching, but with diligence and a small prayer, I was able to find what we needed," he said, noting a look of growing apprehension on Erik's dark and brooding features.

"We," Erik croaked, still not believing what he was ultimately seeing.

"I seem to recall the words, *'I'll do anything for that lovely lass'*," Ian reminded him, eliciting a groan from Erik that bespoke of rapid defeat.

Within fifteen minutes Ian had Erik dressed appropriately, and they descended the stairs together, coming into the foyer just as Brianna entered, having left Monique alone to make last minute adjustments to her makeup and await her signal that the men were in place at the gazebo. When she saw Ian and Erik in all their finery, she blushed with excitement, "Oh, gentleman, don't you both look handsome in those bonnie outfits." She approached both men, gave them each a quick kiss on the cheek, assuring Erik with soft words and an additional hug, that he had made the right decisions. "Now you men take your places, and I will summons your bride," she told Erik.

"I have one last thing to do first," Erik said, and quickly disappeared into the parlour. Moments later he returned, holding a violin that had been mounted on the wall in a glass case. "Do you mind if I borrow this?" he asked, holding the delicate, polished instrument with reverence. "I want to play for my bride as she comes down the isle," he said.

"Oh Erik, how lovely. It will be something she won't be expecting. In fact, I'm sure she will not be expecting any of this." With those words she gave her husband and Erik a most blinding smile, saying, "Now scoot, both of you. It's time for the ceremony."

Monique's stomach was a jumble of butterflies. She had not seen Erik since yesterday afternoon. With all the last minute arrangements of fitting her dress, arranging flowers for her bouquet, the excitement of decorating the gazebo, and planning for today's activities of arranging her hair with Brianna's help and taking a most frivolous and luxurious bath to be perfect for her groom, she decided to sleep alone in the downstairs bedroom. Besides, the groom should not see the bride before the ceremony on the day of the wedding. And Erik had many things to accomplish to get them ready for traveling on to London. The wagon and horses had to be attended, and food and supplies obtained for the two day journey. She was sure Erik would want to do this himself. He had almost totally regained his health and others doing his work was not something he fancied. It was one of many things that endeared him to her.

As she stepped out onto the long flagstone path that led to the gazebo and her groom, she heard the faint melodic strings of a distant violin. The melody was vaguely familiar, but at first she could not put her finger on the tune. She could see the white gazebo away in the distance, at the end of the narrow pathway in which she was walking, its perimeter surrounded with the first fragrant and colorful flowers of spring. Passing through an archway of trellised growing vines, the gazebo came into full view and the picture she was presented with, sucked the breath right from her chest. For several stunned filled moments, she thought she could not breathe. Her cherished and beloved Erik stood at the forefront, beside the preacher, playing the violin, and dressed in the full regalia of her father's Scottish clan, the hunting plaid of the MacPherson's. Her heart was so filled with appreciation for this one simple act of love that it was near to bursting. He had done this for her! The beautiful splendor of the highland kilt, with its grayish-blue background, over-toned with black squares and fine threads the color of heather, was accentuated with a dark blue waist-length jacket and vest, adorned with three square buttons along the cuffs and down the front of the vest. A black leather sporran lined with fur, hung down the front of his kilt, suspended on a chain from his slim hips, and belted down by a wide black leather belt around his waist. A pristine white shirt lay beneath his jacket. Finishing the outfit were heavy black knee-high socks with heather-colored side guards, and a dirk tucked in at his right knee. He reminded her of a highland warrior, raw and primal, his tall, dark, magnetic features, sending a chill down her spine that made every nerve in her body stand on end. Her eyes were brimming with unshed tears. Realizing he was playing an old Scottish ballad, one she often heard her father humming, she offered him a brilliant smile. As he played, his head moved back and forth with the bowstring, and occasionally in concentration he closed his eyes, feeling the power of the music. Her heart filled with over-flowing joy when she realized he had not worn either his mask or his wig, his dark, thick locks splayed about his head, stray strains of hair falling over his forehead as he played, and to her, he was the most handsome man she could ever imagine. She loved him more than life.

Upon seeing Monique step through the trellis of flowers, Erik was struck with the most awesome feeling of wonder that sent heat rushing through his body. A vision of pure and simple beauty was approaching and she would soon be his wife. It was mind shattering for him to even comprehend, how it had all come to this. Please...God! Let it not be a vicious nightmare, like he had experienced so many times in the past, raping his mind and sending him into a vicious rage, after waking to find that it had only been a dream. He concentrated on the vision coming ever closer, a beautiful smile on her face, his own eyes growing wide and his mouth partially open. Monique's ivory dress, accented with pale pink, clung to her petite figure, the bodice pushing her breasts up, presenting every curve to its best advantage, enticing and teasing him, as this most beautiful creature walked his way...to marry him! He couldn't take his eyes off of her and despite the importance of the moment, he felt his lust flare with uncontrolled vengeance, and for the first time he was thankful for his sporran. She was looking at him with an identical desire in her eyes, and he was finally confident that he had made the correct decisions, that of agreeing to honor her father by wearing his clan's plaid, and by being totally himself.

Erik put the violin down, and stepped towards the opening. Taking Monique's hand he walked backwards, leading her up the steps, his wide, ocean green eyes glued to sapphire blue ones, as in mesmerized wonder, unable to even blink, their eyes clung to each other. For a few long moments, it seemed to everyone present, that they were in a world that excluded anyone else. Finally Erik turned towards the preacher, and the ceremony commenced.

It was a typical Scottish ceremony, using the old wording for vows. "I Erik, now take you, Monique, to be my wife. In the presence of God, and before these witnesses, I promise to be a loving, faithful and loyal husband to you, until God shall separate us by death." Erik's voice was slow and purposeful, his commanding tones giving forth a promise of strength, protection and love.

"I Monique, now take you Erik, to be my husband. In the presence of God and before these witnesses, I promise to be a loving, faithful and loyal wife to you, until God shall separate us by death." With her words, her voice and her eyes, as she looked directly at Erik, she told him that not only would she love him for eternity, but she would be tolerant of a man that was overcoming a lifelong history of pain, and that she would do everything in her power to ease it.

As the formal ceremony ended and congratulations were said all around, Monique finally noticed that Ian also had on the formal plaid of his own clan, the McShanes.

"Why do I have the feeling that you had a lot to do with Erik's…outfit," Monique teased Ian.

"Lovely lady," Ian said most seriously, taking her fingers and pressing his lips against her hand. "It was most pleasurable, not only to find a way to make you happy, but to see the most incredible expression on Erik's face when I first presented him with my idea, which I might add was not thirty minutes before the ceremony, giving him little quarter to back out," he said with a chuckle. Erik snorted with pure agitation.

In retaliation, he leaned down towards Monique's ear, and whispered, "Ian assured me most persuasively, my love, that regimental, the true Scottish way, was the only proper way to dress." With that he arched an eyebrow, flashing her the most devilish grin, his eyes promising to take advantage of that most elemental and convenient Scottish fact as soon as possible.

"Erik, you are impossible," she admonished, but her eyes told him otherwise, as they widened in surprise, and in spite of herself she stifled a laugh. What's good for the goose was good for the gander, she thought, an impish grin forming quite naturally. "Tsk, tsk, my love," she admonished, in mock irreverence. "If both of us had been in britches, you declared we would not know who was the groom. Since both of us are in *skirts*...of a sort," she whispered, true devilment in her eyes, "Is it truly possible to know who is the bride?" She batted her eyelashes at him in earnest. The narrowing of his eyes, and the lusty gleam he gave her, as he pulled her bottom tightly against the front of him, pushing his sporran purposefully aside, proved quite satisfactory to his mind, that their was no question of gender. Getting hard evidence as an answer, she tried to wiggle from his grasp, but he held her tightly in place with an arm around her ribcage, as they accepted congratulations from Marta, Bradford and Crocket, who were surprise guests at the wedding.

The ride from London to the outskirts of Cheltenham had been pleasant enough. The weather was constantly warmer on a daily basis, and everywhere you looked, the grassy fields, surrounded by many typically low stone fences, were greener than even one week past. Although the air was not as chilly as it had been closer to the sea, Erik had insisted Monique wear her cape, if only around her shoulders. He would "not have her catching an illness." He fretted about the possibility of her becoming ill, but paid no attention to his own health. The irony of it was preposterous.

Erik had been an enigma on their ride this morning. He was more silent than usual. Since first meeting her husband, she was extremely aware that he did not spit out unnecessary words. In fact, she found him rather quiet, tending to think long and hard about what he might say, before he said it. Unless you discounted those times he was irritated at her, being more than rapidly vocal and annoyingly opinionated. Unlike herself of course, she thought, unwilling to admit otherwise, yet knowing he would certainly beg to differ. Perhaps it was from being virtually alone for two decades. Yet she found his sense of humor to be more than sharp and witty on many occasions, and he possessed the talents of a teacher on important issues, whether they concerned just their own private life together, or things about the world in general. This fact alone had been the most puzzling for her to assimilate, knowing that he had been isolated below the ground for over twenty years. With the vast knowledge he possessed on so many subjects, and on so many levels, both practical and merely book oriented, it was almost unfathomable to perceive that he had taught himself.

She looked back on the last few days with humor, fondness, and yet some puzzlement, knowing she would cherish every moment. Erik had done everything in his power, considering their most peculiar situation, to give them a lovely wedding. That she had fallen in love with her dark, foreboding, and mysterious stranger there was no doubt. She looked upon both the past few weeks and the coming future as an adventure. Much of Erik's past had been unraveled, but with her limited knowledge to work with, she believed there would be more events of heartaches from his past, mingling like a tightly braided rope with the joy of building a future. To her mind's eye, she was instinctively positive that life wedded to this complicated and undeniably commanding, yet gentle man beside her, would never be dull.

The wedding party and guests had spent a few hours talking and getting reacquainted, the four men deep in a discussion about repairs to Ian's ship, what new equipment had been ordered, and when the paddle steamer would again be put into commission. Monique had been rather amused that Erik quickly noticed some special attention she had received from Steward Bradford, who was inquiring rather lengthy about her welfare and if their trip to the inn had been satisfactory, saying that he had missed saying farewell and was glad to have the chance to do so now.

Ian, picking up immediately also that Erik's attention centered on his steward and Monique, gave an amused laugh, and leaning close to Erik's ear, commented, "Don't fast yourself, lad. She's all yours and don't ever forget it! Bradford is just young and enamored with a pretty lady that has spunk. She really did crack a whip, just like I told you. Take care of her, Erik, or someone else will!"

Erik gave a little snort, his eyes a dark, emerald green, as he stared directly at his wife, and when she turned his way, feeling his gaze boring down upon her, he replied, "I can well imagine the picture. I have had the distinct fortune, or perhaps *misfortune,* to be on the other end of that whip you speak of," he said, both humor and respect in his tone. "Do not worry, Captain, no one will be taking care of my wife, except me. I can guarantee you that." And the look on Erik's face assured Ian that Erik would do just that.

Ian only chuckled. "Life with a good woman should never be dull and has many obvious advantages, Erik, but never for a minute believe that you would want them docile and compliant against their will. The spitfires are the ones that you keep for a lifetime. Take my word for it. Believe me, I know," Ian said, his own eyes finding his wife's and clashing in a heated turmoil of promises.

Erik had every intention of keeping Monique safe. In fact, if he had his way, wrapped safe and snug within his arms would commence immediately. He smiled with devilish intent! He had ordered up another honeymoon...one for after the wedding, instead of before. For traditions sake, he wanted to assure himself, once again delaying their journey to London! Looking at the beautiful, enticing figure of *his* wife, one he most certainly intended to keep, his entire body ached to put her beneath him, and show his love the way that he wanted. The sooner they were alone, the better!

The positively smolderingly looks that Erik kept shooting Monique's way, were enough to melt her to a puddle. Erik had indicated that he had a surprise for her, not wanting to reveal it until after the ceremony. Were they starting off immediately for London? The journey would take two days, and the hour was getting late. Marta had come from Weymouth and seeing her had been quite exciting. That her friends had thought enough of them to join in their happiness was overwhelming. It was good to prove to Erik that they did have friends that cared.

As evening drew upon them, Erik came to her side. "Ma petite, we really must say goodbye to our friends," he said, slipping an arm around her waist and pulling her close to his hip.

"Will the ride be long to where we stay tonight, Erik? Will we get there after dark?" she asked. "And should I change into something comfortable for traveling?" she added.

"Oh, love, most assuredly, you will be changing into something comfortable, but it won't be for traveling," he said so only she could hear, a devilish grin just touching his eyes that had turned that dark shade of emerald green that she had learned to interpret so well.

"What do you mean, not for traveling? Where are we going?" she asked, not understanding.

"You didn't think I would spend time traveling, when I could make passionate love to a fiery red-haired sea siren. A Scottish one, at that!" he said, his hand roaming over her sweet derriere that was hidden from view, their backs most conveniently against the trellis.

"Ooohh!" she exclaimed, feeling his hand caress her bottom in a most familiar fashion, her face blushing red. "You are incorrigible, *my dear husband*!"

"Never doubt it, my dear. I fear our one night apart has merely heightened my lust for our union.... *in the physical context*," he said, his breath hot against her ear. "And the most *unusual feeling* that few *barriers* stand in the way of my taking you, does nothing, my sweet, to quell that lust. Are you quite ready to depart, *mon amour*?" he asked, anxious to make good on his promise.

"Where are we departing to?" she asked, still perplexed, yet highly amused, knowing that wearing a kilt in the traditional way would be odd, to say the least, but it also extremely excited her. The very idea that Erik had agreed to this, made her giggle, in spite of herself. To have been a bird on the windowsill watching him dress!

A narrowing of Erik's eyes at her laughter prompted him to say. "Say your goodbyes, my love. You are trying my patience."

After many farewells to the guests, the phaeton was pulled up, the bay's harnessed and ready. Monique had been prompted not to change her clothes, for the ride would not be long. They journeyed not ten minutes down the road to a lovely cottage owned by the inn. Before entering the doorway, Erik swept Monique off her feet, and carried her over the threshold, saying, "not our permanent home, *mon amour*, but one that will do for the moment."

Entering the cottage, they found one large room, decorated in the quaint setting of a rural hunting lodge. In one area was a bedroom set, another a living area with a roaring fire emanating from a stone hearth, and lastly a small dining area. A large basket of food lay packed upon the table. Erik carried Monique into the room and set her on a plush bear skin rug in front of the fire. The light from the flickering flames sent streaks of brilliant light across her lovely face and body, illuminating her hair and gown against the background of the hearth, and the picture it presented took Erik's breath away. Monique was so beautiful. A living and breathing goddess of his every fantasy! And she was *his wife!*

"The cabin is lovely, Erik," she said. "I must admit, I am most thankful not to be traveling to London so late in the day."

Erik fell to the floor beside her, his own body pinning her partially beneath him. "I wanted to make love to my wife… *tonight*," he choked out, his emotions at that moment spiraling out of control, knowing this woman would truly be by his side…forever! "I did not want to be riding in a carriage, or I fear I would have taken you right there, a few leagues down the road." His lips captured hers with a kiss that branded them with his possession, his tongue plunging deep, his body virtually an inferno.

Monique put her hands against the sides of Erik's face, and pushed him gently away, breaking the pressure of his kiss. She looked deep into the eyes of her man, "Thank you for not wearing your mask, or your wig, and becoming my husband as the man I know and love." Gently she traced his full bottom lip with the tips of her fingers, then followed with her tongue and then her mouth, nipping it with her teeth before kissing him full on the mouth.

Erik's nostrils flared, as a flash of impatience whipped through his eyes, his gestures less controlled as pure male aggression became unleashed. He growled deep in his throat, pushing his plaid aside, then took her hand, wrapping it tightly around that rock-hard part of him that said he wanted her. And he wanted her now!

"When other men look at you, it drives me quite insane," he admitted. "I hate sharing you with anyone, even if for one amusing afternoon."

"You can't be selfish, Erik," she teased, knowing exactly what he meant, but unwilling to acknowledge it.

"I'm very selfish, indeed, my love, and you will learn that soon enough. I'll not share you with anyone," he said, pressing his hips against her thigh, even as she demonstrated with her hand that she understood his need. He closed his eyes in momentary ecstasy.

"Perhaps with just one," she said, her other hand resting on her abdomen. "With tiny feet," she added, giving him the most impish smile, as his eyes flew open at her words.

The idea of his child growing within her body ignited his passion to an indescribable level. "You can be assured, my sweet little witch, that our child will know his parents very well. That I will give up the private time we share together... *never*!" he said with such conviction, she was most pleasantly convinced that a child would never diminish their passion. Too many marriages fell stagnant with that occurrence. She was glad theirs would not!

Monique gasped when her gown fell suddenly to her waist, once again surprised at the deft ability of Erik's hands to unknowingly manage small buttons so expertly. He rapidly maneuvered the gown down and over her feet. Her bloomers followed quickly, stripping her naked. Pulling her under him, he caught one plump breast with his mouth, teasing it with his teeth. His touch was tantalizing and tortuous, yet not quite enough. She wanted to feel his hard masculine body naked and rippling against hers. All of it!

"What about your clothes, Erik," she admonished, working furiously at the buttons of his vest. Equally fast, he was divested of his jacket, vest, shirt and socks. When she removed his belt and sporran, and reached for his plaid, his hand grabbed hers, pinning them above her head. "Nay, my love, the plaid stays. I will take full advantage of the amenities offered in donning the dress of a Scottish warrior, if only for one day," he said, his eyes mocking, with an amusement that bordered on possession, and right now she most assuredly wanted to be possessed. What was he waiting for?

"Oh, aye!" she laughed, relaxing against the rug, blue sapphires melting into green emeralds, both dancing with the flames of the fire. "Anything the laird desires," she purred, pulling his body down against her own. Pushing the plaid aside once again, he proceeded to show her exactly what he meant. Joy and wonder played in every movement and expression of love they shared, soaring them to greater heights of appreciation for that love, finally sealed under God's binding power!

Their time together was one of joining and loving, searching and sharing, talking and discovering. All those things, once hidden and too prideful to easily reveal, were laid within an open book to share together. Erik told what he remembered about his time before living in his dungeon under the opera house, and the making of his lair, and Monique spoke about the little she remembered of Scotland, and growing up at *Chappallae*. Two days later they emerged from their cottage, Ian and Brianna much amused at their extended wedding night, yet food had been delivered to their door on a regular basis! A few hours of preparation and they were on their way to London.

The inn being only a day and a half from the old, booming capital of Britain, they traveled until dusk, whereby Erik stopped, much in the fashion they had used in France. He pulled the phaeton off the road into a tiny clearing, yet hidden by trees and bushes, laid blankets under a tree, and after a small meal of bread, cheese, fruit and wine, fell asleep for some much needed rest, Monique wrapped snuggly within his embrace. On the road again before dawn, with his wife's head resting in his lap in slumber, they headed toward the outskirts of London. Mid-afternoon they reached a fork in the road with a sign indicating two directions. Downtown London pointed to the right, and Lower London to the left. Erik paused in silent contemplation. He had told her, they had reservations for one night at a hotel in downtown London, but he swung the carriage to the left, saying, "I want to see the real London, to understand where we will be living. Things are not always as they seem."

Their detour gave her an appreciation for the man she had married, perhaps more than anything else could have done. They traveled though the poorest part of London, its shabby dwellings fallen in disrepair, yet people lived there. Others were small, but well kept, gaily decorated with pride, even though meager. Sweeping through the market area, where numerous wagons and carts gathered to sell their wares to the gentry, as well as the poor, Monique saw children of various sizes running the streets, dirty and scrapping for those items they needed to survive. Throughout this ride, Erik pretended not to notice his surroundings, but she knew that he did. She recognized it in his demeanor...the way he held the reins with his knuckles turning white, and that all familiar pout to his lips when something important was bothering him. That one part of humanity could live in such squalor, while others lived in wealth was quite apparent. Today Erik wore only his wig and gentleman's attire, and again he was stared upon like some kind of leper. Why he had chosen this route, she wasn't exactly sure, but somehow she believed he wanted to prove to himself that nothing had changed, that anywhere you traveled, mankind was just the same. The few that had money and power could cope, caring only about themselves, and those unfortunate enough to be without, would have to suffer. But the children, she noticed, affected him the most. Watching a few of the most pathetic, digging in a garbage can for food, he had turned his head in disgust, mumbling incoherently about *something had to change!*

Arriving late in the day, staying at the Winchester Hotel, Erik had pulled up to the entrance, stopped the phaeton beside the curb and stared toward the doorway. Two doormen, dressed in impeccable red uniforms, stood ready to help the patrons at a moments notice. Through the window, Monique could see a lavish, sparkling interior. Without preamble of any kind, Erik stated simply, "Money and often beauty determines a persons station, and what kind of life you can expect, no matter if you are in need or not." That simple statement was all he had said, and by his attitude from then on, you would have thought he had totally dismissed it from his mind. But she was to find out many months later that he had not.

Erik ordered dinner in their room and they had spent another intimate evening alone. This morning, he had paid a long visit to his new solicitors, settling some pressing affairs, sent a courier to Pembroke Manor to advise them of their imminent arrival, and then taken her shopping.

"I will not be so ignorant this time as to let my wife go shopping alone. It takes only one disaster to learn my lesson, my sweet," he admitted, adamant that he would not take the chance, hating to remind Monique of that unpleasant experience, yet wanting to prove his point. They spent several hours at a ladies shoppe, picking out a dozen dress styles he liked, deciding on the material, then placing an order to have the dresses and gowns made. Most were simple, yet pleasing to the eye, to be used for everyday, but two were for receiving guests. But the detail that was uppermost in Erik's mind, was that they were suited for a woman who was enceinte. He wanted her to have clothes to wear in the coming months, for he did not plan on returning to London again in the near future. And those months would see a drastic change in her body, of that he was certain. He was not totally ignorant of such things, his adopted older sister having had one child. He suspected that Monique was ultimately dreading the idea of her body growing round, due to a woman's vanity, but Erik was looking forward to it with relish.

At first Monique had objected to going shopping. "You are forgetting, Erik," she said quite forcefully. "I do not like to shop."

"Well love in this case, perhaps you might make an exception. I do not think your clothes will continue to fit for very long," he explained with humor.

"Oh, I had not thought of that," she admitted, frowning, thinking he would not be pleased when her body grew large. "Not clothes that make me look fat!"

Seeing the frown spread across her features and predicting what she was thinking, he placed a kiss on her forehead and said, "You will never look fat, my dear! Adorably round and pregnant with my child, most assured! We'll only purchase clothes comfortable and befitting the situation," he said with finality. "Agreed?"

"Agreed," she said, a little concerted that she had not given the need for maternity clothes even a thought. That Erik had, totally amazed her. But then, she mused, his organized and calculated mind thought of everything.

Now they were clipping along a cobblestone road, badly rutted and in need of repair, that led directly into Pembroke Manor, which was fast approaching in the distance. The light brownstone of the building, designed in the Tudor tradition, loomed majestically within the copse of a dozen towering oak trees, their tall spreading branches shading the area and gardens from the noonday sun, casting a charming effect of serenity. That some of the building was in need of repair was obvious also, stones on the exterior crumbling here and there, but Erik had warned her that his plans were to rebuild the entire manor from the ground up, adding additions as necessary. The first revision being the installation of plumbing, he had quite amusingly assured her...with a very large tub.

Erik could see the structure of the manor house as it came into view. There were no surprises, for he had seen both interior and exterior drawings when visiting Bontonae in France, and been properly advised on the condition of the building. He had mentally mapped out many changes in his mind, determined to make a comfortable home for his family. What he did not expect, was the soul searching emotions that would hit him like a brick wall, with the realization that this was not a dream. This was not some fanciful longing in his mind that had been his previous experience, desiring something with desperation, and ultimately being denied, as reality came crashing down. How had this all come to pass? It was as if some timetable that he was not privy to, had meticulously been played out within a labyrinth of twists and turns, letting him find his own way, make his own disastrous and hopefully some favorable choices, but perhaps providing exactly the same outcome, yet teaching him the lessons of humility and the giving of unconditional love along the way. He had been given an indescribably torturous lot in life, not of his choosing. What had he made of it? Had anything good come out of his past? Did his downfall from grace, and the events that followed, culminating with the burning of his home and the necessity to leave, teach him anything? That he would meet the most enticing and bewitching creature within less than a day, that would ultimately turn his entire world totally on end, bringing forth feelings that even he did not know he possessed, was nothing short of a miracle. Did he believe in miracles? Perhaps he did now! Were all the events of his miserable life leading up to this one ultimate experience, culminating with that one person who would love him for the person he was, and not shun him like the majority of the world for having a deformed face? Could he have ever found another woman that would have loved him as she does? He would not dare to even speculate on what he had come to believe was surely fate. At this very moment, every facet of life that he was presently living, was an affirmation that no matter how far into the depths of hell one might fall, it was possible to survive. Yes, there were tears along with the laughter and horrible grief had been replaced with joy, but there was also a burning passion and an indescribable love that for some reason had been gifted upon him, a phenomenon he probably would never fully understand. But he would accept it, in its entirety, because to him life with the ingredient of love was precious, and he would not take this new gift for granted. He had waited an entire lifetime for it! The future lay before them, and it would know only love.

The reins hung limp in Erik's hand, the carriage unmoving, the entrance to the circular drive just ahead. Erik stared at the manor house and then down at his wife, whose body was pressed tightly against his side. "This is a new beginning," he stated softly. "One that I did not relish entering into alone. That you consented to be my wife is the second best gift that you could give me," he said with a smoldering gaze, pulling her into his lap and searing her mouth with his own. Her compliant body molded to his so naturally that he groaned deep in his throat, plunging his tongue deep into the nectar that sweetened his soul, telling her with solid proof once again against her backside that he would always and forever desire her.

When she could manage another breath, she asked quite innocently, her eyes bright with laughter, "My Scottish warrior, his mighty sword ever ready for battle, what would be the first gift?"

A growl came forth from Erik's throat, as he laid one hand over her still flat stomach. "A child of our own making, to complete our new home," he murmured, taking her mouth again.

It was many minutes before the carriage moved again. The approaching phaeton had been duly noticed, and when it stopped for what seemed an eternity to a staff eager to meet the new patrons, a stable hand was dispatched without haste to see if they needed assistance. Within minutes he was back with his distant observation. With a very wide and meaningful grin upon his wise, old face, he announced to one and all, that for the moment, the Earl of Pembroke and his new bride were unavoidably occupied." And with a wink, he added, "And make no mistake about it, the *new* master has indeed, come home."

EPILOGUE

1924

The day was bright and sunny, with a hint of breeze blowing over the landscape. Monique sat in a large white gazebo, sipping a cool, tangy lemonade. A bright red and yellow kite came streaming by, its many-colored tail, dipping and swaying back and forth in the breeze. Following the string down to its source, Monique smiled, spying a child of about ten years, who was maneuvering it so eagerly, on his face a brilliant expression of satisfaction that he could accomplish such a task. In fact, as she gazed out over the lovely rolling grounds of Wiltshire Preparatory School, she could see children everywhere, all happily engaged in wonderful outdoor activities befitting a late spring picnic. Some were playing croquet, others were engaged in more child-like games, but it was always the horse related activities that caught her fancy. Of course, that had been her doing, and she had to laugh just a little, remembering Erik's comment as he arched his left brow, stating most emphatically that horses were a very expensive activity. One that took time, money and dedication, he pointed out most reasonably. But as usual, with almost anything worthwhile, she had won him over, using that special way she had of twisting him to her way of thinking, and of course he had never minded *that* particular way she used to persuade him! And discovering how easily and eagerly the children had taken to riding, you would have thought it was his idea, the pleasure he found in those activities that guided the children in proper horsemanship. But the one that had captured Erik's mind and soul with a passion that had amazed even her, had been in the realm of music. There, he had been a very stern taskmaster, but the years and the events of his new life had mellowed him, and even a child could find a way to wrap this dark, and once dangerous man around their little finger with just a remark, a gesture, or even a wondrous and searching smile.

The Wiltshire picnic was an annual event that Monique always looked forward to attending with great anticipation and fondness throughout the entire year, for it brought back so many memories from the past...memories that seemed as if they had happened just yesterday, rather than many years ago. She reminisced about the beginning of all of this activity that spread before her. And when she brought it to mind, a magnificent gleam was in her eyes for the one man that had made it all happen. It had started out so simple! Really it had, and no one could ever have foreseen that one small event could expand into all of this.

The earlier balmy weather was turning frigid. Thin ice began forming on the deserted cobblestone streets as the temperature dropped rapidly, a fine mist changing into freezing rain. Dark shadows lingered between buildings, where the dim light from fog, shrouded street lamps could not penetrate, the city ultimately pushed prematurely into the first vestiges of winter. Erik did not often go to London, but occasionally, it was necessary to confer in person with his new solicitors, suggested by Bontonae and Seward. With construction underway on expanding and refurbishing Pembroke Manor, in addition to architectural projects that he had promised in America and Spain, it was necessary to do some business himself, a job Madame Giry had often attended to, mostly connected with posting and collecting his work. On this particular occasion, he had finished quite late, not leaving the manor house for London until well past noon, an unforeseen construction matter arising in the newly built west wing, demanding his immediate attention. When he broke free of his meeting with Mister Templer of Collier's Law Offices, and noted the change in the weather, although he certainly would not relish the damp and miserable ride back to Cheltenham and his estate, he did not hesitate, quite uncomfortable with the idea of leaving Monique alone. Especially when the time for their first child's birth was so imminent! Sometime within the next four weeks, in the month of November, he would be a new father. And that thought both excited and scared him immensely. Having a child of his own, only months ago, he believed to be an impossible dream. It was most ironic that such a horrible tragedy of circumstances had changed his life in an instant, like an eternity of darkness bringing forth the dawn. For this timely and coveted gift, he could only be grateful. But it also made him wonder...*why*? Why had he been forced to live twenty years in darkness, when there was a world out here that could accept him for what he was inside, reaching beyond the mask or his disfigured face, to appreciate what he had to offer the world. Why had it taken so long for him to find that one person who could make the difference, bringing him out of the ugly caverns of self pity, denial, and loneliness into the light of a new existence. Now above all reason, all hope, and above anything he deemed remotely possible, he would soon have a family. A family in which love was a reciprocal occurrence, not taken lightly, but judiciously cherished, and he would do everything in his power to protect that entity. But what if the child was deformed like him? If that were to become a fact, his child would never know the horrors that he had known. Never to be hidden away from the world, nor displayed like an animal in a cage for people to gawk and laugh at, creating a feeling within his soul of total rejection and humiliation. His child would know only the emotion of all inclusive love!

As Erik passed a dark, narrow alleyway between a bank and an eating establishment, he heard a banging of metal, as if trashcans were knocked over, and rolling about the pavement. A harsh voice came out of the darkness, cursing and yelling. "Boy, best be off, if ya know wot's good fer ya. Scat now, before I call the bobbies."

"I'm hungry, Mister! Was just looking for some scrapes of food. I didn't mean no harm," a small voice answered meekly. "Ouch, Ouch! Please, don't. Please, please, I'll leave," came a shaky, pitiful cry of terror. Erik took a detour down the alleyway. What he came upon made him furious, his temper rising alarmingly as events of his own past flashed before his eyes with fervor, the physical pain from those images being felt within his own mind, yet radiating to his body as if they were actually happening right here and now to his own person.

A dark bearded man wearing a long white apron stood silhouetted in an open doorway, the light from the interior illuminating a wide yellow pathway into the alley. He loomed menacingly above a small lad, his right arm poised overhead, holding a long narrow stick, ready to beat the lad again. Suddenly his arm was impeded from what he intended, its tortuous pathway blocked and held fast by Erik's silver walking stick. The bearded man looked around sharply, negligently dismissing the hindrance, until he saw the man's dark, ominous features, and then he took pause. "What do ya think yer doin', bloke?" he yelled, clearly irritated by the interruption, stupidly not heeding this stranger's actions, not privy to whom he was dealing with. He tried with no success to wrench his arm free of the uncomfortable position.

"I suggest you restrain yourself from inflicting injury on the unfortunate," Erik replied, his fury sitting heavily on a very thin layer of ice, his control ready to break through at a moments notice. What he really wanted to do was beat the man senseless to teach him a lesson, but he had promised Monique that he would find better ways to deal with *unhealthy situations*, as she called them. Unhealthy indeed! More like disgusting and inhumane! Something he was all too familiar with.

"Can't have these ragamuffin children that run the streets, pilfering our garbage, Gov'nor, now can I?" the man spat nastily, lowering his arm only as Erik lowered his own, giving the man space to move.

"Might be more beneficial to give the boy a meal, rather than beat him for eating what you throw away," Erik said, his satanically dark features finally registering with a look of caution upon the other man's face.

"If I do either, he'll just be back every night and bringin' his friends, causing a ruckus, makin' a mess, and me havin' ta clean it up," the man said, staring suspiciously at this man in a white mask, warily deciding perhaps he had better go inside before something nasty happened. Like to himself! Quickly he stepped backwards, bumping into the doorframe, turned around and was gone, shutting the door hastily behind him. Erik heard a clink of metal as the bolt shot through the lock.

There was little light left in the alleyway, but Erik could see a child of about seven years. He hunched down in front of the boy and looked into eyes that showed sorrow and need, his frail body shivering with cold. He was dressed in ragged breeches with no socks, and worn tattered shoes. Many colored patches covered the light coat, whose sleeves ended just below the elbow. "Where do you live, child?" Erik asked, his voice soft and mellow, almost mesmerizing in quality.

The boy looked up into Erik's face, not in the least frightened by his dark appearance, or the power he obviously possessed. "Around here somewheres," he said evasively, lowering his eyes instinctively, knowing he was telling a lie.

"Don't suppose you could take me to where this *somewheres* might be? Perhaps I can talk to your parents," Erik said, a slight grin playing at the corners of his mouth, realizing the child was not being truthful, but probably had a good reason.

Deciding he wasn't fooling this man, perhaps it would be better to just tell the truth, or face heavens knows what if he didn't. Although he wasn't afraid, he told himself, this man didn't seem like someone to lie to. "I don't have any parents, or a proper home, Mister. I'll just be on my way. Sorry to have troubled you." The lad started to walk away, an obvious limp to his gait from a crooked foot that turned totally inward, as he stumbled towards the entrance to the street. Erik stood up and grabbed the lad by the collar of his coat, pulling him back around to face him.

"What happened to your parents, lad?" Erik asked, a decided frown on his forehead, his eyes boring into the lads bright brown ones, letting him know instantly that no lies would be accepted.

"Took with a sickness a few months back," the boy supplied, his voice shaky and mournful. "Been on my own ever since. Was just looking for food. I didn't mean any harm," he finished quickly, looking up into those searching eyes that showed only understanding.

Erik patted the lad's head. "No son, I know you didn't mean any harm. It would be best if you come along with me," he said matter-of-factly, like the decision had already been made.

"Respectfully, Sir, but I can't leave here. I have things to take care of," he said urgently, his voice full of trepidation, that perhaps the man would grab him and haul him off against his will. He started to back away from Erik, ready to run like a scared rabbit.

Erik immediately recognized the fear in the boy's voice and the terror in his eyes. He knew the lad wasn't afraid of him, so what else could it be.

Cautiously he asked, "What *things* are so important that would keep a young lad like you living here in the cold, without any food?" Erik asked, searching the boy for an answer to this new puzzle. He scrutinized the boy's agitation and found it to be real.

"I would be most happy to leave, Sir," the boy said honestly, " but I can't go without first collecting something very important. Please, Sir, just follow me," he said, and taking a firm hold on Erik's arm, he started tugging him towards the entrance of the alleyway. Erik arched an eyebrow at the boy's insistence, but followed along.

They wound in and around several crumbling building, and through a very narrow opening in a broken wooden fence, which Erik found challenging to squeeze through, but finally came to a small hovel, constructed in the corner of an amazingly dry, mostly sheltered, deserted building. What he found there broke his heart, but supplied the missing piece to the puzzle. A puzzle he felt compelled to put together.

Inside the front door of Pembroke Manor was a small greeting foyer that expanded into an octagonal area from which branched a study, a large dining area, swinging doors to the kitchen behind the stairs, a library, and a circular staircase that led to the second floor. Gratefully aware of the welcomed clip-clop of horses hooves upon the drive in front of the manor house, Monique placed herself in the foyer to meet Erik, the hour extremely late, and the inside servants having retired for the evening. The weather was cold and nasty, and she knew Erik would not abide himself to stay in the city overnight, even though she had insisted. He was diligently over protective of her welfare, and she could almost be irritated, but instead she smiled, thinking upon those times he demanded she do this or that, or refrain from something else, particularly riding on horseback, because it would not be safe for the baby. And he was so gentle while making love, for at least that was still in full bloom that she stifled a giggle at the thought. Perhaps she could find a particularly pleasant way to warm Erik up after his frigid, wintry ride.

The door swung wide as Erik entered, his black cape swirling around his boots from the wind, the front closure of his cloak shut tight to ward off the freezing night air. He closed the door with his foot, and turned around to face her. Stepping forward a few paces, he leaned over further than usual, avoiding the protruding stomach of his enticingly beautiful wife to place a lingering kiss on her soft, warm lips.

"Erik, I wish you hadn't returned in such foul weather," she chided, but her voice told him she was glad he was home. She knew he hated staying in London, where he always wore his mask, having become accustom to going without it here at home, and quite often his wig also.

Erik raised a quizzical eyebrow and smiled lecherously, his eyes green smoldering sparks, "You do not wish me home to warm your bed on such a cold night?" he said with humor, but in turning ever so slightly, Monique caught a sudden movement behind Erik's long flowing cape. Seeing she had noticed, he reached behind with his right arm and pulled out a small boy. The lad had big saucer eyes and was clinging to Erik's leg. "It's okay, lad. This is my wife and mistress of the manor," he said, pushing the boy forward towards Monique.

"Pleased to meet you, Mam," said the lad, and he bowed most courteously.

"Oh, Erik, what have you here?" Monique cried, her heart reaching out immediately to the bedraggled child. His clothes were filthy, and his frail frame shivered either from the cold, or from this new and perhaps frightening situation. His hair was a thatch of brown unruly curls that looked as if they hadn't been combed out in months, and his face was smudged with dirt, but his telling eyes caught her attention first. They were bright and hopeful. Without a moment of hesitation, Monique got down on her knees, and enfolded the lad in her arms, hugging him tightly to her chest.

She glanced up at Erik, who was not moving away from the spot where he had entered, and thinking it quite odd, she wondered why he remained there. As if in answer to her inquiring eyes, he proceeded with an explanation. "Jaxson here, met with some misfortune. He was on the streets, searching through discarded garbage for food, when a shopkeeper saw fit to beat him for his so called *indiscretions*," he said with a bit of temper.

In horror, Monique looked at Erik. "Erik, you didn't..." she started to say.

"No, I didn't. The man is still quite healthy, " he answered, before she could finish what he knew she was thinking. Idly he added, "The child has no parents."

Monique looked at the lad in relief. "Are you hungry?" she asked, and got an enthusiastic shaking of his head in the affirmative. "We must see to that at once," she assured him, getting up awkwardly to her feet, noticing that Erik did not come to her assistance in his usual manner. She started to usher the child toward the kitchen. Belatedly, she realized that Erik was still riveted to the same spot, standing like a statue. "Erik, what is the matter?" she asked, knowing her husband well enough now, to recognize when something was disturbing him, or when he was hiding something important from her.

Erik stepped forward almost hesitantly, opening his cloak in the same motion, and what he uncovered made Monique gasp with astonishment, but also with complete delight. A sleeping girl child was nestled in the crook of Erik's arm, swaddled in a pink blanket, her small face turned towards Erik's chest in blissful slumber. She looked to be less than a year of age, her blond curls tight ringlets against her tiny head. "This is Jaxon's sister. He wouldn't leave without her," Erik explained sheepishly, like that was the only reason he had brought the child along. He looked into Monique's eyes with a passion of experience, reflecting both sympathy and understanding for those less fortunate, and said quite simply, but with questioning in his face, "They need us, don't they?"

"Of course they do, love. And we will see to their care," she said, taking the small girl from Erik's arms and crushing the sleeping child to her bosom. Erik could feel tears beginning to well up into his eyes, as he realized, this was exactly the way Monique would treat their own child, no matter the circumstances...with unconditional love and affection.

Erik peeled off his cape and his mask and hung them on a coat tree in the foyer. As he turned around, Jaxon came limping up to him in a most pathetic manner, tugging on his arm. Erik knelt down on one knee to see what the lad wanted. With the innocence of a child, the boy put his small hand on Erik's deformed cheek and said, "Just like me."

Erik hugged the lad to his chest, tears running down his cheeks, and choked out a murmur above the lad's head, "Yes, just like you." He gave the boy a pat on the behind, sending him back towards Monique, then turned away until he regained his composure. Yes, just like you, he thought. You are just like me!

That one small incident had literally changed their lives forever. The new construction and remodeling of the old part of the manor house continued for many months and did not finish for almost a year. Erik involved himself in every detail, and joined right into the melee with relish and vigor, gaining a healthy respect from not only the workers, but the staff of the mansion as well. Such behavior from an Earl, and master no less, was quite unheard of, raising a few eyebrows in wonder, but not in a negative way. Of course Erik did demand perfection, but was not unwilling to help make that happen with his own sweat and labor. During those times he wore his mask, but had taken to going without it when only the staff were present, for they had easily adjusted to his various appearances, that aspect of the new master of the manor discussed before carefully being hired by the law office of Bontonae.

When they had first arrived and construction had immediately begun, Monique had come upon Erik pouring over drawings in his study. Coming up beside him, she had leaned over his shoulder to look at the plans. Besides the usual replacement of many deteriorating parts to the building and the addition of a huge, two-story circular music room off the back of the manor, there was a large wing with many rooms sketched out, branching off the main living quarters on the second floor. The name penned in large letters on his drawing, indicated, West Wing, Children's Quarters. Monique started to giggle under her breath, and Erik looked up in astonishment that she would make fun of his architectural drawing. "What is so funny that you would laugh," he said, turning around to face his wife, her belly starting to charmingly protrude out in front of her. He pulled her between his legs, his muscled thighs holding her standing form immobile, as he placed one large, delicate hand on her stomach, a gesture of late he had become accustom to doing. He looked up into her face that was merry with undisguised laughter.

"Erik, the children's wing is so large. How many children do you plan on having?" she asked, knowing as often as they made love, it was a certainty they would have many.

"I plan on keeping my wife pregnant and barefoot," he said seriously, but in a laughing manner, his eyes taking on that dark, green color of the ocean, a dead giveaway that he desired her. With that he stood up, swinging her into his arms before she could protest, and was out of the study and headed for the stairs. Noting her two bare feet that wiggled slightly against the air, as her long legs dangled over his muscled arm, he chuckled deep within his chest. Both of them were well aware that the servants were watching, but he paid them no heed, as he continued onward. Climbing the stairs two at a time, and without an ounce of embarrassment, a most wicked grin upon his face, he stated again in a voice that resounded, "Yes, pregnant and barefoot suits you just fine, M'lady." Stopping only momentarily at the top landing, he looked down into her face, and between a string of searing kisses placed upon her sweet mouth, he murmured, "Do you mind?" Moments later the only sound heard within the house, was the door to the Earl's bedchamber, slamming in haste!

Erik was in the study, brooding. The midwife had been summoned and the time for the birth of their first child was alarmingly imminent. But was he ready? If the facts were known…he was scared to death! It wasn't the idea of responsibility for taking care of a child, for they already had two. Jaxson and Mary were darlings, never giving them a moments trouble, that was not part of being a growing and happy child. Both were a joy to have around, their new home already a fast growing pandemonium of endless events. No moments were ever dull! And now another child soon to be presented to the world! But this would be his natural child…one made out of love and need, and even perhaps selfishness to cleanse his own soul. Would this child be made in his own image… a perfect replica? Should he have left well enough alone? Would he be dooming another human being to a life of pain and sorrow, no matter that love would be bountiful?

Suddenly there was a scream from the second floor, and Erik mounted the stairs without realizing it. He had stayed with Monique for hours, pacing back and forth in their bedchamber, between moments of holding her hand and encouraging her when the pain seemed over-whelming. He had left for only a few moments, to get a stiff shot of brandy. His nerves were unraveling as the moment drew closer, yet Monique seemed calm, even in the throngs of the pain of first childbirth, his research into the event telling him that it might be the longest and hardest.

"Erik, it will be alright," she had assured him. How could one woman, he thought, be so completely astute, with caring and understanding all rolled into one, and unconcerned for herself, even amidst grave uncertainty. At that moment he wasn't sure if he was holding her hand in comfort, or she was holding his.

Erik rushed through the door to find his wife pushing, her face scarlet red with the effort. She simply *could not do that yet*, he thought, the midwife was not here! What could she be thinking, he thought irrationally. But before he had a chance to voice that ludicrous opinion, she groaned out a response, "The baby is coming, Erik!"

"Coming?" he said, a little stunned. Damn this indomitable weather, he thought. Where was the midwife?

When Erik stood by the bed for a moment without moving, she prodded him with a suggestion. "I know you have read all about this, Erik. You will have to deliver your own child. We can not wait for the midwife," she said, falling back against the pillows to wait for another contraction. With humor, she added, "You wouldn't want all that knowledge to go to waste, would you?" Noticing an intense scowl spread over his features, she almost had to laugh, for the seriousness with which he would tackle this event, would prove to be...enlightening. Besides, he needed something to take his mind off his brooding thoughts, and she believed this would certainly do the trick! The welfare of the child would be uppermost in his mind.

"Stop pushing while I wash my hands," Erik told her, and immediately set about the task. Monique thought in amazement, that only a man would make that impossible demand, but started to pant with deep breaths as another contraction took hold, hoping that Erik would hurry.

Erik came over to the bed, sitting down alongside her legs, and pulled back the covers. Monique's knees were up and he could see the baby's head crowning, a dark thatch of hair visible. Taking a towel in his hands, and placing it below the baby's head, he said, "Okay, love, push!"

With relief that was most welcome, Monique gave one huge effort and the child's head burst through, the body following without ceremony. Erik used his thumb to wipe out the child's mouth, then turned the baby towards him, rubbing the body dry. One perfectly formed face, ruddy and chubby, opened its sweet little mouth, and out came the most horrendous and adorable cry he had ever heard. He quickly tied the cord with two small pieces of string, then gathered up the screeching form, and hugged it to his bare skin where his shirt front parted, trying to quiet the baby.

"Is it a boy or a girl?" Monique asked, taking in the most cherished scene she could ever imagine.

"I hadn't thought to notice," he said belatedly, through a flow of unembarrassed tears, his throat tight with emotion. He held the child away and looked at the baby closely, noting its gender. "It's a boy," he said, a huge smile spreading across his face and handed the baby to Monique. She took the child from Erik, and placed him on her stomach, his face near one breast. With her hand she guided his mouth to her nipple, and the tiny lips latched on eagerly, his little jaws pumping with vigor.

Erik laughed and looked at Monique with both humor and love. "I had not thought about having to share with another man," he said. He sat on the bed facing her, fascinated with watching his son, who greedily devoured his first meal, his tiny hand splayed out over her breast in comfort. Erik bent his head to capture Monique's mouth in a long and lingering kiss, his arms encircling both his wife and his first child. Could anything be better than this? Today he had been presented with the most precious gift of a lifetime.

Upon this scene, the door burst open and the midwife entered. "Let's get this show on the road," she exclaimed, her rosy cheeks nearly frost-bitten from the snowy weather. When Erik straightened, revealing a sleeping child with his lips still attached to his mother's breast, everyone took a moment's pause, and immediately all three started laughing. "I see I am here in time to clean up the mess," she said, and started preparing to make mother and child comfortable, and finish the birthing process.

Erik stayed awhile longer, sitting on a chair beside his wife, holding his son while the midwife attended to Monique, knowing she would soon need to rest. Looking most captivatingly at his son, his perfect little body nuzzled so naturally into his own massive chest, he asked Monique, "What are we going to call him?"

"I had hoped you would agree on Drew," she said, a little apprehensive.

"Drew?" he questioned, wondering why she had picked that particular name.

"My father's given name was Andrew, and he would kind of be named after him," she said, realizing that Erik did not have anyone to name a child after, except himself, and she hated to hurt his feelings.

But Erik was delighted. "His name will be Andrew, but we shall call him Drew," he announced, because he was not fooled. He knew her reasoning. Leaving them to rest, he kissed his wife, thanking her with his eyes for a most treasured gift. His sleeping son, he placed in a cradle by the bed, and went down to his study, stopping to check on the other two sleeping children. He would tell Jaxon the news in the morning. Sitting in his study, he silently wept, tears running down his face onto his neck, the heartbreak of a lifetime somehow starting to dissolve, as he thanked the Lord for the gift of a child made in the Lord's image and not in his own.

Having a large children's wing became a needed commodity within less than a year, for each and every time Erik went to London, he would somehow discover a child that was homeless, without parents, and in great need of assistance. Monique was positive he made a concerted effort to frequent the poorest sections of town, where many children lived in squalor, for how else would he manage time after time, to find that unfortunate soul that was desperate for help. Where some would collect animals or trophies, Erik had a knack for collecting children. But not just any children! Most of those he brought home had some kind of physical deformity that made their meager existence harder than for most others, and oft times nearly impossible. Those children were the ones that pulled tightly on the strings of Erik's heart, and he could not, would not, leave them to suffer. He knew all too well, what an unfeeling slice of society, preoccupied with self-importance, handed to those that were different, meting out cruelty, when kindness was needed instead. Within two and one half years, there were a dozen children running about the house, three being their own. Although two nannies and two tutors had been hired to help with their care, and their schooling, they had both participated in almost every aspect of life regarding their most unusual motley brood. Being educated in many forms of medicine, Erik was insistent on finding suitable help for those children whose medical condition could be improved.

Sitting on a stone bench one hot and sultry afternoon, resting from a bit of over zealous exertion with gardening, a new past time that Monique found exciting, she spied some of the children playing on the lawn. Jaxon, now age ten, was pretending with childish exuberance to be a teacher of music. Several of the children sat in a semicircle, singing a familiar child's song, as he creatively waved his arms like a musical conductor. At that moment an idea formed within Monique's head, and she could barely contain her enthusiasm while she searched for Erik.

Observing his pregnant wife all flushed from running, Erik laid down the tools he was using to fix a broken tongue on a large wooden wagon that carried hay from the fields to the stables. "*Ma petite*, what's all the hurry?" he said with speculation, unable to hide a small chuckle, for he loved the rosy, glowing cheeks Monique had when she was with child. He caught her in his arms as she stopped, her breath coming in quick little gasps.

"Not so petite, my love," she grumbled, but with a rather saucy grin, aggravated that her middle had expanded so rapidly, but pleased when it had been confirmed she was having twins. Their fourth and fifth children would be born well before Christmas. Erik had certainly held true to his boast of keeping her pregnant, while she happily supplied the bare feet. Married just over three years and with child for the fourth time—Drew being the first born, followed by Claire ten months later, then Giles a year to the day, sharing the same birthday with Claire. But she really didn't mind. Pregnancy suited her, and Erik was of a mind to have a very large family, whether by collecting children off the streets when no one cared about their existence, or by satisfying that unquenchable passion that seemed forever to be a part of his soul. Either way, she never had a day go by that she wasn't thankful that she had married her dark and mysterious stranger.

"I happen to like that belly you have there," Erik mumbled, placing a scorching kiss upon her rosy mouth, using his searching tongue to part her lips, giving him a delicious taste of that sweetness he never tired of taking. He kissed her soundly, until she felt faintly dizzy, her knees buckling just enough that he held her up by his own power. Whispering in her ear with a warm and tantalizing breath that made her shiver, even in the heat of a scorching day, he asked, "Why is my sweet little sea siren running to find me? Perhaps for a quick toss in the hay?" He gave a deep, growling laugh, thinking that sounded like a superb idea! "If you weren't pregnant, my love, I'd carry you off to the loft, away from the prying eyes of small children. But alas, the ladder is steep."

"You may not have noticed Erik, but some of those small children are old enough to climb the ladder," she said, chiding him affectionately for his amorous thoughts, but wishing just the same that he would carry them out.

"Well, yes, I suppose so," he said, releasing her in disappointment.

With an impish grin that he had grown to decipher so well, she said most beguilingly, "We could latch the doors," and with those words, she grabbed his hand and pulled him through the arched doorways of the stable. He quite willingly followed.

After bolting both doors, Erik carefully guided Monique up the ladder to the loft, climbing behind her, least she fall. He spread a woolen blanket over the hay with his boot, then lay down beside her, the golden sun shining through a large window above their heads, shafts of light streaming like arrows into the hay. He kissed her gently at first, then with a climbing and urgent fever that spoke of his escalating passion. Within minutes their clothes were discarded, and they lay naked within each other's arms.

Erik never ceased to marvel at how beautiful Monique was. Even with child, her body excited him to distraction, perhaps more so, because she would once again bestow upon him that most precious gift...a child...or two! Her breasts were fuller, with nipples that protruded, fitting his mouth so perfectly. He bent to capture one rosy peak, licking and tugging gently, until her breasts felt swollen and tingling. She moaned in quick response, wrapping her fingers in his hair, her hips pressing toward him in mutual need, feeling that glorious part of him she longed for, hot and pulsing with desire also. She felt her world spinning with the sheer magnetism of his powerful body, as bone-melting excitement surged through her own.

His dark eyes looked up, boring into hers, and the rampant possessiveness she saw there, made her feel like the most beautiful woman in the world. A dark, husky, erotic sound escaped his lips as he slid lower on her body, his mouth finding the center of her need, his tongue tasting and stroking. She embraced the sensation, kneading his shoulders, then fisting her hands in his hair when first she soared and then shuttered.

He raised himself above her and slowly, excruciatingly slow, entered her. Then he drew back, teasing, then entered slowly again, finally pushing his hard, thick shaft to the very hilt. The sensation never failed to amaze her, as she gripped him tightly. It was forever incredible.

Burying himself deep within her body only tempered the insatiable sensual desire she stirred in him, that crying demand to bind them together. She was a drug he hungered to partake of in very hardy doses, time and time again. Her skin was an aphrodisiac to his senses, and her eyes a love potion that totally captured his mind. His heart beat rapidly in his chest and his shoulders heaved with his skyrocketing passion.

Steadying his weight on his forearms, he slanted his mouth over hers, tracing her lips with his tongue before finally plunging within, mimicking an age-old rhythm that he continued with his hips. It was hard and fast, with no intelligible words, each consumed with the other, hands roaming, tongues melding. When their desires were spent, Erik lay against Monique, his weight eased partially from her blossoming body.

Kissing the top of her head, Erik asked softly, "What was it you wanted to talk to me about?"

She turned in his arms to face him, an excited look on her face. “The most wonderful thought came to mind when I was watching the children playing,” she explained.

“And what might that be, love?” he said, stroking her hair, his body still savoring the feel of hers against him.

“Well…,” she said, hesitating, wondering if perhaps it had all been a ridiculous idea.

“Well, what?” he encouraged, a little amused. She was usually quite vocal about her ideas, and most often they were good ones. Like starting a vegetable garden, planting a row of young trees along the two, mile drive coming into the manor to give it distinction, and modernizing the kitchen to be more efficient and not just up-to-date. Purchasing riding horses for the children at such a young age had taken him months to mull over, but in the end, she had been correct even in that. Jaxson, and a few others, were already amazingly good riders for their ages. But there was a limit! That she had wanted to demonstrate the rudiments of good horsemanship when she was heavily pregnant with Giles, had been out of the question.

“I thought that perhaps…since we have so much land…and you…like to build and design…and are a natural teacher…that maybe…you would like to start a school,” she said, the words finally coming out at the end in a rush. “I mean…. we do have an awful lot of children, Erik. Those besides our own three, I mean, soon to make five! The children’s wing is getting a bit crowded, and if you bring home anymore, we’ll be needing another tutor.”

Erik let her talk, his face showing quiet amusement as she rambled on with her reasoning. Finally he rescued her. “It seems I have entertained the same idea myself, my love. On the desk, in my study, are the plans for a school that would teach classes up to the university level. And although it would consist of the curriculum of a basic education, it would offer some advanced specialties, such as music and architecture.

"Erik, why haven't you said anything?" she asked, quite astonished, but not entirely surprised. The children adored him, a few sharing his love of music, others wanting to help with anything that entailed building. Not that most were old enough to participate, which often caused quite a stir, Erik needing to be rescued so he could get anything done. That he was patient with all of them was his most endearing quality.

"I had wanted to surprise you. But then, I also wanted your blessing. It is not something I would undertake without your support. It will entail much hard work and planning to accomplish such a project, but…it's something I'd like to do," he said with a serious smile. "But then again, you said we were busting at the seams," he added, with a chuckle. "And… we must make room for the rest of those children I plan on giving you," he said laughing, as her eyes grew wide. That he was thinking of more, when buns were still in the oven, was astonishing. And exactly like him, she thought with amusement!

"Perhaps I should put *you* in the children's wing, to give myself a rest," she teased, feeling him grow hard against her hip.

Bending his head to capture her ear with his teeth, he murmured softly, "You know you would miss me in a minute, love." His searching hands stroked her breasts and over her skin, setting her body on fire immediately. He knew her body better than she did. He kissed her mouth, then opened her lips with his tongue, touching hers just enough to make her moan.

When his mouth latched on to one plump breast, as he deftly rolled the hard nipple of the other, he heard her say in short little gasps, "Perhaps I should reconsider."

"I thought you would see it my way," he growled, and preceded to show her why, until at the most inopportune moment, there was a horrendous pounding on the stable door.

"Daddy! Are you in there? Mommy! I saw you go in there. I *want* to be in there *too*!"

A stern voice of reprimand was heard, scolding little Drew. "I told you not to come down here," Jaxon said with commanding authority.

Two muffled voices of laughter were buried in the hayloft, as they scrambled for their clothes.

Monique had been reminiscing alone for quite awhile. The sun had gone behind a patch of clouds, and the wind had become calmer towards the late afternoon. She noticed the beautiful flowers planted around the gazebo, and they reminded her of their wedding day. Each and every experience she and Erik had shared was inherently special, and many quite extraordinary. One particularly painful one, that became a lesson in patience and understanding for both of them, she remembered all too well. When the buildings of the Wiltshire Preparatory School were almost completed, an abundance of trees, shrubs and flowers were ordered to decorate the grounds. Erik decided this would be an opportune time to replant the rounded garden on the inside of the circular drive at Pembroke Manor. It had never been spruced up, remaining somewhat shabby in appearance, lending an unkempt look to the main entryway. Erik ordered an array of colorful azalea bushes that complimented the brown stone, Tudor style exterior of the house, along with various perennial flowers that would need little care from year to year, his sense of design and detail quite obvious. When the plants arrived, the gardeners had set to work that very morning, planting them in a circular pattern that fanned out from the middle of the bed with flowers on the perimeter, lending a beautiful variegated pattern that immediately caught the eye upon entering the main drive. But the household would soon find that a grievous mistake had been made, for the bushes planted were not azaleas, but red rose bushes with gorgeous red blooms, their long firm stems pointing towards the sun.

The day had started out very well. Finally the spring rains had subsided long enough to allow one entire day of work to be accomplished outside, a dozen workers planting a large assortment of small trees, flowers, and shrubs. For the school's location, Erik had chosen an appropriate acreage of land just as you entered the long, two mile drive to Pembroke Manor, taking every advantage of numerous, hundred-year old trees to shade the buildings from the hot afternoon sun, disposing of only those necessary to erect the stone buildings.

As he returned home in the late afternoon, Erik was duly exhausted, the day starting extremely early. Perched on the wooden seat of the hauling wagon, Erik held the reins of the harness loosely, the bay clipping along the cobblestone drive at a leisurely pace. His mind was concentrating on a minor, but troublesome problem with the plumbing system to one of the dormitories. It would mean extra work, but piping had to be put at a deeper angle to run the wastewater off properly. Erik had added inside plumbing to the manor house, and the school would be no different. He would get the solution to this new problem underway tomorrow. From a distance, his eye caught a brilliant, but yet indistinguishable color, coming from the circular garden at the manor house entrance, and he was pleased that his decision to replace that garden would give the entrance the look it needed. As he drew closer, his eyes focused on the newly planted bushes, their distinct blood red color becoming clearer to his vision. He didn't remember ordering anything quite so brilliantly red. His plan had been a softer pink. He reined the horse in to get a better look, and what he discovered made his jaw tighten as he pulled sharply back on the leather straps with a jolt, the wagon coming to a sudden jarring halt.

"*Mon Dieu*," he exclaimed with rising anger, his displeasure immediately felt by all within earshot. He jumped from the wagon, standing both transfixed and momentarily immobile, his eyes converging on two, dozen rose bushes, their plump, blood red delicate blooms stretching upwards towards the sky. In silent fury, he went for the nearest bush, wrapping his strong hands around the stems at their base, ignoring the sharp thorns that tore at the skin of his hands, and ripped the sturdy roots right out of the soft, newly tilled ground, tossing it aside in a fit of transient indignation. With emotions that were running rampant and uncontrollable, like a furious stupor, he stalked from one plant to the other, destroying the beautiful bushes in his wake. His nostrils flared as he breathed in the pungent aroma, its seemingly sweet and delicate fragrance burning his senses like acid, his stomach churning with a sickening feeling that made him weak.

Monique, alerted by one of the servants about the Earl's behavior and displeasure, came bounding down the stone steps of the manor and ran across the drive, not stopping until reaching Erik's side. She could tell by the sneer of disgust on his face, and the incoherent, broken sentences he was muttering that he was more than a little furious. Absolutely livid would be appropriate! But why? His hair was in disarray over his head, locks falling into his eyes as he bent over towards the ground. What alarmed her was his disregard for the thorns. His hands were raw and bleeding, blood soaking the cuffs of his once white linen shirt.

"Erik, Erik, please stop," she pleaded. "You are injuring yourself," she said in alarm, not understanding this sudden, unexplained outburst of blazing temper. She pulled on his arms, trying vigilantly to make him see reason. Her constant and insistent tugging finally made Erik pause and take notice, looking around at Monique as if he were seeing reality for the first time. He appeared truly stunned for a few moments, glancing around at all the havoc he had created, bushes flung in all directions, and flowers crushed beneath his boots in the process of his quick and destructive retaliation. He moved over to the wagon in silence, leaning his forearms over the wooden sides, his shredded and bleeding hands hanging dejectedly inside. Closing his eyes, he hung his head as his rage began to subside.

"I thought I was over that," he said, regret and grief both evident in his tone. "Those were not suppose to be roses," he added simply, as if that explained everything.

"The roses were beautiful, Erik," Monique commented.

"Roses are not beautiful to me," he said, a sarcastic sneer to his tone. He rubbed the back of his hands against his eyes, leaving smudges of blood and dirt on his face and mask. He glanced at Monique with need in his eyes for her to understand his actions *without an explanation*. Something she had learned to do many times in the past.

"Come inside, Erik, and let me tend to you," she said with gentle persuasion. She accepted his answer, knowing it was the ghosts of his past that made him act so irrational.

She had married a man that had vast knowledge of the world around him, learned through the guise of books alone, being denied the experiences that humanity takes for granted—never experiencing love or the human touch, and never being guided as a child to reap the rewards for good behavior. Instead he had been denied everything for being himself. Was it no wonder he found it difficult, in the least, to deal with anything connected with human emotions.

Without judgment or comment, she soaked his hands in clean, hot soapy water, washing off the blood and dirt, and softening the skin. Then she took tweezers and extracted a dozen thorns. All the while, Erik sat stoically immobile, gritting his teeth in pain, but did not utter a sound. She applied a healing ointment to numerous scratches and puncture points. One thing she had learned over the last four years, this complicated, yet wonderfully kind, tender, humane and emotional man, would tell her eventually. Patience, she had discovered, was a virtue!

That same evening, with his hands and forearms wrapped in gauze to facilitate the medicine soaking into the wounds, she helped him undress and bathe. He leaned over to kiss her, his arms hanging at his sides. She knew he felt terrible about what had transpired. The gardeners had put a lot of time and effort into their work, and he had destroyed it all in a matters of minutes. "I suppose I should give an explanation," he offered.

"Only when you are ready, Erik," she told him, placing a loving hand upon his cheek.

As he lay in bed, Monique's body cuddled against him, barely pregnant with their sixth child, he mulled his thoughts over in silence for a few moments. Here was the woman by his side that had changed his entire existence for the better, always understanding and patient with his demands, many times when she certainly should not have been. That she loved him with as much passion as he did her, there was no question. Did he deserve her…perhaps not? From the onset, he had warned her that he would be a difficult man to live with, yet she had offered, what he now considered to be a lifesaving gift, and perhaps restitution for the years he had suffered in denial and pain. He hoped, in some small way, he had given to her, that which she had given to him. He owed her everything.

Finally he was able to speak. "The rose is only a symbol, but it creates an anger in me that I can not totally explain. I gave Christine a red rose adorned with a black ribbon, each time I was pleased with her performance," he said, his voice hoarse with the effort to say those words. "That I harbor a resentment still for her rejection of my affections, I don't believe I do. Those ghosts I laid to rest long ago. That the memories haunt me still…you know they do," he said in simple offering, not really understanding himself, but with the knowledge that Monique comforted him in the night, when his dreams drifted back to a time that he mostly wanted to forget, yet hold within his heart that part of his past that made him the man he was today.

Monique was not jealous and she understood his rash and destructive actions, her heart shredding with empathy as he painfully sought to sort out his past, a never ending process of one eventful encounter at a time. Over the many months of their unique and beautiful marriage, Erik had told her much more about his relationship with the young Christine, and unraveled the details of his life in the lair, along with his years below the opera house. He had made peace with his past, as much as could be expected under the circumstances, but occasionally demons would rear their ugly heads to haunt him either in his dreams or with something like this latest incident, rubbing salt into an old wounds, catching him off guard, sending his mind reeling back to the past in a painful fury of raging and often times, uncontrolled emotions. Those were the times he needed her the most, once again drawing strength from the security of their passion to sweep the demons away, and once again mend that part of his soul that made him whole. She believed it would take a lifetime for Erik to totally bury the ghosts that haunted him, if that were even possible, but she knew with all her heart that she would try to do just that! She snuggled down, trying to avoid his tender, gauzed wrapped arms. In the darkness, he encouraged her to love him, and she did so with pleasure, that thrill of silent communication that was comforting and so familiar, wiping away the cobwebs that threatened to destroy his calm and happy existence.

Many years later, just two years after Christine's passing, Madame Giry had written Erik about an auction at the old opera house in Paris, and Erik had made his only trip back to France. He never mentioned what transpired there, but he had taken with him a ring he kept secreted away in an old velvet box within his bureau drawer. He had once explained, it was a ring Christine had returned to him, but he had kept it for almost fifty years, swearing that someday he would return it. And somehow she believed that he did!

Monique's eyes were misty, and the day was getting late. There were so many memories to think about. Some were the kind you wanted to cherish and others you might want to forget. There was that frightening incident when Drew was only seven, and disaster had struck like a keg of dynamite exploding. Their lives had spiraled out of control with overwhelming grief, like a booming cannon had been unleashed upon a battlefield. In the wake of that catastrophic event, Erik had disappeared from Pembroke Manor without a word, taking his lasso and sword, once again donning his old disguise of a dark and mysterious stranger, and a foreboding feeling had settled within Monique's heart, realizing immediately if she were ever to see Erik again, she would have to leave the children and follow after her husband. Six months had transpired before that incident had ended and they had returned to England and their children.

But this was not a day to dwell on tragedy. It was a time for celebrating with the participation of glorious and fun-filled activities, and reminiscing about happier times. The picnic was delightful and the weather was perfect. She turned around as a young man entered the gazebo.

"Grandmother, it's time for me to play," he said, his mellow voice a pleasing sound to her ears. "I don't want you to miss it, so I came to collect you." He approached with a grace that bespoke of manners and breeding, yet he exuded an aura of dark and mystical power that was unmistakable. He planted a soft and loving kiss upon her cheek, then offered his arm.

"And what will you play, my love?" she asked. They walked along the grass toward the music conservatory, his tall, muscular frame towering above hers and the familiarity of it was uncanny.

"It is one of Grandfather Erik's most fiery and outrageous pieces that he wrote before he met you. It came from an opera that he composed when he lived in Paris," he informed her, his tone excited, hoping she would be pleased.

Monique laughed at his exuberance. He reminded her so much of her beloved Erik. His dark raven hair was worn of a length just below and around his ears and he pulled it straight back from his forehead. His classical chiseled features were strikingly similar to those from the left side of Erik's face, with eyes colored like the darkest green emeralds. When he looked into your eyes, you were instantly mesmerized by his intense stare, one that could either melt you into a pool upon the floor, or chastise you with a solid look that demanded attention. She had seen him on more than one occasion use that look on children and adults alike, and she had been most amused, for he was so infinitely like his grandfather, both in his mannerisms and his talents. He was attending the university and excelled in both music and architecture, something his professors had deemed impossible to accomplish, but he had proved them wrong, excelling in both. Today he was dressed in his uniform, and upon graduation, would join the royal guard, his tour of duty somewhere in the desert. England was expanding her territories and her soldiers were needed in many foreign lands. She would miss him fiercely, but like his grandfather Erik, he would take his responsibilities seriously.

Momentarily they entered the conservatory, and Monique was guided to her seat nearest the stage. Her grandson, Erik's namesake, took his place at the organ and began to play his selection…fiercely outrageous, and totally mesmerizing in quality. Monique was misty eyed with her memories once again. Just last year she had lost Erik at the age of eighty-four. A life that had begun with the horrors of pain and seclusion, sending him cruelly into years of tortuous darkness and denial, had finally yielded to an awakening dawn that brought forth a full and satisfying life. That he tried to atone for those tremendous horrific transgressions that haunted his past, she was well aware. His continuous belief that she healed his soul and made him a whole man, by giving him the love that he was ultimately denied by others, was only half a truth. She knew better than anyone, perhaps even better than Erik himself, that the true healing of his soul came through the tremendous outpouring of love that he so generously gave to others. Would he have admitted it….*NEVER*! Erik Devereau, Earl of Pembroke had left behind a legacy to be proud of…fourteen children called him father, numerous grandchildren had adored him, and hundreds of others thought of him with fondness, calling him teacher, friend and *beloved husband*.

About the Author

Jodi Minton was born in Muskegon, Michigan, but grew up in the state of Indiana. She holds a Bachelors Degree in Education and practises as a Registered Nurse in a NICU. She retired from the Army Nurse Corp in 2005 as a Captain, spending most of her career in a Combat Support Hospital. She enjoys touring with lighthousing groups around the country, visiting and taking pictures of lighthouses and is concerned with their preservation as the castles of America. Some of her favorite things are Scotland, camping, writing, reading, and celtic jewelry and music.

Printed in the United States
50222LVS00003B/151-264

9 781425 929794